*My Name Is Mary Sutter*

# *My Name Is Mary Sutter*

Robin Oliveira



VIKING

VIKING
Published by the Penguin Group
Penguin Group (USA) Inc., 375 Hudson Street, New York, New York 10014, U.S.A. • Penguin Group (Canada), 90 Eglinton Avenue East, Suite 700, Toronto, Ontario, Canada M4P 2Y3 (a division of Pearson Penguin Canada Inc.) • Penguin Books Ltd, 80 Strand, London WC2R 0RL, England • Penguin Ireland, 25 St. Stephen's Green, Dublin 2, Ireland (a division of Penguin Books Ltd) • Penguin Books Australia Ltd, 250 Camberwell Road, Camberwell, Victoria 3124, Australia (a division of Pearson Australia Group Pty Ltd) • Penguin Books India Pvt Ltd, 11 Community Centre, Panchsheel Park, New Delhi – 110 017, India • Penguin Group (NZ), 67 Apollo Drive, Rosedale, North Shore 0632, New Zealand (a division of Pearson New Zealand Ltd) • Penguin Books (South Africa) (Pty) Ltd, 24 Sturdee Avenue, Rosebank, Johannesburg 2196, South Africa

Penguin Books Ltd, Registered Offices: 80 Strand, London WC2R 0RL, England

First published in 2010 by Viking Penguin, a member of Penguin Group (USA) Inc.

10 9 8 7 6 5 4 3 2 1



PUBLISHER'S NOTE
This is a work of fiction. Names, characters, places, and incidents either are the product of the author's imagination or are used fictitiously, and any resemblance to actual persons, living or dead, business establishments, events, or locales is entirely coincidental.

LIBRARY OF CONGRESS CATALOGING IN PUBLICATION DATA
Oliveira, Robin.
My name is Mary Sutter / Robin Oliveira.
p. cm.
ISBN 978-0-670-02167-3
1. Nurses—Fiction. 2. United States—History—Civil War, 1861–1865—Fiction. I. Title.
PS3615.L583M9 2010
813'.6—dc22 2009046312

Printed in the United States of America
Designed by Carla Bolte • Set in Warnock

*For Drew, whose love and generosity never falter,*

*and for my mother,*

*who bequeathed me her muse*

# *Acknowledgments*

I am deeply grateful to my husband, Drew, my daughter, Noelle, and my son, Miles, for their forbearance and support during this book's evolution.

In addition, I am indebted to the stellar faculty of the Vermont College of Fine Arts MFA in Writing Program, with special gratitude to Douglas Glover, David Jauss, and Xu Xi, whose uncompromising commitment to excellence fostered my ambitions. Program Director Louise Crowley and Assistant Director Melissa Fisher (with a nostalgic nod to Katie Gustafson) infuse the entire community with a deep generosity of spirit. And to all the students (current and former) of that fine institution, my deepest thanks for the joyous experience that is being an MFA candidate at VCFA.

I wish to thank Kaylie Jones, Mike Lennon, and Bonnie Culver, the judges of the 2007 James Jones First Novel Fellowship, for choosing my manuscript from the pile of outstanding applicants, and Christopher Busa of Provincetown Arts, who published a chapter of the novel in 2008.

Marly Rusoff, my extraordinary agent, and her partner, Michael Radulescu, brought enthusiasm, competence, and dedication to *Mary Sutter.* I am a very lucky writer to have found Marly, and in turn to have been found by her. My editors, Kathryn Court and Alexis Washam, are insightful women whose eagle eyes and critical acumen drove me deeper into the story, helping me find its best and truest incarnation. The whole team at Viking has been kind and supportive.

Liesl Wilke, my dear friend, read the final manuscript and helped me unsnarl some very reluctant sentences. My husband, a physician, tutored me on the finer points of childbirth. Dennis and Kathy Hogan spent a week one winter driving me around the greater D.C. area visiting Civil

War sites and museums. In addition, Domenic Stansberry read my final manuscript and made several helpful suggestions. For their words of encouragement, I also wish to thank Andre Dubus III and Wally Lamb. And finally, to Douglas Glover, an enduring and heartfelt thank-you for the gift of the question that guided me home.

People have asked me about the amount and type of research I conducted. What follows is a brief and by no means comprehensive account of an effort that spanned several years and myriad institutions and was gleaned from books, Web sites, historians, libraries, museums, and various primary documents, including newspapers, journals, government publications, lectures, and diaries. Most important, I delved into the records of the National Archives for the original documents from the Union Hotel Hospital. The Library of Congress proved invaluable for Dorothea Dix's letters and the records of the Sanitary Commission's visit to Fort Albany. The New York Public Library also provided me with additional information about the Sanitary Commission. The Interlibrary Loan of the King County Library hunted down book after book and untold amounts of microfilm reels for me. The Special Collections at the University of Washington Medical School Library holds a plethora of books on medicine and midwifery that I plundered. I made heavy use of the *New York Times*'s online archives. I would also like to note the Son of the South Web site for posting issues of the magazine *Harper's Weekly*.

A number of researchers steered me toward some invaluable discoveries. I am especially grateful to the online librarian at the Library of Congress who directed me to Clara Barton's War Lecture, which provided firsthand documentation of the aftermath of the Second Battle of Bull Run and South Mountain. I hope Miss Barton won't mind that occasionally I used her specific details; they captured the peril under which the men and women at Fairfax Station and South Mountain were working, particularly her fear of the candles' catching the hay on fire and her conversation with a surgeon who intimated that triage occurred after the battle. The inimitable Miss Barton also was at Antietam, but there we parted ways. I relied mostly on my imagination and on *Too Afraid to Cry: Maryland Civilians in the Antietam Campaign* by Kathleen Ernst.

Other books of great help were *Civil War Medicine* by C. Keith Wilbur, M.D.; all volumes of the *Pictorial Encyclopedia of Civil War Medical Instruments and Equipment* by Dr. Gordon Dammann; *A Vast Sea of Misery: A History and Guide to the Union and Confederate Field Hospitals at Gettysburg, July 1–November 20, 1863* by Gregory A. Coco; *Gotham: A History of New York City to 1898* by Edwin G. Burrows and Mike Wallace; *Mr. Lincoln's City* by Richard M. Lee; *Loudonville: Traveling the Loudon Plank Road* by Sharon Bright Holub; *Reminiscences of General Herman Haupt* by Herman Haupt; and *Doctors in Blue: The Medical History of the Union Army in the Civil War* by George Worthington Adams. *The Personal Memoirs of John H. Brinton, Major and Surgeon U.S.V., 1861–1865* detailed for me some of the history behind the founding of the Army Medical Museum, which eventually became the National Museum of Health and Medicine. Also, his captivating observations about battlefield rigor mortis enlivened the aftermath of battles more than almost any other detail that I read. The six-volume *Medical and Surgical History of the War of the Rebellion,* first encountered at the National Archives and later through interlibrary loan, provided critical medical information. My special thanks to the *Journal of Forensic Sciences,* Volume 51, Issue 1, pages 11–17, "The Effects of Chemical and Heat Maceration Techniques on the Recovery of Nuclear and Mitochondrial DNA from Bone," for the methods and list of chemicals that might have been employed to skeletonize bone.

Historians and rangers at the National Parks of Gettysburg, Antietam, Ford's Theatre, and Bull Run were helpful not only with verifying obscure points of history, but also in directing me toward primary documents that proved pivotal, especially Herman Haupt's memoir. Frank Cucurullo at Arlington House not only educated me as to the significance of the site, but also read a chapter of the book and made suggestions. The director of the National Museum of Civil War Medicine in Frederick, Maryland, George Wunderlich, spent time on the telephone with me early on in my research. I am also grateful to Terry Reimer, director of research at the museum, for her generosity. In addition, the museum's exhibits helped in visualization of battlefield care. Also, the National Museum of

Medicine at Walter Reed has a wonderful Civil War exhibit. The Albany Institute of History and Art's archives yielded critical information on nineteenth-century Albany. To Erin McLeary, Michael G. Rhode, Brian F. Spatola, and Franklin E. Damann, curator, Anatomical Division, National Museum of Health and Medicine, Armed Forces Institute of Pathology, thank you for helping me track down information on bone preservation. Special thanks to the Town of Colonie historian, Kevin Franklin, for information on Ireland's Corners, or Loudonville, as it is currently known. And to Kathy Sheehan of the Rensselaer County Historical Society, thank you for walking me around the historic district of Troy, New York. Many thanks to James Dierks of the New York Museum of Transportation for answering my questions regarding transportation speeds in the nineteenth century. More thanks to Martha Gude, Roger S. Baskes, Joan R. McKenzie, and Jane Estes.

When I read in Louisa May Alcott's account of her brief tenure at the Union Hotel Hospital in January of 1863 that a rat had nested in her clothing and stolen even the meager amount of food that she had purchased at a corner grocer and set aside for herself in hope of augmenting the paltry army hospital diet, I knew I had a view into the destitute conditions under which both the nurses and patients were suffering. I acknowledge that I was perhaps a bit hard on Dorothea Dix, though I believe I portrayed her as she was perceived at the time. I am happy that history has revealed her courage and independence.

For insight into President Lincoln, his whereabouts and state of mind, I consulted a variety of sources. An account of a conversation between the president and Willie's nurse related Lincoln's sudden crisis of faith. John Hay's diary yielded additional perception. *The Lincoln Log,* published online by the Lincoln Presidential Library, was incredibly helpful, and I turned to it again and again. (It was also my deep pleasure to be able to contribute, in a small way, to this invaluable resource.)

I took artistic license as much as I could when it served the story. Of special note, while I stayed true to the public record of Lincoln's activities, I did move the president approximately a quarter of a mile into Arlington House, a license I hope Frank Cucurullo will forgive me. In addition, though the questions on the Sanitary Commission officer's form were taken directly from the actual form, I invented the answers; their report on the Union Hotel is, however, quoted verbatim. And while Appleton's Guides did exist, I made up the entry for Washington, because the true entry wasn't interesting enough.

And finally, to all the women of the nation who braved disease, despair, devastation, and death to nurse in the Civil War hospitals, we owe our endless thanks. Nearly twenty women became physicians after their experiences nursing in the Civil War; it is to honor them and their collective experience that Mary Sutter lives. The willing sacrifice of their own health and well-being to serve the men debilitated by the war deserves our commendation and admiration, but especially our remembrance.

*My Name Is Mary Sutter*

# *Chapter One*

"Are you Mary Sutter?" Hours had passed since James Blevens had called for the midwife. All manner of shouts and tumult drifted in from the street, and so he had answered the door to his surgery rooms with some caution, but the young woman before him made an arresting sight: taller and wider than was generally considered handsome, with an unflattering hat pinned to an unruly length of curls, though an enticing brightness about the eyes compensated. "Mary Sutter, the midwife?" he asked.

"Yes, I am Mary Sutter." The young woman looked from the address she had inscribed that afternoon in her small, leather-bound notebook to the harried man in front of her, wondering how he could possibly know who she was. He was all angles, and his sharp chin gave the impression of discipline, though his uncombed hair and unbuttoned vest were damp with sweat.

"Oh, thank God," he said, and, catching her by the elbow, pulled her inside and slammed the door shut on the cold April rain and the stray warble of a bugle in the distance. James Blevens knew Mary Sutter only by reputation. *She is good, even better than her mother,* people said. Now he formed an indelible impression of attractiveness, though there was nothing attractive about her. Her features were far too coarse, her hair far too wild and already beginning to silver. People said she was young, but you could not tell that by looking at her. She was an odd one, this Mary Sutter.

A kerosene lantern flickered in the late afternoon dimness, revealing shelves of medical instruments: scales, tensile prongs, hinged forceps, monaural and chest stethoscopes, jars of pickled fetal pigs, ether stoppered in azure glass, a femur bone stripped in acid, a human skull, a stomach floating in brine, jars of medicines, an apothecary's mortar and pestle. Mary could barely tear her eyes from the bounty.

"She is here, at last," the man said over his shoulder.

Mary Sutter peered into the darkness and saw a young woman lying on an exam table, a blanket thrown across her swollen belly, betraying the unmistakable exhaustion of late labor.

"Excuse me, but were you expecting me?" Mary asked.

"Yes, yes," he said, waving her question away with irritation. "Didn't my boy send you here?"

"No. I came to see you on my own. Are you Dr. Blevens?"

"Of course I am."

Now that the time had come, Mary felt almost shy, the humiliation of her afternoon rearing up, along with the anger that had propelled her here, looking for a last chance. On her way, she had waded through crowds, barely conscious of a mounting commotion, lifting her skirts out of the mud, struggling past the tannery and the livery, finally arriving at the two-story frame building with its unpainted door and narrow, steep stairs, so unlike the echoing marble hallways where she had just been refused entry. And all the while, newspaper boys had been yelling *Extra!* and tributaries of people had been trickling toward the Capitol, and still she had pressed on.

"Dr. Blevens, I came here today—" Mary stopped and exhaled. All the hope of the past year spilled over as she stumbled over her words. "Today I sat in the lobby of the medical college for four hours waiting for Dr. Marsh, and he didn't even have the courtesy to see me." Mary shut out the memory of her afternoon spent in the unwelcoming misery of the Albany Medical College, where after several hours the corpulent clerk had finally hissed, *Dr. Marsh no longer wishes to receive letters of application from you, so you are to respectfully desist in any further petition.*

"When he refused to see me, I decided to come and ask something of you," Mary said.

"Would you mind asking me later?" Blevens asked, propelling Mary toward the young woman. "I need your help. This is Bonnie Miles. Her husband dropped her here early this afternoon. He said she has lost a child before—her first. I think the baby's head is stuck."

Mary pulled off her gloves and unwrapped her shawl, her quest forgotten for the moment, all her attention focused on the woman's exhaustion and youth. Bonnie was small-boned, tiny in all her features, too young, Mary thought, perhaps fifteen, maybe seventeen. Her hips were too narrow, which might be the problem Dr. Blevens had encountered.

"Have you been laboring long?" Mary asked.

The doctor answered for her, speaking quickly and nervously. "She cannot say. Since the night, at least."

Mary lifted her gaze from the girl to appraise the doctor with a cool, steady glance. "No chloroform, no forceps?"

"Why do you think I called you? I've seen enough of the damage those can do. I'm a surgeon, for God's sake, not a butcher. Please," the doctor said, "I need your help." Of late, surgeons had entered the obstetrics trade, but there had been too many mistakes to make him feel comfortable. He didn't like administering chloroform to ease the mother's pain, because babies ended up languishing in the womb, and doctors had to go hunting for them with forceps. Too many women had bled, too many babies' skulls had been crushed. He would stick with the ailments of men: hatchet blows and factory burns.

"You'll help me?" the girl asked.

As Mary smoothed the blanket, she thought that the girl resembled Jenny, though she lacked Jenny's distinguishing clarity of skin. But the wide-set eyes, the high cheekbones, and the bright lips had emerged from the same well of beauty as Mary's twin. Once, when Mary was very young, she had asked her mother what "twin" meant, and her mother, who had understood the root of the question, had answered, *God does not give out his gifts equally, even to those who have shared a womb.*

"My last one died," Bonnie said, whispering, drawing Mary close to her, her face transforming from a feverish daze to one of grief.

"I beg your pardon?"

"The baby before this," Bonnie said, her eyes half closed. "I didn't know it was labor I was taken with, you see?"

The ignorance! It was *exactly* like Jenny. But Jenny's ignorance was something altogether different, a refusal to engage, to exert herself. A lack of curiosity.

Outside, above the street clatter of carriages and vendors came the hard clang of the fire bell, and cries of "On to the South!"

Blevens rushed to the window and threw it open as Mary whispered to Bonnie not to worry. The rising strains of a band joined the bugle, producing a festive, off-tune march that beckoned like a piper. A swelling crowd hurried along the turnpike, shoulders and wool hats bent against the rain. In the distance the flat pop of gunfire sounded.

"You there! Hello? Can you give me the news?" Blevens cried.

A man who had stopped to don an oilskin looked up, revealing a slick, battered face, pocked, the doctor was certain, at the ironworks where the spitting metal often scarred workers' faces.

"Haven't you heard?" the man shouted. "The Carolinians fired on Fort Sumter!"

"Has Lincoln called for men?" the doctor asked, but the scarred man melted into the stream of revelers pushing down the muddy turnpike toward the music as if something were reeling them in. James Blevens slammed down the window and turned.

"I cannot believe it," he said. "It is war."

Bonnie seized Mary's wrist, and Mary said, "Do you want to scare her?"

"Sorry," Blevens said, but he was agitated, glancing again toward the window.

"I'll need scissors, lard, and any rags you have," Mary said. "And water."

With a last look over his shoulder, Blevens scurried to assemble the requested supplies. Bonnie nodded off into the deep sleep that overcame women between contractions. Mary probed her belly, feeling for the baby's spine. Often it was the baby's position in the womb that caused delay. There were also other reasons, worse reasons, that Mary did not yet want to entertain. Look first, her mother always said, for the common.

Bonnie was thin—undernourished even—but even through that thin wall of belly, Mary could not detect the rope of spine she was looking for.

"Bonnie."

The girl snapped from her deep sleep and fixed her gaze on Mary.

"I have to put my hand inside you. Do you understand? I have to confirm where the baby's head is."

The girl nodded, but Mary knew that she did not understand. "You keep looking at me, do you understand? Don't close your eyes."

Mary slipped her hand into the warm glove of Bonnie's body and began to probe the baby's head for the telltale V, where the suture lines of the scalp met in ridges at the back. Bonnie's water had not yet burst and Mary worked gingerly, pressing gently against the bulging sac around the baby's head, taking care not to snag the membrane. Yes, there was the V. She ran her hand along the lines, keeping Bonnie's gaze locked on hers, smiling encouragement as she searched for the obstacle.

"Bonnie," Mary said gently, withdrawing her hand, wiping it on a rag. "Your baby is coming out face up. That's why you're having so much trouble. I have to turn the baby. It will make things easier for both of you. It's going to be uncomfortable, but I'll do it quickly."

Mary nodded to Dr. Blevens; at her summons, he strode across the room and took Bonnie's hands in his. Mary slipped again inside Bonnie and slowly fitted her fingers around the baby's skull. With her other hand, she felt through the abdominal wall for the baby's arms and legs. She established a grip. She was standing now, her right hand deep inside Bonnie, the other on her belly. The wave of contraction hit hard. Bonnie's mouth moved, but no sound came out. Dr. Blevens was leaning forward, his face inches from Bonnie's, whispering encouragement into her ear. When the contraction relaxed, Mary grasped the baby's skull and made a percussive shove with her left hand, rolling the baby in a wave. Bonnie writhed under the abuse, arching her back off the table, then falling again. Through the tidal swell of the next two contractions, Mary held the child in place, keeping the baby locked in its new position, the muscled womb clamping down on her fingertips. From outside, Mary could hear more shouts, but even these could not distract her now. All her movements, decisions, and thoughts came from a well deep inside her. When she was certain that the baby would not roll back, she carefully withdrew her hands, and the rest of the delivery proceeded. Mary looked only at Bonnie, thought only of Bonnie and the baby. She was authoritative when Bonnie faltered, stern when she panicked, and unflagging when, screaming, Bonnie expelled a boy in a rush of amniotic fluid. Mary wiped the small flag of his gender along with the rest of him, and then swaddled him in a blanket that the doctor handed her. There was no deformation. The child was perfect, if small. She judged this one at nine months' gestation, but maybe less.

"Extraordinary. I was certain the head was too large," Blevens said.

"It's a common enough mistake."

Efficient but tender, Mary went about her work with a kind of informality. She tucked the mewling infant into Bonnie's grateful arms and tied off the cord after the afterbirth slithered out. There was little blood. The girl had not even torn.

"It's the lard," Mary said, wiping her soaked skirts with a towel. "Massage it into the flesh beforehand, a bit at a time."

Blevens tucked in the ends of the blanket that had fallen away, but he knew it to be an insignificant contribution, the act of a maiden aunt after the danger had passed.

"Do allow me to pay you," he said, but Mary dismissed this offer with a wave of her hand.

"Where is her husband?" Mary asked.

"I don't know. He ran in with her and then left." Blevens looked around the room as if the boy might suddenly appear.

"But where will she go?"

Blevens shrugged. His rooms were not made for keeping patients overnight.

"If you like, I can take her home with me. My mother and I have a lying-in room. She can stay with us until she's recovered."

He protested, and Mary shook it off as if it were nothing, but James Blevens knew it wasn't nothing. The girl and her husband were poor farmers. James had surmised that much when the boy had dropped Bonnie off. They would never be able to pay for any care, not even room and board. Her offer was very generous, more generous than James had any right to expect given that she had been called in at the last minute. But now he recalled the earlier confusion.

"Miss Sutter, what was it you wanted from me this afternoon?"

Mary wiped her hands on her ruined skirts. Her birthing apron was at home, along with the rest of her medicine, rubber sheets, scissors, and rags. "You have already seen me turn a child. I am just as skilled with a previa, or twins. But I want more. I want to study. I want to know more about anatomy, physiology. The *something* I cannot see." It was the speech she had meant for Dr. Marsh. She began to speak in a rush, the words tumbling out. "For instance, the problem of why some women seize in labor. I know that headaches and light sensitivity precede it, but do they trigger it? Is it like other seizure disorders? I know that sometimes it's caused by a rapid revolution of blood to the head, or a too severely felt labor, but why? I was reading in *The Process of Parturition*—"

Dr. Blevens swiveled to look at his bookshelf and then turned back to her. "Aren't deliveries enough for you?"

Mary's gaze was covetous. "I want to understand *everything*," she said. "Isn't it all connected? Isn't the body a system? How can I understand a part if I do not understand the whole?"

Mary recognized Blevens's look: the tilting of the head, the gaze of incredulity. Why was she always such a surprise to people? In her childhood her father had often greeted her questions—Is the Hudson's tidal nature a detriment or a help to transportation? What is the height of the world's largest mountain? What is the true nature of the earth's center?—with exhalations of astonishment.

"Miss Sutter, what precisely do you want?"

"I want to become a doctor. The Albany Medical College won't admit me. I want you to teach me."

"I beg your pardon?"

"Many fine doctors have only apprenticed—"

"Miss Sutter—"

"Consider what you just saw, what I just did for you. I work hard. You would not be disappointed. And I could teach you midwifery!" *This is it*, Mary thought. *I have to convince this man.*

Blevens could understand the young woman's enthusiasm for medicine, and he wondered now what William Stipp would make of her. She was nearly as windblown and desperate as Blevens had been a decade ago, when he had accosted Stipp much the way Miss Sutter was accosting him now.

Blevens sighed and said, "I am terribly sorry, but what you propose is impossible."

"It is not impossible."

"It is. I'm going to enlist. They'll need surgeons."

"But you don't know what will happen. You don't know. Maybe this is the end, maybe it's all over—"

"Have you gone mad? The war has just started!"

The baby began to cry and James Blevens cursed. They had been whispering, trying not to disturb Bonnie.

Blevens said, "I am most grateful to you today for your help, and I will pay you, but I cannot—"

"But you *can*," Mary said. "Dr. Blevens, if you take me on—"

He heaved a sigh. "Miss Sutter, even if there were no war, and we were to do this, you would have no lectures. No dissecting lab. You would see no surgeries except the sporadic ones I perform here. And then when I finished teaching you, you would have no credential—"

"Please," she said. "Please. It is all I want."

The kerosene lantern threw shadows across the walls and floor. In the flickering light, Mary Sutter and James Blevens stood as opposed now as they had been united moments before. Only the soft whimpering of the baby broke the silence. James Blevens could feel the strength of the woman's desire. They echoed memories of his own beginnings, his own desperate pleas when he was starting, when getting into a medical college had seemed an impossible goal.

"I'm sorry. I cannot," Dr. Blevens said.

"I see." Even as Mary spoke, she modulated her tone, but it was no use. Yearning and heartbreak combined with fatigue, and even as she turned her attention to Bonnie, dutiful as always, remembering to check Bonnie's belly to make certain the uterus was still contracting, she said, "It would be nothing to you to teach me. Nothing."

"Are you always this persistent?"

"Always," Mary said.

"Miss Sutter, you helped me a great deal today. I am grateful. No doubt Bonnie is grateful. You demonstrated great skill. Remarkable skill. But I cannot help you to become a physician. What you are asking is impossible."

"Well, then," Mary said, nodding, remonstrating with herself not to say *Thank you for your time,* or other like idiocies. *Do not cede,* she thought. *Keep your spine straight.* "You'll have to help me to get Bonnie home. I haven't a carriage."

James Blevens took in the disappointment of the woman who had helped him and felt, not for the first time, that he was hopeless with women. He didn't understand them. His wife, Sarah, living in Manhattan City, would agree. He should be given credit for asking for help from a midwife; no other doctor in Albany would have capitulated control, but Sarah, if she ever heard of this, would only say that he had failed yet again.

"My carriage is in the back. I'll bring it around front," he said.

Blevens tacked a note to his door for the delinquent husband and then went back inside to retrieve Bonnie. Mary followed behind with the child, swaddled against the rain. He had already padded the bed of the open carriage with horse blankets for Bonnie, and as he laid her inside, Mary noticed how tender he was with her, as if he knew what it was to be a woman.

The nearby slaughterhouse smokers were snuffed for the night, but the air felt compressed and humid in the tapering rain. From the direction of State Street, a gaseous yellow haze hovered, a drumbeat speeding the distance from the revelry to their carriage, the brass notes lagging behind. As the horse plodded through the streets, James Blevens and Mary Sutter did not speak. Witnesses to intimacy, they could find nothing now to say except for directions given and clarified. It was awkward to have spoken of desire, revelation, disappointment. Only a mile separated Dove Street from Dr. Blevens's surgery, but the drive felt like a hundred.

The Sutter home was one of the new kinds of row houses made from quarried stone: deep, rather than wide, windows aligned singly one atop the other in three neat stories, an iron railing ascending the steep stairs from the sidewalk of slate. Dr. Blevens tied the horses and carried Bonnie in his arms; Mary cradled the infant and glided up the stairs behind him, letting the maid answer the bell. Inside, an open stairway soared to the next floor and a third beyond. A newel post stood sentry, and balusters supported a carved walnut balustrade. Off the hallway, French doors opened into a parlor; on a small table, tulips bloomed in a glass vase.

Blevens had not expected wealth.

"Is my mother home?" Mary asked, unwrapping her shawl with one arm while managing the baby with the other.

"Out, Miss, on a call." The maid calmly surveyed the pair of guests. "Shall I set the table for two more?"

"A tray, please, upstairs for the new mother," Mary said, and climbed the stairs with Blevens following. Sconces burned tapered candles; on the stairs, brass rods held back a cascading maroon runner. Mary settled Bonnie under a thick comforter in a wide bed in a room at the top of the stairs while Dr. Blevens waited in the hallway outside. A walnut bookshelf lined the long hall, which was open to the stairwell. The shelves held a medical library to envy: *Gray's Anatomy, A Pharmocologia,* and the aforementioned *The Process of Parturition.* Blevens was holding the text open when Mary emerged some ten minutes later.

"Wellon's Bookstore," Mary said. "He gets me anything I ask for."

"You have read all of these?"

"Of course." She excused herself and disappeared into a bedroom. When she emerged she had changed her clothes. She wore a clean, high-necked dress of no distinguishing feature. It was as if she cared nothing for beauty, though it was clear that someone in the home did.

Blevens trailed Mary down the stairs. "Do you often take ladies for lying-in?"

"Rarely. And only if they are destitute."

In the entry, Mary retrieved Blevens's hat from the stand and held it out for him as she opened the door. There would be no dinner for him at the Sutter home tonight, no matter what the maid had offered. Outside, rain was drumming on the red leather benches of his carriage, the cobbles, the stone stoop, the houses opposite.

"Good night, Dr. Blevens."

"You must understand, Miss Sutter," Blevens said, "that I am not in a position to help you." The excuse sounded lamentable. *I am not in a position.* "Surely, with your resources—" He made a vague gesture toward an elegant crystal vase, as if its presence on a burnished walnut table in her foyer could somehow persuade Dr. Marsh to admit her to the college.

"One cannot buy what one truly wants, Dr. Blevens. Haven't you learned that yet?"

Blevens pulled his coin purse from his pocket. "I insist on paying you."

"You cannot buy *me*, either."

"I meant only to thank you."

"Good-bye."

Blevens sighed, replaced his coin purse, put on his hat, and murmured a good-bye. He would have liked to have helped her, would have, too, if he could. But the war. Even now, he was thinking of following the noise of the band still playing in the distance despite the rain, which had become a torrent, wind gusting through the door. He was about to step over the threshold when an open carriage pulled up and two women and a male companion tumbled out, wrapped in horse blankets. A clap of thunder hurried them up the stairs and into the foyer, the women brushing water from the puffed shoulders of their coats and shaking sodden umbrellas. The blankets were soaked through and the women laughed as they unwound themselves and began unpinning wet hats more stylish than the one Mary Sutter still wore perched atop her wild curls. (Blevens thought, *She doesn't care for herself; she neglects even the simplest rituals of dress.*) It was obvious that these two were related in some way, even though there were only hints of resemblance—the same long nose, large eyes, and square chin as Mary, but they were more accurately and pleasingly executed, especially on the younger of the two women, though the older was youngish and alive, with luminescent skin and curls tamer than Mary's.

"A friend of yours, Mary?" The older woman smiled and extended a gloved hand, but, noticing its waterlogged state, laughingly peeled off the glove and then extended her hand again. "I am Amelia Sutter, Mary's mother." If she was surprised to see a strange man in her hallway with her daughter, she did not show it. If anything, she seemed delighted. "How do you do?"

"James Blevens. I am quite well, thanks to your daughter. She saved me. She took over in the middle of a difficult birth and has also taken in the mother and child. I was just about to leave."

Mary became furious, suddenly, at his courtly tone, as if they hadn't been arguing moments before.

Amelia glanced at Mary and then back to Blevens. "Do you teach at the medical college?"

"No, Miss Sutter came upon me when a young woman in labor arrived unexpectedly at my surgery."

Amelia looked inquiringly at Mary, but Mary shook her head. An understanding passed between them, and a fleeting look of pity altered Amelia's features. Mary shrugged her shoulders and the moment passed, but James Blevens knew that the mother had known of Mary's appointment.

"Well," Amelia said. She looked outside, where James Blevens's carriage was thoroughly soaked and his horse shivering in the rain. "Oh dear. This is impossible. You cannot leave now. The weather is beastly. You'll be drenched. And we've just come from the rally. There is no one left, not even the vagrants. Just the band, sheltered under the Capitol's portico. And all the rosters that everyone signed to enlist are wetted to shreds. So you see it's no good. You must stay to supper."

She pulled off her coat, revealing a mourning dress of deep black. Her pleasant affect was in such contrast to the attire that Blevens wondered if she merely liked the color.

"That is very kind of you, but I cannot impose."

"He was just leaving, Mother," Mary said. "It would be rude to keep him."

"Yes, I—" Blevens gestured at the rain.

"But this won't do at all. Jenny, would you please—" Amelia turned and, seeing her other daughter waiting patiently, said, "Do forgive me. May I present my daughter, Jenny? She is Mary's twin. And our neighbor, Thomas Fall." She rested a hand on the shoulders of the two young people beside her. "My son Christian is lagging behind; he could barely part with all the excitement even though he'll be drowned. He'll have to join us in progress, I'm afraid." Amelia patted Jenny's shoulder and said, "Jenny, darling, please ask the maid to send her son to take the doctor's horse to the carriage house. He'll need to be dried down and hayed."

Jenny dutifully went to deliver the message before Blevens could refuse. There was no gracious way to decline the invitation that Mary had so blatantly withheld. But he did not want to stay. His presence would only goad. He thought longingly of the solitude of his rented rooms on State Street and pictured Mary Sutter scolding her family after he left for their guileless welcome. He had withheld the favor she perceived he could easily give, and there was no way to make that right.

Amelia turned her attention to Mary. "A delivery, you said? Is she all right? Did things go well? Do you have any questions?" On Amelia's river of words, everyone was swept down the hallway to the dining room, where a fire blazed in an expansive hearth and maids had already expanded the table to set more places. There were six settings around the linen-covered table. Mary took her place, with her back to the fire, and did not look at Blevens. Jenny and Amelia exchanged glances, trying to discern from Mary's stony silence how her day at the medical college had ended with a guest for dinner whom she was ignoring. Thomas Fall, the only one unaware, it seemed, of the day's expected role in Mary's future, was pulling out his chair and speaking eagerly of the rally and Lincoln's call for men.

It was a subject that Blevens was impatient to discuss.

But it was difficult to discuss anything. There was something unformed about Thomas Fall, Blevens thought as the young man began to talk. His conversation left little room for interruption, though the young man spoke with the confidence of one who had been accepted and encouraged at this table before. Idealistic, ambitious, Fall spoke about the war with intelligence and naiveté both: "Lincoln wants seventy-five thousand for the immediate protection of Washington City," he began. The *Argus*, it turned out, had published a special edition with Lincoln's plea. Virginia threatened to the south; the Rebels could be upon the city at any moment. If they captured Washington, the war would be over. A coup. Slavery forever. Fall was certain that the Rebels would soon be defeated, which Blevens also believed, for the North had the advantage in manufacturing and railroads, but it was the flicker of excitability, the flare of eagerness that showed when Fall babbled on about the glory of battle that betrayed his youth, though his clothes were better cut than Blevens's, attesting to greater wealth.

As he spoke, it turned out that Fall's confidence was well founded: all three women yielded the conversation to him, and not solely for reasons of hospitality. The younger sister, Jenny, was adoring. But Mary attended perhaps more intensely, albeit covertly. Glances of sharp admiration, a softening of her features. Moments when she ceased eating to gaze, then remembered herself and passed the salt or the butter, though no one had asked. When Fall finally solicited Blevens's opinions, Mary became inattentive as he probed the possibility of greater bloodshed than Fall expected, but he did not want to be rude or alarm the women, and so he droned on about the necessity of controlling the railroads, which sounded boring even to him.

Christian Sutter, the brother, arrived during the meat course. He was tall, curly-headed, a mop of hair, a grin, all confidence, younger than his two sisters. Charm had won him everything in life, it seemed, including his mother's adoration. He took the foot of the table. No father had been mentioned. Their mourning must not have been recent, Blevens decided. This was a family adjusted to whatever losses it had sustained. Happily settled at his place, Christian beamed and said, "Did you know that they've already formed a regiment? The 25th. It's a good number, don't you think?"

Amelia Sutter threw her son a fearful, longing glance. Pride muzzled instinct, though it was a battle. A sudden smile turned tremulous, then disappeared altogether as Thomas and Christian agreed that immediate enlistment was required of any self-respecting Northerner.

For her part, Mary had shaped a more formed opinion of Blevens during the soup course than she had been able to do in his surgery rooms. Seated opposite, he comported himself with the manners of a man not unaccustomed to either money or talk. The dishevelment of his surgery rooms did not coincide with this new picture.

Thomas and Christian were arguing about Texas. "If there is to be any fight at all in Texas, it will have to be soon, because they've just emptied the forts of Federal soldiers—"

"Dr. Blevens is going to the war, too," Mary said, interrupting.

It was as if someone had declared war in the dining room. Blevens hurriedly said, "Yes, as a surgeon. One doesn't wish for bloodshed, but—"

"But you do, don't you, Dr. Blevens?" Mary said. "You want to see what can happen to the human body. You want to see inside it. You want to solve its mysteries." She had sharpened her voice and set down her heavy silver knife. The roast was delicious, but unimportant. "Not that you should be ashamed. It is no less than I would wish to do. Given the opportunity."

"Mary," Amelia said.

"It is not shameful to press one's point, Mother." She turned again to the doctor. "I haven't misspoken your aspirations in going to the war, have I, Dr. Blevens?"

Mary Sutter was calling in his debt. He was to be made to apologize in front of everyone. "Miss Sutter, I am very sorry that I cannot help you. But with your gift for persistence, I doubt very much you will not someday claim your opportunity."

"Help you how, Mary?" Amelia asked.

Mary ignored her. "But I will only be able to claim it if I am offered it. Tell me, Dr. Blevens, in your opinion, is there a limit to how much knowledge one person is allowed to accumulate? Have I reached my quota?"

Blevens thought again of his rooms on State Street. He could be beside his own fire right now, looking through his microscope. "Miss Sutter, you have my deepest respect and gratitude. But I cannot help you."

"Dr. Blevens, do you know of the woman Miss Nightingale?" Mary asked.

"Do I seem as illiterate as all that?"

"Have you read her *Notes on Nursing*?"

"Yes, as a matter of fact, I have."

Mary registered surprise, but forged on. "One of the reasons my mother and I are the best midwives in Albany is that we read the latest medical literature."

"You speak, Mary, as if our accomplishments were daggers," Amelia said.

Mary Sutter laid her hands in her lap and rearranged her expression into one of tolerant hospitality, but behind the benign visage sparkled the same intense determination she had shown in Blevens's rooms that afternoon. She fixed him with a stare.

"Are you aware, Dr. Blevens, that in the last year, Miss Nightingale has refused to leave her room?" Mary asked.

"I beg your pardon?"

"Miss Nightingale, brilliant lecturer, member of the Royal Statistical Society, the woman who saved the British army in the Crimea, has shut herself in a hotel room in London and refuses to leave it. I am not saying that she is mad. Apparently, she is quite coherent. But averse to society for some unrevealed reason."

"It is possible the war both made and unmade Miss Nightingale. The deprivation, the difficulty—"

"That's possible, but I believe Miss Nightingale has hidden herself away from society in order to be heard. I think she knows that people would not listen quite so intently to her if she were always parading her achievements in front of everyone. I myself think that no woman should have to hide." A pause. "Or perhaps Miss Nightingale *is* mad. It's interesting that no one really knows."

Glasses clinked and throats cleared. Jenny wiped her lips with her napkin. The halting silence around the table was characterized not by shame, but by a vague weariness. Mary unfurled was formidable and her family all knew it and, it seemed, sometimes despaired of it.

"I do beg your pardon, but are you suggesting that my refusal to help you will somehow render you mad?" Blevens said.

"I fail to see how comparing female intelligence to madness is going to help your case, Mary," Thomas Fall said, emerging from the hush to jolly along his future sister-in-law.

James Blevens raised his hands in concession. "You did not want me at your table tonight, Miss Sutter. You have had to endure my company after I disappointed you."

"How? How did he disappoint you?" Amelia asked, but Thomas Fall stepped in once again.

"Our Mary is not quite as inhospitable as she seems." Thomas threw Mary a gentle smile, which she returned with a flicker of her own. "If you wish to receive a pass from Mary, you need only be a woman in the last throes of childbirth. She likes the needy best, I think."

"Yes, she was remarkable today," Blevens said. "As I suspect she usually is."

His compliment earned him no correspondent smile from Mary, who took a sip of wine and looked away. Amelia reached her hand to Mary, but Mary shook her head.

Taking charge of the table, Thomas abruptly changed the subject, accustomed, it seemed, to navigating the family's more difficult shores. "Dr. Blevens, before we all go off, I'd be happy to take you out to Ireland's Corners. I keep orchards on the Loudon Road. Apples and cherries. I have hopes that the New York Railroad will one day extend a line northward. Think of the prospects of fruit picked in the morning being delivered to Manhattan City by evening of the same day."

"Is this a family business?" Blevens asked. He reached for a glass of water, giving sidelong glances to his dinner companions, all of whom suddenly held Thomas Fall in a sympathetic gaze.

Thomas set down his fork. "It was, yes. But last October my father and mother died in a carriage accident. Hit by a runaway."

"I beg your pardon. I didn't mean to—"

"No. Your question was welcome."

Jenny reached out her hand and enfolded his hand in hers.

"I do beg your pardon," James said. "That is very recent."

"We had just moved into town. Father was not used to the traffic."

"I am sorry." Blevens wished now that Bonnie Miles had never walked through the doors of his surgery this afternoon. Nothing had gone well from that moment. Upstairs, he could hear the baby crying, and footsteps climbing the stairs. A maid, going to Bonnie's aid. He cast around for something to say. "If you don't mind my asking a practical question, but with no one to give your business to, how will you enlist?"

Amelia said to Thomas, "If Mr. Sutter were still with us, he would have gladly taken control of the orchards until your return. And have built you a rail line."

Of course, Blevens thought. Why hadn't he registered this before? This was the family of Nathaniel Sutter, of the New York Railroad. This explained the beautiful home and furnishings far better than did the income of two midwives. He tried to remember exactly when Sutter had died. Less than a year ago also? Their mourning had been brief, but perhaps they had found solace in one another.

"Nathaniel would have built you two rail lines," Amelia said, extending an arm across the pale linen to the beautiful daughter. The quiet one, too, it seemed, for she hadn't yet spoken a word, though Jenny appeared unruffled by her own silence. She had the prize, the boy next door, and therefore did not covet the spotlight for herself.

"I have an excellent overseer," Thomas said, "who knows the business far better than I do. I rely on him."

Cake was being served, coffee poured. A few more minutes, fifteen at the most, and then James could beg fatigue. He wondered now whether Amelia regretted her hospitality as much as her daughter Mary did. So far, he had insulted Mary twice, revived grief in all of them, and invaded a family dinner on the brink of a war. It seemed there was no way he could redeem himself. He was picturing the Sutters' conversation after he left—*Mary, how did you ever bring such an odd man home?*—when a maid flung open the door.

"She's bleeding, ma'am."

A flash of skirts and Mary was out of the room, Blevens racing after her up the stairs two at a time.

In the lying-in room, Bonnie's bedclothes were saturated with blood, the baby stowed safely on a pillow by the maid. Bonnie's eyes were saucers of astonishment.

"I felt something warm," she said.

"A tear," Mary said, thinking of her hands deep inside Bonnie earlier that day.

But Dr. Blevens was already raising Bonnie's reddened nightgown while shielding her nakedness with a blanket. "Lie back; don't be afraid." Swiftly, he palpated the pillow of her abdomen, and after a few minutes began a circular massage. Behind him, Mary Sutter stood reluctantly impressed. He had been hunting for the uterus, to see if it had relaxed, which obviously it had, because as soon as the massage began, the flood had stopped. The massage contracted the uterus, shutting off the open blood vessels where the placenta had been attached. This was the first step in any maternal hemorrhage.

The tide abated, Blevens took Bonnie's hand and pressed her fingers deep into her stomach.

"Do you feel that?" he asked, helping Bonnie find the hard ball of her uterus underneath her navel.

"What is that?" she cried.

"Your womb," Blevens said, smiling now. "Yours is a bit recalcitrant for some reason. You'll need to rub it every few minutes so that it will keep contracting and you won't bleed. Can you do that?" Over his shoulder, he called to Mary, "Have you any ergot?"

Reduced to the role of nurse in her own lying-in room, Mary dispensed the medicine and then called the maids to help her change the bedding. While everything was made right, Dr. Blevens scooped up the baby and retreated to the window, where he bounced the child in his arms. Then Mary led Blevens to the kitchen so he could wash his hands. His frock coat was edged in blood.

Mary said, "You know far more than you let on this afternoon, Dr. Blevens. Did you even need my help in the delivery?"

The maids scurried out, pretending not to pay attention. Later, this conversation would be told in the kitchens on Arbor Hill in the Sixth Ward: *And then the doctor said. And then the Miss said.* Outside, the pigs would be rooting in the garbage and the maids would be saying to their husbands, "And her so haughty."

Blevens said, "I don't practice enough to feel successful in deliveries, but I am not completely ignorant of the needs of women. Bonnie's hemorrhage was easily controlled, merely atony of the uterus. You would have done the same."

She could barely contain her humiliation. She would not have done the same, and the failure of her usual unerring intuition made her furious. She would have hunted for the tear, wasting precious time. "Why do you think I knocked at your door today, Dr. Blevens? Did you really think that I would prefer to apprentice when I could attend a college? Did you really think I wasn't at the end of my choices?" She was pinning and unpinning her hair, the curls disobedient, refusing to be locked in place.

Laughter echoed from the upstairs, where Amelia had gone to supervise, having already taken graceful leave of Blevens in the hallway. Jenny and Thomas were closeted away in the parlor, lovers with shortened time. Christian had gone out again after shaking Blevens's hand.

"I'll say good night," Blevens said, bowing.

The front door swung shut behind him, sounding like the end of something. Outside, the rain had not let up, and he remembered too late that his horse and carriage had been quartered in the carriage house in the alley behind. He should have exited from the kitchen, where the door led to the yard and alleyway. For a moment, he paused on the stoop, but then hunched his shoulders and walked down the windswept, rainy block, turned right, and turned again into the alley, where he located the Sutter carriage house and led his horse and carriage from the warm confines into the dreary night.

# *Chapter Two*

Amelia Harriman and Nathaniel Sutter had married for reasons of family; his land near Ireland's Corners abutted her parents'. Their union was to expand the Harriman orchards and to support Amelia's midwifery practice. It was not a loveless marriage, however; economic cooperation was the added bonus of a childhood affection. As Amelia saw it, Nathaniel Sutter was the man least likely to complain about her profession. Her mother had been a midwife, and her mother before her, in a line that extended back to medieval France. Her great-great-great-great-grandmother had once delivered a dauphin, afterwards using ergot she had culled from the rye in her garden to stem a hemorrhage in the queen, earning the La Croix family a parcel of deeded land near Versailles, which they fled during the revolution.

In America, the tradition continued. Amelia's mother married James Harriman, but everyone knew who she was—the French midwife. There was simply no question of Amelia not being a midwife, and yet while American men might want good midwives for their wives, they did not wish to marry one. Nathaniel Sutter was different. And so the knowledge that had once saved a dauphin was preserved for the women of Albany County. In addition, the proximity to Amelia's parents ensured that when Amelia was called away on a delivery—staying at the home of a woman in confinement days beforehand in anticipation of the onset of labor—her mother, who had retired after decades of sleepless nights, would be nearby to care for any children that arose from the marriage.

Nathaniel soon discovered that he had little desire to tend flowering cherry trees, as his deceased mother and father had. A year after his marriage to Amelia, he sold the bulk of their land and bullied his way into a job with the New York Railroad, where his engaging, gregarious, and tireless personality disguised a rapacious capacity for stealing freight contracts away from the Erie Canal. As soon as the canal was finished in 1825, it proved to be slow and feeble in comparison to the speed of the railroad. Nathaniel believed that despite the inherent dangers of rail travel—the crashes, the bridge collapses, the derailments—no one would want to put their goods on an open barge in Buffalo to be dragged by a team of mules when you could place the freight on a railcar and have it arrive in Manhattan in two days. Two days when the canal took at least two weeks! The railroad was in constant battle with the legislature; the state's debt from the canal was still a financial burden, the railroad an upstart that threatened the state with bankruptcy if the canal could not retain enough contracts to pay off the cost of building it. Nathaniel thrilled to the battle, Amelia less so. The job rendered him frequently absent.

Two years after the marriage, Amelia's parents died, and Amelia and Nathaniel moved back into her childhood home, a three-room clapboard on the rise that ran toward the Shaker settlement. When children finally did come, five years after their marriage, their lives became a negotiation. Amelia could no longer stay in a woman's home for days before the woman gave birth. Husbands had to come and find her when labor started, always risking that Amelia wouldn't be able to respond if Nathaniel was away.

One dawn in June of 1842, Amelia sent word from a neighboring farm that she was just about to return home. An hour, two at the most, the boy reported to Nathaniel. But Nathaniel had to catch a train at eight a.m. He was due in Buffalo that evening. He stood at the bedroom threshold and made a calculation. Amelia was just a half mile away. Their two-year-old twins were asleep in their cribs—Mary restless, but still sleepy, Jenny quiet, her thumb in her mouth. The boy had said Amelia was coming in an hour. Two at the most. He could wake the twins and load them into the wagon and hurry them cranky and unfed to Amelia, or he could let them sleep alone in the house for an hour. The light was soft; a breeze billowed through the gauzy summer curtains. An hour. That was all.

When Amelia returned home that evening after failing to save her neighbor from a sudden hemorrhage, her girls were standing in their crib, their faces wet with tears and mucus, their nightgowns stained with urine.

The argument when Nathaniel returned home went like this: *I had to go to Buffalo. The railroad needed that lumber contract.*

*But you should have brought the children to me at the Stephensons'.*

*You sent word that you were coming home.*

*Dolly bled suddenly, I couldn't leave.*

*I didn't know. If I had known, I would have brought them to you.*

*But how could you abandon them?*

Amelia's distrust, once roused, could never fully be put to rest. From then onward, she took the children with her, even in the middle of the night. She ordered them to dress, don shoes, bring their blankets. While Mary sleepily complied and Jenny and Christian cried, Nathaniel argued, even as the husband of the laboring woman stood leery at the door. But Amelia would not relent. The children went—on with the bonnets, on with the boots—the twins propelled by a watery memory of an echoing stretch of time inhabited by terror and hunger and finally, their mother's tear-stained face, bent over the crib in which they had been confined. That vestigial memory of abandonment made them follow Amelia out the door to fall asleep in the wagon as she barreled down washboard roads after worried husbands.

They became vagabond children. When they were younger, they played with the children of the laboring mother; when they were older, they hauled and boiled water, and listened to birthing cries in houses high and low, becoming accustomed to joy being predicated on misery. This accounted for their assured nature; prescient, possessed, they would later feel at home anywhere and in the face of anything.

The first time Mary asked to help was in a brooding house along the Shaker Road, not far from home. The house was two stone stories, with looming windows and a narrow stairwell. Well along, the woman shrieked upstairs. The walls were drab, the bed a ticking upon the floor. Two toddlers sucked thumbs beside their mother.

"Are you certain?" Amelia asked, when Mary pulled the bonnet from her head and said, "I would be grateful, Mother, if you would let me stay."

Her mother's eyes pierced, giving her the look that Mary would later learn to ignore: the tilting of the head, the gaze of incredulity. But then she said, "So, it's you," having wondered which of her daughters would become a midwife.

Jenny, never eager, was happily relegated to the dull tasks of water and childcare, while Mary seized opportunity.

Mary was not given a corner from which to watch. No clinging to territory, no adult separation of *I know better than you.* Amelia said, *Hand me this, hand me that. You might not want to see this; turn your head.* At times it seemed to Mary that the world over was rent with the cries of women giving birth. But when at last the baby emerged, slippery, fighting, squalling, the woman's thighs trembling and then collapsing, and Mary was given charge to kneel beside the mother and wipe—gently—the writhing baby dry on her stomach, the battle of labor proved a war worth fighting. What did Mary remember most? Not the mother's bulging flesh, the bullet-shaped head of the infant, the gasp of love when at last the mother encircled the infant in her arms, but Amelia's stillness. Her grand remove. Competence incarnate.

And so the tradition continued. With Mary, not with Jenny. It could have hardly been otherwise, for Mary had set her heart. Within two years, it was she who said, *Hand me this, hand me that.* Fifteen, and already precociously able. She was spoken of: *It is something about her hands; it is something about her voice.* And around the city, at suppers and church socials and dances and even upon the streets, when an alert matron spotted a newly expectant mother, Mary Sutter's name was whispered.

When the success of the New York Railroad made Nathaniel his fortune, they sold their land and moved into Albany and the Dove Street home, eschewing old-money Eagle Street for the outskirts of the city. There followed the consequent ease of wealth and servants, and with it no longer any need for Amelia to take the children along with her. But Mary continued to go to deliveries with her mother, while Jenny and Christian stayed behind. It was said that Amelia Sutter had ruined Mary for society, and that she had nearly ruined Jenny. That Amelia's running about risked her marriage, that only her charm and beauty saved her. For

Amelia Sutter was indeed charming. She was at ease in conversation, knew how to deploy a hand to a forearm at just the right moment. And in the childbirth room, her presence was a gift. But the combination of social status and occupation puzzled. Midwives were supposed to be matrons beyond childbearing age, with years of life in which to have been disappointed enough to wish to spend all one's time delivering babies. Not that the women of Albany County were not grateful; instead they were envious, which took its form in criticism. The problem, they said, was that she neglected her family. Never mind that they never left her side. Never mind that Mary took first place at the Girl's Academy. Mary Sutter, talented as she was, couldn't string two words together unless they were combative ones, and Jenny Sutter, why, that girl was destined for trouble.

When the girls turned eighteen, there was a trip to Wellon's Bookstore on State Street for Mary to purchase *Gray's Anatomy*, newly published, resplendent with illustrations, and *Notes on Nursing* by the celebrity Florence Nightingale. For Jenny, there was a party and dancing. Amelia enjoyed both equally, though perhaps, if pressed, would confess to having liked Jenny's more, for the frivolity of dancing past midnight. And though in her daughters, their mother had cleaved—Jenny had adopted Amelia's charm, Mary her persistence—no one could say that Amelia Sutter was not proud of each of them.

Mary turned twenty years old the day her father died in September of 1860. Her first delivery had been nothing compared to the utter helplessness of watching death stalk her father. Even the memory of the woman's dreadful house, the hard work, the boiling of water, the jack towel tied at the head of the bed for the mother to pull on, the screams, the fatigue, paled in her mind as her father suffered. In the face of her own ignorance, she peppered the doctors with questions. *Why are you bleeding him more? What is the matter with him?* But they could not answer her. She studied the *Gray's* at his bedside, employed every tenet of Miss Nightingale's, seeking to alleviate his pain, but he died in an agony that not even copious doses of whiskey and laudanum could dull. The day after her father's funeral, Mary wrote her first letter to Dr. Marsh. It was the day that the Fall family moved into the new home next door, and a then young and diffident Thomas Fall, not yet having suffered his own great grief, tipped his hat to Mary as she went out to post the letter. The new neighbors did not go to Nathaniel Sutter's funeral, not wanting to press the burden of hospitality on their newly bereaved neighbors.

It was Mary and Thomas who met first, at a show at Tweddle Hall, two weeks after Nathaniel died. Amelia had insisted that Mary get out of the house. *Go somewhere, do something, you'll shrivel up if you stay inside a moment longer.* Gas leaked from the chandelier; the smell was very strong, and everyone had covered their mouths and noses with handkerchiefs. Thomas arrived late, and chose a seat next to Mary, whom he did not at first recognize because of the makeshift veil. But it was impossible to mistake her for anyone else; he had watched her comings and goings from the window of his house and had admired the dignified way she carried herself, the resolute set of her shoulders, the graceful neck that stood out from her otherwise plain appearance. The simple act of walking down the street seemed to communicate that she knew who she was. That he did not completely know yet who he was or what he wanted was a discomfort he kept at bay with industrious endeavors toward happiness that daily seemed, in light of Mary's apparent self-possession, an insignificant enterprise. He was pleased to find her here, though a little surprised to see her at entertainment so soon after her bereavement, though Thomas decided he admired even this break with convention. He noticed, too, that Mary did not wear the traditional black, but a shimmering deep navy, and that the rich color suited her dark brown eyes, which he decided were the most remarkable feature of her face. From time to time during the performance he glanced her way, but Mary kept her gaze fixed on the dozen jugglers from Boston who first lobbed balls and oranges, then plates and cups, followed by chairs and stools, and finally knives and swords, but decided against lighting their flaming batons because of the gas.

Absorbed as she was by the spectacle, Mary blinked back tears. She was not usually so vulnerable a person. She knew that it was said of her that she was odd and difficult, and this did not bother her, for she never thought about what people usually spent time thinking of. The idle talk of other people always perplexed her; her mind was usually occupied by things that no one else thought of: the structure of the pelvis, the fast beat of a healthy fetus heart, or the slow meander of an unhealthy one, or a baby who had failed to breathe. She could never bring herself to care about ordinary things, like whose pie was better at the Sunday potluck, or whose husband she might covet should the opportunity arise, or what anyone was saying about an early winter or an early thaw or if the wheat would blight this year due to the heavy rains, or if the latest couple to marry had any chance of happiness. Perhaps it had been foolish to come to the theater, where potential death was being offered as entertainment, though Mary knew that no matter what she did or where she went, she would always see mortality where others saw frivolity. As a dozen swords sailed effortlessly onstage between the performers, all Mary could think was how precarious life was.

The performance ended, and Mary rose. She lowered her handkerchief, the opening Thomas had been waiting for. He touched the tip of his program to her gloved hand and said, "I am terribly sorry about your father."

It was this simple gesture that immediately made her like him. He did not say, *How do you do*, or *Pleased to meet you.* Instead, he said the essential thing. She liked his directness; she liked that he did not inquire why she was out so soon; she liked that he hadn't even introduced himself.

Thomas guided her by her elbow out of the auditorium to the street, conscious of the whispering their pairing induced in the other patrons. *Mary Sutter? Out so soon? And who is that young man she's with?* As they started up State Street, his fingers moved to the small of her back, and for the first time in a long time Mary felt that someone was taking care of *her.*

Thomas was pleased to have made himself so easily acquainted with his new neighbor. He'd been nervous how she might take his overture so soon after the loss of her father, but she seemed untroubled by, and even grateful for, his boldness. He glanced over at her, uncertain what to say now that they were alone. In the twilight, Mary Sutter appeared to be older than her age. *The midwife*, everyone said of her. But there were no claims to her affection among any of the young men of Albany. They did not attribute the cause to intimidation, but rather named the distraction of the more beautiful twin sister. All this Thomas had learned one night at the Gayety Music Hall, where he had gone last week to make himself known. He would make his mark among the society of men in Albany; he would not feel unsettled, as his mother did, by the change from the country. Her preference for Ireland's Corners was something she hid; the country was generally viewed as unsophisticated, except as a summer escape from the dust and heat. Thomas liked the city; he liked the novelty of the noise and the ready proximity to theater and dining saloons. He liked being out and about. He liked being a young man.

Though their families came from the same village, they were barely acquainted. The Fall family had lived on Loudon Road, the Sutters on Shaker Road. The Falls were Presbyterians, the Sutters Episcopalians. And though the Sutters had once owned an orchard, Nathaniel's sale of the family land and Amelia's practice had rendered them acquaintances only. Amelia had not delivered Thomas; another midwife had, for Thomas was born just as the twins had confined her to her bed. He was three months older than Jenny and Mary, but now he felt much younger. Years in the company of women in agony had conferred on Mary an aura of wisdom; she inspired respect and trust; it was this, Thomas thought, that made him feel so young.

The whitewashed brick homes and St. Peter's Church reflected the last of the light; it was an Indian summer night of hypnotic beauty. At the top of the street, a few farmers' wagons lingered in the market square; soon coal fires would acidify the air until the springtime winds scrubbed the skies clean.

In the park by the Boy's Academy, they rested on a bench. Just across Eagle Street the pillared white marble of the medical college reflected the ghostly beauty of the evening light. Mary gazed at the building, thinking of her letter of application on Dr. Marsh's desk and how she might soon hear from him. Twice a day she accosted the postman at the door, only to be told there was no letter. Amelia said she was being impatient, and Mary said that she could not help it. The anticipated letter was her distraction from grief. It was also her future.

Gaslight flickered in the lamps along State Street. Thomas and Mary sat together, the conversation arising naturally as between old friends. Soon she was telling him how just before her father died, he had apologized to her for once leaving her alone when she was a baby. Her father said he attributed her independence to this, his worst mistake, thereby taking credit for her accomplishments while completely ignoring the fact that her twin sister, likewise abandoned, was utterly uninterested in midwifery.

While she talked, Thomas studied her. She had a way of carrying her grief that gave the impression she was doing well and would continue to do well. "I am certain you were a comfort to your father," he said.

"He died badly. I never want anyone to die as badly again."

Mary leaned forward. Did Thomas have any ambitions?

"I am to take over my father's business." He explained about the orchards in Ireland's Corners.

"My family once had orchards there," Mary said. "Are you passionate about farming? Will the endeavor sustain you?"

Thomas thought Mary asked this as if he should question everything, but she did not appear disappointed when he said that he had no idea; rather, she nodded, as if she too found uncertainty the expected state of existence.

"You, however, have already accomplished quite a lot," Thomas said.

"Not enough," Mary said. Her eyes shone, and the stiff posture with which she held herself disappeared. "I want someday to attend medical school." And she lifted her gaze to the wide pillars and high windows of the school; off to the right was the hospital wing; under its golden cupola was the lecture hall. The surgeries and laboratories resided in the wing to the left. She knew its layout by heart from having once sneaked past the clerk guarding the school from behind his desk.

Thomas studied the building, and Mary held her breath, though not consciously, but having revealed herself she felt exposed. She hadn't meant to say what she wanted so clearly. Desire had burst out of her, as if it could not be contained. And the goal seemed within reach. Any day now, she would receive the answer; any day now, she would be the first female student of the Albany Medical College. She waited for the puzzling, troubled look from Thomas, the one that said, *You are overreaching,* the one that said, *What an absurd idea.*

Instead he said mildly, "You want to be a doctor?" There was only a slight tilt to his head, only a brief, quizzical glance, as if she had spoken in a foreign language that he had had to translate in his head, and then a wide grin blossomed on his face. The evening light was beginning to wash the color from the sky, but Mary could see clearly that Thomas's eyes were sharply blue. Boyish, happy, his face shone with generosity. He seemed incapable of guile, incapable even of finding her ambition extraordinary. As if the entire world were an open place, holding out its arms to everyone. As if munificence were the normal course of things.

"Wouldn't that be something?" he said, leaning back, holding her in a gaze of respect and admiration.

For the first time since her father died, Mary smiled.

They walked homeward in a companionable silence, a damp gust of wind scurrying up State Street behind them. By the time they reached Dove Street, leaves were already beginning to fall from the maple saplings lining the street. From the corner of her eye, Mary could see the curtain parting in the Sutter parlor window. Jenny had been aghast that Mary would follow her mother's suggestion that she get out of the house; Jenny still spent most of her days in tears. The curtain's lace shielded her face, but it was Jenny, watching.

"I am pleased to have met you, finally," Thomas said, cradling Mary's hand in his. She was a surprise, he thought. Though the frame was large, the hair unmanageable, the chin too square to do her credit, there was something about her manner that drew him in. He did not want to say good night.

"Thank you," Mary said, "for the diversion of conversation and your company. I have been very sad."

"Perhaps our families could dine together, after your mourning is over," Thomas said.

"My mother would welcome an invitation."

"Good night," Thomas said. And he watched her climb her steps and enter her house before taking the adjoining stairs two at a time into the Fall home, whistling.

Jenny was seated in the parlor, looking at a book, turning the pages too quickly to be reading them. Amelia was staring at the fire, but turned when Mary came in, a look of expectation transforming her features from the sadness that had haunted her the last few weeks.

"Did you have a good time?" Amelia asked.

"Yes."

"Who was that?" Jenny asked. In her pale face, her eyes snapped with color. Since the death of their father, she had been uncommonly quiet, when usually she was voluble, joyful. Jenny found it difficult to be serious about anything for long. Of Mary's intensity and seriousness, she often said, "You really ought to laugh more."

Mary turned, unpinning her hat. "Our new neighbor."

"Did you meet him on the street?" Jenny was forcing her voice toward blandness, turning the pages of her book three at a time.

"No. He walked me home from the hall." Mary set her hat on the table in the corner, near her mother.

"And he didn't think you odd for going out so soon?"

"He didn't say if he thought me odd or not."

"Well, I thought you odd."

"Girls," Amelia said. The word came automatically now. She could sense tension before either of them did. She and Nathaniel had often wondered how two such different individuals had come from her womb. *Nathaniel.* She sighed. No one had ever told her that grief was a leveling of all emotion, that life would stretch before you, colorless and endless, devoid of any hope.

Mary said, "He wants us to come to dinner."

"All of us?" Jenny said.

"Yes," Mary said. "At least I think so. Perhaps he just meant me."

"Oh," Jenny said. "Well." And she rose and left the room.

Amelia shot Mary a disapproving glare. "This is not a competition," she said.

But they both knew that it was.

A week later, Mary stood in the alleyway behind the Dove Street house, waiting for the maid's son to finish shoveling coal into the chute so he could come and harness the little sorrel to her gig. Last night, Amelia had been called to a delivery on Arbor Hill, but one of the Aspinwall daughters out in Ireland's Corners was due, and Mary was going to stay at their home, Cottage Farm, until the infant arrived. Her bag rested at her feet; she might be away a week.

Though the Sutter family was in mourning, women continued to have babies. Amelia and Mary set aside their sadness to answer any summonses that arrived. It is the inescapable rule of caregivers that they have to be available despite how they themselves might feel. But Mary had found it a relief to plunge again into the intricacies of childbirth. Amelia yielded now to her in almost every respect, reserving only the most difficult deliveries for herself, but even then she taught Mary all she could. On those occasions, Mary observed over Amelia's shoulder, mimicking her movements, mumbling to herself, finding that she remembered Amelia's instructions better if she narrated. Twins: mother exhausted at second pass; it may be necessary to use smelling salts to rouse her. In case of cord entanglement, ease the child back into birth canal to lessen tension and slip cord quickly over neck. For asynclitic presentation (fetal head tilted toward shoulder) check carefully for bleeding afterwards; use rags to compress. Bedrest for two weeks while the mother heals; movement could cause hemorrhage. In cases of stillbirth, give child immediately to mother in order to preserve maternal sanity. Mary inhaled the information her mother dispensed. Centuries of wisdom resided in Amelia's muscles. Often, when Mary asked questions, Amelia could not answer unless she was in the act itself, able to remember only as she performed. Instinct as textbook.

And work as distraction, for no invitation had come from next door.

No word from Dr. Marsh either. Mary wrote another letter. *Perhaps my first letter of inquiry was lost in the post?* It seemed as if the universe was conspiring to teach her patience. What does Mary Sutter most desire? Let the stars withhold it.

Now, in the distance, thunder rumbled. A day of contradiction: Mary's bonnet shaded her from a sun bright enough to strain her eyes. The alley percolated: a privy tilted a half block away; the neighbor's poorly kept chickens flapped in protest at the confusion. An ice wagon lurched into the narrow ruts and climbed the slow rise, its wintered-over ice blocks crusted with sawdust. The last of the last, before winter set in and ice would be everywhere. The verge of deprivation and plenty.

"Miss Sutter?"

Thinking it the maid's boy, she turned and scolded, "I thought you would never come."

"You've been waiting for me?" Thomas Fall shut the gate and grinned, leaning against the whitewashed fence that separated the Fall home from the eyesore of the alley. "But perhaps you should have come around the front and rung the bell. I do not normally meet ladies here."

"And where do you usually meet them?"

"At Tweddle Hall, where they need walking home."

On his own ground, Thomas was self-assured, in command of his supple frame; he wore a hat to offset the flash of amusement in his eyes.

"I'm going today to Ireland's Corners to await a birth. The maid's son is supposed to harness the gig, but I fear he has fallen asleep on the coal."

"May I drive you? I was on my way there myself. Father is at the farm and wishes to instruct me about preparing saplings for the winter, a concern that is not unlike your profession, which is, I believe, nursing things along."

Not dinner with his family, but something much better. Time alone. Mary tried to discern: merely kindness or real interest? She was seeking not to make a fool of herself, as she had sought not to every time she had left the house in the last week, feigning nonchalance as she descended the stairs, as if she were glancing to the right only to contemplate the chance of catching a cab and not hoping for the Fall house door to open and for Thomas to appear.

And now here he was, more confident than she had at first supposed.

With an exaggerated sweep of his hand, he bowed, and then righted himself and smiled again. Lines radiated from his eyes, a product, Mary believed, of an abundance of happiness.

"Miss?" It was the maid's son, blackened by coal dust. Mary turned him away.

Mary told Thomas she was headed to Cottage Farm, to the Aspinwalls'.

Thomas raised a mocking eyebrow. "The manufacturing king? So you're delivering royalty?"

"Of course not. Every woman is royal when she is having a child, whether her family owns a brass foundry or not. No one should be without good care, no one. When I become a physician, I will open my doors to everyone—" She stopped. She was being combative, when Jenny would beguile. "Everyone deserves the same care and help."

"I know what you meant."

Thomas navigated the narrow alley and the riotous traffic on the city streets with an assured hand, driving past the clatter and boom of the Lumber District, the hiss of the ironwork's open forges, the Irish taverns and the city liveries. On the Erie Canal, the mule drivers sang while they waited for the locks to fill, their songs drifting on the autumn air.

At the base of the Loudon Plank Road, the young Palmer boy saw Mary and turned the barricading pike without requesting payment of the toll.

To Thomas's astonished inquiry, Mary said, "Midwives travel without charge."

Two dozen cattle lumbered through, coming south from Saratoga. The Palmer son collected an exit levy of forty cents from the farmer driving them to the river, which they would swim. They would then climb the embankment to the Hudson River Railroad depot and entrain for Manhattan and their slaughter in the city's abattoirs.

"You just saved me twenty-five cents," Thomas said. "Tell Dr. Marsh. He'll admit you to the medical school as a cost-saving measure. Of course, you'll have to accompany him wherever he goes. You'll be a scandal."

Mary laughed. No one teased her, not even her mother. He was easy, she thought, when everyone else was so hard. "I don't think Dr. Marsh has to pay."

"I would charge him, just for keeping you waiting." (He had asked whether or not she'd received word yet almost as soon as they had turned down State Street; when she told him she had not, Thomas denounced Marsh as a pigheaded dimwit.)

Under the carriage wheels, the road planks thumped pleasantly. A heavy scent of ripe persimmons and apples wafted from the orchards of the Van Rensselaer lands that stretched westward all the way to the New York Central Railroad yards. The orchards brimmed with wagons and pickers placing red and green apples into bushels; flat persimmon crates burst with purpled fruit. A flock of sheep swelled toward Mary and Thomas, who veered into a grove of cherry trees to allow the beasts to pass. (Pleased with their frolic, the sheep too were ambling toward their deaths, unknowing.) Autumn had burned fire into the trees; the canopy above shone like a stained window. The sheep were an aggregate mass, a vast, woolly cloud drifting down the road; the air, the clack and bleat of the animals, the laughter from the fields eased Mary back into memories of her childhood. Her youth and his, while separate, had both been spent here. They had this in common.

"Where exactly is your family's farm?" Mary asked.

"A mile or so past the Corners. I've been thinking about you since we last talked," Thomas said. Offhanded, but he met her gaze and held it.

*And I you,* she wanted to say, but could not. The language of courting was not her language. Jenny would tilt her head, invite more confessions with a smile. Mary, who could coax reluctant babies from unwilling bodies, could not now coax words of flirtation from her mouth. Would that Thomas would ask her instead about the physical workings of the heart, its struts and valves, the music of the blood that swished through an infant's heart when she pressed her monaural stethoscope to a woman's belly. She grasped at the shepherd's arrival with desperation. "See now, the flock has passed."

Thomas looked away. Languid, his movement, but Mary thought she detected disappointment. Recovery seemed impossible. (The brief swoon of a mother after delivery, when her body gave in to the shock.) Thomas took up the reins and reentered the road, but looked at her once again. "I did not take you for being bashful."

"Not bashful. Rather, unpracticed." Now, thank God, her reluctant tongue.

"But you are such a courageous woman."

He would steal language itself from her. She turned to hide her blush.

Around a bend, Cottage Farm hurried up to them, and Mary cursed the efficient road.

Thomas helped her down, but retained her elbow in his and walked her toward the door, which flung open, revealing the Aspinwall son-in-law. He was young, recently married; his beard struggled to make a statement of age, but failed. "She's early, she's early, you must come, I was about to saddle to ride to you." (An early baby, yes, but the infant would be fully formed. A miracle, everyone would say.)

Thomas handed Mary her bag, and his hand lingered in hers. The son-in-law looked from one to the other, recognized the symptoms, and would have left them alone, for he too had suffered such an attraction (which had earned him a swift marriage and a premature baby), but his wife—would he ever get used to saying that?—had already frightened everyone with her screams.

"Please, you must come now; she might die."

Mary put her hand to the young man's forearm and soothed. An essential element of midwifery was mastering the art of distracting fathers, husbands, and brothers from their alarm. And women, too. Mortality was the ever-present companion of women brought to bed, to say nothing of the myriad postpartum ailments: childbed fever, prolapsed uteri, and fistulae. Peril was Mary's working conversation. "Could you help me? It would save time if you could carry my bag inside, and clear a table so that I might lay out my things. I'll be right in."

The promise and the nonspecificity of *things* seemed to assuage him, and he took her bag and dashed up the steps to the house, calling, "She's here, she's here!"

"See how everyone wants you?" Thomas said, smiling, and then one by one tugged on the fingertips of her glove, and then slowly pulled it off, turned her hand over in his. "May I come by on my way home this evening and ask for you?"

Mary pictured being called to the door, just for five minutes even, to say hello, imagined the surge of pleasure, double, perhaps triple the anticipation she felt now. How easy to forget, with his calloused hand in hers, the labor that was waiting her attendance. To breathe, for a moment, in ease, as Jenny might.

"I am sorry, but I cannot allow it." But even as Mary spoke, she wanted to snatch the words back. What would Jenny have said instead? *Oh, it would please me so much, but I'm terribly sorry, our next visit will have to wait for another day. When I get home, perhaps?* Ensuring both that they would see one another again, and that Thomas would think it was his idea. But it was too late to say those words. A wave of futility came over Mary, even as she worried about the laboring girl. Mary had been home for a *week.* Why hadn't Thomas called for her then?

He looked from Mary to the house and withdrew his hand. "Of course. I apologize."

*It's nothing,* she wanted to say. But it wasn't nothing. Nearby, a chestnut dropped from the grove of trees, its spiky shell splitting open with a thud when it hit the ground. She thought, *He is done with me.*

And then Thomas was gone, striding toward the wagon. The cant of his shoulders made Mary feel suddenly cold, as if autumn had turned to winter in a moment. She took in everything as he swung onto the seat: his muscled forearms clutching the reins, his cheeks, clean-shaven in the morning, now shadowed, his gaze, set resolutely ahead.

"Perhaps if you were to send someone for me when you are finished here? I could drive you home. Would that be acceptable?" he asked.

An arc of sunlight struck the firm contours of his body, and for a moment Mary thought she could see right through to his heart.

"Yes," she said. "Entirely acceptable."

And then he turned onto the road toward the Corners, and the stand of chestnut trees hid him from her sight.

After a mild labor of only ten hours, the Aspinwall girl produced a healthy son of small size at midnight, a feat that boded faster and faster deliveries in her future. The girl recovered well, and was even able to leave her bed on the third day and walk across the room without any help, despite a small tear that Mary treated with cold compresses. The entire clan of Aspinwall sisters, aunts, and friends, including the girl's mother, who herself had been delivered of a baby only the year before, were on hand to provide attentive care. After assuring herself that the girl showed no signs of childbed fever—no chills, discharge, or lassitude—Mary sent a note to Thomas, along with word to her mother that not only had the birth gone well, but that Thomas Fall had offered to bring her home.

Thomas drove first north up the Loudon Plank Road, and then east down Menands Road toward a small lake hidden in a thicket of poplars. He helped Mary out of the carriage and down the treed slope to the edge of the water. The late afternoon air was tinged with woodsmoke; the surrounding trees concealed them from the road.

"This was my favorite place as a boy. In the winter, my father shoveled snow from the frozen surface, and we ice-skated until our toes and fingers were numb. I caught round-fish and chased bullfrogs here in the summers. It seems smaller now, though." He looked about wistfully (as former children do), nostalgic for the irretrievable past. "Did your family ever come here?" he asked.

The Sutters hadn't. The small lake was unimpressive, as lakes went, better considered a pond, and certainly nothing like Lake George, where Mary and her family had once taken a summer excursion.

Thomas brought a horse blanket from the carriage and spread it on the grass near a small outcrop of dying bulrushes. They had very little time before the sun's warmth faded and they would have to leave. Mary forced herself to focus on a series of ripples emanating from a shallow spot in the middle of the pond.

"Are you always so long at a lying-in?" Thomas asked.

The question accelerated Mary's already high regard for Thomas. Most men could hardly bring themselves to say *lying-in*, let alone *brought to bed*, and certainly never *pregnant*. "Actually, that stay was very brief. I usually stay a week."

He whistled and said, "What a life you have set for yourself."

"My mother was able to marry."

Thomas did not answer, and Mary flushed and hurried to her feet, cursing herself for having leapt to the ultimate question, which had sprung from some buried place to betray her. "Forgive me. I must be exhausted." She could not look at him, but compelled herself to, to thwart awkwardness. "Please, could you take me home?"

Thomas rose and folded the blanket, his expression a combination of concern and something else she could not discern. Disdain, probably.

"I'm not usually so outspoken," she said. "You must forgive me."

A bemused, tender smile crossed his face. He drew close, out of mercy or desire, the air between them suddenly turning.

Mary thought, *He might kiss me*; she had to fight to keep still, to not lean in and invite the intimacy.

Thomas thought, *She requires forgiveness for candor; is vulnerable, but only in love.* A contradiction that intrigued. Her mind had already voyaged to the frontier and was unafraid. But all he had anticipated so far was the leisure of time, entertaining but not yet subscribing to the possibility of a mutually interesting life.

He thought, *She is near enough to kiss* (would allow it, he believed), but he was not ready to decide.

"If I may," Thomas said. "I want to tell you with what respect I regard you. You are someone extraordinary, someone exceptional."

It was a gift, this compliment, but even in her pleasure Mary could only think that worship was dangerous, for it established irrevocable boundaries.

He helped her into the carriage. They followed the road down to the river and then the canal towpath that offered an unobstructed view of the river, with the river schooners' sails like clouds, and the distant hills aflame in orange and scarlet, but nothing could dislodge Mary's sense that something had changed. On the towpath, Thomas had to maneuver around the tethered mule teams crowding the approach to the locks before the Albany Basin. From the barges wafted the scents of stagnant water and the acrid smell of anthracite carried in their hulls; the high bank to the west only partially obscured the ugliness of Arbor Hill and Broadway.

At the Lumber District, Thomas turned off the path and onto Quay Street and then veered up Maiden Lane, avoiding the parade that was State Street. As they crested the top of the hill, the shadows of evening had already encroached, and glimmers of candlelight and whale oil broke from the windows of the medical school. The park where they had sat on a bench only a week before was a mere silhouette.

When they arrived in the alley behind the house, the homely approach signaled familiarity, neighbors having had an outing. In the mullioned window of the Sutter house, a curtain slipped aside, revealing Jenny's blonde hair. A wedge of light spilled out the back door, followed by the door slamming and Jenny appearing at the gate.

"Mother says you are to invite our neighbor in for a meal."

Thomas's gaze alighted on Jenny and lingered.

There was nothing else for Mary to do. She said, "Thomas Fall, may I present my twin sister, Jenny."

Mary could see him making the comparison, not unlike everyone else who ever heard the word *twin* in the presence of the two of them. The envy she thought she had mastered years ago opened inside her, swelling and pressing against her diaphragm, making it hard to breathe while she tallied which of her inadequacies stood out the most: her posture, her bone structure, her chin, or her hair. Thomas bowed slightly, a courtly gesture, and then said, "Forgive me. This is very kind of your mother, but my mother and father expect me at home tonight. However, please thank your mother for the invitation, as it would be my deepest pleasure to accept it for another time." And then he smiled at them both and raised his hat, but there was something magnetic about the way he ignored Jenny as he led his horse into the carriage house.

---

Less than a week later, Thomas Fall knocked at the Sutter door. He was clutching his hat in his hands, a look of pain and despair on his face.

"Is your sister here?"

"Mary is away," Jenny said. Having been summoned to the door by the maid, she was at first delighted to see him, then disappointed when she understood it was Mary he wanted. "Is something the matter?"

He cupped his hand to his mouth.

"Oh. Please. Are you all right? What is the matter?"

"My parents." His voice broke and he doubled over, placing his palms on his knees.

Jenny coaxed Thomas into the parlor and called for a maid to send for the Episcopal priest. Then she poured Thomas a glass of whiskey, which he could not hold steady in his hands. She took the glass from him and set it on the table. Outside, the day was burgeoning. Inside, the clock's pendulum struck ten. A maid brought a tray of tea, spied the whiskey, and quickly retreated. Only when the Episcopal priest arrived did Jenny learn that a constable had knocked on Thomas's door to report that his parents, on their way to Ireland's Corners for the day, had collided with a runaway rig on Broadway. After the priest had prayed and left, she sat beside him on the divan, her hands in her lap, waiting, reliving her own grief, remembering what it was to feel the firmament slide away from you.

When Mary and Amelia returned at noon, they found Jenny and Thomas still huddled in the parlor. They had passed the scene on the way home and spared Thomas the details of the tangled carriages, the broken axle, the chestnut horse suffering in the street, and the drunken carriage driver sitting stunned in the gutter as the coroner's black-draped wagon swayed past with its burden. Mary, exhausted from the delivery they had just attended—unlike the ease of the Aspinwall delivery, the child had died at birth—had nonetheless wanted to leap from their carriage to run up State Street. But here in the parlor, Thomas's grief had already found comfort. Mary, usurped, lowered herself to the couch, a hand to her heart, but no one noticed.

This time, Thomas was made to stay to dinner.

Amelia probed over the soup. "Of course, your parents made plans?"

"I don't know."

*What child listens?* Amelia thought. *Or what spouse?* The end is unimaginable, therefore not to be imagined.

"You will allow me to help you." Amelia was past asking questions. She had another child now; in Thomas's eyes she saw the same helplessness as she had in Jenny's when Mary had descended the stairs, saying, *Father has died,* and she, Amelia, had looked into Jenny's eyes and seen the searing likeness of her own anguish.

"I will host the reception. And you must eat with us every day. You cannot be alone in that house."

*Alone in that house.* Jenny sprang from the table to retrieve a handkerchief. All that was left for Mary to do was to whisper to the maid to pour their guest another glass of whiskey.

The Falls had not made plans, it turned out. At the funeral, the Sutters sat with Thomas. He was young, at twenty-two, to be left alone without uncle or aunt or cousin to help him. St. Peter's echoed with the sounds of the organist's mistakes. Amelia apologized for the false notes, but Thomas did not seem to notice. Amelia had chosen the Albany Rural Cemetery and arranged for a hearse to ferry the caskets up the Menands Road, with its restorative view of the Hudson River. The Falls' graves adjoined Nathaniel's; neighbors forever now. At the reception afterwards, the servants laid hams, cheeses, breads, and nuts on the Sutter dining-room table; black crepe draped every picture, balustrade, and door handle of the two houses. Thomas Fall drifted from one grieving circle of his parents' friends to another.

But it was to Jenny, with her calm demeanor and ease with his distress, to whom he turned in the days afterwards.

Thomas Fall called often for Jenny after that. A smile for Mary, but an invitation for Jenny. He did not mean to be cruel; it was not so much a choice as it was affinity. In his grief, Jenny would not ask too much of him, while Mary, who had showed such courage after her father's death, might expect similar strength of him.

"Did you ask Thomas to dinner?" Mary asked her mother one day, lowering the curtain as Thomas once more escorted Jenny down Dove Street, having been both congenial and kind to Mary while he waited for

Jenny to appear in the parlor. "The night I came back from the Aspinwalls'?"

"I beg your pardon?"

"Did you send Jenny out to invite Thomas in?"

"I don't remember," Amelia said, remembering very well. From labor to death, she thought, despite every moment at the breast, every reprimand, every tender tousle of hair, every fever fought, every night spent worrying, it came to this: you couldn't protect your children from anything, not even from each other. "Mary, did anything happen between you and Thomas? Did he say something, insult you that day he offered you a ride home?"

"No," Mary said. "He was more than polite."

"You are certain?" Amelia asked.

"When am I ever not certain, Mother?"

"You know I am sorry."

"Don't be, Mother. He never promised me a thing."

In the month following, Jenny and Thomas embarked upon walks, mostly heading west from Dove Street into the wilds that ran beyond the city. There was talk of making a park around a little lake between rocky outcroppings, like the great park Frederick Law Olmsted had designed for Manhattan. The Presbyterians might build a new church. Albany was expanding. The rumble of Southern discontent had provoked an Illinois lawyer named Abraham Lincoln to fight Stephen A. Douglas for the presidency. Even November's cold did not turn Jenny and Thomas from their rambles. They stooped to gather fallen horse chestnuts and fingered the curved surfaces in their pockets. Their grief was a shared bond, and they spent as much time together as they could, finding a soothing happiness in one another's company. Life seemed, suddenly, too brief for either reticence or formalities. They needed one another. Of Mary, Jenny was unconcerned. Why, Mary and Thomas had only spoken with one another two or three times—hardly an understanding. And if Thomas preferred her to Mary, then what was she to do about it?

In December, Jenny persuaded Thomas to abandon the trails west of the city for the warmth and bustle of the quay and lower State Street. She drew

Thomas with her along the granite pavers, dodging block-and-tackle loaders in the din of the thuds and whistles from the Lumber District. One afternoon, Thomas steered Jenny into the Delevan Hotel, where they settled into a pair of high-backed chairs next to the fireplace in the dining room. It was nearly four o'clock; Amelia and Mary had left that morning for East Albany to tend a birth, and Jenny and Thomas had spent the afternoon on the banks of the Hudson, watching sleds dash up and down the frozen river. Jenny pulled off her gloves, unwrapped her cream coat, and leaned back into her chair. The angles of her face were delicate, her skin so white she was nearly colorless. Even the blush the wind had brought out could not enliven her appearance of pale, cosseted beauty.

"Don't you want to be a midwife, too?" Thomas asked, as a waiter brought tea.

*Here,* Jenny thought, *is the question. Also, the end. He will tell me that he finds me high-spirited and pretty, but shallow.* "Do you perceive a fault in my not wanting to?" (A question of her own, in defense.)

"No. Not at all. But it seems the family occupation."

"I am not like Mary. I am not nearly as clever as she is." She preferred the definite, rather than the indefinite; in this again she was different from her twin, whose intelligence could easily tolerate the undefined.

"You are different from your sister, but it does not follow that you are less desirable."

Jenny flung him a look, trying to discern. She had not yet permitted courting; she wanted Thomas's affection to blossom from joy, not sorrow. Passion won in the hours of grief was cheating. But was it still the hour of grief? It was two months now since his father had died, three since hers. Once he had asked her, *Do you dream about your father?* She had told him that once in a dream she had discovered her father reading by a fireplace in the house across the street. *You've been here all this time?* she'd asked.

(She believed her father had loved her best, not knowing it was the clever parent's trick to convince every child they were the most beloved.)

Thomas had dreamed the same dream, and believed not in the universality of the dream but in its singularity.

He leaned across the table and said, "Have I told you that you are the most beautiful girl I have ever seen?"

(Observed by other patrons in the high-ceilinged tearoom, Jenny's grace and reticence forced admiration; Thomas's youthfulness and ardor, an abundance of goodwill. The onlookers forgave them their lack of decorum because their preoccupation and beauty cheered them; they secretly feared they might never survive a future bereavement of their own.)

"You prefer beauty to cleverness?" Jenny pressed the point, because it seemed to her that sisterly betrayal demanded a firm foundation. And if Thomas wanted her, she had to know the terms. Beauty and grief, over time, would fade. A memory of shared anguish would be no match for the persistent glory of Mary's intelligence.

Thomas Fall saw Jenny's insecurity. He closed his hand around hers and said, "I prefer not beauty, but you."

# Chapter Three

After returning his horse and carriage to the livery on Pearl Street, James Blevens unlocked the door to his rented rooms in the Staats House and viewed his surroundings with eyes fresh from the ordered comfort of the Sutter home. His weekly maid despaired of his clutter. She flicked at his piles of books with her feather duster and suggested in her thick Irish accent that he might not want to ruin his eyes with so much reading. The memory of the old country was in her, as it was in him; these rooms were a step down. Coal dust and noise seeped in from the streets. But they were a step up from Manhattan, whose filth and cacophony James had fled for Albany. Good chairs, two of them, near the fireplace. A bedroom. Coved ceilings, wainscot, crown molding. Fine rooms, as hired rooms in Albany went. Enervated after his dinner with the Sutters, yet still alert, he laid his coat and hat on the bed to dry, lit a candle, and, after a brief toilette, set a microscope on the cluttered table.

From the velvet grooves of a mahogany case, James plucked a pair of tweezers, a rectangle of glass, a blade with a tortoiseshell handle, and a dropper. He removed from the pocket of his coat a small portion of the baby's placenta wrapped in cheesecloth that he had cut away when Mary Sutter had been preoccupied with Bonnie. With the blade, he carved a paper-thin slice and mounted it on the rectangle of glass. He lit the small candle under the microscope's stage and affixed the slide with the brass appendages. Fiddling with the focus, he peered into the lens until the edges of the image sharpened.

He was not unacquainted with cellular theory. In New York, he had studied Jean-Baptiste de Lamarck: "Every step which Nature takes when making her direct creations consists in organizing into cellular tissue the minute masses of viscous or mucous substances that she finds at her disposal under favorable circumstances." Recently, he had spent an entire week engrossed in Darwin's *Origin of Species.* That he attended the Presbyterian church on Sundays, where he worshipped out of obligation, did not trouble him. He had learned to divide himself between what he could do and what he could not do, in addition to what he could believe and what he could not believe. He had almost stayed in Manhattan City to do research, but had found compromise instead in Albany, in these hermit-like rooms and in private practice. Less than orderly, his research was meant to satisfy longing and curiosity. He was not intending to publish.

He bent over the microscope, taking in the faint outlines of life.

It was late when he finished; the clock on the bank tower having struck three o'clock a while before. What had he learned? That though the placenta was wholly different than any other organ—a tumor supported by the mother, disposable yet indispensable—its unique function was nonetheless imperceptible in the cell, as undifferentiated from any other cell he had studied.

Mary Sutter's appeal: *Please, it is all I want.* Such an unusual request from so young a woman. How the extraordinary blossomed from the ordinary, though he suspected that Mary Sutter might have always been exceptional. He understood so little. If only one could take a microscope to a person in whole, not just in parts. What would he understand then? Perhaps his own life, with its peculiar introspective lens. His patients were puzzles to be solved, enigmas to be dissected. He could not look at a person without reading the curve of his spine, the meter of his breathing, without wondering about the condition of his internal organs. Before he knew it, his mind would race through the body's systems, trying to detect just which deficiency hobbled them. He was, at all times, interested in life.

From outside came the distant rumble of a train rushing through Patroon Canyon: the New York City Railroad's night train to Buffalo. Briefly, he wondered whether at the Sutter house the thunder was a nightly reminder of Nathaniel's absence. His mother would have taken it so. The Blevens family had lived north of Manhattan City on a stretch of farmland the Hudson River Railroad would bisect within the decade. James had lived with his father, mother, two older brothers, and the ghosts of two dead babies, for his mother was a woman who could never forget. The family worked the fertile land and never once ventured southward into the large city that occasionally spat weary residents northward seeking respite from the grime. The family was aware of its good fortune: the land was good, their lives filled with work, and despite the occasional lamentations of their mother, the boys, immune to the hazards of maternal grief, lived a life unremarkable except for its lack of want. A life sublime, as lives went in those years; across the globe, good fortune was scarce. In Ireland, the potato crop had failed and famine was spreading; in Mexico, war was raging; in France, Napoléon III was escaping from the fortress of Ham.

But all of that changed one night in the middle of the spring thaw of 1846, when James was thirteen years old. Drawn by a strange noise, he left his sleeping brothers behind and opened the door to the dark hallway, where his father stood breathing like the bellows in a blacksmith shop. In a high rasp, his father said, "Get your mother."

Skirting his father, James shook his mother awake. Together they coaxed his father back to bed, and only when he would not lie down, when he fought to stay sitting up, did his mother understand that what her husband was suffering from was no latent fever.

She whirled on James. "Get out! Get out!"

Terrified, he backed into his room, climbing into the bed he shared with his brothers. He lay awake, listening to his mother's tearful entreaties for his father to take water, to take anything, to breathe, to *try*. The night crept on, dark and moonless. James nudged one of his brothers awake and tiptoed behind him to stand horrified at the door. Now both his mother and father lay slumped against the headboard, gasping and feverish. The lamp sent leaping shadows against the wall. James rubbed at his face with the back of his hand, wiping away his tears, looking to Jonathan, who always knew what to do: how to skin a deer, clean a musket, set a rabbit trap deep in the tangles of brush where the hares thought they were safe. But in the dim light of the lamp, Jonathan's face had turned bloodless.

For the next two days, James did not eat. He sat at the doorstep of his parents' room. Even in their suffering, his mother refused him entry, but James would not leave, not even at night, when he curled up in a quilt and dozed at their door. When their end came, two days later, there was a *rattle*, a snake-like, intermittent hissing. And then silence. He entered the room, pulling his quilt around him. He lit the welled sperm oil that had long ago smoked out. He touched his mother's curled, gray hand. Her eyes, blunted and staring, her head at an angle, twisted. Her mouth, open. And across the back of her mouth, a thick, clotted, gray curtain.

His father's throat was similarly occluded. Later, James would learn to recognize diphtheria in an instant, but that night he sank onto the bedclothes, still twisted and damp with sweat, and thought, *Why would the body grow something that would kill it?* The thought consumed him, even as he helped to bury his parents and incinerate the ruined bedclothes.

His parents' deaths altered his sense of balance. James began to fear that life made no sense at all. It was not as if he was unacquainted with death. The soil had already accepted two brothers that his mother could not save from mumps. But a membrane? Made of what? And to what purpose had it grown? There was no doctor for miles, no one to explain the myriad vagaries that presented themselves. The tangle of life and death, so closely associated, fascinated him. He caught rabbits in the field and dissected them before he cooked them. He observed his brothers, watching for signs of mysterious, random assaults on their health. He collected dead animals and made a museum of them in the barn until his brothers, fed up, flung them out with a shovel and made him bury them.

In the winter of 1851, the year James turned eighteen, he sold a plow and left the crisp air of the country for the city. He took a room in a boarding house near the East River in Manhattan City and asked for directions to a hospital.

"You sick?" the clerk asked, snatching the pen away. "We don't want no sick here."

"I'm not sick."

The suspicious clerk looked him up and down before he spat out directions to the New York College of Medicine and Bellevue Hospital. It took a week of haunting the hospital entryway for James to learn the names of the surgeons who were taking apprentices. One, a Dr. Stipp, seemed more inviting than the others. He was thirty-five, maybe, with a neat, combed beard and glasses perched on the end of an aristocratic nose. James followed Dr. Stipp home, running to keep up with his carriage, darting through the rain-swept streets, pulling his inadequate coat tight around his chin while he dodged the trash-filled gutters.

The housekeeper let James in when he knocked, dripping clothes and all, and retrieved Dr. Stipp from his brandy to come see the insistent boy at the door. The doctor led James to his study and sat behind his desk with a pipe in his hands and his eyebrows raised. The office, full of leather-bound books and a desk as wide as a kitchen table, was a room of such warmth and civility that James nearly did not pull from his sodden coat the dead cat he had just collected from the alley. It was newly deceased, dead of one of the many diseases that regularly slayed them. He unwrapped from its protective chamois cloth the butchering knife he had also hidden under his cloak, spread a newspaper across the doctor's desk, and before the doctor could stay his hand, slit the cat open from chest to pubis.

Dr. Stipp lay down his pipe and pushed away from his desk, protesting.

"Before you stop me, if you would please just show me," James said, expertly separating the jiggling yellow fat, carefully slitting the taut, opaque membrane, letting it curl back to reveal the organs underneath, so carefully arranged, a genius of a puzzle.

"Here," James said, pointing the knife tip at the gizzard-like organ lying behind the stomach. "What is this? I think it must be for digestion, but I can't imagine what it does." He lifted the stomach with the knife. "You see, just under there? It has a tube, or a duct, and it feeds into this coil of gut here." He looked up then, because Dr. Stipp had not spoken. The doctor's hand had retreated to his vest pocket, but he was leaning over his desk, holding his smoking pipe aloft.

"Why, it's the pancreas. A little different from ours, but not much." The doctor moved closer. "And there, the liver. But that's obvious."

"But what does the pancreas do? Why is it there?"

The doctor stepped back, pursing his lips. "How many times have you done this?"

"Enough. I've got it pretty well figured out. But I don't have any books."

The doctor leaned over the table. "It's easier if the animals have been dead longer, but this will do." He poked his finger at the stomach. "Make the cut there. It will expose the organ without ruining your understanding."

James made the cut.

"Yes, that's it, but for God's sake, don't saw," the doctor said.

They worked into the night, breaking for a dinner of beefsteak and potatoes and whiskey, served in the doctor's elegant dining room by a maid wearing an apron of snow-white cotton and a cap of lace on her head. She and the doctor's wife, Genevieve, seemed unfazed by this strange, windtorn guest and his project in the front room. Afterwards, under the wavering flame of a single sperm lamp, the doctor and James worked until the digestive system of cats was no longer a puzzle for him.

Dr. Stipp installed James in an attic room in his home next to the East River. James's education began the next day, and continued for a year. In addition to following the doctor from house to house, learning what he could, James twice attended the six-month run of courses at the medical college. It consisted of lectures in anatomy, with a cadaver on a table and the professor making cuts and explaining to the students, kept at a distance in their seats, what each revealed organ did. There were other courses in Surgery, Chemistry, Theory and Practice of Medicine, Institutes of Medicine and Materia Medica, and Obstetrics and Diseases of Women and Children. Never once, however, did James perform a surgery. Never once did he see general patients, at least not under the auspices of the college. That possibility presented itself only because James was apprenticed to Dr. Stipp. James was, by far, one of the luckiest, for not everyone taking the courses was given the opportunity to see a doctor in actual practice.

At first, James was just charged with carrying the doctor's instruments in their leather case, but about a month after Dr. Stipp had taken him into his practice, he found himself ducking and darting down Worth Street, following Dr. Stipp on a call. Everything about Manhattan City—the noise, the filth, the traffic, the wailing of its street denizens—had battered James in the month since his arrival. An argument could be made that he was beginning to find his feet in this strange, clamoring place where the air bore no resemblance to the sweeter perfume not thirty miles north, but here in Five Points the dirt and crowding overwhelmed. The streets veered off at angles and the ramshackle tenements were peppered with advertisements for tailors, painters, oiled clothing, and every manner of commerce. Broken windows were stuffed with newspapers and rags against the cold. Grog houses, tanneries, bakeries, and houses shouldered up against one another; wooden stairs jutted from their windows to zigzag down to the street. Dr. Stipp avoided a block and tackle, its hook swinging wide out into the street, the crowds screaming and ducking, the children gleeful, running shoeless in the muddy puddles that collected in the sunken cobbles, the origin of which was best not contemplated. James dodged the great fishhook and scuttled after the doctor, surprised by the older man's agility and confidence among the hustlers and harlots who thronged the streets. Over coffee that morning, Dr. Stipp had been eager: *What you'll see today, you'll see nowhere else; disease has an affinity for the broken.* After navigating a sinuous, seemingly nonsensical path—James was now hopelessly lost—Dr. Stipp darted down a narrow alley, where from the windows of a tavern drifted a plaintive Irish song. Five Points, for all its faults, was Ireland transplanted, absent the dales and green hills of which the patrons now sang melancholy and gorgeous tribute.

The groggery before them was tumbledown, and James could not understand why they were now stationary after so much activity. Dr. Stipp opened a door hidden under a slantwise post, and they descended a stairwell to a dark basement, where they arrested momentarily to let their eyes adjust in the gloom. The cellar's stone walls leaked mud. Small rivers of murky water collected in buckets positioned at strategic points; billowing sheets hung from the ceiling simulated rooms. The effect was of a small sailing ship, marooned underground, doomed. Someone, or some thing—an animal?—was crying. The noise drew James's gaze, and he peered into the filtered light shed by one rectangular, thick-paned window high in a corner. Under it, a girl of indeterminate age was bending over a cradle tending a mewling child.

When she saw them, she righted and said, "Mother died a week ago. He's been crying since she died."

Her accent was thick with the sound of Ireland, though the family couldn't have been new to the Five Points, because no immigrant could afford such a treasure as this falling-down tenement. It could have been a century since her family had come over. It would have made no difference in how she talked. A round of "Danny Boy" sifted through the floorboards from above, as if to magnify her tragedy, though the girl did not cry or even register any great disappointment. Her message delivered, she bent back over the child, as if she assumed that absent their ailing patient, the doctor and his guest would now leave her, but Dr. Stipp crossed the muddy floor, leaned over, and lifted the crying child into his arms. His voice was as kind as James had ever heard it when he said, "I am so sorry, Sarah. I wish you'd let me know." But when he turned to James, his voice came in telegraphic pedagogy: "The mother was a tubercular. Rusty sputum. Cough like a storm." He renewed his attentions to the child and the girl, who could not have been more than eighteen, but whose breasts James now assessed as plump enough to confer womanhood, whatever her age.

"How old is the boy again, Sarah?" Stipp asked.

"He was born two years ago. February, I think it was? Or maybe January."

If this date was truly the child's birth date, then he was far too small for his age. Listless, he whimpered as Dr. Stipp bent his head to his chest. The boy's fingers were blunted and blue with cold and his chest thrust in and out in his efforts to breathe. Whether the girl was aware of the child's danger was difficult to tell, for she had about her the air of someone quietly resigned. After some time had passed—time in which Sarah continued to gaze at Dr. Stipp with a dazed, apprehensive, exhausted look reminiscent of cows that James remembered from home, the doctor lay the child in its bed and touched the girl's elbow.

"Sarah, I'm going to speak to your father now." He left James behind as he climbed the stairs to extract the father from the grog house to tell him he would lose another family member within the week. Sarah's gaze drifted over to James, then back to the ailing child in its bed. She placed a longing hand on the cradle's wicker frame and began to rock the bed back and forth. The song from above roused to a stomping jig, one James would later learn was a marital melody designed to incite a groom's desire, and which came to a dwindling halt as the news was delivered. James could think of nothing to say to the girl, who finally leaned against the moist cellar wall and shut her eyes.

Dr. Stipp returned and pulled a vial from his bag. "Tincture of opium to give to the boy when he struggles too hard. Give it all," he said, saying without saying that the opium would kill the child, and that she was to be the merciful executioner.

She took that vial with slender, beautiful fingers. It was impossible to know if she understood; she displayed neither gratitude nor reluctance, merely the same cowed resignation.

Once outside, Dr. Stipp took James by the elbow. "Breathe deep to cleanse your lungs when we leave this place. This part of the city will kill you."

But James returned to the slum the next week, and the week after that, reluctantly drawn by a place—and a person—mired in helplessness. Ostensibly, he went instead of Stipp, to provide encouragement where there was clearly none to be found. The ruse was not remarked upon by the girl, who accepted James's lurking sympathy. (Was that what it was, sympathy? Or perhaps instead, voyeurism?) She only marked his presence with a numb and tolerant patience that he interpreted as gratitude. The predicted final week passed, followed by another, and then another. Every time James arrived in the cellar, he expected to find the boy dead and the girl destroyed, but remarkably, the boy still breathed. Looking at the boy's puckered blue lips, his feeble claim on life, James fell in love. The child's achievement was somehow heroic, and for one uncomfortable moment cast James's parents' failure to breathe after contracting diphtheria as somehow a failure.

For several hours at a time he cradled the child in his arms while the fatigued Sarah slept on a musty mattress. In those hours, James felt as if his father and mother were dying all over again. It was not grief that kept him returning, not consciously at least, but instead a sense of utility that he had not been able to give his parents; though armed only with two months of medical lectures, any help he offered now was rudimentary at the most. From time to time, he cleared the child's throat of phlegm. He would lay the child over his knee and gently pound his lungs to loosen the tenacious stuff that soon required another round of clearing. Through all these ministrations, the child, withdrawn and passive, peered at him with eyes the color of a pale Irish sky and did not once protest. Such calm acceptance and perseverance evoked in James an admiration and devotion he had never summoned for anyone since his parents' death, so that when the boy died a month after his mother had succumbed, finally hastened by Sarah, who, having spent night after night walking the dark cellar tormented by the boy's wheezing resolve, ended it all by dropping the whole of the opium in a draught of whiskey and forcing it down the boy's throat, James grieved far more than she did.

James would not ascribe what happened afterwards to pity. Rather, as he held the girl's hands and vowed before the same gaggle of guests as had attended the boy's funeral the day before that he would love, honor, and cherish her, he truly thought that he would. He took Sarah to live with him in his room at Dr. Stipp's, a situation viewed by Stipp as an ironic and unexpected turn of events for his gifted student, and by his wife Genevieve as romantic, but suspect. Immediately it was apparent that the marriage was not a great success. Separated from her father, adrift in a part of the city where no one reminisced about County Cork or hailed one another with a slapping of backs and an invitation to drink, Sarah dwindled like her younger brother, until James was fraught with worry. Fearing illness, he took her on day trips on the Hudson River Railroad to the north end of Manhattan Island for the fresh air. They wandered over the hills and rocks and perched themselves on the bluffs overlooking the Hudson, picnicking on sausages and cold potatoes. She soon rallied, and on those afternoons they tried to find common ground besides the death of her brother. But Sarah was not interested in microscopes or disease; neither had she had any schooling, and her speech turned so thick with brogue that at times James couldn't even understand her. Free now from her grief, she would ramble on, relating raucous, at times unintelligible stories of life in the slums, the breeze off the river forcing them to huddle close to one another, even as James began to realize that it was lingering love for the dead child and not the living, mercifully murderous sister that had captivated him. And now there loomed the inevitable, irrevocable tie of children. Only two months into their marriage, he resolved to withdraw from lovemaking, or at least, when that proved intolerable, to withdraw early during the act, an insult that the newly bold Sarah could not tolerate.

"Children," she said, "are what marriage is for."

(Her Catholicism, too, had been a shock, though he was at fault, for he was the one who had acted on impulse, disregarding everything because of a supposed idea of romance.)

When he refused to comply, the same cool determination that had allowed Sarah to kill her brother also allowed her to pack up their one pot and feather bed and depart for her father's basement and grog house, moaning that annulment would be impossible, because he'd already sullied her.

James went on with his studies, depressed by his foolhardy foray into love, determined to learn as much as he could. He helped Dr. Stipp examine his tubercular patients, learning to prescribe brandy for some, eggnog for others, and when it did not compromise their modesty, to listen for the faint signs of a lung slowly hollowing out, his ears pressed up against the ribcage, sometimes using a stethoscope, sometimes not. Medicine was devoted to diet and air and brandy, for there was little else. He never saw Dr. Stipp give out morphia to the dying again; he wondered what had prompted him to ease Sarah's brother's death and not others. Perhaps, James thought, the offer of marriage and the offer of morphia had leapt from the same impulse: to take away the sadness in her eyes.

Even Dr. Stipp rarely performed surgery, and only then to cut out sores that would not heal. He was judicious with his knife, for he believed that there was little one could do for the living, really, besides touch and comfort. Chloroform was new and untested, and ether had become a flammable nightmare. Surgery was always the last resort. So it was only in the autopsy lectures that James learned some of what he craved to know: the levers and pulleys of the muscular system, the placement of the bones, the ball and socket of the joints, the clever role of tendons to bind the structure together.

Still, after his year of apprenticeship with Dr. Stipp, there was something *invisible*, something *electrical*, that James did not understand. Something sparked the body to live, propelled the heart to beat, the brain to think, the structure to live on, to sometimes win over typhoid, measles, pneumonia, and even diphtheria. The body was a structure, yes, with struts and piping, but something else, some miraculous, invisible fabric made it work. But he had no idea what that was, and no idea how to repair the structure once it failed. No one else seemed to know, either. He left his apprenticeship with the surgeon with a medical degree and an insufficient understanding, but it had to do.

Only in his current work at the microscope, alone in his rooms in Albany, did James begin to fathom that the invisible fabric might be something that no one had ever imagined. And it had taken him years to understand that his mother had kept him and his brothers from their sick room that night not only because she feared their death, but because of an emotion stronger than fear—an unseen loneliness for her dead children.

Every year, James traveled back to Manhattan to visit Sarah. A marriage of inconsequence, but a marriage nonetheless, for the love that had turned out to be pity had not hardened to disregard. He could not completely abandon her. He was a boy from a farm who had moved to the city to chase his curiosity and had married an Irish girl for whom he had felt sorry. It was as if he had lost his mind one day. But he did not regret the marriage. Rather, he regretted his impulsiveness, and the loneliness that had accompanied him northward.

And he regretted that he did not yet know what real love was.

Across town, Mary was sitting in the rocking chair in the lying-in room worrying about how she had misdiagnosed the cause of Bonnie's hemorrhage when Blevens had discerned its cause right away. She wanted to believe that if he hadn't been there, she would have recognized the issue herself, but she couldn't be certain that she would have. She was embarrassed. She knew more than Blevens did about midwifery, but she had been angry and distracted. *A tear.* When a relaxed uterus was the most common problem after a delivery. She had allowed emotion to cloud her thinking.

*Pride goeth,* she thought. *And now I have lost my chance.*

"Mary?" Jenny was at the door, whispering through the narrow opening Mary had left for the light. Downstairs, the clock struck three a.m.

This was a rare visit to the lying-in room for Jenny. Ordinarily she avoided it and everything to do with midwifery and, by extension, Mary. Since Thomas, the two sisters had defaulted to distant politeness in their interactions, though neither of them ever mentioned it. An unspoken truce with unspoken rules.

Mary stood and motioned Jenny in, and Jenny paused to admire the baby asleep in the bed beside Bonnie before drawing Mary to the window, where she fell into her arms.

Jenny had been crying. Thomas was going to war. Did Mary think the war would last beyond three months?

Like an actor on a stage, Mary deflected self, her usual and instinctive response to need. *Do not mention your regard for Thomas; do not admit it.* The sudden intimacy surprised her. It was unlike Jenny to seek her out for solace. They were unpracticed at it, and Mary could feel a latent resistance in her sister's body, even as they embraced. She looked over her sister's head outside, to the dark street, which was as still as death.

The baby stirred and Mary pulled Jenny into the hallway. Sitting on the top of the stairs together in the light of a single candle burning in a wall sconce, the sisters marveled. Always astonishment, the world over, when one is affected by upheaval. We are bored by the familiar, but terrified by the unfamiliar. The added lament: Christian, too, was leaving.

"Our hearts will break," Jenny said.

Mary didn't want to think of her brother at war. He was asleep now behind his bedroom door, where she wanted him to stay, safe and protected. As strained as her relationship was with her sister, her relationship with Christian was as easy as if they were mother and son. No competition, only joy. But now, with their full skirts gathered around their ankles, whispering like they used to when they were younger and shared the same bed, Mary felt a thaw between herself and Jenny, and the veil of night working on her, inviting disclosure.

"I wanted to be a surgeon," Mary said.

"No woman is a surgeon. Besides, how can you think about a thing like that when we are losing a brother and I am losing Thomas? You are too cool, Mary."

*Too cool.* Cool about everything but achieving her goal? Perhaps everyone viewed her that way, even Thomas. *No woman is a surgeon.* Mary smoothed her skirts and tucked the stray curls of her hair back into a comb, tired now, the full weight of the day's disappointment bringing tears to her eyes. She felt like a failure. Wanting to become a surgeon when she couldn't even take proper care of Bonnie. Believing she could sow intimacy again with her sister, when they were unalike as twin sisters could be. From the lying-in room came the mewling sounds of the baby, needing to be fed.

Rising, Mary said, "You could help sometimes, you know."

"I don't want anything to do with babies," Jenny said.

"You might someday," Mary said, though she hated acknowledging the prospect, for it seemed a prediction.

In the glimmer of light from the sconce, Jenny smiled shyly. "When I do, then you will be here to help me, won't you?"

But Mary didn't answer her, only turned her back and headed for the lying-in room door.

# *Chapter Four*

James Blevens sat at his desk in his surgery pondering what to write so that Colonel Townsend, the newly appointed commander of the 25th Regiment from Albany, would choose him over the other physicians applying for the position of regimental surgeon. Time was short. The North was rallying, troops were assembling. That very morning, Wednesday, April the seventeenth, the Sixth Massachusetts, the first regiment to venture southward in defense of the Union, had set out from Boston for Washington City.

James Blevens dipped his pen in the inkwell and began to write.

*Dear Colonel Townsend, I am offering my services as Regimental Surgeon for the 25th Regiment. My credentials are impeccable. I studied medicine for one year at Bellevue Hospital in New York, repeating the requisite six-month course of lectures to enhance my understanding. I then moved to Albany, where my surgery is located on Washington Avenue. I am well acquainted with serious fractures and their repair. The most recent fracture I set was on a boy who'd been run over by a wagon.*

Mention of this accident reminded James of Thomas Fall's parents. He had inquired around, learned the details. Had the policeman called him instead of that drunkard Fin McDonnall more than a year ago, he was certain he could have saved them, setting their broken limbs on the street before they were even moved, unlike McDonnall, who'd let them be picked up and hoisted into the wagon bed, where they had both died. In his care, Thomas's parents might have lived, and he would have visited them often, and perhaps encountered Mary, who would no doubt have been sitting at their bedside, stalwart and useful. Mary would have been curious about the fractures; he would have answered her questions: "You see here is the break of the femur. It's important to splint it strongly so that it can't move. In this case, I used a plaster with a splint and assigned them both to bedrest. Rest is very important. How long have you been interested in medicine?" Cast as the hero, the indulgent pedagogue, he might have held a different position in Mary Sutter's eyes. It had been five days since he had eaten dinner with the Sutters, and he had not been able to stop thinking about her. With difficulty, he pushed her from his mind and again dipped his pen.

*The injured boy walks now without a limp. In addition, I am conversant in all manner of violent injuries sustained in factory accidents. Albany being a great manufacturing hub, I have attended victims of the ironworks, tanneries, lumber district, and railroads, learning skills that I believe will be appropriate to the situation thrust upon us all. Please return your decision at your earliest convenience. I am yours most sincerely, etc., James Blevens, Surgeon.*

"'Scuse me?" A young man was standing at the threshold of James's surgery. Dark brows over large eyes gave the impression of thoughtfulness, though his pants hems were ringed with dirt and manure, and his skin was sallow. James could not remember having left the door open after dismissing his last patient an hour before. With some degree of certainty he recalled at least latching it. He had not heard the rasp of the catch, nor a knock, and he wished now that he had shuttered his window so that the candle burning on his desk would not have alerted passersby to his presence.

"Are you sick?" James asked, squinting at the doorway.

"I'm Jake Miles. Bonnie's husband."

James could have passed him on the street and not recognized him.

"I've come to claim my wife," Jake said. He waved the note from the door that James had posted nearly a week ago and said, "Can you show me where Dove Street is?"

---

In the foyer of the Sutters' home, James removed his hat and introduced Jake to Mary Sutter.

"This is Bonnie's husband, Jake Miles, who is eager to see his wife and baby." He was perhaps assigning more emotion to Jake than Jake himself felt. On the ride over, Jake had been taciturn, maneuvering his cart over the cobbles with the deliberation of a farmer unused to carriage traffic. He had not mentioned the child, or seemed all that eager to see Bonnie, either, but it was possible the boy was just uncertain.

"How do you do?" Mary said.

Jake ducked his head in greeting, his hat clutched tightly to his waist. He gestured toward the parlor doors, where a maid had laid tea. There was an iced cake and yellow daffodils in a crystal vase. "I can't pay you for taking care of Bonnie."

"Don't trouble yourself. Payment is unnecessary," Mary said. "I am very happy to tell you that Bonnie is well, but she must stay with us a bit longer. She's not strong enough to travel. And certainly not at this hour of the night."

"But we've got to get home," Jake said. "The ferry doesn't run past eight."

"Your wife has had a difficult time. And the baby shouldn't be out in the evening. Perhaps you could wait until the morning?"

"But in the morning the animals will need me," Jake said, his voice polite but adamant. "We need to get on."

Mary emitted an almost imperceptible sigh of frustration, but she called a maid to show Jake up the stairs, his shoes leaving pebbles of hardened dirt on the floor. When he disappeared into the lying-in room, she turned on James and said, "Where has he been?"

James shrugged. "I have no idea."

"You should have dissuaded him."

"He is her husband."

"He is a seventeen-year-old boy who knows nothing."

They stood in the foyer, opposed. The maid padded down the stairs, her gaze skittering between them before she ducked into the kitchen and told the cook that she had better come listen at the door because Miss Sutter was at it again.

All the way over, James had planned what he would say to Mary in order to put the evening of Bonnie's delivery behind them. He owed Mary a great deal and wanted to mend the rift, which had seemed impossible only an hour ago. But Jake had given him a legitimate entrée, which he had been eager to take. True, help had been given both ways that evening. Mary had helped with Bonnie's delivery; he had stopped Bonnie's hemorrhage. In his mind, the debt was already paid. But this wasn't completely about a debt. He wanted to help her, as Stipp had once helped him. He gestured with his hat and said, "I was glad that Jake came by, Miss Sutter, because it gave me an opportunity to return. You and I didn't part on the best of circumstances."

"No, we did not."

"I have an offer for you. Why don't you let me speak to Dr. Marsh on your behalf? I know him; perhaps if I recommend you, he might be inclined to rethink his decision." He was going out on a limb, because he doubted very much that Marsh would take to it, but it was the help he had to offer. And she *was* skilled. That he himself might not be chosen as Townsend's surgeon he did not mention. He was going to go to the war no matter what occurred, in any fashion that he could.

Mary regarded him for a moment. "You want to speak for me?"

"Yes, with your permission."

"The last thing the clerk said to me was that no woman would ever attend Albany Medical College."

"A clerk is nothing. I'll talk to Marsh. You could just as easily have asked me to intercede on your behalf as ask me to apprentice you."

"But Dr. Marsh didn't even return my letters. Three medical schools have turned me down. Why would he change his mind for you?"

Blevens considered carefully what to say next. He wanted to fully discharge the perceived debt and thereby gain Mary's trust; here was a way, but not a certain way. He feared her disappointment should he fail, and it was very likely he would fail. "To be truthful, Marsh may not change his mind."

"Then I do not want intercession from you. It is ungenerous of you to dangle hope when none exists."

How was it that she stirred both exasperation and sympathy at the same time? In her presence, it was like being at war, arousing simultaneous urges both to fight and to run away.

"Are you always this stubborn?" he asked.

There was a bout of laughter from behind the kitchen door, followed by a stern warning of reprimand as the door flew open and the maids scattered. Jenny and Thomas emerged from the kitchen after them.

"Those maids think they know so much," Jenny said. "Eavesdropping at the door again."

"At least they strive to know something," Mary said, straightening.

A look flew between the girls, and then just as quickly dissipated. Venomous or sweet, it was difficult to tell which, because Thomas Fall intervened again with news, smoothing the air. They had just been downtown. A phalanx of volunteer militia had arrived on the New York Central Express from Buffalo; the city was filling with soldiers and there wasn't a room to be had in any hotel. Not even the elegant, expensive Delevan, where they had all greeted Abraham Lincoln at a special levee held there on his way to Washington in February, had any vacancy. And now Lincoln had called for men, and everyone around the state was reporting to Albany to muster in. A crowd had gathered this afternoon at the Capitol, and a band was still playing in the park near the medical school, and the whole of the city was seething with excitement.

"You should have seen it, Mary, it was glorious. I think even you would have declared it a spectacle worth seeing. You might have even learned about something other than midwifery," Jenny said, and then she and Thomas disappeared together through the French doors into the parlor, apparitions of happiness stirred into deeper intimacy by the threat of Thomas's imminent departure. Mary held herself very straight; her gaze did not follow her sister and her companion. James Blevens suffered a surprise stab of jealousy, certain that he was right about Mary's regard for Thomas, but he could not understand the attraction. Whatever affection Mary suffered for Thomas Fall seemed misplaced. She was not the same confident woman when Thomas Fall was near. Or perhaps it was the sister she minded, though they were each so different as not to be in competition at all. Blevens wished very much that he could say, "I have it fixed for you. Dr. Marsh said yes, and you will be admitted tomorrow," convinced that by saying this he could erase the sadness from her eyes. Through the open door, the lovers could be observed seated upon the divan, familiar but formal. James thought that there was something not quite right. Years of reading people's bodies had instilled in him an instinct for the hidden.

He said, "I do beg your pardon, but they seem not quite suited for one another."

Mary said, "Well, they are in love."

Not even a hint of wistfulness.

"You want something you think you cannot have," James Blevens said.

Mary looked at him then, startled, and a flare of anger flickered in her eyes before they cooled. "You have brought your charge, and now you must go."

On the steps outside, James turned to apologize, but Mary had already shut the door.

"Come on, now, Bonnie. Get up. The ferry's leaving soon."

Upstairs, Bonnie pushed herself up in bed. She had almost forgotten that Jake would come for her. Her previous life had seemed to disappear, erased by meals in bed and gentle inquiries regarding her well-being. Before Jake had awakened her, she'd been dreaming of feathers, a consequence of five days' rest in a comfortable bed. "But Jake, I haven't even been out of bed yet. I don't know if I can walk."

"Sure you can. Just get up. I only left you because I had to take care of the animals. You'd 'ave delivered at home if things hadn't come on so fast. You can't stay here. We got to get on." The clock struck seven. They had an hour before the ferry to East Albany was to leave. "Get yourself dressed."

"But you haven't even looked at the baby," Bonnie said.

Jake Miles edged toward the bed and peered at the squashed-up face and pimply cheeks of the boy. "What's the matter with him?"

"Nothing. He's just new is all. You're not used to him." Neither was she. She held the infant shakily in her arms. She was afraid to go home. She didn't know enough. Not yet. It was terrifying having a baby. They sucked hard at your breasts and cried for no reason she could understand.

Jake edged closer.

"Don't you like him?" Bonnie asked.

"Sure. Sure I like him." Jake sidled up to the bed and sat down. "What's his name?"

"I didn't name him yet. I was waiting for you,"

Jake broke into a sheepish grin. "You were?"

"Wouldn't name him without you. What do you think?"

"I don't know."

"How about Jake?"

"You think?"

"He looks like you."

"He does, doesn't he?"

By the time Mary had shut the door on James Blevens, Jake had nudged Bonnie into getting dressed, which Mary reluctantly helped her finish doing when she arrived upstairs. Jake held the boy in his arms, a stunned, marveling expression on his face. His hushed awe had the effect of making Mary a little less worried about the two of them leaving, but all the same, she said, "If you're going to take him home tonight, you'd better learn a thing or two." And she made him diaper the child and swaddle him tightly against the night cold. Then she packaged six doses of ergot powder into an empty jar and pressed it into Bonnie's hands. "This will keep you from bleeding. You must take a teaspoon—twenty drachms—each night until it is all gone. Do you understand?" Bonnie nodded and lifted the smooth round stop from the bottle. A token of loveliness to take home with her. She took a last look at the vacated bed, the flowered wallpaper, the panoply of hot-water bottles, the feather pillows.

The young couple went off in their wagon with the baby, the wheels clattering over the cobbles, the farm horse skittish, unused to the paved city streets.

Bonnie might have been any young mother, required too soon to fend for herself, Mary thought. It should not have upset her as it did, because it rarely ended disastrously, but you could not say that it frequently ended well.

She sighed and shut the front door and walked past the parlor, not even glancing inside.

On the brocade couch in the near corner of the parlor, half hidden from the door, Jenny and Thomas were locked in an embrace.

Jenny said, "I cannot bear to think of you going, Thomas." He was kissing her cheeks, her lips, grazing her shoulders and neck with his hands. Not yet coupled, Amelia's vigilance having imposed strict virginity, they were eager, as imminent lovers are, when time threatens. Thomas heard Mary's footsteps echo in the foyer, and withdrew from Jenny's arms with difficulty. Respect was such a taskmaster. The parlor as bedroom; he would consume Jenny here and now were it not for his regard for Amelia and Mary.

Jenny's love had saved him. From shared grief, more than devotion. She cupped his face in her hands, and the intimacy of palm to cheek promised imminent surrender.

"You'll come back?" she asked, but Thomas heard *when* you come back.

Oh, he would die if he had to wait another three months.

"I don't even want to leave," he said. Such lies men tell, but it was true that he did not want to leave her arms. He would take her into battle with him, if he could. What was a handkerchief, or the memory of a kiss, compared to the sweetness of Jenny, yielding?

"Then don't leave."

He kissed her cheek, and Jenny read the lie.

"You will go away and forget me," she said, dissolving into doubt, for his protestations of love were always given in the thrall of touch, and only honor bound a man and woman when distance intervened. And what effect would the enticement of war have? In becoming more of a man, he might mistrust his boyish choices.

The beginnings of love, when the phsyical and the spiritual, seemingly aligned, disallow hesitation. Thomas put his hands in her hair, undid a single pin, and loosened a lock of her curls. Like Mary's thick mane, but Jenny's were more easily tamed.

She suffered his caress, but wanted permanence instead, believing it to be more real. "Thomas? You do love me, don't you?"

Thomas whispered into her ear, breaching doubt with a proposition. A question to answer a question. Such is the enigma of love.

# *Chapter Five*

"It's too much, Mother," Christian Sutter said. On his back, he carried a haversack stuffed with food, a blanket, two pairs of socks, a change of pants and shirt, an oilskin, a knife, plate, fork, spoon, and a new canteen, all purchased at an outfitters' store that had sprung up on the quay overnight. There was also stationery, a bottle of ink, a pen, and money for posting letters.

Amelia drew Christian's shoulders down to hers in an embrace. He had been up since before dawn, rattling about in his room. She had brought him coffee at seven, and they drank it together in his bedroom while he finished packing, though Amelia thought he was secreting far too little in the haversack's ties and pockets to sustain himself for three months. He could not contain his eagerness, though he tried to for her sake, and in her unhappiness she had been unable to think of anything to say to him. The hours sped by until ten, when he and Thomas joined the regiment at the armory for the farewell parade down State Street. Amelia and her daughters searched the marching columns as they passed, but they had not been able to find either one of them. The act of joining an army had somehow transformed them into strangers. Now the 25th was massed at the base of Maiden Lane, and she and the girls had pushed through the crowd until they had found them.

The *Lady of Perth* ferry had just left the dock with another hundred men, but it would return soon, for it would take ten trips to ferry the entire regiment across the swollen Hudson River toward the railroad depot on the far side. On the quay, there was a band, in uniform, and a flag, brilliant blue. The day had the crisp promise of spring; the freshet had receded, leaving the cobbles muddy and slippery. Saying farewell was a noisy business this April morning. There was so much vibrant feeling, a willful ignorance of what was to come. It had been almost a hundred years since Albany had been taken up with a war, and in between there had been years in which to forget the consequences.

Amelia released Christian and took his hand. She would not let go until the last second. Mary and Jenny and Thomas stood now in a tight circle in the milling crowd of soldiers who hailed from all over New York, from high and low, farms and offices. Later in the war, only the poor would go—the Irish off the boats, the Italians, paid by wealthy young men like Christian to take their place. But now it was an honor to be going. Not an obligation, but a lark. Even among strangers, kisses were laughingly demanded and freely given; there was a new sense of freedom in the air. All over the North, men had begged women to marry them, and all over the North, women had said yes.

Jenny had said yes.

Yesterday, at City Hall, at four o'clock in the afternoon, Jenny and Thomas had gotten married. Mary, Amelia, and Christian had stood with them in the justice's chambers as witnesses. Before the ceremony, the justice of the peace had questioned Thomas.

"You are my third couple today. Is it merely the war nipping at your heels like all the others?"

"No," Thomas protested.

Though he seemed unconvinced, the justice nevertheless assumed an air of sudden industriousness and proceeded briskly with the ceremony. Even during the portion when he said, *Do you promise to take this man, this woman*, he did not linger on the words.

During the brief rite, Mary disciplined her expression and posture with the same control she reserved for managing a difficult labor. The week before, when Thomas and Jenny had announced the engagement with glasses of sherry raised and Jenny more deeply happy than Mary had ever seen her, Mary had kissed Thomas's cheek in chaste welcome and then suffered the long dinner and her mother's concerned glances and Christian's jubilant oblivion before escaping to her room early with the excuse of a headache, which a spate of silent weeping soon obligingly produced.

Amelia, her arm protective around Mary's waist, fought to hold her doubt in check, though withholding consent had been impossible, for the world was caught up in love. Love and war, it seemed, worked by the same rules. One had to hurry, before the fires flared out.

That night, another celebration. A good last meal, though no one said it, deferring of speaking of the war until the next morning.

As the cake was served, Amelia touched Mary's wrist. "You aren't hungry, dear?"

Mary stretched her face into a smile and said, "The meal didn't agree. Just an upset stomach," but she was thinking, *It is done. They are married. This is what a newborn must feel. Cut from its mother, the twin pulse that has kept it alive, ceasing forever.*

A maid appeared and whispered in Mary's ear.

"Don't wait for me," Mary said as she got up from the table, relieved to have an excuse not to have to smile or to pretend happiness any longer. "Don't let me spoil the celebration. I'll be just a moment."

In the foyer, Bonnie was clutching her bundled infant in her arms, obviously exhausted, dark circles shadowing her eyes, tendrils of hair escaping from underneath her cloth bonnet. A week, Mary thought. That was all the girl had lasted.

"There is something wrong," Bonnie said, rushing toward Mary as soon as she saw her. "The baby fussed and cried all night and all today, but he stopped crying on the way here. Is he all right?"

"Bonnie, how did you get here? Where is Jake?" Mary asked, drawing Bonnie close to her. She unwrapped Bonnie's shawl, untied her bonnet. The girl was trembling.

"Jake drove me to the ferry, and then I walked from the landing. There's something wrong, I know there is."

It was perhaps a mile uphill from the quay to the Sutter house. For the mother of a newborn child, it would have been an exhausting walk. Mary took the baby from Bonnie and guided her to the stairs, where she sank onto a step. Mary sent for Christian, who bounded out of the dining room, ready as always to do anything she asked of him. It was all Mary could do not to weep; tomorrow, he would leave for the war.

"Could you please carry Bonnie up the stairs for me?" she asked. "Take her to the lying-in room," she added, as Christian swept Bonnie up in his arms.

Lagging behind, Mary unwrapped the heavy blankets, certain of what she would find. The baby's budlike mouth and tiny, curled hands seemed slightly unformed. Unfinished. Even in death, the skin was translucent, revealing a glimmer of the veins and bones within. *It is the stillness,* Mary thought, *that stuns. The complete absence of life.* It was always a shock, even to her.

"Bonnie," Mary said, when she reached the lying-in room.

She had tried to keep her voice even, but Bonnie moaned and sank onto the bed. Mary handed Christian the baby to hold while she gave Bonnie laudanum, and then after washing the dead child and wrapping him in a new blanket and laying him in the cradle beside the bed, she said to Christian, who had lingered to keep her company, that he ought to go downstairs.

"No. I'll stay with her," he said. "You go down to the party."

"No. It's your last night at home," Mary said. "You should be downstairs."

But Christian insisted. "Jenny is your twin. I'll change places with you in an hour or so."

Christian placed a cane chair outside the door. He was glad for a quiet moment. For all his eagerness, he was frightened suddenly, and he didn't want his sisters or his mother to know how afraid he was. He and Thomas had been to the armory in Troy earlier in the day, and there had not been enough muskets to go around. He, however, had gotten a hold of one, and it was the feel of the gun in his hands that had suddenly made the war seem more real than it had been in his imagination. He was frightened of being afraid, frightened of dying. He hadn't told Mary, but he thought the dead baby was a sign. He hoped she didn't tell Jenny. A wedding shouldn't be spoiled with news of a dead child. He rarely entered the lying-in room; having lived since his father's death in a world of women, he had developed boundaries for his own survival. But he had spied Bonnie's husband a week ago, when he had come to take her away, and had taken an instant and unreasonable dislike to him. And where was her husband now? His dislike seemed entirely justified. In his arms, Bonnie had given the feather-light impression of a bird, marooned. She was like Jenny. Small-boned, hair streaked with gold, fragile. He was contemplating this when the sound of crying came from behind the door.

He tapped on the door, and immediately the tears ceased, as if someone had shut off a gas jet: the last flare and then nothing.

"Are you all right?" he called, opening the door.

There was the swift rustle of the coverlet as Bonnie sat up, a thin form in the dimness. Her hands, like wings, were folded over her breasts, where two damp circles on her dress bodice smelled of curdled cream.

Perhaps, he thought, he should call Mary, but there was something about Bonnie's sadness that drew him into the room. For a moment he stood in the doorway, uncertain about what to do, but then he opened a cabinet, rummaged around for a length of toweling, and offered it to her. She took it from him and pressed the cloth to her chest to absorb the milk. In the darkness, the liquid appeared clear, like tears. The thought came to him that she might never recover if her breasts mourned like this. She would not look at him, but he did not want to leave her, so he sat in the rocking chair, where, had her baby not died, she would be nursing him now from those swollen breasts.

He did not know what to say, but instinct kept him there. Between them there was perfect stillness. He did not move, only breathed in silent rhythm with Bonnie's muffled sobs. Time flickered and then flared, with its peculiar ability to alter perception. In its throes, we enter another life, one of possibility: *I will overcome.*

When Bonnie stopped crying, Christian took the sodden toweling from her. He was clumsy, new to physical expressions of comfort, though as a boy he had flung himself into Amelia's arms in full view of anyone. Though his chest still had yet to harden completely, he felt Bonnie's wet cheek cushioned against it. In his shirt pocket was his gift for Jenny, a rose sachet with a lock of his hair tucked into a tiny pocket stitched in its side. He rocked Bonnie until she fell asleep, and then, as careful as a mother with a child, cradled and shifted her so that her head rested upon the pillow.

Then he left her to give Jenny the sachet, damp now with Bonnie's tears.

On the quay at the base of Maiden Lane, the Sutters were all crushed together; it was agony waiting to say good-bye, watching the ferry wallow across the river to deliver a load of enthusiastic soldiers. Mary's elbow was linked in Christian's. That morning, he had shyly asked her whether or not he had done the right thing by Bonnie, though she already had known of his kindness, having slipped upstairs to bind Bonnie's breasts after Christian returned to the dining room for the rest of the celebration. "I never knew any man so obliging," Bonnie had said, as Mary tucked cabbage leaves against Bonnie's breasts and then bound them with a tight length of toweling.

Christian was not a man yet, Mary thought now, but soon the war would make him one. Neither she nor her mother could bear to let him go. Amelia was blinking back tears; Mary was stroking his arm, trying to forget what had happened later that morning when she and Jenny had met unexpectedly in the kitchen. Jenny had been unable to hide her blush. The newlyweds had spent the night at Thomas's, but were breakfasting with them, for Thomas had let all his servants go.

"They'll be off soon," Mary said, busying herself with assembling cold compresses for Bonnie. "Thomas will need things. Have you helped him pack?"

Jenny set down her coffee cup. "Mary, you have everything. Do you see? I'm a shadow. I haunt our house, I watch you go off wherever it is you go. You understand things. Women respect you. They come and ask for you." She straightened. "Thomas married me. Not you." Then she walked out of the kitchen, the door swinging in her wake.

Now, looking away to avoid having to talk to Jenny and Thomas, who stood as near one another as decorum allowed, Mary studied the crowd, thinking that she should remember it was Bonnie who truly held the capital on grief today, tucked in bed back at the Sutter house. Mary wondered, how had her brother learned such an essential thing? To be with grief, and to say nothing? Now Christian had one arm slung around Amelia's shoulders, and Amelia looked as stricken as Bonnie had that morning. Each of them losing a child, though Mary refused to believe that she wouldn't see both Christian and Thomas again.

Through the maze of people, James Blevens, his tall frame soaring a head above the others, was working his way toward her.

When he arrived, he said, "They took me as regimental surgeon," as if Mary had been anxiously waiting to hear of his appointment. They hadn't seen one another since he had brought Jake Miles to the door. Blevens had kept his promise to her, but Marsh had said, *No, absolutely not.* Blevens would not tell Mary about this now; he did not want to taint his good-bye with bitterness and disappointment. He was going to war, and, unreasonably, there existed the vague hope of kindness.

Mary said, "Bonnie came back to us last night. Her baby died."

"I am very sorry to hear that. How is she?"

"Grieving." Out of the corner of her eyes, Mary could see Thomas kissing Jenny. "But that is nothing to you, is it? You have your opportunity now to see what you can see. You will learn everything you want to know."

"Yes," Blevens said. "Though it is only for three months." This was all the time Lincoln wanted the volunteers for. Everyone believed that the war would be over soon. "It's likely I'll see nothing of surgery."

"Have you no family, Dr. Blevens?" Mary asked. She could not forgive him, but she noticed that he was by himself, when no one else was alone today on the quay.

"I have two brothers, but they live near Manhattan City. I haven't seen them in a long time." How was he to explain the rest? Even he himself did not understand. He had not even written Sarah to tell her of his plans. Illiterate, she took his letters to the priest, who read them to her in a pew of the dark church where they had wed. He tried to imagine what she would feel upon hearing the news, if this adventure of his would matter to her at all. But perhaps she did not even take his letters to the priest anymore. It had been a long time—six months—since a single vellum sheet in the priest's spidery handwriting had been delivered to the Staats House.

"Not even a wife? Even Thomas Fall has a wife," Mary said.

James Blevens sharpened his focus, his blue-eyed gaze darting to find the couple. She was making light of it; perhaps he had been wrong. Inscrutable in her expression, Mary did not even show envy, though he suspected it simmered alongside her well of dissatisfaction with him.

The *Lady of Perth* docked to make its last trip across the river, and the crowd surged, huzzahs and cheers and cries and a wild, thrilling excitement pressing all the parting together. Mary saw from the corner of her eye, though she did not want to, the deep kiss that Thomas Fall impressed upon Jenny, while Blevens and Mary met face-to-face. Mary averted her head, the only possible way to cope, for nothing would induce her to kiss a man for whom she felt only antipathy. But it did not keep her from speaking.

"You could have helped me," she said. "It would have cost you little enough in time and trouble."

"I am sorry," Blevens said, and lifted his cap, offering this lackluster farewell, and then the surging crowd caught him in its current and carried him away. Mary watched him go, feeling the breeze of a last door slamming shut.

Amelia was drawing Christian's wide shoulders downward, clinging to him, unable to let him go, but he unwrapped her arms from his neck, kissed her cheek, and then turned and walked away. The three men stepped onto the ferry together, James the tallest of the three, but not watched, as Christian and Thomas were, by the three women now huddled together. A hush fell on the crowd as the ferry slipped from the dock to cross the choppy river. Not one of them noticed Jake leaning against a bulkhead, a sad, sullen expression contorting his face, looking up State Street toward the Sutter home, from which he had just come.

It was Amelia, not Jenny, who needed assistance walking home, who, arriving there, fell upon her bed, pained by the futility of giving birth to a boy only to have him board a ferry for war without even a backward glance.

In the adjacent room, Bonnie Miles, seventeen years old, was weeping, having told her departing husband an hour ago that she never wanted to see him again. For how could she, when a man like Christian Sutter existed in the world?

# *Chapter Six*

Six weeks later, on a warm afternoon on June the fifth, 1861, a petite, dark-haired woman, often mistaken from afar for a child, strode three diagonal blocks down New York Avenue in Washington City. Crossing the cobbled street, Dorothea Dix dodged bands of drilling soldiers on Pennsylvania Avenue, then swept up an ill-tended slate walkway to the tall double entry doors of the president's house, where roving sentries let her pass with a nod. Presenting a letter confirming her appointment with Mr. Lincoln, she took in the tattered rugs and dingy walls that adorned the entryway of the Mansion and decided that chief among the needs of the new president was a better housekeeper. A butler disappeared down a shadowy hallway and returned with a man who introduced himself as John Hay, the assistant secretary, who had at first suggested that she join the long line of office seekers that gathered each morning in hopes of an audience with the president. But Miss Dix had insisted on an appointment instead, because her aim, as she had replied to Mr. Hay by return post, was not to become the tariff collector or postman in some distant town. Her aim, she had written, was to save the Union's men.

John Hay guided her upstairs, where the president's office faced north, overlooking Pennsylvania Avenue, situated on this public side to avoid viewing the boggy southern White Lot into which, until recently, the house sewer had drained. But the open windows still let in its lingering stench, augmented by the City Canal that ran at the base of the property. Since the inundation of the capital by the seventy-five thousand men for whom Mr. Lincoln had sent, the canal itself had turned decidedly unpleasant. Miss Dix was no newcomer to Washington City, having passed in and out for years to make pleas to the legislature, but the city's southern torpor and accompanying odors were always an unwelcome surprise. That it had been built on a swamp had only recently been made known to her. A maid had related this morsel of information as she went about netting the mirrors of Miss Dix's newly rented town house. "For the blackflies," the girl had said ominously, tucking a fold under the edge of a mirror. "They like to lay their eggs on the glass."

Miss Dix had heard Mr. Lincoln described as rough, but when he strode into the room the word *elegance* came to mind. It was not his shocking height that gave her that impression. Rather, it was that taking charge of his long limbs and torso seemed to demand a great deal of his attention; this self-consciousness communicated a kind of solemnity. Despite the heat this afternoon, he wore a black suit with a long jacket, and his tie, though knotted, dangled loosely. She had the impression that he had not slept, though whether that was due to the deep set of his eyes or the sigh that escaped him, she could not be certain. He took her small hand in his enormous one and apologized for the heat and the distinctive scent.

"I must move to a better part of town," he said, a mischievous grin breaking out on his face. She came barely to his chest, and this, combined with the sense that she was on a mission of more gravity than any she had ever undertaken, made her feel almost as shy as she usually led men to believe she was. Demureness was a helpful weapon, she had discovered, and it was a practice she had nearly perfected. She allowed the president to guide her to an armchair far away from the windows and smiled a faint but grateful thanks. The president folded himself into a large chair that barely contained his frame and said, "It is an honor to meet you. I've heard extraordinary things about your work with prison reform and the insane."

"Thank you," Miss Dix said. She had learned over the years to say nothing more when people offered compliments. She found it counterproductive to retrace old victories when her interest lay in accomplishing new ones. Politicians especially were most extravagant with their praise, and always after the fact, but it was generally a feint to forestall any new proposition, which she always had ready and which would always require work on their part.

"You've read the notes I sent you?" she asked.

Lincoln's expression gave away nothing, but by the firm set of his shoulders she feared she was about to be patronized.

"Your suggestions are well-intended," the president said. "But I am worried that your newest petition, while both ambitious and admirable, is unnecessary. My generals tell me we have surgeons enough to take care of any needs. And, frankly, they are concerned that women in the hospitals will be"—he broke off for a moment and then found the word she was certain he thought was least offensive—"distracting."

The president was wrong about there being surgeons enough, but Miss Dix did not yet want him to know how much she knew. First she had to address his primary concern. And in it, he was being circumspect. So far in her life, the words *indelicate, hysterical, meddlesome, obstructive, uncooperative, immodest, indecent,* and the worst, *superfluous* had been flung at her in both the press and in person, usually as she embarked on some new endeavor. And somehow, her latest plan, spoken of only to her closest friends and outlined in detail by letter to the president, had been made quasi-public. She had not been in the city five days when a senator visited her town house to say that her reputation for admirable social reform would be reversed should she continue to pursue this inane idea of nursing. "Do you think," he had said, "that any mothers in the country will let their boys enlist if they are going to be exposed to women of that sort?"

"And what sort is that?" Miss Dix had asked, though she knew very well what the senator meant. After all, she herself had once witnessed a prostitute employed as a nurse consorting with a patient in the halls of Bellevue Hospital.

Flustered, the senator had leaned forward in his chair. "I apologize for my directness, but no doubt you have seen enough in your lifetime, Miss Dix, that neither of us needs to outline what indecencies could occur should women's presence in army hospitals be condoned. Do not sully your reputation by pursuing this."

"My reputation, Senator, will be sullied if I do nothing."

Armored now by that inauspicious welcome, Miss Dix folded her hands across her lap and said to the president, "My nurses will not be distracting," letting his euphemism roll off her tongue. "They will be at all times modest and circumscribed, not leaning in any way toward the nocturnal activities of some of our lesser sisterhood."

This allusion to the sexual was perhaps too much for the president's comfort. He nodded and took another tack, which was the usual strategy of men unprepared to do battle with her.

"But won't you be complicating things? More people than are necessary for the job?"

In addition to embarrassment, the president's voice betrayed an air of weariness. Thousands of men were now encamped in the Capitol building and on its grounds. Already, boys hailing from isolated farms and small towns were falling sick with mumps and measles, victims of overcrowding. It was the unwritten rule of assembling armies that a third of their population would be lost to disease within the first month. Most had arrived with nothing, not even arms. And they were a hungry lot. They'd taken to slaughtering the cattle penned beneath the stunted Washington Monument when they weren't parading up and down Pennsylvania Avenue. The chore of managing an untrained army of volunteer militia was turning out to be a far greater task than even Mr. Lincoln had expected, with unforeseen repercussions and consequences. In his eyes, Miss Dix knew, she was one of these repercussions.

"Your generals tell you there are surgeons enough. Have they told you how many surgeons they have?" Miss Dix asked.

Lincoln shifted in his seat. "Not specifically, no."

"Twenty-seven. And only seventy-one assistants for the regular army of thirteen thousand men. And now you have an additional seventy-five thousand volunteers. Did you know that in our recent conflict with Mexico, ten men fell ill for every one injured? And in the Crimea, Miss Nightingale discovered that in one month, 2,761 soldiers had died of contagious diseases, while only eighty-three died from their wounds?

"The sick of our army are languishing even now on the floors of churches and government buildings. There are not enough proper hospitals and the war has not even yet begun. Have you considered where the wounded will go? How they will be fed? How they will bathe? Who will care for them? Do you really think that twenty-seven surgeons will be able to handle everything? Do you think they will bother with bedding? Do you think they will even have enough medicine?"

Miss Dix leaned forward. "Mr. Lincoln, I am your ally. If the war ends in one battle, then you will have no need of me. But if the war does not, if it goes on, if it becomes anything like what happened in the Crimea, then you will see our conversation today as one of the most auspicious of your career."

Mr. Lincoln fell silent. Looking into the future was his greatest skill. It was hers, too, and together they regarded it in both its forms: disastrous and more optimistic. Each seemed possible, though outside a lively band was leading an unruly swarm of soldiers down the street, as if to highlight the city's uneven and unbalanced preparations for war.

The president waited until the last strains of the music died away. "My compliments, Miss Dix. It would appear that you are a politician."

Now that she had a receptive audience, Miss Dix described Miss Nightingale's outline of the hospital conditions during the Crimean War, her reforms, and the nurses who had enacted them, explaining exactly how a nursing force could change everything.

"But why can't you just pass this information along and let the generals sort it out?" the president asked.

Miss Dix paused, trying to appear as if she hadn't already planned what she would say if Mr. Lincoln suggested this. "Perhaps the generals would appreciate this burden being lifted from them?" she asked mildly, as if the thought had only recently occurred to her.

Mr. Lincoln's manner now lost all its courtliness. She recognized this invisible passage, for all of the men with whom she engaged in conversation crossed it at some point. There came a time when she was no longer a petite woman that courtesy demanded they hear out; instead, she became the woman who might actually save them.

"We have one remaining problem," he said. "What will you say to the skeptics, Miss Dix? Those who would worry about the delicacy of the situation you are proposing?"

She produced the circular she had composed after her meeting with the senator, the one she planned to have published in all the major newspapers across the country.

After another half hour, Dorothea Dix was in possession of three things: Mr. Lincoln's blessing, a written order to see Secretary of War Cameron, whose responsibility it would be to appoint her Female Superintendent of Army Nurses, and the troubling sense that despite her intentions, she had generated more worries for the president than she had allayed. As she said good-bye, she finally settled on the reason for her concern. She pitied him. Not because he had taken on a thankless job. That impetus she was entirely familiar with. No, she pitied him because he seemed to possess an endless capacity for grief.

# *Chapter Seven*

**Circular Number 1**

Hospitals are being established for the care of the soldiers of the Union Army who will sacrifice themselves for the good of the Union. We are in search of ladies to serve in them in the tradition of Florence Nightingale in her recent successful work caring for British soldiers in the Crimea.

No young ladies should be sent at all, but some who are sober, earnest, self-sacrificing, and self-sustained; who can bear the presence of suffering and exercise entire self-control of speech and manner; who can be calm, gentle, quiet, active, and steadfast in duty. No woman under thirty years need apply to serve in government hospitals. All nurses are required to be very plain-looking women. Their dresses must be brown or black, with no bows, no curls, no jewelry, and no hoop skirts.

If any willing lady should meet the above requirements, please send references directly to me at the corner of New York Avenue and Fourteenth Street in Washington City.

Miss Dorothea Dix
*Female Superintendent of Army Nurses*

That Mary Sutter would read the circular was inevitable. The daily perusal of the newspaper for information of the 25th Regiment had become a ritual for her, in search of reassurance. The paper had progressively reported that the 25th had traveled via steamer and landed at Annapolis, thereby avoiding the city of Baltimore and the fate of the Sixth Massachusetts, who had been set upon in that city by Southern sympathizers while marching from one railway depot to another. Four soldiers were killed and not a few civilians. Rebels had also sabotaged the railroad that ran south from Annapolis into Washington, but undaunted, the Sixth Massachusetts had gone to Annapolis and marched from there along the rail lines, repairing them as they went. The 25th had followed, becoming among the first troops to enter Washington. They set up camp near the unfinished Capitol building, absent its crowning dome, and then took over Caspari's Guest House on A Street, sleeping in its rooms and stable and backyard and fouling the neighborhood round about. On May 24, however, they had decamped from the city of Washington, whose citizens had been at first thrilled and then appalled by the surfeit of so many rowdy volunteers for their safety, and had invaded Virginia, where they were now chopping down trees to build a fort.

So far, the war was quiescent. Rarely a shot fired. Only Colonel Ellsworth from East Albany, a member of the Fire Zouaves, had suffered, shot and killed by an inflamed hotel owner after Ellsworth had removed a Rebel flag from an Alexandria hotel the night of the Virginia invasion. Ellsworth's war had been extravagantly personal; Abraham Lincoln was his friend. In death there was glory, but for the 25th only drudgery, throwing up fireworks and fortifications along the ridgeline on the Potomac River.

"You're not thinking of going, are you?" Jenny asked, after Mary had read the circular out loud by the fire, laid it on the table, and looked around at Amelia, Jenny, and Bonnie gathered in the parlor before dinner. The windows were open to the last of the sweet June air. Soon the heat of July would sour Albany's peculiar drafts and perpetual odors beyond tolerance and the windows would have to be shut.

Jenny did not see the possibilities.

Neither did Amelia.

The four women had risen, the tea things abandoned. Bonnie, their permanent guest—until, at least, Christian returned home to claim his room—was thinking not about Mary going, but about how soon Jake might be coming to reclaim her.

"It will be drudgery," Amelia said.

"No less than what Christian and Thomas are suffering. If I am in Washington, I could see them." Mary thought of Washington as she thought of Albany, a city of ready transportation, of ease, the prospect of calling on a friend no difficulty at all. The work of an afternoon. She did not yet comprehend the vastness of the capital, or its provincial, unwieldy, and besieged condition. "And think of what I will learn. Oh, Mother, it's an opportunity."

In the intervening month and a half since the 25th had left, Mary had delivered five babies. Only one delivery had proved mildly challenging, while the others had proceeded benignly. The thrill of learning she had experienced in becoming a midwife had been replaced of necessity by the more quotidian habit of vigilance, and though she was always on the lookout for the disasters of childbirth—the rare inverted uterus, a developing maternal seizure, a placenta that refused to detach, and of course, the more common event of maternal hemorrhage—day-to-day midwifery now held only the slightest appeal for her. The truth was that you had to know very little to deliver a baby. Babies mostly delivered themselves. Only rarely did the process take on the need for extraordinary skill and urgency; as a practice, the procedure had become routine, almost dull.

"An opportunity," Mary said again, "that I do not want to miss."

"You won't defeat me on this. I won't allow it." Amelia was staking her position. Having a daughter like Mary had been both boon and travail: she was excellent company when engaged, sharp of mind, quick with insight, but a formidable antagonist when crossed.

Mary said, "James Blevens is not the only one who knows an opportunity when he sees it."

"But you cannot become a surgeon by going to Washington to be a nurse." Sometimes Amelia worried that Mary was too much like her, too willing to follow responsibility through. She shuddered, remembering that evening long ago, when she had returned to the house when Nathaniel had left for Buffalo and had found the girls in their beds. She was glad now that they had been too young to remember it, that Mary could not use it now to goad her into acquiescing.

"I cannot become one by staying home, either."

Across the country that night, other mothers were saying, *Think of the deprivation. Think of the scandal. Consider the danger.*

From her quiet corner, Bonnie was suffering envy. Her mother had died when she was very young. That is how she had come to be married so young to Jake Miles. Her father had forced the match; he had not wanted her anymore. And here was Mary, wanting to leave, when she had everything that anyone could ever want.

"Do not mistake me," Amelia said. "I do not think you are overreaching, Mary. But you will not find satisfaction in Washington. You will only be discouraged and beaten down. And besides, you are not thirty years old. This Miss Dix won't accept you." Amelia had already lost Christian to the war, and she did not want to sacrifice Mary too. Besides, Mary had no idea what she might be facing. Amelia had no idea, either, but she did have fear. Mary's ambition and curiosity was not worth the price of venturing into the unknown. She had always wanted too much.

Amelia's opposition was unprecedented. "Help me, Jenny?" Mary asked.

But Jenny hoped the war would never begin. It had been weeks and weeks now since the 25th had left, and to her great relief, nothing terrible had yet occurred. "They will all be home very soon. And you will have exhausted yourself for nothing," she said.

Mary perceived the caution, but also the abandonment.

"Don't look at me like that," Jenny said. "Incuriosity is not a crime."

"Neither is curiosity."

"I'm sorry," Jenny said, touching Mary's wrist. Then she let go and sat down quickly on her chair.

Mary reached her hand across the divide and took Jenny's elbow; Jenny had turned a peculiar shade and had lifted her hand to her mouth.

"Jenny?"

Amelia knelt at her daughter's side. Bonnie, Jenny's twin in ignorance, stepped backwards to better allow the Sutter women she admired to administer care.

Jenny was not dramatic; there was no wish to divert attention. Of this, Mary was certain, even as Jenny broke free and rushed down the hallway.

The unmistakable sound of retching came from the open door of the water closet.

"I'm sorry," Jenny gasped from the closet's confines. "I don't know what the matter is."

A cold rag was fetched, hair was held back. Mary loosened Jenny's corset, and it was this untwining of the cords, with its implication of intimacy, that caused both midwives to look at one another and say at the same time, "When was your last monthly, Jenny?"

On Jenny's part, there was a display of confusion and then a long, embarrassed exhalation of recognition.

At the dinner table, Jenny sipped broth. An assumption of victory prevailed on the part of Amelia, who, both delighted and paralyzed at the news that her less hardy daughter would be facing the perils of labor by the end of the year, was failing to remember that Mary had a mind of her own. She considered the subject of Mary's leaving forgotten. It was the same at dinner tables all over the country that night. Mothers assumed that having put their feet down, their daughters would comply, while daughters, pretending to have listened, made secret plans. The topic of new babies was also general conversation around the country. January of 1862, when Jenny was due, would be the busiest month for midwives in ten years. Farewell babies, they would be called. Three months later, in April, there would be another round of newborns nine months after Lincoln called for yet another hundred thousand men.

It was not that Amelia was insensitive to Bonnie or Mary, though the news had a differing effect on each of them. Bonnie was determined not to spoil Amelia's or Jenny's delight, because women went on having children, didn't they? What did it matter that her arms ached from emptiness, that yesterday she had had to stop herself from sweeping a baby from its carriage? She might one day have a baby that lived; it was this hope that sustained her. Mary was aware of everything; the queasy happiness of her sister, the cautious anticipation of her mother, the generous restraint of their guest, but mostly she was aware that the *Argus* carried on its front page a listing of the arrival and departure times of both the trains and the Hudson River day boats. She excused herself to make certain that the maids had not thrown out the paper in a flurry of efficiency.

Very early the next morning, a hired hack pulled to a stop on Quay Street. From it climbed a young woman carrying a hastily packed valise. She walked briskly along the granite sidewalk, steering her formidable frame past the closed storefronts of dry grocers and brothels toward the wharf, where at a booth, a young man sold her a ticket for two dollars. The young woman walked through the gate and down the slanted gangplank to the deck of the steamer *Mary Powell.* Though it was six a.m., a band was playing on the deck, a circumstance that the brothel dwellers along the quay had long despaired of. The woman took a seat on a bench at the prow as the ship's horn blasted three times and steam roared from the two stacks in the center of the boat. Crewmen uncoiled thick ropes and threw them onto the deck. The paddle churned and the boat backed away, the reversed engines blowing coal smoke, fouling the morning air. The engines reversed again and the ship steered away from the dock and maneuvered around a ferry and a river schooner laden with lumber. Out in the channel, the ship's boards vibrated with the thrum of the engines. A rising breeze played with the loose ends of the woman's hair as the black river water slipped underneath the sharp prow.

The young woman imagined her mother finding the note she had left behind.

In her valise, she carried forty dollars, three dresses, and her stethoscope. In only six hours' time, she would be dropped at the docks in Manhattan.

# *Chapter Eight*

A few weeks earlier, when the 25th Regiment had abandoned Caspari's Guest House to march west under a full moon along the filthy streets bordering the southern perimeter of the capital, they left behind the liquor they had managed to find on every street corner, the prostitutes in Swampdoodle, the daily drilling, the press of men, the unfinished Capitol dome, the stunted Washington Monument, and the doomed cows who grazed in the vast pastures that lay between. They did not know what drudgery lay ahead of them, though when they dropped their haversacks and took up axes to fell the tall, bowed firs of Arlington Heights, they soon understood. The men who had come to fight, who had been roused to enlist in granges and community halls to take back the Union from the infidels, instead chopped wood and shoveled dirt to build redoubts. It was raw work. They suffered blisters, chiggers, mosquitoes, and then the cutting began in earnest. In ever-widening circles, trees fell. Soon they could see southward across the Rebel hills and northward to the capital they were protecting. The 25th named the piece of earth they were clearing Fort Albany, since it was their hard work that was accomplishing the task and since they missed home so much. The Albany men were not alone. From the Long Bridge in the south to the Chain Bridge far to the north, barricades made up of Virginia fir and clay blighted the landscape, hewn by men from Connecticut and Ohio and Pennsylvania, all of them dreaming of home. They posted pickets and rotated night duty, but it was difficult to equate what they were doing with soldiering.

They mostly tried to find food and wondered why the army had sent them out of the city without even a thought to their nourishment. They ate what they could gather from the nearby farms or foraged from the hills, the best being the hogs that wandered through the newly cleared forests, confused, easily caught. The men urinated and defecated in camp and failed to build sinks. They drank from the streams that the neighboring fort used as its privy. They did not wash. They slept without blankets upon the impervious Virginia clay. When it rained, tributaries of mud coursed through the camp, bringing with it a plague of enteric disease that rendered James Blevens, miserably, a privy constable.

The doctor was seldom agitated, except when the lack of sanitation infuriated him. He hurtled through the camp, surly at the state of the streets and his need to monitor them, ordering men to pour lime into the privy trenches and to shovel dirt upon garbage piles humming with flies.

On a day in early June, a Sanitary Commission officer visited the camp. Lincoln had called the group, formed by women but led by Frederick Law Olmsted, the fifth wheel to the coach and complained that the army already had a medical department. Nonetheless, he appointed them "to inquire into the subjects of diet, clothing, cooks, camping grounds, in fact everything connected with the prevention of disease among volunteer soldiers not accustomed to the rigid regulations of the regular troops." This was now read to James by the inspector, who peered over the top of his glasses with a seriousness that he clearly felt befitted the gravity of his dull tedium. James had stopped listening.

They sat on chairs at the door to Colonel Townsend's shack, the most palatial of all the camp abodes—shanties built from scrap branches and bark—as the usual uproar of shouts and swearing and fights careened up and down the mostly orderly lines of lean-tos.

*Are the men required to bathe under the eye of an officer?* "Yes."

James refused to observe the men bathing. He thought the sanitary officer could detect this lie, though the man continued to read questions from his form in a measured, nonjudgmental fashion, writing down the answers with a thick-nibbed pen that he dipped into a bottle of ink set precariously on the ground.

*If so, how often each man?* "Regularly." (Another lie.)

*Does each man (as a rule) wash his head, neck, and feet once a day?*

James gazed mournfully at the heat rising in dust clouds off the baked

Virginia clay. Spring in Virginia was an oven compared to Albany. "Undoubtedly."

*Are the men infected with vermin?* "Yes."

*If so, has any application been made to remove them?* "Yes."

The inspector did not ask if James had been successful. No one had been successful. Carbolic acid, turpentine, nothing worked. Fort Albany was, in fact, an encampment of lice in which men were allowed to live.

*Do the men void urine within their own camp?* "Yes."

(Bland, noncommittal gaze from the officer. What had he seen in other camps?)

*At night?* "Yes."

*In the day?* "Yes."

There was the crack of an axe against a tree. More Virginia trees falling to the Federals, all that the men of Albany had been able to conquer of Rebel territory. In their single distinguishing moment, two of their regiment on picket duty in May at the Long Bridge had arrested a Rebel sneaking across to Washington City, but other than that, soldiering for the men of the 25th Regiment had consisted of construction and endurance. It was, however, a matter of pride to the regiment that their fortification, one of a dozen forts of earthen walls and ramparts on the Arlington Heights, guarded the Columbia Turnpike, the main road that led to Washington City, two miles away.

On and on the sanitary officer read: *Does each soldier have a pair of trousers? Do they as a whole take pride in their camp? Do you observe odors of decay within the camp? Does the surgeon make a daily inspection of the camp, with respect to cleanliness? How many paces from the body of the camp is the privy? Is the privy trench provided with a sitting rail?*

James had dug a private privy nearby in the disappearing woods. He had gone there the other morning only to discover the forest had been clear-cut the previous day.

*Is any officer required to examine and taste the food of the men before it is served at any meal, or is this done generally by the captains or other officers, either by order or voluntarily?*

James Blevens's skin had been burned red by his long days outside, his lips blistered and his neck rendered crimson. He had lost, he estimated, perhaps a dozen pounds. He was a picture of the life they were all leading. Soldiers were starving. When they did get rations, most often it was beans and flour, which they fashioned into cakes they fried in lard rendered from the hogs they shot.

"The officers test only the potatoes and caviar. For the rest the men are on their own, although we do serve high tea at four with crumpets and scones."

(Small twitch of left eye, barely distinguishable.)

*Is there a regimental band?*

Memories of Tweddle Hall surfaced. An orchestra. And once, Jenny Lind, her voice soaring above the crepe and crinolines of the beautiful women in attendance. James Blevens had not seen a woman in a month and a half.

"No, no band."

The inspector wrinkled his nose. "You do understand the necessity of amusements for the men?"

James said that there was nothing amusing about necessity.

*Is there much intoxication?*

"Some." James thrice had taken up pen and paper to write to Washington, then abandoned the prospect. Who would he tell? Released from the spell of decency, nearly every soldier had at least dabbled in the general revelry of the most untamed troops: liquor purchased from privateers who had set up shop in shacks just off the fort's grounds; women obtained from the shanties of Swampdoodle, the quagmire village of lawlessness adjacent to the Capitol. Already he had seen three cases of gonorrhea.

*What are the prevailing diseases?* (Pen into mouth while awaiting answer to question. Nothing unsanitary about that.)

"Malaria. Typhoid."

James held two sick calls each day: one at seven in the morning, after drill, and the other at seven in the evening. So far, he had seen measles, mumps, scarlet fever, colds, bronchitis, and pneumonia. He had sent men to hospital with icterus, constipation, but mostly with diarrhea. The entire decamped city of Albany was ill with it. In fact, the entire Union army was. He often wondered whether anybody would ever suffer anything requiring surgery, and if they did, what he would do. He had nothing beside the instruments he had brought with him. Not plaster, morphia, gauze, ether, chloroform, nor charcoal either; the paucity alarmed. But nary a shot had been fired during their tenure. His idle instruments daily mocked him from inside their wooden case.

*Is there a moderate supply of medicines?*

"I believe I just answered that."

*Are the men required to regularly wash their underclothing?*

A bout of raucous laughter from a nearby fire. Dinner today appeared to be griddlecakes.

"Perhaps by their mothers."

(A stern and altogether earnest gaze.) "Dr. Blevens, you are their mother in absentia."

"I am in desperate peril if I am now a woman. They are in scarce supply."

The inspector shifted on his seat. He could be a preacher from the depth of his blush.

"There are 180 questions on this form and I still have to get to Fort Runyon today."

"From time to time I do observe the men nude, swishing their clothes in the stream that runs at the base of the hill. You understand, I do not encourage it, as it is the same stream from which we get our drinking water." Dr. Blevens took unreasoned pleasure from the expression on the inspector's face, as the inspector had, in fact, quenched his thirst at that very stream upon his arrival that morning.

(An intake of breath.) *Is there a regimental library?*

"I did try to have the contents of the Library of Congress transported here for our use, but I was unsuccessful."

"Now you are just being sarcastic."

"Who wrote this form?"

(Deep sigh.) *Are the common military signs of discipline punctiliously enforced or practiced, as the salute between men and officers?*

"You do understand that two months ago these men were plowing fields?"

"I will take that as a no."

The inspector took the rest of James's comments as a no also, except when he asked the final question: *Does the surgeon understand that he is responsible for all conditions of the camp or regiment unfavorable to health, unless he has warned the commanding officer of them?*

James Blevens, who had come to conquer bullet holes and shattered limbs, but was instead camp supervisor of hygiene and sewerage, and also, apparently, military salutations, musicianship, literacy, and gastronomy, sighed and said, "The surgeon does."

# *Chapter Nine*

The Baltimore & Ohio Railroad Station in Washington City squatted mere steps from the Capitol building, but the shabby wooden structure teemed with hustlers and pickpockets. The trip from Albany had taken Mary more than thirty hours. She had grown confused at the pier in Manhattan City until a hack driver helped her find the ferry to Jersey City. The train had overnighted at the depot in Philadelphia, and Mary had had to sleep sitting up in her seat. Near Baltimore, the train had slowed and stopped so that the engineer could walk the tracks ahead to make certain the rails had not been torn up. As Mary disembarked, she thought that no delivery she had ever attended had been as exhausting as sitting in that humid train car, en route to the rest of her life. Now moist heat billowed through the depot doors left open to the street; a horde of people, horses, and carriages crowded a wide, circling avenue. Mary gathered herself. Just one more hurdle, she thought, and then she would be there. She elbowed through the crowd and hailed a hack from the line of cabs and directed its driver to take her to the corner of New York Avenue and 14th Street.

The capital was unexpectedly seedy, a cross between a swamp and Versailles. Rare islands of marbled grace reared up between linked villages of squatting shanties, vacant lots, rollicking taverns, and slovenly grocers. Squalid creeks and deep gutters formed moats around the fine and unsightly both. Even the receding Capitol building itself, viewed as Mary twisted her head in search of something to admire, disappointed. Under a pale sky blunted by heat, it towered upon its hill, a skeletal dome awaiting marble blocks, looking like the Union itself, gutted and uncertain. As the hack traversed a long angled avenue of broken cobbles and rutted tracks, the driver became a tour guide: here is this, here is that. The Saint

Charles Hotel. City Hall. In between, muddy hog wallows and seedy ruin. The avenue made a turn: here is the Treasury, here is the Mansion. Set behind an iron railing, the president's house needed a new coat of paint and a gardener.

"That will be a quarter dollar. It costs more for the tour," the hack driver said, grinning, pleased with his larceny when he stopped a few blocks later at a row of new town houses on a street like Dove Street, with slate sidewalks and stone stairs and windowsills of granite. Mary knew it was more than she should have paid, but the similarity to home boded well and so she handed over the exorbitant fare, glad to finally have reached her destination.

The maid who answered the door was crisply capped and insolently aired and she sniffed as she inspected Mary's travel-stained clothes. Mary touched her hand to her hair, twisted into wildness by the humidity. It occurred to her that she should have taken a room at a hotel and made an appointment, but it was too late now.

"I'm here to see Miss Dix."

"Miss Dix is not seeing anyone today," the maid said.

"But I've come a long way—"

The maid shut the door. She was worse even than the hissing clerk at Albany Medical College, who had at least received Mary's initial visits with amused courtesy. Mary turned on the stoop, hoping that the hack was still at the curbside, but he had gone, and the long street now looked unwelcoming. She had just started down the stairs when the door reopened and the maid said, "Follow me."

Dorothea Dix was sitting in a low armchair in the bay window of her town house. Though it was warm, no one could accuse this woman of a lack of decorum or of surrendering standards to the Washington swelter. She wore a black, long-sleeved, high-collared dress fastened with a white rosette. Her black hair was parted in the middle and collected in a low bun at her neck. She had been shuffling papers, but she extended a long, bony hand and waved Mary in.

"How do you do? I am Miss Dorothea Dix." She said her name with a strong emphasis on the vowels, as if she were pronouncing it carefully for someone to get the spelling right. "Please sit down. You came, I see, from the train?"

Mary managed a wan smile to cover her embarrassment. "Please forgive me. Forgive my appearance," she said. She stumbled over her words, her fatigue conspiring with the heat. She thought how she must appear, and fought for composure. "Perhaps I should have engaged a hotel," she said. She settled into a velvet armchair next to Miss Dix, acutely conscious of the dirt and perspiration that sullied her dress. It did not help that a forest of potted ferns emanated a mossy scent that somehow intensified the oppressive heat. Nor did it help that she was now two days into her journey, a trip she had thought would last fourteen hours at the most. Not a drop of sweat, however, glistened on Miss Dix's high forehead.

"I brought them with me," Miss Dix said, referring to the armchairs. "You cannot buy anything in Washington to compare."

They were as alike as women could be. Each sat with her hands folded, ankles crossed, demonstrating a certain discipline about backs not touching the seat. One woman was small, one was large. Neither was beautiful to look at. The world would have looked at them and thought, *Odd.*

Miss Dix studied her guest. She appeared to be in that category of women who, by their lack of aesthetic appeal, appeared ageless and would remain so for the rest of their lives, while the fairer of their sex would wilt into decay. Miss Dix shifted her pile of papers with a noncommittal nod of her head and drew out a blank sheet. Dipped pen in hand, she said, "Your name?"

"Mary Sutter."

"May I see your letters of recommendation?"

"I have none," Mary said.

Miss Dix laid down her pen. This woman was her first applicant, and she had no idea what to do now that the woman didn't have references. Character was everything. A letter from home, preferably written by a minister or a church deacon, would back up her judgment and silence her critics. She wanted no more visits from the senator. And the truth was, she'd been wrong about people before. She still suffered haunting memories of the one man about whom she'd been most wrong. Her engagement to Edward Bangs had been brief. She frequently wondered what would have become of her had they married. Sidelined, strapped to a house and children. Certainly she would not be here, indecisive herself, wheedling about references. "You wish to work in the army as a nurse?"

"I do."

"And on what basis am I to hire you if you do not provide me with letters? These are essential. Surely you know this."

"I have none," Mary said. She'd been in such a hurry to leave Albany that somehow the issue of references had seemed an unnecessary impediment to her escape. "But I am very qualified."

"I published that circular two days ago, Miss Sutter. You came very quickly. I did expect that you would send references first. I specifically stated that references were required."

"I came out of urgency," Mary said.

Miss Dix understood that sense of urgency. She had felt it herself, carried away on a wave of anticipation not unlike the men's eagerness for guns and battle. At sixty, Miss Dix felt as if she knew things that no one else knew, cared about things that no one else did. This understanding was both a blessing and a curse. She had seen the worst that one human being could do to another. The insane handcuffed to bedrails, fed almost nothing. Men accused of crimes kept in filth for days, dying for lack of water. She entirely agreed with Miss Nightingale that improved sanitary conditions for the sick would improve this war for everyone, if war could ever be improved. Miss Dix had felt it so keenly that she had talked her way right into this moment: choosing the first nurse for hospitals that were already burgeoning with the sick. They had already opened so many. Every public building in Washington, it seemed, was overflowing with men suffering from measles, mumps, and dysentery.

"Miss Sutter. I imagine there will be many more applicants who will conceal from me their true reasons for their desire to become a nurse. Some will be chasing their beaux. Is this your sense of urgency?"

How could Mary explain what she wanted? That she had come to be a surgeon? Indeed, in the thirty-six hours that she had been traveling, she had begun to question her own reasons for running here. She had a feeling Miss Dix wouldn't understand any of it.

"I am well acquainted with the sick room," Mary began. "I am a midwife. I have delivered over fifty babies." Mary almost added, *A significant number given my age*, but age was another of Miss Dix's rigid requirements, and she did not wish to give this woman another reason to dismiss her.

"There will be cleaning and laundry and cooking," Miss Dix said. "Distasteful and difficult work which must be borne without complaint and will be best performed by women who do not think they are above other nurses because they have more experience." Miss Dix's voice, while sharp, had an acuity that made it seem as if she was on the verge of dismissing Mary outright.

"You misunderstand me. I would do anything required of me," Mary said.

"In my circular, I also specified a certain age, which you obviously have not yet reached. I'm afraid, Miss Sutter, that you have traveled to Washington for nothing."

No marble hall, no muttering clerk, nothing but a diminutive sixty-year-old woman in a black frock.

"If we had met in the street, you would have thought me thirty," Mary said.

"I have established strict rules for a reason, Miss Sutter. Age has a way of molding a person that will be advantageous in the extreme circumstances in which my nurses will find themselves."

"But I have come all the way from Albany. Surely the distance traveled is worth consideration."

"The surgeons are already furious. They say no woman will pass the doors of any army hospital. I have battles ahead, and I do not wish to have to defend any youthful indiscretions."

"But I am qualified," Mary said.

"Miss Sutter, no man in the army is going to have a baby." Logic of a specific, narrow kind. *Aren't deliveries enough for you?* And there was the matter of the expectant Jenny. Somehow, it was more than Mary could bear. *Don't be foolish,* she told herself. *You did not flee, you advanced.*

Both women said, "I need—" and stopped. The maid was intruding with the tea tray. She was pleased to see Miss Dix in an attitude of refusal, her bothersome guest on edge. The maid took too much time arranging the milk and sugar. Miss Dix waved an impatient wrist, and the gleeful maid floated away with an air of victory.

Miss Dix said, "I need to establish precedent."

Miss Sutter said, "I need to stay."

Miss Dix recognized her twin in Miss Sutter, but instinctively, perversely, pressed for authority more than affinity, as siblings sometimes do. The elder, to the younger: "You do not understand what will be asked of you."

"I am not here on a whim, Miss Dix."

Miss Dix opened her hands. She was confident, as she would never again be, in her judgment. Within days, she would be besieged by hundreds of young women. But at this moment, she pictured the future in a certain way and was confident she could control it. "You shouldn't have gone to the trouble of coming."

"Yes, coming here *was* trouble. It was a great deal of trouble." Mary, unfurling. Any member of her family would have recognized the signs. A certain straightening of the spine, the impression of a gathering storm. All sense of supplication evaporating, though her next utterance did resemble a question. "May I ask? Is it true that you are a friend of Miss Nightingale's?"

Miss Dix preened, ashamed and delighted that the war had brought her such quick celebrity. "I am greatly pleased to be acquainted with Miss Nightingale. I made a visit to Europe in order to meet her."

"Would you have considered Miss Nightingale incapable of her work in the Crimea before she went, merely because she was young?"

In all of Miss Dix's preparations, she had pictured complaisant, polite women of a certain age, widows perhaps, seeking to devote themselves to the dear boys. Dependent upon her for courage. Instead, she found insolence. Youth. "When Miss Nightingale went to the Crimea, she was thirty-four years old."

"But I believe she was twenty-four when she began nursing."

Miss Dix and Mary Sutter sat opposed, each armed with facts. Outside, a wagon clattered by on the new cobbles. The tea cooled in its pot.

"But we are speaking of a war," Miss Dix said, stating the irrefutable fact.

"You cannot possibly be as intractable as you make yourself out to be," Mary said.

On the contrary, Miss Dix thought, she had accomplished everything in her life by being intractable.

"If I may say, Miss Sutter, you are, as a person, a great deal of trouble," Miss Dix said, then remembered that the same complaint had been uttered about her by the mayor of Harrisburg, Pennsylvania, when she built a lunatic hospital in his city.

"I have hopes," Mary said, whispering.

"Everyone has hopes, Miss Sutter. This does not earn them a position as a nurse."

As the gloating maid ushered Mary out, it occurred to Dorothea Dix that as a young woman, had she been going to have a baby, she would have liked very much to have seen that able young woman come purposefully through the door, intent upon helping her.

# *Chapter Ten*

*You see, it is a war.*

*The war will keep you from everything. Except, of course, me. Us. Those deemed suitable for volunteering for a war in which few shots had yet been fired.*

Mary stopped at the bottom of the town house stairs, her bag clutched to her side, fatigue in full assault, looking from right to left, trying to decide where she should go, as a new film of dirt and sweat coated her face. A long line of soldiers passed by, drilling in uniform down the dusty street, heading toward the Mansion whose parapets she could just see over the roofs of the busy street. Why had she not seen this evidence of the war as she had traveled in from the train station? Here the city thrummed and rumbled with life, and boys as young as fourteen and fifteen were armed with not just drum, but musket.

*Yet you are not thirty, which I have decided is the minimum possible age for any female to involve herself in a war.*

Mary resolved to find a hotel, to prove herself capable of at least that, when, for the first time in a long time, she felt herself incapable, unseated and disoriented, not only by travel, but by Miss Dix's implacable resistance. It was Sumter all over again, when James Blevens had said, simply, *No.* He was going to *the war,* was in fact here, somewhere, along with Thomas and Christian, but Mary wasn't allowed. She had recovered herself, and was on the verge of setting out in search of a cab, when a young man who had been nimbly working his way down the street stopped at the bottom of the stairs and said, "How do you do? Have you just come from seeing Miss Dix?"

There was something about him, though Mary couldn't say what, that made her ask, "Can you tell me of a good place to stay?"

The man removed his hat, revealing wetted hair, parted on the left, youth, and a forehead that looked already well acquainted with worry.

"The Willard Hotel is good," he said, "but I suppose—" He stopped, appraising her dishevelment, but not impolitely. "You might try Mrs. Surratt's Boarding House on E Street." He spun around and pointed through a wall of buildings. "But you would need a cab."

"I need only a room and privacy."

"Then the Willard. A couple of Vermonters have done good work there. Shall I walk you?"

"Thank you, but no."

He stepped aside as Mary started down the street. "I do beg your pardon," he said, "but did you say whether or not Miss Dix is in?"

Mary turned back. "She is. Though what good it will do you, I have no idea."

"Is that so?"

"She is in charge of the war."

"Is that right?"

"Yes."

"How very interesting. May I introduce myself? I am John Hay," he said. "Secretary to the president. I am certain Mr. Lincoln will be delighted that he is no longer in charge."

"Then would you tell the president something for me, please?"

"I would be delighted to," Hay said, suppressing a sigh. Daily, he went about his errands, retrieving tooth powder or fetching soup for the president, only to return from the streets with a dozen messages, rarely urgent and often ridiculous. *Just let 'em go. What good is the South anyway? Nothing but cotton growers and pickaninnies.*

"Would you please tell the president that Miss Dix is turning women away?" Mary felt great shame in tattling, but she was tired and hungry.

John Hay felt oddly vindicated. He had told the president that it had been a bad idea from the start to appoint Miss Dix. Now he took stock of the young woman before him, who was as tall as he was, sturdily built, not beautiful, but compelling all the same. "You wish to become a nurse?"

Mary had the feeling of being once again a specimen. Gathering her pride, she cried, "Why do people think it is such an odd desire?"

"I don't. Not at all." He assessed her, his gaze raking her body, but not impolitely. "May I escort you please? You look very unwell."

Mary shrugged and gave in, and, bowing, Hay took her by the elbow and walked her toward Pennsylvania Avenue, which they crossed. They followed a street next to the Mansion until they reached a set of grand stairs rising to the entrance of the Willard Hotel. He tipped his hat and said, "May I ask your name?"

"Miss Mary Sutter."

"May I say, Miss, that it will not be good, not any of it."

She knew he meant *the war.* War. Warning. Warned. The words rattled around in her head. She was on the edge of feeling.

"I'm sorry," she said. "I didn't mean to be rude. I've come a long way, and now—" She held up her hands in apology.

The powerful seethed around them, though Mary could not know it. John Hay did, and stood fast.

"She is well-intended," he said, meaning Miss Dix, though he did not know why he was defending her. He thought her restrictions far too stringent. That he had hoped that the circular would bring a flux of eligible young women into the capital, he had not mentioned to the president and did not mention now.

"You cannot make up for her," Mary said, and turned to climb the stairs to the hotel where Vermonters had done well.

"I met the most remarkable woman on the street," John Hay said. "She complained that Miss Dix had turned her away."

After returning to meet with Miss Dix and asking her about Mary Sutter, he had found his interest stymied by the woman's stubborn self-regard. Now he entered the president's office and found Mr. Lincoln locked in his study, reading a telegram. Lincoln often seemed caged to Hay, as if the woods of Illinois, those much-vaunted forests invoked to shore up the image of him as woodsman, were indeed his natural domain. Woodcutter. Frontiersman. Lincoln had not chopped wood these ten years, at least. Still, restlessness dogged the president. Even when sitting, he wiggled his foot. Impatient, always, in face of the elusive. But in the time it had taken John Hay to meet Mary Sutter, Lincoln seemed to have aged ten years.

Lincoln looked up from the telegram. He loved a young man who knew what was important and what was not. Colonel Ellsworth had known, and lost his life for it. John Hay was beginning to learn, and was losing his youth to it. Already, gray flecked the curls above his ears.

"Our troops at Fort Monroe battled a contingent of Confederates near Big Bethel. We lost eighteen men. We had twice as many men as they did. We didn't last an hour."

*It won't be good. Not any of it.* Hay sank to the edge of a chair and hoped Miss Dix would turn away no more eager women, because they would need as many eager women as they could find.

Across the street, Mary was looking out from the room of the Willard Hotel toward the president's mansion. The hotel room cost three dollars a night, one and a half deliveries' worth, a rate that was even more expensive than the Delevan's. Mary was fairly certain that Amelia would send her more money if she asked, but she did not want her mother to know exactly where she was quite yet. She needed time. The link between becoming a nurse and becoming a surgeon was further apart than it had ever been, and now she wasn't even certain that it had ever been clear. She was beginning to doubt everything, especially the impulsive decision to come to Washington, which had seemed straightforward enough when she had made it, but now appeared rash and unfounded.

Laughter floated up from the dining room downstairs. Mary was hungry, but she could not imagine dining alone in public in a strange city. Even in Albany, she would have been too uncomfortable, though she was well known and might have found someone's table to join. Mostly though, she was tired. The maid had drawn her a bath, and as Mary towel-dried her hair, she thought of Thomas Fall and Christian just across the Potomac River, which she had not yet even glimpsed. Dr. Blevens, too. The thought came to her that she might try to find a way to visit them, thereby garnering at least some purpose in her defeat.

Such a long way to come for hope.

The summer evening was warm and Mary opened the window, but quickly shut it again. The air was foul, worse than the pestilential air of Albany, though it was hard to imagine anywhere that could top the odors of that city in the summer.

She sat down on the bed, running a comb through her curls.

If perhaps she couldn't get across the Long Bridge, it was possible she would run into Thomas and Christian in the city. Though the shape of her future seemed as indistinct as the last forty-eight hours of her life, now she imagined serendipity, coincidence. *Oh. How lovely to see you here. We're just in from the fort. Let me take your arm.* But it was Blevens saying this, bowing, offering his arm. She must readjust; Blevens was not the man she wished to see.

Mary put aside her comb and lay back on the bed. Perhaps they would meet nearby, or even in the hotel. Downstairs, the orchestra was playing a waltz. Thomas, her brother-in-law, was guiding her to a linen-covered table, Christian proudly following behind, James Blevens now lost in the crowd. Pure white walls trellised with gilded vines; dancers weaving to a Viennese waltz played by a string quartet, their violin bows rising and falling in unison; candles flaring in sconces, trays piled with food. Grapes and bananas and a roasted hog with an apple in its mouth sailing by on the arms of jacketed waiters. The dancers in white turned and turned on a parquet floor. *You dance so well. Thank you. I am a very good brother-in-law.* Dr. Blevens cut in and asked, *Is this enough for you?* Christian cut in and said, *Isn't war splendid?* In her arms, her brother was untouched, safe, because she was here. Their mother would be so pleased. In between sweeping dips and turns, Mary found time to deliver the baby of a woman laboring in a corner. *Oh, thank you,* the woman said, swiftly recovering, holding up her baby for the men to admire. *See how clever that woman is? See how she helped me? There, the one dancing in the arms of that young man, the one that looks as if he loves her. He knows who she is. He knows what she can do.*

The music raced and the men took turns twirling Mary in circles until her heart raced and she held her gloved hand to her chest, her beautiful neck rising from her white, square-collared dress. *You have a fine neck and lovely carriage for a woman who is not attractive. I know. My neck is my best feature. I know how to carry this ungainly body. That's good, because this is a war, you know. But you shouldn't have come. You're far too young. You've come too far. You shouldn't be here.*

*You shouldn't be here.*

Thomas glided her off the floor and then rejoined the dancing soldiers, now absent their partners, turning in perfect rhythm in their white waistcoats and white gloves and white powdered wigs as the band played faster and faster, until they vanished, every one.

Mary woke up, startled, not remembering having fallen asleep.

*It will not be good, not any of it.*

At ten o'clock the next morning, on the top floor of the Widner Building at 17th and F streets, Mary stood at a tall oak counter that separated the dozen clerks writing in ledgers from inquirers.

"I am in need of the addresses of all the hospitals, makeshift and established."

A tall, clipped man looked up at Mary from behind his pile of papers and observed that the woman enquiring carried a valise and an open notebook, and that flowers of perspiration had already bloomed under her arms this sweltering morning. "That is not information I am able to give out." The clerk had worked in the Surgeon General's office only two months. In that time, he had become happily stingy and presumptive, playing out the eternal imperiousness of clerks who caught the disease the first day on the job and ever afterwards never recovered. Doomed to their fate, they succumbed to stinginess without argument, as if to death.

"John Hay sent me." Mary said the name without remorse, having decided to hazard everything.

"We sent him a report last week."

"But now it is this week," Mary said.

The clerk looked her up and down, as much as he could from behind the counter, his arms propped upon its smooth, caramel surface, king of his fiefdom. "Is John Hay now employing his own secretary?" He was angry that he had not heard the job was available, admitting to himself the dissatisfaction he rarely let surface. It was a volcano to be capped, for life was long. He managed to notice, with pleasure, the state of her clothes; they were traveled in, and recently. To be a secretary to the secretary to the president did not confer advantage, it seemed, only discomfort, a circumstance that rendered only a modicum of satisfaction. He said, "We do not make duplicate reports."

Mary set down the pen, a simple action the clerk would later remember for its threat. She might have been taking up a sword. *You are my last. Not hope, not chance, but impediment.*

"If you do not give me the addresses, then the president himself will be forced to come here."

The clerk would have liked very much to see the president up close. Mr. Lincoln had never visited the Surgeon General's office, though he was frequently seen striding through the park on his way to the War Department across the street. *Will be forced.* The clerk tried to picture a scowl from the famously congenial man. A reprimand, possibly even a dismissal, might follow, all from wishing for a moment of recognition.

The clerk reached for a thick ledger. "It will take a moment for me to copy them out for you."

"It will be more efficient if you read them to me," Mary said.

The clerk sighed and began to drone.

A few minutes later, examining her notebook outside, Mary hoped that John Hay might forgive her the use of his name. She had considered calling at the Mansion to obtain some sort of letter of introduction, but had decided that she would make her own way, though it was the desk clerk at the Willard who had said, "If it is information of that sort you are after, you could really do no better than the Surgeon General's office," and had provided her with a map drawn on the back of her hotel receipt.

Mary tucked the notebook into her valise. She had given up her room at the Willard; whatever was to become of her, would become of her today.

The morning was dusty and already insufferably warm. As she marched up the rise as if *to war*—thought it herself, in celebratory defiance of Miss Dix—she had no way of knowing that John Hay watched from an upstairs window of the War Department, and was marveling that the young woman had found her way so quickly, sorry that he had not been the one to help her.

Across the river at Fort Albany, a wagon train materialized from the Columbia Turnpike. Christian's back and arms flamed as he set down his axe to watch the procession turn from the road into the unfinished fort. He'd been felling trees to create an unobstructed view to the road, and any chance to leave off for a moment was welcome. His body had grown hard with the manual labor, but he still ached, especially in his joints. The pain was worse at night, when he had only his haversack for a pillow, and even the ravishment of a night sky painted with stars could not distract him from the pangs of a body adjusting to hardship. A wagon train of supplies was a rare occurrence, although last week a train had arrived out of the blue bearing thousands of loaves of freshly baked bread. And now, it appeared, they were the recipients of new tents, if the canvas ties and fir poles were any indication. Christian flung down his axe and called to Thomas, and together they ran after the wagons and followed them through the crude stick-and-post gate of the fort.

"Four to a tent, four to a tent," the sergeant called, and the men lined up. The sergeant had counted the canvas rolls, divided a thousand exhausted men by the amount, and come up with the crowded answer as the men lined up for the unexpected gift of shelter. In the hot sun, the prospect of tents made the men long for home and all its comforts, including liquor, the last of which they'd seen in Washington City. But not Christian. He had once tried the cheap still-gruel that passed for whiskey brewed out of Swampdoodle and had found it foul. All he really wanted was to go home, a fact he hid from nearly everyone, including Thomas. It was only June 12 and they wouldn't be going home at least until the end of July. He had been so eager to come, but now he could barely picture his mother's and sisters' faces. Had he said good-bye properly? He wasn't certain that he had.

"Bedfellows now," Jake Miles said, having fallen in line behind them. Since coming to Washington, Jake hadn't seemed to recognize either of them, though when Christian had first spotted him on the steamship down to Annapolis, he had thought that Jake might have. But he either hadn't or it didn't matter. Besides, it had been only for a moment at the Sutters' that Christian had even seen Jake. Even so, he had avoided him.

Colonel Townsend said, "Clear out the lean-tos and pile them for firewood."

The colonel was on horseback, patrolling the hill on which Fort Albany was rising, where three weeks before there had been only trees and scrub and wild hogs. In this endeavor, there was pride and disappointment both, but shouting about construction was not leading troops into battle. Nor could he even call this motley band of brigands troops. Men only, dignity an elusive thing when professors and drunkards both had answered Lincoln's call.

"Mind your neighbors; five feet between tents. Dig a trench for drainage; there are no shovels, use your hands. Or a rock. Who's on picket duty? Take up your muskets, damn it. Your tentmates will finish." Ever reminding, a parent to grown men. Townsend sighed. It was exhausting. There was pride only in his position on horseback, saved from manual labor by his status.

Jake flung the heavy bundle onto a small rectangle of dirt and rocks that sloped from the top of the hill where they were building earthen ramparts. On either side, knots of men puzzled out poles, ties, and wooden stakes. In the making up of tents, the absence of women had never been more felt, and the men all silently decided that the male species was inadequate to the task of comfort.

"Kick away the rocks, or they'll kill us," Jake said, dictating to his three tentmates, who in Albany had been his betters, but not here. War was the great equalizer, and no one knew it better than Jake, who reveled in telling the city folks how to take care of themselves. He rarely shared the squirrels and rabbit that he shot, though sometimes he did in exchange for fruit. Of his future tentmates, Jake was the only one to whom living outside had not been a shock. He had grown more robust, not less, in the hills of Arlington, exhibiting none of the signs of scurvy that were beginning to plague the rest of them. His joints did not ache; his gums had not begun to bleed.

Jake unfurled the rolled canvas across the newly cleared dirt, releasing a clutch of fir poles that clattered to the ground.

"Should've sent oak," he said, shaking his head. "These won't last four months."

A thousand men couldn't all know each other, and now they exchanged handshakes and names. Thomas Fall. Jake Miles. Christian Sutter. Ali Baba, and they all laughed but Jake, who didn't understand.

"I beg your pardon. Edmund Wellon, son of the bookseller." He was the skinniest of the four, having rarely ventured out of the stuffy confines of his father's shop on State Street. "The tents," he said, by way of explanation. To Jake's still puzzled gaze, he said, "*A Thousand and One Nights*? The story of the queen who told stories to save her life?"

Jake pressed his lips together and turned away, shaking his head over what some people thought was important.

Christian said to Edmund, "You must know my sister, Mary Sutter?"

Thomas jabbed Christian's side.

"Mary Sutter?" Jake wielded one of the poles. "Is that midwife your sister?"

"That's right."

No one wanted a war in the tent. By the looks of the rude structures going up all around, they would all be sleeping toe to cheek, and have to turn in unison. Edmund Wellon watched, wary now, his hands on his hips, sensing something in the air.

"You close with that doctor?" Jake asked.

James Blevens was marching by with a tent all to himself, a treasure of privacy in the public nightmare of being physician to a thousand men around the clock. He stopped and said, "At least now we won't have to sleep in the rain."

"Bonnie." Jake and Christian each said her name: Jake in a kind of strangled cry, Christian with disdain, for it was not he who should have been comforting Bonnie that night, but the boy before him, now down on one knee, gripping the pole with which he had pierced the ground, tears spilling down his face.

In the six weeks that the men of the 25th Regiment had been living without women, they had seen fights, anger, laughter, bawdiness, drunkenness, challenge, affection, but not tears. What tears they shed were shed alone on picket duty, at night, when a man was free to admit that his quest for adventure had turned into a test of endurance and deprivation.

"Who is Bonnie?" Edmund Wellon asked.

Christian abbreviated the story: "My sister delivered his wife's baby. The baby died." He put a hand on Jake's shoulder, taken by his grief, but Jake shrugged it off.

"She never would've left me if it weren't for your sister."

There had been no letters.

"She left you?"

"First thing I get home, I'm going to go get her."

"Where is she?" Blevens asked.

"At the Sutters'," Jake said with a sneer. "Because you couldn't take care of her."

"She is still at our house?" Christian asked.

All the remaining traces of Jake's sorrow twisted into anger. "She wouldn't go home when I went to say good-bye. Treated too nice, is what I think."

Blevens said, "No one can be treated too nicely, least of all a woman who has lost a baby."

Jake, startled again into sadness, ducked his head and gripped the tent pole as ballast.

That erecting a semblance of home could evoke such emotion.

It was like that all around, evocations of sorrow and sadness as the men received their first comfort of the war. But as Jake Miles and his uneasy tentmates untangled, pitched, and tied, and James Blevens climbed the hill to erect his own tent on the flats above, they all resolved to sleep lightly. Not because Jake had alarmed, not because his emotions had flashed recklessly between sorrow and anger, but because the dangers of childbirth had penetrated even their fraternity on the hill. Thomas thought of Jenny, James thought of Mary, and Jake and Christian thought of Bonnie, each fearful that that their love for a woman might one day bring them to their knees.

# *Chapter Eleven*

It was past three o'clock that same afternoon that Mary sank into the shade of a single oak tree standing outside the E Street Infirmary in Judiciary Square. Named in the hope that it would house a series of courts, the square instead featured City Hall, with its heavy towers, steep chimneys, and court system hidden deep within its Gothic confines. In Judiciary Square, there were no other courts, only the infirmary and medical school, housed in a large winged building that stood between a series of rising row houses that would forever usurp the concentration of courts Pierre Charles L'Enfant had envisioned for the capital. The square was also a thoroughfare for farmers taking their product to the nearby market, and the lively plaza seemed as familiar as State Street on Market Day, except that Mary had never felt more out of place or more tired. Her hair had gone wild in the humidity, and her calico dress, right for warm weather in Albany, was far too heavy and stiff for the southern summer. The day's heat had incinerated her resolve almost as quickly as had the Sister of Charity at the infirmary. Dressed in a hot black gown, the nun had been doppelgänger to the keeper of the door at Albany Medical College. No, they didn't need anyone to nurse. Was she interested, however, in becoming a sister?

After leaving the Surgeon General's office that morning with her list, Mary had hired a hack for the day, first visiting the Patent Office, which had become an overflow hospital to house the flood of sick soldiers. Invalids lay on pallets of straw on the floor between inventions and displays. There were small piston engines arrayed under glass, great winged contraptions hanging from the ceiling, drawings of apparatuses for sawing the skins off calves, smoke-consuming furnaces, and even more devices that crowded the large, echoing rooms. To find someone in charge, Mary climbed two staircases of cool echoing marble. Near a display of blueprints for mousetraps, a surgeon shrugged off her plea.

"Nurses? I have no need. The men take care of themselves, mostly."

"I could help. I am a midwife."

The surgeon, a thin, freckled man who had introduced himself as Major Edwards, said, "But no one here is going to have a baby."

From the Patent Office, she traveled to the Capitol, where invalids housed in the basement furnace room languished on cots fashioned from canvas. The answer there was also *No.* At the New York Presbyterian Church, where plywood lay across the pews, the ladies of the sanctuary asked, already knowing the answer, *Was she a member of the church? You must be a member of the church.*

An invisible fence surrounded *the war.*

The earth was turning, carrying her with it. At the medical college, she had even asked the sister whether they took female students now that the rest of their classes had left for the war. She had learned this after overhearing a sister complain of all the work. No, came the answer, they did not.

A man appeared at the door of the infirmary, speaking to the refusing sister. He had a leathered, permanently sunburned face and a beard of tight, graying coils. His voice carried in the airless doldrums.

"Surely, one of you could come, even if just during the day. You could return here at night."

"I'm sorry, but that's impossible. Our work is here."

He turned and walked with caged ferocity toward a run-down cart, which he handled poorly in the traffic.

The last hospital on Mary's list was the Union Hotel.

Her driver crossed the flat city and clattered over a bridge and climbed the hill to the village of Georgetown. A bustling place, it was full of people, even at this hot hour. Genteel homes lined the narrow street, but soon gave way to commerce. The driver stopped opposite a tobacco warehouse that occupied the whole of a block.

"Here?" Mary asked.

All day, the driver had been solicitous, asking whether or not she was well and whether she needed to stop for refreshment. Now he surveyed the dilapidated building from which hung a sign declaring it to be the Union Hotel. Rows of small windows were crookedly set or broken. It was unpainted, three stories, ill configured, added on to, subtracted from, ramshackle, severe, looking more like a prison than a hotel.

"You cannot go in there," he said.

"I've been inside worse places," Mary said, though she hadn't. Once, she had been called to a tenement on the quay, where a hurly-burly girl was having a baby, but even there the façade had invited, and the stairs, though narrow, had given way to a room of some comfort. Mary felt herself sway in the humidity. A knot of laughing Union soldiers passed by, heading down a side street toward a canal. Like the Erie, Mary thought, and grasped at this as a sign. She opened her purse. "How much do I owe you?"

"Twenty cents."

The price made her realize the extent of her mistake of the day before, the wide grin of the cab driver. *Extra for the tour.*

"Are you sure?" the hack driver asked, and when she nodded, turned and clattered down the cobbles toward Washington. She could tell by the hunch of his shoulders that he did not think her wise to have sent him away.

The rough door lacked a bell. She summoned memories of success: she had delivered three sets of twins; had driven ten miles in the rain one night to a house where a shrieking mother cried for six hours before she was delivered of a baby the size of a fist; had managed to survive her sister's marrying Thomas Fall.

Inside, the fetid air overwhelmed. A single gas flame flared in a broken sconce, revealing, as her eyes adjusted, that it had been a long time since the walls had seen paint, as long, it seemed, as the room had been cleaned. Barren rectangles remained behind where pictures had recently been removed. Save the brass railing circling the abandoned reception desk, no ornament of the hotel's faded utility remained. Dust sifted from creaking floorboards above. Across the narrow rectangle of lobby, a set of narrow stairs rose to a blind turn at the landing.

She made for these.

A second floor crouched between a third and the first. Low ceilinged, claustral, darker even than James Blevens's surgery that day in April, the hallway angled through the series of squat additions that made up the Union Hotel. Dull brass room numbers marked the open doors of rooms, where men in various states of undress flung bony legs from under sheets. Listless, they barely noticed her as she passed. The smell of illness, stronger now, permeated the walls. Little light penetrated to the hallway. At tunnel's end, she came to another stairway, and took that up. All was misery. The men were coughing and crying out. Occasionally, a rare burst of laughter made its way down the hallway. Mary descended again to the savage lobby and stood there, uncertain. To the left was a wider hallway and from it came the sounds of whistling. She followed the noise to a door that retained a sign boasting that it had once been the hotel library. There, sitting in a spindly chair at a small round table made for a café tête-à-tête, was the man from the E Street Infirmary, his beard dipped to his chest as he read intently from a book. The room was protected from the outside heat by half-closed shutters, but it was still beastly hot all the same.

Mary said, "I saw you earlier. At the infirmary."

The man looked up, his eyes squinting to take her in, as if he was still blinded by the light that had bathed them earlier in the square.

"And what were you doing there?"

"The same thing I am doing here, inquiring after a position as a nurse."

The man's head tilted to one side, inspecting her carefully. "Did the sister send you?"

"Actually," Mary said, "I don't want to be a nurse. I want to be a surgeon."

He raised his eyebrows. "And you propose to do this here?"

"I propose to begin here."

His gaze, not intrusive but inquiring, took in the length of her. Mary no longer cared that her skirts had wilted in the heat, or that her hair had tumbled from its ties and was now a hot mess about her neck. She had come to her last chance and wanted to look like it.

He put a finger between the pages of his book to hold his place. "I do not need a doctor. What I need is a charwoman and a nurse. You do not look like the sort of woman used to menial work."

"And what sort do I look?"

"The sort that wants to be a surgeon."

The hotel creaked and snapped in the heat.

"Have you been to see Miss Dix?" he asked.

"Yes."

"She give you trouble?"

"Yes."

"She would." He closed the book and said, "You think because you know an herb or two, or because you are unafraid of men, or because you have sat by the bedside of a dying relative, that you know what it means to attend the sick. I can assure you that you know nothing of what has been going on inside this hovel for the past month. If you did, you would follow my advice and leave. There are sights and sounds upstairs that would offend anyone, man or woman, surgeon or no. The work is unfit for a human being. It is unfit for the most robust of men. If I were you, I would run north, find a place of beauty, and remain there. It is my advice to you. It is my advice to anyone."

Mary took a deep breath and allowed herself to smile, because she had come too far not to recognize a yes when she heard it.

"I warn you," he said. "I don't need or want a medical student. I offer you nothing but the position I need filled."

"I'll take it."

"You won't last," the man said, eyeing Mary.

"I will need a room and bedding," she said.

"I fear you will need much more than that." Shaking his head, he stood, a look some might describe as pity shadowing his eyes, softening the hard set of his mouth. "My name is William Stipp," he said. "The surgeon in charge of this misery."

"And my name is Mary Sutter."

# *Chapter Twelve*

After depositing Mary Sutter in a closet of a room under the stairs with only a porthole of a window, William Stipp returned to the library and his copy of *The Practice of Surgery*, given to him by the Surgeon General's office when he'd arrived in Washington in March. Something about Mary Sutter was unsettling, though it was not her interest in medicine that bothered him. He'd seen enough eager students in his career, and besides, he wasn't going to teach her anything. What bothered him was that she reminded him of Lilianna, the lithe, brown-eyed daughter of the Mexican cook in Texas, whom he'd left behind when Texas seceded from the Union. It was nothing specific, except perhaps the way Mary Sutter had looked at him as if she knew how to find his heart, as Lilianna had. Stipp set the textbook on the table and leaned forward into his hands. Grief was such an avid stalker, surprising him when he least expected it.

After Genevieve, his wife, died in the cholera epidemic in the spring of 1855, he had thought he would never recover. The outbreak had spared no family in Manhattan City; the Episcopalian church on Fifth Avenue had been booked for two solid days of funerals, while the Catholic services went on for weeks, the poor in Five Points having suffered more. Neighbors brought picnic baskets to the church, and in the final hours of the second day, funeral corteges wound through the streets to the landing on the East River, where steamships carried the bodies around the tip of Manhattan for burial to Jersey City, far from the overcrowding that had killed them. Stipp had been inconsolable. His friend Thomas Lawson, the surgeon general, had written a condolence and offered an amnesiac: the Mexican War, though long since over, had spawned permanent forts along the Rio Grande. They needed a good doctor.

Upon Stipp's arrival at the post at Davis Landing, the southernmost fort on the border, the commander had taken one look at Stipp and said, "The sun will burn it out of you."

Glinting off sand and scrub, penetrating every rocky crevice, the hot light was superior to most defenses, but Stipp had loved too strongly. Head cocked, chin back, blue eyes sharp, his hands to his hips, he confronted everyone he met as a possible disappointment. The two hundred men of the garrison, however bored with one another, soon gave up on him as a possible source of entertainment, and he began a solitary life, so different from the one he had led before that he was certain he had found grief's antidote. In the sun's brilliant glare, in the fort's isolation, bachelorhood was assured, and slowly, grief shriveled. The smiling Mexican women who laundered for them in the muddy water of the Rio Grande shunned the men who fought their countryman, Juan Cortina. The men at the post had to travel to New Orleans for feminine comfort, but Stipp never went.

On an afternoon in the second year of his stay, he was dreaming of his wife when he awoke to a hand caressing his face. Lilianna was sitting lightly as a bird upon the edge of his cot. She was perhaps fourteen. Dark haired, small-boned, but armored with Mexican sturdiness, she was leaning on one hand, her head tilted, a shoulder shrugged into one ear, her other hand wrapped around her supporting arm. She was making a study of him, her gaze running over his chest dusted with gray hair.

"The women laugh and call you '*virgen*.'" Her voice, with its dark foreign song, magnified the distance he had traveled.

"Go back to your mother."

"I'm going to have a baby," she said. "It is by one of the men here."

Stipp never could make out if she'd been raped. Upon his promise to help her, she adopted him, keeping to his room and doing his laundry and preparing his food, his shoes shined to a polish every evening, water hauled from the river for his use. "Enough!" he'd yelled one hot evening when she brought him a pile of freshly mended shirts. But she kept on. Though she slept elsewhere, the men suspected nonetheless, grumbling aloud about what the girl could see in a forty-year-old man when their caresses would have been much more vigorous.

The commander frowned, but said, "I told you the sun would work."

When her time came, and the light-skinned boy slipped at dawn into Stipp's hands, Lilianna wrapped one arm around Stipp's neck and pulled him to her and whispered, "*Gracias, mi padre.*" Suddenly, Stipp's grief had no boundary, for now the world was flooded with possibilities of love, a terrifying and dangerous prospect for a man who still mourned.

He would have stayed in Texas forever, he thought now, gazing out the library window. He would have stayed in that sun-soaked land had not the state of Texas voted in February for secession and demanded a surrender of all Federal property. The speed with which the army had evacuated the forts scarcely gave Stipp time to bid his little family farewell. He stood on the boat at Davis Landing as the cloudy waters of the Rio Grande, dark as chocolate, lazed by. Lilianna raised her arm against the pale Southwest sky, while the boy cried out, his arms thrust before him, his fingers wiggling, calling Stipp to him. The boy had developed the habit of flinging himself into Stipp's arms and wrapping his legs around his waist, laughing, saying, *Abuelo. Grandfather.* As the steamship pulled away, Lilianna turned her back. Stipp's last memory of her was her slow, deliberate return to the adobe hut the three of them had called home: he, his adopted daughter, and her son.

The steamer whipped around Florida, having collected three surgeons from New Orleans and another from Galveston. Celestial bodies at a distant remove observed this rearrangement of humanity—displaced Northerners northward, dismissed Southerners southward—the national chess board realigning. The steamer captain raced up the coast past flat islands of sea grass, but he was receiving too little a sum to be happy about burning coal at such a clip. He was a Creole, fast-talking in a nearly unintelligible mash that resembled nothing of the Spanish Stipp had picked up from Lilianna. Stipp spent the eleven days at sea braced against the pilothouse at the bow, out of the way of the rigging, under the ship's bronze bell as the ship rolled and bucked in the breezes of the Atlantic and the coal smoke sent black cotton puffs into the bleached blue sky. At night, he slept with his window open to the sea. Lanterns flared and bobbed as ships passed. The Atlantic had become a game of dodge and hide; Lincoln had declared a blockade, and though he had few ships to enforce it, already a Union naval officer named Garrett Pendergrast had captured upwards of a dozen sympathetic ships trying to supply the Confederates.

By the time William Stipp reached Washington at the beginning of March, he had armored himself with reticence, but knew it to be a pretense. He was forty-five years old, and the desert sun had opened his pores; life would run in and out at will. The watery boil of Washington shocked; he'd grown fond of an arid night, the clicking of lizards, water contained in a single brown ribbon slicing through scrub. At night, he drowned in moisture and awoke in sweaty confusion when neither Genevieve nor Lilianna answered his summons.

And always, when on the street he heard the laughter of a little boy, he turned involuntarily, and was destroyed.

Stipp blinked back his watering eyes. He needed no more loves, no more attachments. What he needed was to relearn everything he had forgotten about medicine in Texas. Five years had been too long; the absence had softened his brain. He picked up his book and began memorizing the passages about amputations, all the while wondering what form of grief had driven a young woman as self-possessed as Mary Sutter to a hellhole like the Union Hotel.

# Chapter Thirteen

The needle jabbed and poked. The young bride Jenny Fall threw down the yard of unbleached muslin and sucked this latest puncture wound to her thumb. Her irritation was made worse by the morning sickness ravaging her insides. Since five this morning she'd been up depositing the churnings of her restless stomach into the bowl beside her bed.

Being with child had not been, so far, a pleasant experience.

In the filtered light of the Episcopal church's stone-walled basement, chosen for its coolness as the Ladies' Auxiliary meeting place late this July morning, Jenny's fingers were the only ones not flying through the heavy cloth. The place was full of ladies gossiping and sewing havelocks to send to the boys in Washington to protect them from the ravages of the southern sun. No one quite knew how havelock fever had caught on, but it had. Jenny lifted the odd, Arabian-inspired hat up by its frame. It seemed silly to her to be sewing so many of them when the war would soon be over and Thomas would be home.

"Are you hurt?" Bonnie asked.

In her modest dress, Bonnie looked out of place in the church basement among the wealthy women of Albany, though her stitches were as small, even, and assured as the oldest matron's. Bonnie had the oddest ability to blend into the background when she wanted to, Jenny thought. Hardly any of the women, usually so clannish, had even given her a second glance this morning. Since Mary's departure, Bonnie had been Jenny's ever-present shadow, going with her everywhere. Jenny suspected that Bonnie was drawn to her because of the baby, though Bonnie displayed none of the envy Jenny believed she harbored. The need she felt not to show even the smallest amount of anticipation, out of respect for Bonnie's loss, had been a kind of usurpation of her happiness. Just last night, Jenny had dreamed that each of them—she and Bonnie—had birthed a single child, but that afterwards, the baby would suckle only at Bonnie's breast. Jenny had awakened sad *and* nauseated, and she answered Bonnie's solicitation now with a furious shake of her head and began again to sew, slipping a silver thimble onto her finger. Lately, the satisfaction she had harbored over her wedding had completely faded. She'd heard nothing from Thomas, not one letter. She supposed that in wartime the mails were inconsistent, but they'd had a letter from Mary. Piercing the cloth once again with the needle, she set to work, shrugging off Bonnie's shy smile.

Across the low-ceilinged basement, Amelia was speaking to a group of women at the far table, some of whose children she had delivered.

"Yes. She traveled on the day boat to Manhattan and then on to Washington by train."

Glances were flying across the tables. What had Amelia Sutter been thinking? None of them had let their daughters go off to nurse.

"Is Jenny going, too?" Frances Ellis asked. She had been down at the quay on the morning Mary had left, seeing her aunt off to Manhattan, when she'd spied Mary embarking the boat alone and unchaperoned. Frances had flown up the hill to tell Amelia, and by the look on Amelia's face she was fairly certain when she'd reported the news that Amelia had had no idea that her daughter was even gone. Too independent, those girls. She threw a quick glance at Jenny, over the tables spread with old bedding, needles, scissors, and spools of thread.

"No, Jenny won't be going. Jenny is . . . not able."

Amelia let the implication find its target, and then sighs and smiles were directed Jenny's way. This was how such announcements were usually made, though most of the matrons present had already noticed the girl's pallor and lain bets.

"But Jenny wouldn't have gone, in any case. She has a different temperament. Mary is more like me."

Determined pride was Amelia's public armature against her terror at Mary's disappearance, a shield against the rising fear that had been her constant companion since she'd first read Mary's note, pinned to her pillow in parody of an elopement. Had she known what Mary had been planning, she would have tied her to her bed that night, and every night after that, if necessary. Thinking back, Amelia knew that Mary had been too complaisant at dinner that night, too accepting of her objections. And Mary was never accepting when she wanted something. All through the evening, she had smiled benignly at Jenny, when in fact the Mary Amelia knew so well would still have been pursuing her argument, even at the expense of ruining Jenny's moment. She had sent a letter saying that Amelia was not to worry. The hotel was lovely in every way, rivaling even the Delevan. It had a view of the C&O Canal. There was a laundress and a cook. It was ideal. Amelia was not to send for her. The surgeon had sought to make her comfortable in every way. A feather bed, an armoire. There were a dozen women working there as nurses. Privacy was at a premium. An entire wing to themselves.

Amelia tried not to imagine her daughter's real circumstances. The day Mary had disappeared, Amelia bought an Appleton Guide from Wellon's: *A Companion Guide to US & British Provinces*. The note on Washington had done nothing to quell her fear.

> Washington is a city of villages, neither enlightened nor beautiful. The denizens of the capitals of Europe would laugh at the city's paucity; no head of state should go. Keep tight to your purse; choose lodgings with discrimination; and leave the city as soon as possible for the more graceful attractions of the hospitable state of Virginia.

Amelia looked up to see that Jenny had abandoned her sewing and was gazing at her with an inscrutable expression. *Mary is more like me.* How loudly had she spoken? It was difficult to have two daughters with such different natures. Though she was terrified for Mary, she was also proud of her, and besides, she had not meant to disparage Jenny. She was terrified for Jenny, too.

All this Jenny read from her bench, hunched over the unfinished havelock in her lap. Already, in the three weeks since Mary's departure, Amelia had kept up a running commentary no doubt intended as soothing, but which had only increased Jenny's disquiet. *The war will certainly be over by the time you are ready to deliver; Mary will be back; I think it would be best if Mary delivered you; did you know that once Mary delivered a pair of twins to a girl whose hips were as narrow as yours?; drink plenty of milk, I think, not the water; tea toast will help with the nausea.* Amelia delivered all this with a brittle smile, a fountain of enthusiasm that was so unlike her.

Jenny tried to picture Mary in Washington. No thimble and thread for her. Instead, midwife to grown men, the half of the species her twin sister did not understand. To Jenny, Mary's departure had been swift and curiously timed and had told her all that she needed to know, had feared but not voiced, until the day after her wedding, on the morning of the 25th's departure, when she and Mary had met in the kitchen. *You understand things. Women respect you.* She'd never been able to admit her envy to Mary before, and she'd hoped that the revelation might quicken their sundered friendship. In the weeks since the wedding, she had tried to find her way back to her sister, feeling sympathy, even, for how Mary had managed in the months in which Jenny had blatantly campaigned for Thomas. But Mary had been averse to any hint of pity.

And now a baby was coming, hers and Thomas's, and Mary was not here to deliver it.

The thimble, the size Jenny imagined her baby now to be, rolled from her grasp. The tiny silver cup tumbled to the uneven stone floor, and the clatter of it striking sounded, absurdly, like a baby crying.

That night, Amelia wrote two letters.

*Dear Mary,*

*I do not believe that you are as well off as you say, nor do I believe that working in Washington as a nurse will help you achieve your aim of someday becoming a surgeon. If you have left because of Jenny, I cannot imagine you being so foolish. They are married and it is done. The truth is, I need you to come home, Mary. A mother shouldn't have to deliver a daughter, and perhaps a sister shouldn't have to deliver a sister, either, but I already know that my worry over her condition will cloud my judgment. Perhaps if you return, you will be able to persuade Dr. Marsh of his unreason. I will do everything I can to help you. Please come home, Mary. It will all work out. Please, find Christian and see that he is well. I haven't had a letter from him, and I worry about him almost as much as I worry about you.*

*Your loving mother,*

*Amelia*

*My dearest Christian,*

*I think of you every day. I am both proud and fearful for you. Please be careful. The papers print such stories of illness and unhealthy conditions that I fear you will become ill, and will be far from me when it happens. I know this is a mother's letter, full of concern and worry, and that you will think I am foolish. I do not mean to deprive you of your glory, or of your adventure, I only say, please, take more care, not less, than you think you need. And if you can, write to me.*

*But this is not the only reason I have written to you. Mary left home in June to work in Washington City. She is at the Union Hotel in the village of Georgetown, which is very near Washington City. Please find her and convince your older sister that leaving home is not the answer she seeks. If you need to, take Thomas with you. You know how she listens to him.*

*I love you. Come home to me,*

*Your adoring mother*

# *Chapter Fourteen*

**Sanitary Commission Report**

*The Union Hotel Hospital, July 10th, 1861*

The Union Hotel Hospital, Georgetown, was occupied as its name implies, until recently hired for its present use. It is considered capable of accommodating 225 patients, and at present contains 189. It is well situated, but the building is old, out of repair, and cut up into a number of small rooms, with windows too small and few in number to afford good ventilation. Its halls and passages are narrow, tortuous, and abrupt, and in many instances with carpets still unremoved from their floors, and walls covered with paper. There are no provisions for bathing, the water-closets and sinks are insufficient and defective, and there is no dead-house. The wards are many of them over-crowded, and destitute of arrangements for artificial ventilation.

"Just think what they would have said if they had visited before you arrived, Mary."

Stipp was leaning up against the wall in the second-floor hallway, watching Mary run a ragged mop over the uneven floorboards, which was the only flooring in the entire place that took mopping, but even if Mary were to remove each rug and beat it until it approached cleanliness, she would never accomplish anything even approaching clean. It seemed that no cleaning had been attempted in the eighty years or so since George Washington had eaten at the hotel, when the humble building was still only a tavern on the turnpike north. Neither had anyone cleaned the single water closet in an age. (The Sanitary Commission had gotten it wrong; there was only one, and its fabrication of more seemed somehow gracious, as if they could fill the need by wishing them into being.) Its box seeped through the floorboards to the cellar, where a shimmering lake of sewage pooled in the corner before bubbling into the unseen swamp that lurked beneath the city. Not even the linens were clean. The laundresses, hired by Stipp to work once a month, frequently did not show, and the sheets soured for weeks at a time under the patients' backs. The cook knew how to prepare only two meals, oatmeal and boiled beef, but since there was no beef to boil, oatmeal was the mainstay of the 189 inhabitants of the least sanitary building in a hundred-mile radius of the nation's capital.

"What the commission should have said is that this place is an apocalypse." Mary wiped away the streams of perspiration cascading down her forehead. Her back ached; her palms were blistered from the mop handle, last sanded, she was certain, on George Washington's final visit. She sank against the wall and sighed.

"I warned you that what I needed was a charwoman."

"This is not sport, Dr. Stipp. Men cannot get well in such a place."

"In all the world, there is not medicine enough to heal what ails the Union army, mopping or no."

Stipp was at his wit's end. He had no patience for dysentery, the disease that had seized most of his patients even though he had attacked the tenacious ailment with a cocktail of drugs that the steward, Mr. Mack, had cleverly pilfered from the medical supply at the quartermasters' in Foggy Bottom. But not a single doctor in the army knew what to do. In light of the ever-present and rampant diarrhea, Stipp had had to improvise. He had at first suspected malarial fever as the cause, and had pushed the normal quinine dose to its limits, and for good measure added mercury and Epsom salts. But then he had changed his mind and thought the cause might be typhoid, and so now he was using Dover's powder and the occasional opiate. When pain presented, he administered blisters by cupping, and ordered good slugs of whiskey. Several times, however, calomel had proved useful, as had castor oil. And if the sufferer was immune to all of the above, he gave ipecac, to induce vomiting. But it was a nasty business, every bit of it, and nothing he did was working. The Sanitary Commission had been generous in its assessment; the conditions in the hotel had reached unbearable long ago. Only Mary and her efforts were keeping death by enteric asphyxiation at bay.

As if to prove him right, Mary splashed the mop back into the bucket.

"You cannot drown disease, Miss Sutter."

"I can wash away its residue."

"You are the most stubborn young lady I have ever met. You were certainly not a charwoman in your former life."

"I want to be a surgeon."

Stipp sighed, regretting ever having invited this headstrong young woman to stay, though it hadn't been bad to have her about. She had made remarkable progress on the hygiene situation. And the men had perked up in her presence, though Mary was no beauty and certainly gave no indication of any of the usual weaknesses of her sex. But it was demoralizing to have her see that day after day, week after week, none of his patients improved, and that he had no idea what he should do for them, and that this seemingly most simple of medical problems was in fact the most baffling one he had ever faced. And Mary turned up everywhere, looking over his shoulder at the bedside, inquiring whether or not such and such a dose of quinine had worked yet, whether or not the Dover's powder was at all effective, had he thought of tapioca and rice as a palliative, did he wonder whether there was some collective problem afoot in the land, would the intestinal lining of the patients tolerate the repeated onslaught, did he think they would survive?

It wasn't ego, he told himself. He was not really so small a man as that. It was that he was done with teaching. James Blevens had been the last of his students, and he had been sharp, that one. Cleverly taken with the body and its vagaries. But that was when he himself had been sharp; now the Texas sun had dulled his memory, and he was fighting to remember what used to come to him without any trouble at all. Sometimes, he felt himself not so much at his wit's end, but witless. How much there was to know; how little he knew. Mary would be much better off anywhere else, even if she couldn't see it. Still, she was remarkably resilient. It seemed nothing would bring her to her knees, not even the despicable state of this building. But as happy as he was to have finally obtained responsible help, he would not engage in dishonesty.

"You will not become a surgeon here. I cannot help you. I tell you this as a warning. I want you to understand. There is nothing for you here."

"I will become a surgeon here," Mary said, but she would not look at him, because she did not want to see the unwavering honesty in his eyes. "I am learning things."

"This is no place to become educated. This is no place at all, in fact, or can't you tell that?"

"I will learn what I can."

"By mopping floors?"

"Yes, by mopping floors. And by washing sheets and by beating rugs and by any other means necessary." She was shouting now, her voice carrying down the narrow hallway, penetrating the old timbers of the hotel that had seen murder, adultery, generosity, desperation, and grief, but never such ragged disappointment.

"You're a fool," he said.

He left her then and Mary finished mopping the hall, furiously slopping the water onto the floorboards and then whipping the mop back and forth, banging it into the walls. She felt like she was fighting the entire history of the country, all its residue, all its neglect, all its ignorance. In the dim light, it was impossible to tell whether or not she was making any progress, on the floor or in her education. What had she learned so far? How to unplug an ancient water closet, how to bathe in a building without bathing facilities, how to pitchfork boiling linens from a wash cauldron to a rinse one, but nothing about medicine. What was striving for if all you learned was that your stubbornness led you places you never wanted to be in order to do things you never thought you would do?

She flushed the water closet with the waste water, and set the mop in the corner to rinse once she went downstairs. She was soaked though with perspiration and dirty water; the hotel walls also hoarded heat. She unpinned her hair and ran her hands through her curls, twisting them back up again into their pins. What had she wanted; where had she come? The men called to her as she careened down the hallway, begging her for help to write a letter, for something to drink, for her smile, but she dashed past their open doors until she reached her room under the stairs, where she peeled off her dress and threw herself onto the hard, thin mattress in her camisole and pantaloons. Drab walls, peeling wallpaper, a wardrobe in which a rat had made a nest in her nightgown.

*It will not be good, not any of it. You will have exhausted yourself for nothing.*

Her mother's letter was folded under her pillow and Mary pictured now, as she rarely allowed herself to do, home: the bounty of the dining table, the clean, scented sheets on her bed, the yellow orchid gracing the hallway table, the airy rooms, freshly laundered curtains billowing from tall windows open to a spring breeze.

A pot of tea, served on a tray, with a pitcher of milk fresh from the icebox and crystals of sugar in a silver bowl.

Who was Stipp anyway? He was not the keeper of the gate, just as neither Blevens nor Marsh was. But she couldn't help but feel now that she had made a huge mistake, had gone backward, not forward, had made her life worse, not better. The sweat was beginning to evaporate now from her skin, cooling her, but there was still so much to do. There were sheets to boil and bedpans to clean, and then she had to try to find something to eat, because mealtime as the only woman among hundreds of men was a fight for survival.

She reached under the pillow and pulled Amelia's letter from its envelope. *Please come home. Please find Christian.* The pages were already beginning to tear, though she had only read the letter half a dozen times. She supposed Jenny would want to hear of Thomas, too, though she wasn't surprised that Amelia hadn't mentioned it. Nothing was as she had imagined coming down on the train, when the resolve propelling her had seemed as right and true as love. It was terrifying to have miscalculated; she rarely did that, and feared that her stubbornness—yes, she would admit she was stubborn, Stipp was not wrong about that—might not be enough to sustain her.

Do one thing, Mary thought. Have control over one thing. Wasn't this how she had conquered uncertainty in childbirth? Steadiness, patience, deliberation, then action. Gathering herself in the melting heat, she rose from the bed, smoothed the sheets and her petticoat, and stepped into her still damp dress. After tucking the letter back under her pillow, she collected her purse and a parasol she had purchased to ward off the southern sun (no havelock for her), marched out of the disease-ridden Union Hotel, hired a hack, and headed into Washington, retracing for the first time the route she had taken a month before. Dust flew up from the street traffic and shimmered in the waves of afternoon heat. Mary held a handkerchief to her mouth and the parasol over her head as she climbed the stairs to the run-down building the hack driver had pointed out when he had come to a rest outside the Department of the Army.

Inside, the clerk—cousin, Mary thought to the one at the Surgeon General's office—sighed and asked why she wanted to go to such a rough place as Fort Albany.

"To see my brother."

"I am sorry, but there are no passes for civilians to visit soldiers at the forts." In the heat, his wool uniform smelled like a wet dog.

"I have to see him. My mother begged me, and I've come all this way—"

"We are aware that many mothers are worried. That is why the Sanitary Commission is allowed across the Long Bridge for inspections, but under no circumstances are family members allowed."

"But I have to see him."

"Pardon me, but are you a Miss or a Mrs.?"

"A Miss. Miss Mary Sutter."

"Write him a letter, Miss Sutter," the clerk said, "and be done with it."

"But—"

"Virginia is enemy territory. There are no passes to be had for sisters or mothers or anyone else. Unless you are a bawdy girl, and then that is an entirely different matter, one for the provost guard to attend to. We are not issuing passes. Go home."

He walked away from her then and busied himself with something in the corner. Mary slipped outside. Her hack driver had gone. She stood for a moment, watching the traffic swell in the streets, then walked toward the Willard, where the bellman would hail her another cab.

A charwoman. Not yet a nurse; certainly not a surgeon. Not even a good sister or daughter. Perhaps it didn't matter, she thought, as she dodged traffic on the avenue. The war could end tomorrow and they'd all be back in Albany anyway, just like before, except that Jenny and Thomas were expecting a baby, and Mary would certainly have her chance to be a good sister then.

On the way back to Georgetown, she wondered what ambition was worth, and whether her family would love her if she failed. She had grieved the loss of Thomas, had resolved on this other path, and it was further away now even than it had been in Albany. And now she wasn't even able to comfort Amelia on the state of Christian's well-being. She had never felt so defeated in her life.

At the Union Hotel, the walls throbbed with heat. She hid her purse, repinned her hair, and went upstairs to begin stripping sheets from the beds.

# *Chapter Fifteen*

"We have received certain information that the Confederates are at Manassas," John Hay said. "Are you aware of this?"

It was Monday, July the fifteenth, six a.m., two weeks before Lincoln's seventy-five thousand men were to return home to their plows and wives, and not a thing between the warring states had been settled. Apart from incessant drilling and parades, the growing ring of forts beginning to encircle Washington, and the increasing public outcry for a resolution to the seemingly insoluble conflict, you could barely tell there was a war on. In the past three months there had been the occasional skirmish—small battles scattered here and there, most notably in western Virginia, where a general named George McClellan was successfully harassing the Confederates in the interest of protecting both the C&O Canal and the railroads—but for the most part, the willing civilians-turned-soldiers who had engulfed Washington City had fired no shots, engaged in no battles, and achieved only the dubious distinction of having fallen ill by the thousands. If the issue of secession was ever going to be settled, it had to be settled soon, before the idle seventy-five thousand returned home. On this point at least everyone agreed.

Everyone this morning included General Winfield Scott, seventy-four years old, a brevet lieutenant general who had commanded forces in both the War of 1812 and the Mexican-American War and then served as military governor in Mexico City and had once even run for president. He was the commander general of all the Northern forces. General Irvin McDowell, forty-three, also brevetted, was in charge of the Army of Northeastern Virginia, the Northern contingent encamped on the Virginia side of the Potomac. They had ridden down Pennsylvania Avenue through the simmering dawn to the Mansion for this meeting. McDowell felt himself subordinate to everyone in the room, even the annoying Hay, and was holding himself in an exaggerated posture of diffidence that was making him vastly uncomfortable, not the least because he knew that both Scott and Lincoln had preferred Robert E. Lee for McDowell's current position before Lee had decided to secede with his home state of Virginia. The president, who had slept that night in the Mansion rather than at the Soldiers' Home where his wife, Mary, and their children were spending the summer away from the sweltering bog of the Potomac, was leaning over an incomplete map of Virginia spread across his desk that the two generals had brought with them.

Hay cleared his throat. "I asked, gentlemen, are you aware?"

Both Scott and McDowell sized up Hay, with his linen vest and oiled hair, and decided these dandifying vanities were further evidence of his youthful ignorance and that he was far too young to be advising the president, especially in military matters. Besides, how did the impertinent boy know where the Rebels were? Manassas was thirty miles away—in Virginia, no less.

Punishing Hay with a humorless smile, Scott instead directed his answer to Lincoln.

"Of course we are aware of the situation. Our scouts reported last night that the enemy recently moved a large force through the Shenandoah Valley. If they have indeed settled at Manassas—and of course," Scott said, both bowing and smirking in Hay's direction, "given the delays between reception of intelligence and any corresponding reaction, a *military* man never assumes that the information in his possession is either current or accurate—however, now might be our best chance to destroy the Rebel force and win the war. And then we can shame the Rebels back into submission."

The four men could almost hear the clock ticking. Even the public had lost patience. *Forward to Richmond!* the newspapers were crying, splashing their impatience across dailies all over the North.

McDowell shifted. He didn't agree with Scott. Despite intensive drilling, his troops were still unready to face an army, unready even to march the proposed thirty miles to Manassas. They were an undisciplined lot, who despite having wielded shovels more than muskets these past months, were out of shape for a hike of that length, not in the least because a good number of them were still unshod. To say nothing of the fact that he didn't know how he would feed them once he got them there. Ammunition was scarce, the supply trains hadn't been established, ambulances were unmanned. That the Rebels would have none of this in place either did not comfort him. An army needed to be prepared. Politics and the military should not be bedfellows; he had believed it at West Point, and he believed it now. Of course, that Lincoln wanted the war to end swiftly was not a crime. He did too. The trouble was, under these circumstances, he needed an advantage. His only hope of victory was surprise, and his unprepared troops, much as he disliked sending them in their inexperience, should have already been on the march. And yet here they were, conferring, when they should already be five miles down the road.

Lincoln seemed not to have heard Scott's answer. He was still perusing the inadequate map, his palms flat down on its curling edges to hold them back. The president's easy manner, so often interpreted as ignorance, seemed now almost disinterested to McDowell. The president's enemies called him a monkey, an ape, with arms far too long, a head too large, a long gawky string of a man, who wanted war. But McDowell didn't think so. He thought instead that the man was resigned to the tactic, was courageous in fact, in not backing away from it, even though he knew nothing.

Scott sighed and heaved himself into a chair. He was too old to wait while a new president, totally ignorant of the mechanics or stratagems of warfare, dawdled in indecision.

Lincoln finally looked up at McDowell and asked, "What of the train depot?"

Both McDowell and Scott exchanged glances. They had bet on the way over that Lincoln wouldn't be able to tell a regiment from a company, to say nothing of understanding the battle plans that McDowell had prepared.

Straightening, though at six feet he was nearly as tall as Lincoln, McDowell said, "Our best chance of victory is to destroy the railroad leading from Manassas into the valley, just as you suggested, Mr. President. I'll have to get a better look on the field, but I'm thinking of a five-pronged attack. One division to attack the Rebels holding the bridge over Bull Run. Another to run to the right over Sudley's Ford, there." He made a large circling gesture toward the map. "Possibly another on the Centreville Heights. Our troops, however, are untested in battle, and I should have left with them yesterday."

John Hay said, "But can you win?"

Before McDowell could answer, General Scott said, "It's a good enough plan." But he was still thinking of his own plan, one that called for control of the Mississippi and a blockade of key Southern ports that would strangle the South without having to fire any ammunition. He was tired of war, tired of fighting, and too infirm to travel into the field, and he would feel a good deal more confident of the success of this plan if it were Lee standing now before the president instead of McDowell, but he would never upset the president's confidence in the proposed action.

Hay asked again, "Will you win?"

Irvin McDowell, a general for as long as Hay had been alive, wished that he could speak plainly, but it was past time for that. He'd already lodged his objections, and no one, not even Scott, had listened. "Mr. President, I promise you that I will not tolerate defeat."

No one else in the North would either, least of all Abraham Lincoln, who, after a moment's more perusal of the maddeningly incomplete map, said, "God's speed, then."

"They don't seem to like you much," Lincoln said to Hay after the generals left, but he said it with a glimmer of amusement at his young secretary, whose company he trusted far more than he did the generals'. They were standing at the window overlooking Pennsylvania Avenue, watching their carriage clatter out the gates.

"It was good you hired that spy," Hay said, "or else I do believe those two would have denied the Rebels were anywhere near here. For generals, they don't seem to like war very much."

"They don't, do they?"

"At least we'll know in a few days who has won," Hay said, "and then the matter of secession will be resolved."

"You think so?" Lincoln said, and Hay turned to him to discern whether it was hope or doubt that had so altered the president's voice, but Lincoln had turned away, and would say no more.

# *Chapter Sixteen*

"You. And you." Room by room, floor by floor, Dr. Stipp flicked his index finger at the recumbent dyspeptics who had been his patients for the past three months. He spared only the most feeble, expelling the rest. Men who that morning couldn't even wash themselves now had to pack up their belongings, retrieve what goods they had stored under their beds—an extra shirt saved for Sundays, another pair of pants—and limp down stairways they hadn't navigated since their arrival, clutching the railing as they descended to finally spill from the hospital that Mary Sutter had named the Pestilential Palace. They pressed Mary's shoulders and palms as they passed her where she stood in the doorway, murmuring good-bye, scarcely able to believe they had been cut off to fend for themselves. They climbed the hill toward the omnibus stop, but most failed to make it, instead crawling under awnings and trees to get away from the July sun searing their pale skin. Watching from the hotel step, Mary could not help but think that they all looked as helpless as newborns.

That morning she had already set fires under the laundry cauldrons and stripped all the beds, but not one of the laundresses she had summoned had yet shown her face. And they had so little time. Even before the messenger had arrived with the directive to empty the hotel, the men had thought they heard the percussion of artillery.

"Our boys are at it now!" they had cheered, thrilling to a fight they were secretly grateful to be missing.

Stipp had rushed to the window, cocked his head, listened, and shouted, "It is heat thunder, you idiots."

When the last of the discharged patients had left the hotel, Mary found Stipp in the basement kitchen.

"Is there any food?" she asked.

"The cook left some oatmeal," Stipp said.

Mary fished a bowl and spoon from a basin of rinse water and ladled a glob of the congealed cereal into the dish.

As she fought the oatmeal down, Stipp said, "Your life in your hands," but newly wiped from his features was any disdain, replaced by a raw terror whose twin Mary had attempted to suppress in herself with frantic work.

He leaned forward now, abandoning, for once, his banter. "Prepare what you can. If you have any sheets to spare, tear them into bandages. If you find any of those stupid havelocks the women up north have been sending, rip them in half. Get the cook to make a vat of beef tea, to bake egg puddings if he can. Send someone to root out the last bit of whiskey from the neighbors. I will send the guard if I have to, to get it out of them. I'll be back in an hour, two at the most—"

"Where are you going?"

"To get chloroform and morphia powder."

Mary yanked her hair back and twisted it into a rope. "We need whiskey and iodine, too. Our cupboard is nearly empty."

"How did you manage to find that out? Mr. Mack guards those keys as if they unlocked heaven."

"I took them last night while he slept." Mary had begun calling the steward the keeper of the key, since he never once gave up possession of the fat ring from which dangled the single skeleton key that unlocked the downstairs closet.

"Thief."

"I needed soap," Mary said. "What will you do if you can't get any morphine?"

Stipp leaned back in his chair. "There is nothing for you here but trouble." But even he knew it was a useless statement. The railroads weren't running. Anyone leaving town was doing so via carriage, but even which direction to flee was in question.

Upstairs, a door slammed. Absent the groaning and scrabble of its former residents, sounds that had gone unheard in the hotel now sprang from the walls: the restive settling of the roof, the ravenous gnawing of carpenter ants at post and pillar, the squeak and wobble of mice, the slow hiss of imprisoned air escaping through cracks and crevices as if the entire hotel were audibly sinking into the swampy shores of the Potomac River.

Outside, the smoke from the cauldrons sent black clouds high into the sky. Line after line of clotheslines, like battalions at the ready, awaited the boiled sheets of the Union Hotel, while inside, Mary looked to the south, where Thomas and Christian were, and began to pray.

# Chapter Seventeen

It was Sunday, July the twenty-first, and the first rumble sounded like horses' hooves drumming the road. Thomas and Christian, assigned to picket posts on the low bluff of Fort Albany above the Columbia Turnpike, merely glanced over their shoulders down the dusty road and sighed. Five days earlier, they had twiddled their thumbs while Irvin McDowell marched thirty thousand men down the road toward battle. The entire 25th had been left behind, charged only with the humiliating assignment of guarding the road. Five days, and still the battle hadn't begun, though this morning festive sightseers in a contingent of buggies and barouches had rolled past in the direction of Centreville, champagne bottles protruding from laden picnic baskets. Only Dr. Blevens had marched out with McDowell, added as surgeon to a regiment from New Jersey, which had none.

The 25th's three months' service was nearly up, but Christian's back and arms were still aflame from the hard work of erecting the fort. He cracked his neck and shifted his gaze to the blue sky. Thomas wasn't in great shape, either; without the suspenders he had fashioned from twine, he would have been pantsless. Christian had never been so hungry. He missed home, and somehow Amelia's pleading letter had made it worse. What had Blevens said when he'd told the doctor that Mary was in Washington? That she was the most remarkable woman he knew. No, they were going to miss all of it, the entire war, and all they would have to show for it would be three months blistering under the southern sun guarding a length of highway, while Mary would show them all up. Their only glory was that two of their number on guard duty at the Long Bridge had arrested a couple of Rebel soldiers disguised as farmers. But it would soon be over. They were due to go home in just a few days.

A second rumble echoed in the distance, and Thomas and Christian looked again at the sky and then down the road and fingered their triggers. They were twenty-five miles from Centreville, but even they knew the sound of artillery when they heard it.

A bullet smacked the dust five feet in front of them, sending a puff of dirt whipping into the air. They hit the ground full out.

"Sorry!"

Jake Miles was heading toward them from the fort's gate, a grin erupting even as he held up his hand in contrition. "Just for fun, boys. Just practice in case those Rebels get too close."

Christian scrambled to his feet and flung himself at Jake, grabbing him around the neck, even as Jake, unresisting, laughed.

"I was just waking you two up. You looked kinda sleepy."

"Not funny, you bastard." Christian, spooked more than he wanted to say, let Jake go. Sometimes Jake's cockiness unnerved Christian, but he was well liked in the fort. He was good with a rifle, and had bagged more birds and hogs for dinner than anyone else. Even Colonel Townsend had praised him, though twice he'd locked him up for drunkenness and had warned him more than a dozen times to lay off the alcohol. But he was the sharpest shooter in the regiment.

Jake picked up the hat Christian had knocked off in the scuffle and looked in the direction of Centreville. "So they're doing it, are they?"

"They're doing it," Thomas said.

Jake sniffed and pointed his cap at a boulder down the bluff. "That's where the colonel wants me, just in case," he said, and loped toward his post as coolly as if he were a ten-year-old sent off to play by his exasperated mother on a fine summer morning.

After he left, Thomas kneeled into the dirt and said, "I'm not too sure about that kid."

"Oh, he's all right," Christian said.

The noise of artillery reached even the streets of downtown Washington, and rumors began to run through the city's streets, arriving in Georgetown via the canal boat captains and hack drivers. By two in the afternoon, reports came that the Union was winning; hills had been taken, the Rebels had been pushed back. By three, a rider raced through the streets proclaiming a Union victory. But by five, the telegraph operator at Fairfax Courthouse telegraphed the news that he had to abandon his post because the Rebels had overrun them and the Union army was skedaddling toward Washington. Stipp and Mary burned oil lamps waiting, and when the lamps ran low, true night fell, darker than dark. At dawn on Monday it began to rain, but not until the afternoon did returning soldiers begin to cross the Aqueduct Bridge and stumble up Bridge Street. At street corners, they told their stories: the Rebels were defacing the wounded, the Rebels were ruthless, the Rebels were legion, the ambulance drivers had abandoned five thousand dying men on the battlefield. By nightfall, the rain ended its drumming, leaving behind a haunted silence. That night, at the sound of every passing carriage, Mary leaped from bed, only to watch empty wagons rattle past, their ghostly lanterns bobbing in the dark. Five days of waiting had whittled her nerves to shreds; the beef tea the cook had steeped had spoiled, the egg puddings had curdled, all her preparations had been for naught.

It was not until Tuesday morning that the wounded began to descend on the Union Hotel. Most had staggered the full thirty-five miles from Centreville, ignored or missed by the roving ambulance crews sent back in after the battle under a flag of truce. Disoriented, feverish, a few had mistakenly stumbled into the tobacco warehouse across the street and expired on the drying floor. They continued to arrive for another two days, and by the time they reached the Union Hotel they were dirty, ravenous, and parched to the point of delirium. By midnight on Thursday, four days after the battle, Dr. Stipp had made full inventory: 254 wounded, most with extremity wounds from slow-moving musket balls that had entered their bodies but not exited. A few of the balls had managed to break bones: the right elbow joint of one man, the right shoulder of another, the femurs of perhaps half a dozen poor souls who had suffered torturous rides in two-wheeled jitneys that pounded into every rut and pothole in the ruined roads, two with missing jawbones, one with a broken hip, one whose feet had been crushed by a runaway wagon, and a dozen flesh wounds of the breast or shoulder or calf.

Three boys needed their legs off. And he had no idea how to go about it.

# *Chapter Eighteen*

In the dining room, Stipp lit candles, assembled rags, and wrestled his amputation knife and bone saw from the velvet-lined case issued to him when he'd returned from the post at Davis Landing. In the days leading up to the battle, he had pored again over the surgery manual, but tonight his lethargic mind could remember nothing about amputating a leg. Across Washington City, it was the same in all the hospitals. No one knew anything about amputating legs or arms; all anyone knew had been gleaned from the government-issued manual. Now Stipp took a strong dislike to the dining room: it was a room of ghosts, of expired conviviality, the walls reeking of decades of sweat and stewed mutton and boiled oysters and spilled beer. Its view depressed: the dilapidated stable in the back fallen in on itself and the smaller tumbledown shed supporting a roof gone to thatch. But dislike would not dispel panic, which was beginning a serious incursion, tightening Stipp's throat, shortening his breath, peaking as Mary Sutter, Mr. Mack, and one of the discharged dyspeptics who had limped back from the streetcar landing stumbled into the room carrying his first patient. Mary backed in first, supporting the boy's shattered left leg, and the two men carried the patient between them in a sling of their joined hands. The trio grappled with the boy—he was a mere boy, but big, with a florid complexion and massive hands—and finally got him onto the cleared table. Though his left calf muscle had been torn to shreds, he did not display the terror that would overcome Stipp's later patients, who would know what a wound like his portended; instead, the boy manifested only a sweating, confused fury, punctuated by shouts of pain.

"Can't you even get a man properly drunk?" Stipp shouted at Mary. He had told her to give the boy as much as he could handle, and Mary had given him the better half of her flask; she pulled the silver container of whiskey from her skirt pocket and waggled it at Stipp, who fought the urge to swipe it out of her hands and down the rest of it.

The steward was not a man the doctor admired, but tonight Stipp needed the wily and resourceful lieutenant. Two assistants would be better, but the dyspeptic, who until the other day had been bedridden for two weeks, had already crawled into a nearby room and collapsed on the floor. Mostly though, Stipp did not want Mary Sutter in the room. It was not pride, he told himself, it was not that he did not want her to witness his ignorance; no, he needed to maintain discipline. Yes, he told himself, discipline and a sense of command; these were vital. He was vaguely aware that he wished he could sit down.

"I'll need you to hold this boy's leg," Stipp said to the steward.

But Mr. Mack was already at the door, his skin a sickening shade of gray.

"God damn it, man," Stipp said, "I order you." But the steward vanished, leaving Stipp alone with Mary, who, with a possessive hold on the boy's shoulder, showed no sign of retreat. Instead, a mixture of anticipation and something Stipp could only think of as voraciousness flared across her pale face.

"Get out," he said.

"I'm staying."

"I don't need you."

"Don't be a fool. You need someone."

"Not you."

The boy lifted his head from the table. "Don't you talk like that to this nice lady," he slurred.

Stipp forced the boy's head back down and inverted an open cone over his face, the larger opening hovering just above his nose and mouth. Into the smaller opening, Stipp stuffed a ball of cotton, onto which he dripped the clear chloroform, which he had kept in a cupboard to avoid exposing it to the light. Averting his own head to avoid the fumes, he couldn't remember how much to give, but he remembered the process, how the body seized and shuddered as it went under. The boy did struggle, but soon he began to breathe rhythmically and fell asleep, and Stipp lowered the cone, watching the boy's corneas slowly dilate. When they contracted, Stipp lifted the cone from the boy's face and set it far away so as not to be overcome himself.

Now he considered manhandling Mary out the door. Why wouldn't she leave? He could not let her see that he didn't know what the hell he was doing. If the prospect of blood wouldn't run her off, then . . . he peered at her, trying to think of something, anything, to get her out. It would take an extreme measure, he thought, and then he knew. In a single flourish, he undid the boy's pants and stripped them off, exposing him. Lifting his head in triumph, he expected fury or at least embarrassment to have washed across Mary's face, but she did not flinch. Instead she crossed her arms and said, "I have a brother." And then she said, "You don't know how to do this, do you?"

"Don't be ridiculous," Stipp said, but a warm flush of blood was rising in his face. Despite all their preparations, he had never thought that it would come down to the two of them standing opposite one another over real need. He, along with everyone else, had not feared this moment in the way they ought to have done. And now the boy's leg was rapidly taking on a bluish aspect. Twilight was seeping in on the edges of the candlelight.

"Just leave me be to do this right," Stipp said, and then feared what would happen if she did. How he would falter; how the boy would die. Mary tilted her head to the side: her face was a shining sphere, as warm as the Texas sun. It was then he suspected she might reach out and touch him. He wished she would. He was terrified. A drop of wax from the burning candles spat onto his arm. Stipp glanced at his knives.

And then, just as he had thought, Mary laid her hand on his wrist. It felt like a caress. He did not know how long they stood there together. It was as if time had swallowed them; all that mattered was her generosity. Over the last month, he had seen her employ this elixir of womanhood, a trick that transformed misery into pleasure and made the men do things they would not otherwise do: walk when they wanted to rest, live when they wanted to die. But in that moment of intoxication—a second, a minute?—he began to believe he could do the job; he told himself that what he was about to do was little more than basic butchery. Any farm boy could cut up a chicken or a hog. Was this really so different? He reached for the small knife and whispered, "On the table beside my cot is a book called *The Practice of Surgery.* Would you get it for me, please?"

Mary withdrew her hand. "My God, you really don't know how."

"If you faint on me," Stipp said, "I will personally take you to the train depot and buy you a ticket home."

Mary drew herself up. "And if this is a ruse—if you lock that door behind me, I swear to you I will get a ladder and climb through the window."

"I need that book," Stipp said. "I have, if I am lucky, half an hour before this boy wakes up."

Mary regarded him for a moment, no more, and then she was gone. An eon passed in which Stipp feared that Mary had deserted him, but then she surged through the door, riffling through the dog-eared pages of his surgery manual.

"Above the knee?" she asked. "Is that what you want to do?"

Desire for her swelled. Quixotic, passionate, it fogged his mind. He turned to assess the boy's mangled calf. It would have to be above the knee. That would be best, because then there would only be the one bone to manage.

"Yes," he said. "Above the knee."

"Then it says to apply the tourniquet mid-thigh."

"We don't have a tourniquet," Stipp said.

Another drop of wax fell on his arm. He flicked it away before guiding Mary's thumb to the fold between the boy's left thigh and hip. "Femoral artery," he said. "Press hard."

"Will it stop all the bleeding?" Mary asked.

"It will stop some of it. Now read me the instructions."

She read, "An assistant is to firmly grasp the thigh with both hands and to draw upward the skin and muscles with some force while the surgeon makes a circular incision as quickly as possible, through the integuments, down to the muscles."

"Fuck," Stipp muttered, worried now because Mary couldn't do all three: read, apply pressure to the artery, and draw back the muscles as well. After a moment of dread, in which he contemplated with great affection his lazy days in the gentle sunshine of his beloved Texas, he leaned over, placed his left forearm against the boy's thigh, and drew back the muscles as well as he could. He then put knife to skin above the knee. Though the flesh resisted like a tough steak, he managed to make a series of awkward cuts, working the blade in a sloppy, imprecise manner. There was no telling how long it took. Time was its own meter, stretching to magnify his incompetence.

At the first sign of red muscle, he pulled back. It was one thing to cut skin, another to sever muscles. Would they snap back? Disappear under the flesh? To what would he anchor them afterwards? Oh, curse his medical training! Six months of courses at Yale; not one surgery performed under anyone's auspices. In New York, little surgery, more management of epidemics. Any latent skill he possessed was merely guesswork augmented by common sense. What would a cut muscle do?

Into these rampaging thoughts came Mary's wavering voice. "It goes on and on about muscle dissection. I can't find a single direction that is clear."

"Read down, read down!"

Turning the pages with her thumb, Mary skimmed, flying past words like *flap* and *oblique division* and *vastus internus*. Finally: "Many excellent surgeons, whom I have seen operate, do not cut at once obliquely down to the bone, after the integuments have been divided and retracted; but so far adopt the principles of M. Louis, as to divide the loose muscles first, and lastly, those which are intimately attached to the bone, taking care, with a scalpel, to cut completely through the deep muscular attachments, about an inch higher up, than could be executed with the amputating knife itself. This last measure causes very little pain, and has immense effect in averting all possibility of a subsequent protrusion of the bone, or of a bad sugarloaf stump." She looked up. "Why can't he say something straight out?"

Stipp began his assault. He nearly closed his eyes. He had no idea if his attempts at division would make any difference for the boy in the end. There were moments ahead that he did not want to think about: how best to cover the bone afterwards, whether his stitches would hold; recovery, if the boy didn't die now.

When knife hit bone, his hand jerked to a stop. He held the knife up for a moment, hardly able to believe what he had accomplished.

It was his first but not his last amputation. One by one, he would grow adept with a knife, skilled, quick, efficient, in conditions much worse than these. In time, he would wield that blade as an extension of himself, grow to love its heft, its curves, the way the blade caressed and then sliced a portion of a man away. And he would grow to love himself: how he would know just what to do and how to do it, could do it, would be forced to do it for days on end, his knees buckling with fatigue, his heart numb to all but necessity. By the end of the four years the war would take, he would perform this operation in under five minutes, his record being nine legs in one hour in a drafty barn in Gettysburg beside a welling stream that would flood one stormy night and carry away all his surviving patients. In the end, he would perform 607 amputations, though he would lose count at fifty and cease caring at a hundred. By that time, loss would be a mere fact, mourning an extravagance he would not indulge. But he would have compassion. It would swell inside him, not for his patients, but for the inept, flawed human being he had once been and was now on a muggy night in Georgetown, mosquitoes diving into the rivulets of blood that percolated from other arteries buried in the boy's thigh with names like *profunda femoris* and *deep femoral,* names that resurrected themselves from his sun-addled brain when he had only a few minutes, ten maybe, before this boy lost so much blood that nothing he did now would matter.

Mary was fumbling, trying to turn the pages.

"Find where it says something about a retractor," Stipp said. He was beginning to remember whole paragraphs, not the details but the gist. "Hurry," he said, tying off the arteries he could separate from the muscle.

"I can't find it—" But finally she lit on it, joy rising in her voice as she read the instructions and Stipp, following them, tore a rag into a strip and ringed the upper flesh and pulled it out of the way. He was remembering, he was remembering, oh the joy of memory, but it was memory of a peculiar nature, as if his competent future self had returned to help his present fearful self. He turned and seized the saw from the buffet table behind him. The danger, Stipp remembered—how could he?—was splintering the bone with too much force.

"I'll need you to steady the leg," he said.

Mary shook her head.

For the first time, her eyes glistened with indecision. He had infected her with his uncertainty; he would remember never to do that again.

"I know what to do now. Cradle his thigh in your elbow and steady it against your shoulder."

To what did she respond? The confidence in his voice? His sudden, alloyed briskness? But with her left thumb still pressed on the boy's artery, she obeyed. It was the first time she had ever done anything he had asked without an argument. She thrust her right shoulder into the flesh of the boy's thigh and slipped her right arm underneath to hug the limb tight against her upper arm. Her hair curled and twisted against the pallid flesh.

Stipp brushed it away. He was glad her head was turned. He did not want her to witness his inexpert thrusts and parries. After several swipes, the saw stuck. He removed it and shook free the bits of bone, then wiped it against his thigh and reinserted the saw.

The break came clean. He had a moment to contemplate what a pristine thing a cut bone was. Then he thrust the severed limb aside.

"Now release the pressure," he said.

Mary lifted her finger. The stump reddened slowly, from intact top to mangled end. Stipp held his breath. His ties needed to hold. He willed them to hold. Sweating, fighting, trembling, he watched that stump grow plump and bright, and the ties tighten against the resurrected arteries and flesh, and when he was certain that the boy had not died, not yet anyway, he began to sew a flap and said, "Bring me the next one."

Ten hours later, a silvery dawn threw shafts of pale light into the hallway outside the dining room where Mary Sutter sat slumped against the sweating plaster walls. Throughout the hotel, feeble cries for water drifted through the crevices of the ceiling and walls, though in this place in the last few days since the battle, calls for water were unceasing.

Last night, uncharacteristically, they had gone unanswered.

And they would go unanswered still.

The sound of the saw had been akin to nothing in Mary's experience. Not the cries of mothers in labor, nor the cries of mothers bereft. Clutching not one but three thighs between her cheek and arm last night, she had closed her eyes and tried to close her ears, but she had discovered that there was no barrier between a person and sound. No way to shut ears as you can shut eyes. The other two attempts to sever legs had been a disaster. In the first, the chloroform had worn off mid-surgery. The boy had flailed, ended up on the floor. Mary's hold on his artery gone, he had watched himself die, uncomprehending and stuporous. The second—she would not think of the second. She could not. A whole success, easier than the two others. Bone cut. Ties holding. Skin flapped. They'd been congratulating one another, she and Dr. Stipp. And then they had turned, only to discover that the boy was dead. Dead, Mary thought now, because of an excess of chloroform, given in an effort to overcome what had happened before. Dr. Stipp had been sawing away on a corpse and neither of them had noticed.

Stipp emerged now from the dining room, and a look of intimacy, of conjugal remembrance, passed between them. Their shared failure—two deaths coming upon the heels of their first success—conferred on them the self-conscious shame of failed lovers. It was difficult to look one another in the eye, but they did, reviving that moment when they'd first realized that the boy was dead.

"What do we do about the legs?" Mary asked. The hallway walls were cool; later in the day the heat would render the lathe and plaster unbearable.

Stipp looked down at his own legs. What delicate, sturdy things they were, he thought, wholly irreplaceable. He wondered what it would be like to awake and find one gone.

"I thought to carry them out," Mary continued, her voice wavering.

"But I didn't know where to take them. The trash heap seems wrong. I don't want anyone else to see them. Or to find them." And if by chance someone did stumble on the legs, at least that unlucky soul would be able to shut his eyes, she thought. At least he would have that, while over and over, she was hearing the saw doing its work, scraping and grating. She thought of Thomas and Christian. Where were they? Was someone thinking of the best way to dispose of their limbs? She was proud of how she had acted during the surgeries. But if it had been Thomas or her brother on the table, could she have been so detached?

"Who were those boys? I don't even know their names. I don't even know where they came from. How will I tell their mothers? What will we do with the legs?"

"I haven't any idea," Stipp said.

"Do we bury them?"

"I don't know."

"Who should I tell to come get them?"

"I don't know, damn it." Stipp slammed his hand against the wall. He had not wanted Mary by his side, and then he couldn't have asked for anyone better. She had stayed calm. The only requisite that really mattered, but she had given more: intelligence and charity. When that boy had died, flailing, disoriented, shouting, reliving the battle, the blood arcing everywhere, Mary had thought to kneel by the boy's side and to sing. To sing! The boy had died to the unsteady voice of a tone-deaf, blood-covered angel. And the next one? Stipp couldn't even think of how long that boy had been dead. A colossal error on his part. What was basic? Breathing. The boy had done none of that for who knew how long. Eight hours together in a room, and he and Mary had accomplished two terrible mistakes and only one good outcome. The army had thought of nothing. They needed coffins, a dead house, a way to let headquarters know who had died and who had not died. But none of this was in place. How do you forget coffins? How do you forget to supply tourniquets? How do you forget that people might die?

"I'll tell you again. Go home, Mary Sutter. You don't need to be here. You don't need to witness any of this."

Mary could go home. She could go home and watch Jenny have Thomas's baby. Perhaps even she, and not Amelia, would deliver the child. She could go home and midwife Jenny through what was certain to be a difficult labor. She would hand Thomas his progeny, the beginning of a Fall-Sutter line of which she would have no part but midwife. Her brother would be home, too, if he had survived the battle. The Sutters and the Falls would be rid of the war, having acquitted themselves with bravery. No one, not even Mr. Lincoln, could ask anything more of them. Albany would think well of her, too. The woman who had gone to war. And she would go on delivering babies. She would apply to medical schools and wait for their letters of rejection. Her life would be certain. Safe. And with time, the noise of the saw might diminish, and she would no longer hear boys crying for water, for their mothers, for release.

"I can't go home," Mary said.

Stipp seized her by the shoulders. She smelled of last night, their joined efforts. "Why are you here? Tell me."

Mary's eyes filled with tears. "I'm tired," she said. "I'm so tired."

"Oh sweet Jesus," Stipp said. "I can't scare you off. I can't fight you off. I can't even reason you off. What the hell is the matter with you? What do you want with being in a place like this?"

Mary pulled away. Her skirts had stiffened with the splatters and stains of the blood of three men. The saw sang in her head. She hated Stipp now. Hated his brutal persistence, his fumbling, his ignorance, his lack of preparation. Was this what medicine was? Barbarity? By comparison, even at its worst, childbirth was artful. Even when women bled or seized, there remained at least the elegance of hope. The flickering promise of life.

Stipp watched her, read her fury and hate, and wanted to slap her. What did she want from him? There wasn't a surgeon in all the army who could have done better; they were all a bunch of sorry fools, every one of them, given manuals and instruments and nothing else. If the army had been smart, they would have sent for surgeons from England, all those doctors from the Crimean War who had already treated these injuries and would have known what to do. But that would have meant that someone would have had to have foreseen this night, have known that politics would shatter into massacre. My God. What was going to happen now?

"How long will this go on?" Mary asked, whispering.

Stipp stepped backward, irritated suddenly, with Mary and the labyrinthine turns of her curious mind.

"They're done? This is the last of it? We're two countries now?" She turned, lifting a bloody hand in the direction of the dining-room door and the legs behind them, then began to twist her apron in her hands, as if to wash them of men's foolhardiness. "No one will allow this to happen again. No one wants this."

Stipp gaped at her. "What do you want me to say? That men are *reasonable*?"

A rectangular patch of early sun trembled several feet away, thrown onto the floor from the unseen panes of a high window hidden around a turn in the hallway. Mary yearned to hear the wail of a newborn, a sound as unlike the scrape of the saw as a symphony was from cannon fire. Women labored until there was life. If that wasn't reason, then what was? But women waged war, too, and it took little between women to make one another miserable; sisterhood sacrificed when desire scalded the veins. Jenny's belly would be starting to show now. But it was not just that, Mary told herself. Neither was it a crime to be uncertain, to be fearful of what she had wrought. She had left the world of women, and now all she had was tomorrow, and men, and their unreason.

Stipp was staring at her as if she had lost her mind, as if she were the one who was unreasonable.

"Well, what is it that *you* want?" Mary said. "Why are you always asking me? Are we so different?"

Stipp rocked back on his heels, as if she had slapped him. "You're deranged."

"Yes," she said. "But no less than you."

Afterwards, Stipp would acknowledge that the urge had been irresistible, but he entertained, in that moment, the lie that what he did next was a choice. He reached out his hand and caressed the sharp angle of Mary Sutter's chin. Mary closed her eyes and let him. He was not particularly gentle, not being a particularly gentle man, but his fingers traveled from her chin, around the edges of her lips, across the prominent expanse of her cheekbones to her temple and then, feather light, into her matted hair. When his hand left her—she couldn't be quite sure when, for his fingers lingered in her curls—she cried out and opened her eyes.

But he had not left her, as she had not left him.

"We are fools, you and I," Stipp said. He felt enormously fatigued, but he suspected it was not the surgeries that had exhausted him. "Go. I will take care of the legs."

"I am not afraid," Mary said.

Stipp smiled. Then he broke into a chuckle and turned to the dining room, wondering how Mary Sutter could believe that anyone would ever think that she would ever be afraid of anything.

# Chapter Nineteen

On Tuesday, July the twenty-third, two days after the battle, Irvin McDowell, his riding boots covered with mud, his collar sticky with sweat, verified to the president that the Rebels were indeed entrenched at Manassas Junction and there inexplicably remained, even though in the hours after the battle he had telegraphed that twenty thousand Confederates were fast behind him. But the Rebels had not pursued them. Extraordinary, that decision. Inexplicable, though attributable, perhaps, to the rain that fell the day after the battle. Meteorological mercy. An entire divided nation was learning the vagaries of combat.

Lincoln, however, was shaking his head, unable to comprehend a victorious army that did not follow up its victory. This morning he had ridden out to Fort Corcoran on the Arlington Heights with William Henry Seward, the secretary of state. On their way they encountered straggling soldiers still separated from their units, ambulances filled with the groaning wounded jouncing over still-wet roads, and knots of alarmed citizenry who, astonished to see the president crossing the drained Aqueduct Bridge into enemy territory, followed his retreating form with shouts of worry. Lincoln acknowledged these queries, but did not speak except to the wounded, his expression growing more grave as their number increased—ten by the time they had reached the timbered palisade of Fort Corcoran and the New York 69th, who vowed to reenlist—so that when McDowell had suggested that they repair to his headquarters a mere half mile away, far from the excitement of the milling troops, Lincoln had acquiesced, unable to shake from his mind the vision of the last of the men, sprawled in the bed of a farm wagon, his face the color of chalk, his hands encircling his ruined leg, which in the sun-blasted heat had grown blistered and flyblown.

Lincoln, McDowell, and Seward were seated in one of the parlors at Arlington House, the plantation home that Robert E. Lee's family had evacuated just after Virginia had seceded. McDowell had been careful to explain to the president as they rode through the now trammeled gardens that he lived in a tent behind the great house out of respect for Lee's property, though the Union army had gladly seized the house, for it occupied a good portion of the land across the river from the capital and commanded a view not only of the entire heights but also of the citadel of Washington glinting across the brown moat of the Potomac.

Lincoln, ill at ease in a spindled armchair of red velvet, surveyed the elegant paintings that had belonged to his preferred but traitorous general, and sighed. Would that Lee and not McDowell were seated in the twin armchair opposite; then perhaps they would be about to discuss a victory and not a humiliating defeat. No matter that Robert E. Lee hadn't commanded the troops that had decimated the Federal army at Bull Run, something told Lincoln that perhaps, had Lee acquiesced to Scott's request to take command of the Union troops, they might even now be planning the swift reannexation of a chastened South, eager to return after its resounding defeat. But no, only this sad little meeting in Lee's former home.

Between the three men, a delft china teapot steamed on a marble table, a swirling tendril of white vapor rising from the graceful arc of spout; there was even sugar, and milk, and delicate teacups arranged with care by one of McDowell's aides. The wounded soldier's face floated before Lincoln. The edges of the man's wound had been blue. He'd been blue and white, like the teapot. Lincoln shook his head. He was exhausted. Since the night of the twenty-first, he had slept only a few hours, having spent the intervening hours designing a new war strategy after hearing witnesses describe the pell-mell retreat. He had it in his coat pocket now.

**Memoranda of Military Policy Suggested by the Bull Run Defeat**

*July 23, 1861.*

1. Let the plan for making the Blockade effective be pushed forward with all possible despatch.
2. Let the volunteer forces at Fort-Monroe & vicinity—under Genl. Butler—be constantly drilled, disciplined, and instructed without more for the present.
3. Let Baltimore be held, as now, with a gentle, but firm, and certain hand.
4. Let the force now under Patterson, or Banks, be strengthened, and made secure in its position.
5. Let the forces in Western Virginia act, till further orders, according to instructions, or orders from Gen. McClellan.
6. Gen. Fremont must push forward his organization, and operations in the West as rapidly as possible, giving rather special attention to Missouri.
7. Let the forces late before Manassas, except the three months' men, be reorganized as rapidly as possible, in their camps here and about Arlington.
8. Let the three months' forces, who decline to enter the longer service, be discharged as rapidly as circumstances will permit.
9. Let the new volunteer forces be brought forward as fast as possible; and especially into the camps on the two sides of the river here.

Lincoln's head swam with still more ideas, so many that he longed for a pen and paper, but he had no real idea what he was doing. He had relied, he thought now, too heavily on the men who were supposed to know how to conduct wars. He looked in shock at McDowell, in whom he had placed such trust, and recalled the man's dispatch of yesterday: "I have reached Arlington after turning stragglers and parties of regiments upon this place and Alexandria and am trying to get matters a little settled over here."

*Get matters a little settled?* How did you win a war by getting matters *a little settled*?

McDowell, too, had not slept in the previous week more than four hours a night, if that, and his trembling hand was barely able to guide the delicate teacup safely back to its saucer. Only the bellicose Seward, uncharacteristically silent, impatiently slurping his tea as he waited for one of the two to speak, had slept well the previous night, aided by two glasses of fine brandy at Willard's.

When Lincoln finally arched an eyebrow, McDowell, his voice hoarse from days of exhorting the troops, began.

"If I may respectfully say, sir, I was forced to attack before the troops were ready."

Seward's face began to bloom purple, and McDowell stopped short of saying, *Including you, Mr. President.* He was ragged with exhaustion. It was true that he'd been forced, though he disliked excuses, disliked even more having to point out that he'd been right. Three months' men. What would it have been to have issued an order for them to stay on another month? Nothing, evidenced this morning by the 69th's ready offer to reenlist. It had been absurd to expect that a raw army of volunteers could not only fell a forest to build a ring of forts but also become an army capable of winning an easy victory. Still, excuses were shameful. Unmilitary. Yet even as he thought this, out came another torrent, his own retreat from accountability, even in the face of Lincoln's tolerant impassivity.

"They had fresh troops, sir. Reinforcements. While mine were thirsty, ill-supplied, exhausted."

Lincoln had already heard that McDowell had known that the Confederates were able to ferry in fresh troops via the infamous trains he had warned him about. Commanding an army was like managing recalcitrant children. Or his wife, whose recent expenditure for four chandeliers defied understanding. What had she said in defense? *But we must be able to see, Father.* Now Lincoln wanted to say, *George McClellan knows the value of trains.* But he held his tongue, as he had with his wife; losing his temper wouldn't help a thing.

"I maintain that the arrival of the train cars during the night preceding the battle was not certain evidence of the arrival of Johnston's forces or of their ability to refresh their army. That information was mere rumor, and could have easily been passed our way by Confederate spies. I wanted to turn their position and force them from the Warrenton Turnpike. I wanted to destroy that railroad, as you wanted me to. Before their troops were reinforced, we were winning. We were." McDowell fell silent, and his left hand floated into the air of its own accord, as if its peripatetic wanderings could illustrate the frustrating nature of the panicky army of which he was in charge.

"Nonsense." Seward pushed his drained teacup into the center of the table in a fit of impatience. "General Scott says it was you who failed. You alone. You ought to take the blame for this."

The aide stationed outside the door whipped his head around to look in and McDowell shot him an icy glance before holding himself rigid before the pugnacious Seward. They had pushed him against his better judgment.

"I was ordered to attack, Mr. Seward. So I attacked. I've explained my impediments. Three months was hardly time enough to turn farmers into soldiers. Why some men fight when others do not—"

"Is a matter of discipline."

"With respect, Mr. Seward, you are not a military man. Neither were you there."

"But you *were* there, and therefore hold the responsibility for the failure."

In the heavy boil of midday, a frosty silence descended. McDowell touched his teacup, marveling at its fragility.

"What is it you wish me to do now?" he asked, addressing Lincoln alone. Seward wasn't even the secretary of war. Why had he accompanied the president and not Cameron?

Lincoln's chair scraped against the oak plank floors as he rose to his full height, and as he did, his coat swept the table and a teacup tumbled slowly to the floor, the blue-and-white flowers blurring as it spun, irretrievable, even by the fumbling McDowell, who reached in vain for the falling china and then knelt to pick up the two imperfect halves, holding them in his hands for a moment before handing them over to Lincoln.

Lincoln examined the broken pieces in his hands, the soldier's white face and blue lips and devastated leg and shattered cries sharpening in his memory, all the beautiful hope of the last three months retreating.

Lincoln set the pieces on the table. "I think we ought to repair this, don't you?"

As Lincoln turned his horse in the muddy grounds of the plantation and set off for Washington shimmering across the river, McDowell did not hear the president remark to Seward that he was very glad that he had already sent for George McClellan. Nor did McDowell hear that his title as the commander of the Army of Northeastern Virginia would be subordinate to the newly promoted Major General McClellan, who would be named commander of the Division of the Potomac by Lincoln himself. Nor did he know that later, in the fall, he would have to defend himself before the halved Congress, who, pressed by a restive public and enraged by the defeat, would investigate his command at Bull Run, intent on finding a national scapegoat.

McDowell gathered the pieces of the teacup and set out across the central hall in search of glue, while in Wheeling, Virginia, a gleeful George McClellan was writing a note to his wife before he boarded a train for Washington.

In it, he was bragging that his star was ascending, that a nation waited on him, that he was the savior of the world.

# Chapter Twenty

"We can't go home to Amelia and say we didn't try. She'll be furious."

Thomas was holding Amelia's letter in his hand. That morning, July the twenty-eighth, the 25th Regiment had marched from Fort Albany back into Washington over the Long Bridge, retracing the steps of their invasion two months before. But no amount of remembering that they had been ordered to stay behind could shield the members of the regiment from the shame that engulfed them when the army began to trickle back into the Union camps that lined the Virginia banks of the Potomac. Thomas and Christian felt the defeat double on their shoulders. They had come to war and done nothing and now it was time to go home. After months living outside, the city seemed strange and foreign, and even the dirty waters of Tiber Creek appeared exotic. The Capitol grounds teemed with the three months' men, all waiting to board a train for home. The crush and noise were tremendous. Seventy-five thousand men were all trying to get out of Washington at the same time as the hundred thousand more coming to replace them were trying to get in. Lincoln had put out the call immediately after the defeat, but this time he had specified that any man who signed on would sign on for three years. No more volunteer army. If McDowell had been right about anything, it was that a volunteer army was never going to beat anyone. That the victorious Rebel army was a volunteer army no one wanted to contemplate.

The march back had been hard on Christian. He was lying on the ground at Thomas's feet, using his haversack as a pillow. Since standing guard in the rain with his carbine trained on the Columbia Turnpike the day of the retreat, Christian had been having trouble breathing, and though he wanted to get up now, he couldn't. The world had begun to spin that last bit of the march, but it had slowed down again. The uncompleted Capitol dome seemed to look down on him benevolently. Oh, good and faithful soldier. It was almost pleasant. If he closed his eyes, he could imagine himself already at home between clean sheets, his mother bringing him tea.

Thomas kneeled beside his brother-in-law. Even in the swirl of shout and fury, he thought he could hear a tight whistle in Christian's chest.

"Have you seen Blevens?" Thomas asked, and craned his neck, looking for the physician, not remembering if he'd seen the man since he'd gone off to the battle, not remembering hearing if he'd returned.

Christian shook his head. He had hunted for the doctor when he started to feel bad, but he hadn't been able to find him.

"If you hurry, maybe you can find Mary before our train leaves," Christian said.

They had already asked directions to Georgetown, had plotted to go together to persuade Mary to come home with them, but that was before the march, before Christian had had such a hard time catching his breath.

Allegiance to Amelia pulled Thomas both ways. He didn't know what to do. He could either return without Mary and keep Christian company, or do as Amelia wished and persuade Mary to return but leave Christian to fend for himself. Three months' proximity had knitted the two men as close as real brothers, and he didn't like the looks of Christian. He thought maybe Christian might need a doctor, but it was nearly impossible to find anyone, and it seemed that no one knew where Blevens was. All the regiments were mixed together, milling around on the Capitol grounds. It would take days to sort everyone out and get them on a train. He had time, he thought, to find Mary and get her back here before the 25th left.

Just then, Jake Miles sauntered by, a bottle of whiskey tucked under his arm.

Thomas snagged him by the shoulder. "You think you can put off your toot for a while and come sit here with Christian? He doesn't feel all that good."

Jake plunked down on a square patch of dust next to Christian. "You bet."

Never had either of them seen him so obliging.

Thomas knelt beside Christian. "If I miss the train, I'll get the next one. Tell Jenny I'll be home soon."

Christian punched Thomas's shoulder. "Don't make a liar out of me."

Thomas hoisted his haversack. "Take care of him," he said to Jake. Of all the people to leave Thomas with, Jake was the worst, but what choice did he have? After a last glance at Christian, he strode through the crowd in search of transportation to Georgetown.

Christian shut his eyes. It was getting harder to breathe, harder even than on the march. He wished he were home. He could almost see home, could almost see Amelia's face. It would have been nice to have seen Mary. But he would, soon. And Bonnie, too. Christian was a little ashamed of coveting Jake's wife, but he decided there wasn't really any harm in it. He would never let on. Not to anyone. Especially not Bonnie. And poor Jake, he'd lost that baby, too. Jake wasn't really so bad. Quiet, maybe, and a little rough, but he was here. They'd slept beside one another for two months, and that was a kind of brotherhood, wasn't it?

"Hey, you need a little something?" Jake asked, uncorking the bottle he'd bought down on the Tiber Creek. It was moonshine, not real whiskey, but something to make the heat tolerable.

The liquor bit and choked, but after a few swigs, Christian found that he didn't have to work so hard at breathing. He closed his eyes and began to drift. This was better. Yes, this was so much better. Jake kept the whiskey coming, and when the call came to board the train three hours later, he helped Christian rise and limp to the depot, where he dosed him with another good swallow before tucking him into a corner of a train car to sleep.

# Chapter Twenty-one

Across town, at the Union Hotel, the steward, Mr. Mack, said, "You have someone asking."

Mary was in a room on the second floor, giving a spit bath to a soldier with a broken arm.

"Who is it?"

"He wouldn't say." Mr. Mack turned on his heel to leave and said, "I know you made a copy of the supply closet key." Embarrassment did not sit well on the steward's frame. Since fleeing the surgery that first night, Mr. Mack had become even more parsimonious and officious.

At the bed next to Mary, a woman named Fannie Warren was changing the linens. In the last five days, four women—good, strong women—had shown up, papers in hand, sent by Dorothea Dix: Mary Abbot, Fannie Warren, Helen Steveson, Monique Philipateaux—all married, all serious, all over the age of thirty. Miss Dix's darlings, but they were more help than Mary had had since she'd arrived. Still, she was exhausted. Sleep came in two-hour naps, stolen whenever someone forced her to lie down.

Someone asking. Most likely it was the milkman. Mary had written down a daily order, had explained to the stout farmer that they would always need twenty gallons of milk, but he liked to double-check, fearful of not being paid, a suspicion Mary did not begrudge him, since the only cheques she had written were promissory notes.

Downstairs, in the dim lobby, a bony figure was leaning up against the reception desk, the last trace, along with the brass room numbers, of the old hotel. Mary thought the figure might be another soldier, sick and weak and in search of a bed. She was suddenly furious with Mr. Mack, for he could have easily found space for him somewhere without having called her away from her work. The man was as ungenerous as a goat.

"May I help you?" she said.

"Mary."

Why is it that voices break hearts?

"Thomas," she said, as he stepped into the light, his name an exhalation, as if she had been expecting him. Thomas Fall. *Thomas, I did not dream of you. I never wanted you. We never danced in a palace.* He was too thin, and his face had lost all vestige of youth, but here he was, and relief surged through her. He was alive, safe, well.

Mary slipped into his arms and laid her head on his chest, marking the surprise of tenderness, which had been the first, and most mourned, casualty of war.

She could hear Thomas's heart, could feel the river of blood surging inside him. Mary knew things now about men that she hadn't known before: how in illness and infirmity their vulnerability shocked them; how they needed reassurance, even more than did women in labor; how they feared their mortality.

To Thomas, Mary looked shockingly undone, though her famously wild hair was safely tethered in a tight bun. Her cheeks were thin, as if she too had not been eating, just like the entire Union army had not, but she carried herself with that same odd grace that he had always admired. He saw something in her, too, of Jenny, a kind of hidden beauty, revealed in the way she tilted her head, and in the rush of concern as she pulled now from his embrace and said, suddenly fearful, "But why have you come? Is Christian all right?"

"Christian wanted to come, but—"

"He's not wounded?" Mary said, her hand flying to her throat.

"No. It's just a little fever." It was possible that Christian was ill with more than just a little fever, but Thomas didn't want to upset Mary, though he was ashamed to be holding back information. But he was almost certain that Christian would be all right. All Christian had to do was get home to Amelia and everything would be fine. "He is back at the depot, waiting for a train home. The 25th is departing."

"Is Dr. Blevens with him?"

"Blevens disappeared. He never came back. We don't know if—"

"You don't know where Blevens is?" Mary asked. "He wasn't with your regiment?"

"No, he was, but the day of the battle he went off with another troop. They were short of doctors."

"The 25th was in the fight?"

"No. We sat at Fort Albany and watched it all unfold on the road."

"On the road?" She looked at him quizzically, and he waved his hand. There would be time later to tell their ignoble story.

"I've come to get you. Amelia asked us to find you. She wants you to come home."

*Amelia asked.* She searched Thomas's face for any sign of their former intimacy, when his gaze had communicated more than friendship, even, once, interest. But the starkness of his fatigued expression was absent anything but exhaustion.

"I am not going home," Mary said.

"You don't look well, Mary, and this place . . ." His voice trailed off and Mary saw her surroundings as if for the first time. The ugliness of the building had fallen away for her long ago, but now she felt slightly ashamed of the rotting floors, the dingy light, the smells emanating from every doorway. She thought Thomas must think how odd she had grown to prefer this hellish place to home.

"I'm fine," she said. "I'm perfectly fine."

"If Amelia were to see—"

"Don't tell her what it's like."

Always the surprise of Mary, the quick turn, the sharp word. He'd forgotten how easily she could be angered. All the Sutter women had melded together in his mind, though somehow in the last few months he'd forgotten even what Jenny looked like. He remembered beauty, certainly, and affection, and most vividly the intoxicating caresses of their wedding night, but not the *whole* of her.

"Jenny wants you home, too," he said, invoking his marriage of a single night, making it up as he went. He had to get Mary to come home with him. It seemed more essential now than anything he had ever done.

"Tell Amelia not to worry. She'll be fine when it comes to Jenny."

"When it comes to Jenny? What do you mean?"

The knowledge came to her in a second. He didn't know. Thomas stood there, gaunt, fatigued, having come all this way to find her, and he didn't even know. What to do? Where did her obligation lie? To tell, or not to tell? She saw Jenny, disappointed, her smile falling away. *Mary already told me.* No. It wasn't right. It was not her news. She felt a slight release then, a shift toward happiness.

"It's nothing," she said. "You'll be home soon."

"I'm not leaving without you."

"Well, I'm not leaving. I want to be a surgeon." It wasn't exactly the Albany Medical College, but she'd assisted in amputations, hadn't she? She pushed away the memories of the two failed surgeries, though she still dreamt nightly of the sawing noise, always relieved when she woke up that she didn't have to hear it anymore.

"Let me show you," she said. She led Thomas upstairs, eager to tell him about her months here, leaving out the worst parts, painting a picture for him that was better than the one he saw. She pictured him telling Jenny and Amelia, *She can't leave. She is learning so much.* She didn't tell Thomas that she was still more maid than anything else. Instead, she told him about the operation, about how in the last few days the amputee's stump had been discharging a large amount of pus that Dr. Stipp deemed healthy. To support him through the process, Stipp had dosed the boy with quinine, beet essence, and milk punch. It was her responsibility to come by to see him in the mornings and in the evenings, no matter how busy she was. She was watching to see how he healed, she explained to Thomas, how the diet and suppuration were working to make him well. Lately, with the increased suppuration, the boy's pulse had risen from 80 to 96 to 124, his lips had paled, and the stump had swelled and reddened. Dr. Stipp was applying water dressings. To draw the pus out, Mary said. Mary reported all this to Thomas as they navigated the dim hallway's abrupt turns and low ceilings. She was thinking, *You see how well I have survived without you, how I have no need of you?* They turned a final corner to the small room where Dr. Stipp had sequestered the boy.

But the boy was not lying in the bed, but on the carpeted floor; it looked as if he had fallen trying to get out of bed by himself. His bloodied dressings had unraveled or been pulled away, and his stump lay exposed. His skin was hot to the touch, and he was staring at the ceiling, his parted mouth roped with white bands of saliva.

Mary gripped Thomas's forearm. "Don't let him move."

"What do I do?" Thomas asked, but Mary had already gone. Thomas knelt down, trying not to look at the limb or grow faint from its vinegary smell. He wondered if the boy was dying.

Mary rushed through the halls, hurrying from door to door. "Dr. Stipp?" She didn't know if she was yelling or whispering. She wasn't even certain she was breathing.

"Mary?" Fannie Warren asked, slipping into the hallway as Mary flew by, but Mary had already rounded a corner.

"It's the boy," she said, breathless, when she found Dr. Stipp downstairs in the ballroom. They'd developed a shorthand: *How is the boy? The boy is well.* It had bolstered them: their first success.

Stipp rushed to the boy's room. "Damn it," he said. He glanced at Thomas, who had risen from the boy's side. "Who the hell are you?"

"A friend of Mary's," Thomas said, forgetting to claim himself as brother-in-law.

"Everyone is a friend of Mary's," Stipp said.

Mary straightened, and in her posture Thomas read satisfaction at Stipp's compliment, recalling that night when James Blevens had come to dinner and she had been railing against him. *She likes the needy best, I think,* Thomas had said. She did, he thought now.

"Help me," Stipp said, and he and Thomas wrestled the large boy back into bed, his weight leaden, even his good limbs falling slack and awkward at his sides. After positioning him on the bed, Stipp immediately put his fingers to the boy's wrist as, unnoticed, Thomas backed out the doorway into the hall. He peered into the rooms at the men who had fought at Bull Run. Heat pulsed from their rooms, as if they, and not the men inside them, were bandaged and battered. All of them appeared to be slowly dying, though Thomas couldn't say for sure.

---

Later, Mary found Thomas sitting on the front stoop. The summer heat had leached any color from the sky, and he had long ago emptied his canteen of water. Mary sat down beside him.

"How is he?" Thomas asked.

"He died," Mary said.

Her voice was flat, but Thomas knew she would not weep. This was why everybody loved her. She balanced pain with anger and so was able to survive. *Everyone is a friend of Mary's.* She had slipped away from them. He noted the pride and the sadness, how they worked together to make her beautiful. She held her hand to her chest, and her long, exquisite neck rose above the ruin of her dress. In her dishevelment, in her intelligence, Mary was something to admire. He looked away, down the cobbled street toward the bridge and the creek, where trees arced over a deep culvert. If there had been no Jenny, maybe. But he would not betray. A choice was a choice. He let out a long sigh, as if he were very tired, and he was tired, though mostly he was ashamed.

He said, "Compared to you, I've done nothing. All I did was build a fort. I haven't done anything else. I haven't even seen a Rebel; I haven't seen anything, except when the ambulances went by, and then I couldn't even look at them. You have done more in this war than I have."

"Of course you've done something," Mary said, though she was stunned and weary and only half listening now. She didn't see Thomas bury his face in his hands, didn't see him look up finally, newly uncertain. She and Stipp had stood together at the foot of the bed. *How is the boy? The boy is dead.*

"I cannot leave you here. Amelia will have my head."

"It isn't your fault that I'm staying."

But Thomas couldn't help but feel that it was, somehow. There was a long silence, broken only by the traffic of Bridge Street running at their feet.

"I admire you, Mary," Thomas said.

Admiration was not love, though less than a year ago Mary had been pleased to hear him say just those words to her, believing they represented love.

"Jenny is waiting for you. Tell my family I am well. Tell my mother everything will be all right." Mary touched his forearm then, and said again, "You've got Jenny waiting."

*And a baby.*

Everything of any consequence that had ever happened in her life had been because of babies.

Now she would admit it, as she had been unable to ever admit it to herself before; she had come to Washington because of the baby. She had come because she couldn't watch Jenny grow large with Thomas's child. But now Thomas was going to go home and see Jenny, and Jenny would tell him, and then they would have the baby together and Mary would stay here.

Thomas held Mary's gaze for a long time. It seemed a betrayal to leave her, as wrong as it had felt to leave Christian at the Capitol grounds. He had failed again. Mary would never come home, and it had been a fool's errand to think that he could ever dissuade her from doing something she wanted to do. But he had had to try, for Amelia, for Jenny, for Christian. They were all his family now, though he could not help but feel that they all deserved more acclaim than he did, especially Mary. He climbed to his feet and took Mary's hand and pulled her up and then enfolded her in an embrace, then he released her and turned away without another word, and Mary watched him go, her heart rising in her throat. She forced herself to go back inside before Thomas reached the bridge, and so did not see him stop and look back, a shadow of regret crossing his face.

# *Chapter Twenty-two*

In Albany, there was a parade to celebrate the return of the 25th. The Lumber District carters came first, having had to wait because the day boat docked two hours later than predicted and then was delayed another half hour while there was some confusion. The Fifth Street Marching Band followed the carters, playing an Irish jig. Then the juvenile Zouaves, the Fire Department.

Stationed near the Staats House, Jenny strained to see over the crowd. She was disappointed that they were not able to meet Thomas and Christian at the boat, but all of Albany wanted to welcome the 25th home with a parade. Now, from the base of State Street, a blue flag waved in the summer afternoon, and the regiment finally came into view. Jenny and Amelia strained to catch sight of Thomas and Christian, but all the men looked the same, their clothes worn to rags by the sun and hard work. Amelia pushed through the crowds, leading the way for Jenny. In the past week, Jenny had finally emerged from her long stretch of morning sickness, months and months of violence that had ravaged Amelia. They followed the 25th as it marched up the hill, but neither of them was able to spot the men. The parade ended at the park on Eagle Street, where Thomas and Mary had sat on a bench one evening. Cries of reunion were erupting everywhere. The two women held hands.

Standing on a bench, Colonel Townsend was scanning the crowd, his wife and daughter fretting behind him, wanting to take him home, where a turkey was roasting and two pies were cooling on the windowsill. But now it seemed that those would have to wait. The crowd was already beginning to disperse when he spotted the two women standing apart from the crowd.

"Are you Mrs. Sutter?" Townsend asked the older woman, after crossing the distance between them in a moment.

"I am."

"I am Colonel Townsend."

"This is my daughter, Mrs. Fall."

"Mrs. Sutter and Mrs. Fall." He seemed dismayed to find them together. "Won't you follow me?"

They trailed behind him to the bench. He insisted they sit down. Unknowingly, they occupied the exact postures that Mary and Thomas had a year before.

Townsend turned first to the younger, Mrs. Fall. A departing soldier took the liberty of patting the colonel on the shoulder as he passed, as if to offer comfort.

"Mrs. Fall, when we left the fort, we accounted for everyone. But then, when we boarded the train in Washington, we walked through all the cars, taking roll. And your husband was not on the train. Please understand, he was never in any danger. He was not in the battle. It is entirely possible that he engaged another way home."

"Another way?" Jenny asked.

He felt terrible that he could not picture Thomas Fall. A thousand men to command; he couldn't know everyone. "Would your husband have had any reason to stay behind, do you think?"

"He's not coming home?"

"He could have just not made the train. Perhaps he went to get a meal." (Townsend was thinking of the turkey his wife had promised.) "The taverns were offering, and everyone was hungry. It is possible that he is on the next day boat."

Colonel Townsend's mantra: *It is possible.* Where had the man gone? He had left the fort with 757 of his thousand; had sent his lieutenants to the hospitals to roust the rest from their beds. Like a proud father, returning children to their mother. But on the train, taking roll, he had realized he was missing two. Townsend hadn't forgotten about Dr. Blevens, but as far as he knew, the doctor had no waiting family. *At least,* he thought, *I am to be spared that.*

The girl stared at him; her delicate features were drawn by illness. After losing nearly a third of his regiment to sickness, he had become an expert.

"No doubt you'll hear from him soon," he said, even though the man could be in Kentucky by now, for all he knew, but it was hard to see what he would be avoiding. Two beautiful women waiting for him. He had not really feared for Thomas Fall until this moment.

"Mary," Amelia said suddenly, seizing Jenny's hand, smiling at the colonel. "Of course. I wrote the boys about her. My daughter Mary is a nurse. He's just waylaid. He's gone with my son. He's with Christian, of course. They've gone to get Mary." Pleased to have the boys doing what she needed, pleased to have them taking care of her. Soon, everyone would be together.

Colonel Townsend reached over and touched Mrs. Sutter's hand. He remembered now who she was. She was the midwife, the woman everyone in Albany admired, Nathaniel Sutter's widow. And her daughter Mary was the young woman his wife had written him about: *Did he know that Mary Sutter, Amelia's daughter, had left her mother and her practice and gone off to nurse in a hospital in Washington City? Before she left, she had even applied to medical school. Why, Mary Sutter was the talk of Albany. Had he seen her there in Washington? Did he not think her peculiar?*

"Mrs. Sutter, by the time we arrived in Albany, your son—"

Amelia recognized the change in tone, had used that same tone herself. No slow cognition here, but swift and violent apprehension. Defiance quickened, like the sudden violence of the mother of a stillborn: *He's just asleep, wake him up, wake him with a slap.*

"But he's fine, isn't he? Dr. Blevens is with him? You called the doctor to be with him?" Amelia was calculating whether or not there would be enough hacks left in the city to hire one to get Christian home from the wharf. Jenny would have to be strong. She would have to keep her disappointment at Thomas's late return at bay. Amelia would send Jenny home to get their carriage, yes, that would be best—

"Mrs. Sutter," Colonel Townsend said. He was an attorney. He had given bad news before. But he did not want to say too much now. In that rocking train car Christian had not even had the energy to hold himself up. The pink froth bubbling from the boy's mouth, the sudden pallor and exhaustion had tormented the colonel, whose single act of courage in the war had turned out to be staying beside a dying boy. Nearby, a group burst into laughter, but the joy sounded far away, farther even than death. Townsend gestured now to Jake, skulking a few feet away, who came forward, hat in hand, head bowed. "This fellow found him. You understand, without a doctor, it was impossible to help him. We thought a disease of the lungs, perhaps. We had to wait to take him from the boat, that was why the parade was delayed. We arranged for an undertaker—"

Later, everyone in the square would remark how the sky dimmed the moment Amelia Sutter crumpled into the arms of Colonel Townsend. A permanent shift in the intensity of the light, some said, while others claimed it was only a passing cloud. But everyone in the square watched Colonel Townsend pick up Amelia Sutter and carry her in his arms to his waiting carriage, trailed by her daughter Jenny, who was being helped by Jake Miles. Townsend wheeled his barouche up Washington Avenue toward the Sutter home, where it was said that he carried Amelia Sutter inside and up the stairs to her bed. Jake Miles's wife, a solicitous girl named Bonnie, received Jenny into her arms, but when she heard the news of Christian Sutter's death, Colonel Townsend had to call for the maids, though Bonnie's husband was right there. It was odd, people said later, that Mrs. Miles hadn't gone down to meet her husband at the park.

By the time Colonel Townsend sat down to dinner that evening, the turkey his wife had roasted had dried to leather, which he thought only fitting for a returning soldier. Too rich an amount of food and he too might become ill. He was glad to be home. His wife and daughter had not left his side; there was bourbon in his glass, and upstairs clean sheets on his bed.

# *Chapter Twenty-three*

*Dear Mother,*

*Thomas has written me a letter, trusting the mails better here, I think, to say that he has reenlisted and for me to write to you and Jenny to tell you of his decision. As reason, he claims a measure of shame that the 25th did so little. I do not understand why he has done this, nor why he should feel dishonor over his service. He visited me here at the Union Hotel and tried to get me to come home with him, at your behest, Mother. I wish I could make you understand how I am needed here. Thomas was to have delivered this news to you on his return home, but today I received his letter and so am writing you now. I wish that we were not separated, but the grave need here prevents my coming home. Please do not fear, you will do fine by Jenny when her time comes. I know that her safety is your purpose in asking me to come home, but I trust you, as you should trust yourself. Please do write and tell me how Christian is. Thomas said he had a fever. I do hope that he is better now.*

*Please do not worry about me. The hospital is very clean and I am well rested and happy in the work.*

*Your loving Mary*

"He doesn't love me," Jenny said, through lips that barely moved. A hopeful, spectral apparition in black, she had spent the last two weeks on the quay, meeting every day boat. Now she lay coiled on the counterpane on Amelia's bed.

"He does love you," Amelia said, her hands entangled in her daughter's.

"But even if the post failed, even if he didn't get my letters, Mary would have told him about the baby. Wouldn't she have?"

Amelia paled, having already asked herself this question. A man could forget a woman, but not a woman and a baby. Surely Mary wouldn't have hidden that news from Thomas? Midwives did not let husbands abandon their wives. It was not in their makeup.

"He has his reasons, Jenny," Amelia said.

Their dresses and petticoats, made from the same bolt of stiff black crepe and sewn in haste just a day before they had buried Christian, rustled together as Amelia spooned Jenny into her arms. They were celebrities of a sort; the first in Albany to grieve from the war. But the community pity, rather than comforting them, only made them feel isolated and alone. Their hallway bowl was full of calling cards that Amelia could not bear to answer. *Dear Amelia, we are sorry for your loss.* She could not bear to hear or read those words ever again. Better to stay inside, where no one could say them to her. Jenny had been the brave one, bringing the disappointing news day after day from the quay that neither Mary nor Thomas had returned. Christian's funeral had been impossible, the coffin disappearing into the ground, the dull eternity of the soil hitting the casket. Awaiting Mary's return had been Amelia's salvation, and now she had to write and tell Mary the news of Christian's death.

"My baby," Amelia whispered into Jenny's ear. But of whom she spoke—Christian, Mary, or Jenny—even Amelia didn't know.

At that moment, across the Hudson River in East Albany, Jake Miles had drunk a good portion of the morning away. The liquor served the important purpose of blurring his ferocious desire into something a little dizzy, something manageable. He was standing at the window that overlooked his back field, which in the middle of August should have been studded with ripening squash. But he'd not planted before he left; across the nation, no farmer had planted before he left. Soldiers were all returning to fallow fields. Beyond the small scrub of the Mileses' land stood a line of poplar trees by the stream. And under them, Bonnie knelt among the marigolds she'd transplanted from a bunch she'd found growing wild by the road. Their baby's grave was how Bonnie had begun to refer to that patch of land since they'd returned from the Sutters'. That the baby was buried in the Albany Rural Cemetery, in a grave paid for by Amelia Sutter, did not sway Bonnie in the least from her curious fixation.

As Jake often did these days when he spied on Bonnie, he unbuttoned his fly and encircled himself and stroked, resting one hand up on the wall to support himself for when his knees buckled. But the curve of the log was no substitute for the soft curve of Bonnie's hip, and he had to think hard to remember what it had been like to touch her, taking away from his present gratification and causing a small headache to blossom above his left ear. It used to be that just the memory of Bonnie's slender waist sent him over the edge in under a minute. But of late he'd had to concentrate harder, which took away from the pleasure. In truth, he was sick because if he'd just let her stay at the Sutters', she wouldn't have blamed him, and then the baby's death would belong to both of them, not just her. Recently, Bonnie had caught him in the throes of self-pleasure several times, an act she viewed with disdain. But bodily deprivation had whittled Jake down into a state of pure longing. She did not understand what it was to look at her and want her and not be able to be inside her. Night after night after they'd returned from the Sutters', he had begged her, but she always said, *You leave me alone.* It had taken all his charm and a good dose of talk to persuade her to leave the Sutter women in the first place, but he'd done it. Since then, however, she'd been more sorrowful than he thought she ought to be, and sometimes she acted as if she wished he had died and not Christian Sutter. He'd told them all the story, sitting in their fancy parlor the night he'd arrived home with the 25th. How Thomas had asked him to help, how he had dosed Christian with whiskey to ease his discomfort. No, he'd said, he didn't know where the doctor was, not since he'd gone off with that other outfit. And he had no idea where that Thomas had gone off to. He'd done the best he could by her boy, Jake said. Gave him as much whiskey as he could take. Amelia took in what he said, a peculiar expression on her face, as if he had hurt Christian instead of helping him. *Yes, ma'am. We slept near one another every night. No, ma'am. Right as rain until the end there. Yes, ma'am. We became friends.* Which wasn't exactly the truth, but a version of it.

Though Jake no longer cared whether or not Bonnie found him pleasuring himself, when the door handle rattled he fastened his fly and wiped his hand against his pants leg. He tried to will himself into the picture of abstemiousness as Bonnie entered with a posy of the cut orange and yellow flowers.

"You been at it again, Jake Miles?"

"There are places I can go, you know," he said. "Places with women that aren't shy of a man."

Bonnie laid the flowers on the table and turned and walked purposefully across the room. At the stove, she dropped to one knee and snaked her hand between it and the wall until she located the chink where he kept his secret cache of coins. She carried the jar over to the bed and upended it onto the quilt. Sitting beside the pyramid of silver and copper, she began to count out the coins into two separate piles.

"Two dollars and thirty-three cents for me, and the same for you. You go right on over to the quay and get yourself taken care of, Jake."

He stood openmouthed, feeling the loose talk of the liquor drain away from him, and with it any recollection of why he had ever mentioned the hurly-burly girls in the first place.

"Go on," she said. "You need it so much. Go get it."

All the way across the Hudson on the *Lady of Perth*, Jake planned how he would stay in the city for the night to scare Bonnie, and then afterwards sweet-talk his way back into her heart. But climbing up the Albany pier thirty minutes later, he decided he was not too happy with her, not one bit, and so he sidetracked into a tavern on Quay Street, where after a half dozen ales he led one of the hurly-burly girls upstairs. Fifteen minutes later and a dollar poorer, he was halfway up State Street, heading toward the Sutter house on foot to ask Amelia Sutter how you kept babies from dying, when a recruiter lurking on the sidewalk noticed his inebriated state and invited him into his storefront bedecked with a red, white, and blue banner. Of all the ways to shanghai a man, the recruiters had recently discovered that drunkenness was best, for even in the short run the disastrous casualties at Bull Run had already begun to stymie their efforts. The recruiter convinced Jake that an aggrieved man in his misunderstood circumstance was best served by joining the Union army. The illogic of this was not apparent to Jake until he sobered up in a train car somewhere south of Poughkeepsie, clutching a set of papers that assigned him to a regiment in the newly renamed Army of the Potomac.

# *Chapter Twenty-four*

*17th August, 1861*

*My dearest Mary,*

*I do not know how to write you this letter. I must tell you that our Christian died on the train on his way home from Washington City. He was ill with something in the lungs, or so Colonel Townsend thinks. It breaks my heart that neither you nor Thomas was with him when he died; Jake Miles was, but that is no comfort to me.*

*We have already had the funeral, but you must come home now. I cannot suffer you in Washington any longer. I have lost both my men. I should not have to give my daughter also. And I need you, Mary, for Jenny. I am her mother, not her midwife, and I trust only you. You cannot deny me the comfort of your presence. It cannot be good for you there. I hear the worst stories of starvation and filth, and I believe nothing of what you have told me about the Union Hotel. You have been very brave, and I am proud of you, but I need you now. Jenny does, too. Please do not let your courage keep you from home. I am not blind, Mary, I know how you have been hurt. But that is nothing now. You see this, I hope; of course you do.*

*I shall expect you soon; any day.*

*Your loving mother,*

*Amelia*

A memory of Christian surfaced, swimming slowly to consciousness. He, younger, happy, beloved, protected, flinging himself into her arms, even though she was the serious one, unlike Jenny's easy joy. His curly hair wild in the breeze, shouting, running up State Street, impossible to collar, though Mary rarely tried, so much she loved him. Even when he left for war, his skin was still so soft that he did not yet shave, his cheeks smooth and given to smiles. Just a fever, Thomas had said.

Beautiful boy.

Mary had witnessed death and still, she was unprepared.

She cried out, "Christian. Christian."

And dropped her mother's letter on the bed.

# Chapter Twenty-five

*22nd August, 1861*

*Dear Thomas,*

*I waited and waited for you and despaired that you were lost or sick or killed. You should know that I am with child; it will come some time in December. I can tell that Mother is nervous. She wishes Mary could deliver me, though she says nothing. You do not require my forgiveness. But please tell me that you love me, for I miss you more than anything.*

*We buried Christian eighteen days ago. Did you know that Christian died? Did Mary reach you? Can you see her? Mother is years older. Overnight, she has become an old woman. How I wish you were here to ease our pain.*

*Bonnie Miles has come here to live with us. Mother took her in after Jake left and went no one knows where. Mother believes that Jake did something that hurt Christian, but she cannot say for certain. Bonnie is enamored of me and the baby to come. She pets over me and tries to hide her envy, but is unable to. Heartbreak scalds her face every time she looks at me. She wants a baby more than she wants anything, even her husband, who I wouldn't want back at all.*

*Your wife,*
*Jenny*

# *Chapter Twenty-six*

In mid-August, Washington teemed with wounded from Bull Run, as Dorothea Dix had said would happen, and though the first estimates—eighteen thousand Union wounded—shriveled in the days following the battle to about fifteen hundred, Miss Dix was satisfied that there were patients enough to forever erase the word *frivolous* from the common vernacular as far as she was concerned.

What concerned her now was lack. Though hundreds of women had stormed her doors, Miss Dix had found only some of the kind of woman she had been looking for, and had installed them in various hospitals across the city—the E Street Infirmary, the hospital at the Presbyterian church on New York Avenue, the Patent Office, the Treasury Building—where she remained determined that they, and they alone, prevail. But she was already losing control. In the weeks following the battle, women had besieged the doors of hospitals and rolled up their sleeves, crowding the rooms and entangling their skirts in dressings and catching nursing fever and making all kinds of trouble. Dorothea Dix ferried from hospital to hospital, segregating the true nurse from the interloper, instructing legitimate recruits to sleep on the floors if the surgeons resisted—which they often did—their rightful claim to stay, and in the process earned herself the nickname Dragon Dix.

Just recently in the *New York Times*, a letter had criticized her. She remembered the missive in almost every detail:

> The people of your city are laboring under the delusion that the Sanitary Commission and Miss Dix have the charge of the hospitals here and take a very active part in their internal management. Simple truth and justice to the medical officers of the Government, make it neces-

> sary that facts should appear which however unpalatable, will rob both those parties of a great deal of their newspaper glory. The Commission and Miss Dix are simply occasional visitors to the hospitals—weeks, and even months intervening between their calls to some of them—calls which are seldom of longer duration than an hour or two. Miss Dix does not live in the hospitals, but in her comfortable house in Washington, and has never nursed a sick soldier, nor folded a shroud over a dead one since the war began. The greater part of her time is spent in writing to Governors of States and having her "Commission" copied and sent to them and to "Associations," and instead of immediately distributing the supplies sent her for the sick, she has even now a large quantity of things sent to her as long ago as June, which are piled up in an old barn in this city—jellies spoiling and leading, and shirts and linen never unfolded—unused, while many need them. So much for Miss Dix.

She was remembering this letter once again as she pulled up to the Union Hotel. It was true, she had never been to this hospital, but since it was so far out of the city it had been impossible for her to come here, and so out of her consideration. Only recently, after that nasty letter was published, had it occurred to her that she ought to see every hospital.

Now, inside, the heat stifled. Even the two perfumed handkerchiefs she pressed to her nose could not smother the overwhelming fog of illness that hovered in the halls. Miss Dix was glad there was no one to see her stagger and place her hand against the wall. Perhaps it *was* true she did not understand what her nurses suffered; to sleep in such a place! Miss Nightingale had always said, "Suffering is my raison d'être." Now Miss Dix expanded it to suit her vision of herself: "Suffering is my raison d'être, my medium, my métier," which she thought more musical and now repeated to herself as she started down the hallway, fumbling for the water closet, for just as in Manhattan City, finding a place to relieve herself as she visited around Washington was nearly impossible. After several minutes, she emerged, a third handkerchief pressed to her nose, and made a note to submit a requisition for a privy to be dug in the back because the water closet was an abomination. Drawing herself together, she forged on in search of Dr. Stipp, glancing shyly into rooms full of languishing men. She found him, finally, not in a patient's room, but emerging from a room under the stairs, his face more haggard and pale than she remembered it.

He did not at first place the small woman hidden behind a curtain of handkerchiefs who said, "Have you dismissed Mary Sutter yet?"

Stipp peered at the diminutive woman. "Miss Dix?"

"I sent those new nurses to you with orders for you to dismiss Miss Sutter immediately."

"I never received those orders," Stipp said. He had, in fact, read them very carefully and then torn them up and thrown them into the burn barrel.

"She is in there?" Miss Dix nodded at the door behind him.

"She is."

When Stipp had heard Mary's cry from the third floor, he had instinctively known where she would be. He did not like to think how he had known where to find her. He marked her comings and goings as if by intuition, knew her schedule, where she was likely to be at any given time of day. *Life would flow in and out at will.* So much he had to guard against. Sometimes at night, he deceived himself that he could distinguish her breathing from the moans and rasps of his patients' exhalations. Hers, an imagined metronome of calm, the imagining of which was the only thing that allowed him to fall asleep.

"You were alone with her in her room? Let us be clear, Dr. Stipp. You are never again to enter Miss Sutter's or any other nurse's room. Mr. Mack keeps me well informed of the goings-on here."

Stipp seized Miss Dix by the elbow. "Hush now. Mary Sutter has just received word that her brother has died," he said.

"Her brother, you say?"

"Yes," Stipp said, releasing her, shocked that he had clutched the woman.

He suddenly regretted his indiscretion. It was a betrayal to share this news with Miss Dix, who would like nothing better now than to see Mary gone, whatever the reason, but Stipp himself was discomposed. It had been staggering to see Mary in such a state. She had been shattered, inconsolable. Something about her guilt, though he could not imagine what that could be.

Miss Dix set her shoulders and immediately swept past Stipp, entering Mary's room without knocking and quickly shutting the door behind her, her gaze as determined as if he intended to seize her once again.

"Wait! She's sleeping!" Stipp said, hovering outside the door, ready to burst in, but in truth he did not know what to do. He did know that Mary would leave now. Of that he was certain. Not by what Mary had said, but he had read the letter. Anyone would go. And perhaps, Stipp thought, disclosure had not been betrayal if Miss Dix could speed Mary home to her mother. It was possible Miss Dix could do far better things for Mary than could he; with her connections, she would merely have to ask a senator to deliver Mary home in his private railcar and it would be done. What could he offer Mary now but a shoulder for her tears, and he had already done that. His chest and shoulders were damp, his two handkerchiefs knotted in a sodden lump in Mary's fists.

He listened, uncertain, his hand hovering over the doorknob, then turned and walked down the hallway, his footsteps heavy on the floor.

Later, Miss Dix found Dr. Stipp in the ballroom, where twenty men still occupied straw tickings on the floor, two weeks after the battle. She was so small that picking her way across the room did not in any way disturb the recumbent men, a detail that Stipp declined to admire, though not even Mary could have accomplished such a nimble passage. When she reached his side, he refused to look up, though the knee he was bandaging was unremarkable. He was taking care not to turn and greet the dragon, who would breathe the bad news of Mary's departure.

"Mary will not go home," she said.

Stipp abandoned the knee to rise. Unconsciously, he assumed his posture of defense: chin out, hands to hips. "I beg your pardon?"

"Mary will not go home, which I do not think is for the best, but I cannot bodily remove her, can I? She claims dedication, which is admirable, considering her bereavement. I even offered to accompany her home, but she will not leave the men here." Miss Dix was pulling on her carriage gloves, fastening the buttons one by one.

"Mary is staying?"

Miss Dix finished buttoning the last button and looked up. "You rely on her, don't you?"

Stipp attempted a dismissive shrug, but neither the men in the room nor Miss Dix were fooled by this diffidence.

"I will take this moment to clarify that Miss Sutter is not your charge, Dr. Stipp. She is my charge, my responsibility, as are all the nurses. I expect that you will not be hiring any more of your nurses from off the street. One is quite enough. I expect you will not be so lucky in the future."

She turned on her heel and picked her way out of the room, and Miss Dix thought that the writer of the *New York Times* letter would be pleased by her decision today. Dedication, yes, this was who she was; she might even write a letter herself to say that the writer had been quite in the wrong. If he only knew what effort it took to take care of the nurses who were sacrificing themselves for the good of the broken nation. She had handpicked every one of them, too. Why, she could use Mary as an example of the kind of young woman she had chosen, and with this thought banished any memory of Mary's previous dismissal at her hand, a circumstance that elevated Miss Dix in her own mind to the kind of woman who did not deserve any of the criticism flung her way, for after all, just look at what she was accomplishing through the nurses she managed.

The horses kicked up a great deal of dust on Bridge Street. Miss Dix checked her watch. It was nearly four; she was famished, done in. She would go home to rest rather than visit the Seminary Hospital. It was quite exhausting to do the work she was doing. Quite exhausting indeed. No one appreciated her. No one at all.

That night, very late, Mary and Stipp abandoned the boil of the hotel for the weedy backyard, where the nightly terrestrial exhalation was beginning. Stipp had gone to her room with dinner, made her eat, and then brought out two chairs from the dining room. Above, the August night boasted Cassiopeia, the upstart queen, in her crooked, jagged imagining. A woman with thoughts of her own.

They sat quietly. Stipp was recalling the way he and Lilianna used to walk to the arroyo behind the house to watch the stars fall from the sky. Lying on their backs, she would ask, *Do you think we are happy?* He had not wanted to tell her that happiness was the province of the young, that with each passing year you lose your hold on it, that it was as fleeting a pleasure as the falling stars. But now he was glad he had not said those things to her, because it was possible that at this moment at Mary's side, he might actually be happy.

Mary was pondering the celestial queen rising to prominence in the southern sky. Ambitious, doomed, reckless. It was unfair, Mary thought, that the stars couldn't rearrange themselves. That a queen who dared to question the gods would be forever stuck in such an unappealing posture. All afternoon, her bed a watery grave, Mary had hardly been able to move, unable to discard the feeling that she was at fault. *It breaks my heart that neither you nor Thomas was with him when he died.* Thomas had come looking for her to persuade her to return home, and she, in a fit of vanity, had delayed him. *You see how I am needed here. Don't worry about me. I never mourned your loss.* (Even laying claim to more accomplishment than was her due; such poverty of spirit she was capable of.) Perhaps, if Thomas would have been traveling with Christian, or if she had ignored Thomas's assurances that Christian was fine and had gone with him to the capital, her brother would be alive now. The pain was almost more than she could bear.

"Your mother will want you home," Stipp said.

"I would feel as bereft there as I do here," Mary said. She did not think she could face Amelia and Jenny; she might break if she did. "And here I can at least do some good."

"Grief is meant to be shared."

"I have quite enough of it on my own."

"Who was that man who came to visit you the other day?" Stipp asked, striving for nonchalance, for equanimity.

"No one. My sister's husband."

Stipp let the contradiction go. "He wanted you to go home, too."

"Yes."

"You turned him down."

"I want to be a surgeon."

"I think you will regret not going home," he said.

Above Mary's silhouette, the queen tilted crookedly on her throne.

"I will never regret not going home."

"If you change your mind—"

"I won't."

"But if you find yourself—"

"If I go, I will never come back."

She said the thing that would silence him, but this was the first time Mary had seemed young to Stipp. The young were always so certain they knew what was best. His heart broke for her mother, even as he gave silent thanks that Mary was going to stay.

The night settled around them. A waning disc of moon lit Mary's face. He had already learned that she did not want to talk about Christian anymore. *I can't,* she'd said after Miss Dix left. He would give her time. He himself had not spoken of Genevieve for at least a year afterwards. To Lilianna, when she'd asked, he'd said only, *She loved me.* He had traveled to Texas to purge himself of that loss; Mary had not yet even had a day.

The crickets provided melodic comfort as, for once, time did not reign preeminent. A chance, a rare minute to breathe. Neither was aware of the other in the consoling way that friends are not; only the crickets spoke. Grief as the proof, the revelation. From Bridge Street, laughter drifted in their direction, as alien a sound as if it were descending from the sky.

"Now you must make good on your promise," Mary said.

"What promise?" Stipp asked. "I never promised you a thing."

"You knew what I wanted when I came. And now we have help. There is no obstacle."

"You barely sleep." Hedging. Appealing to fragility, which she lacked. Even this morning, with her head pressed into his shoulder, weeping, she had asked about the broken hip in room thirty-nine.

"Teach me everything you know. I want to understand what makes the body work. I want to see what you do, how you do it. I want to hear what you think. I want to know which medicine to give for which condition. I want to change dressings, see the wounds, understand why the boys are dying, how to make them well. Not just after a battle, but all the time. Every day. At your side." Not a request, but a repeated demand. *I want more.* The *more* being extorted skillfully on the basis of grief and the unspoken threat of her remove. It reminded him of someone, an echo from the past, but the past was so far distant that it seemed now to have nothing to do with him.

"But who will run the beds? Who will run Mr. Mack?" he asked.

"That protest is beneath you," Mary said.

"Forgive me, Mary, but after today? After all this? This is what you are thinking of?" A falling star streaked across the sky, a river of white against the dark. They both saw it. Cassiopeia shedding tears.

"Yes," Mary said, "this is what I am thinking of," but Stipp could hardly hear what she said next, because she was whispering. "Because then," she asked, her voice wavering, "what would all this have been worth?"

Stipp thought now that he ought to say that no matter what she did, no matter how hard she worked, no matter how much she learned, resurrection was only a tale in the Bible to save men from their fear of death, from eternal loneliness, from despair. But to assert now the truth that death was final seemed as cruel as confessing his joy that she was going to stay in spite of her loss.

"It would be worth nothing," he agreed.

Above, the stars grew pale and reserved, as if in judgment. The queen from her throne, seeing his duplicity. Double the guilt.

He would tell her a portion of the truth.

"I am not a patient teacher," he said, thinking that if he warned her, he might be able to shed some of his culpability and preserve something of the intimacy they now shared. Innocence, yet.

But Mary knew there was no more innocence.

Not looking at him, she said, "You'll regret everything that happens between us."

But she reached out and took his hand, as if he were the one in need of comfort, and they sat together as the night sky fell around them.

# Chapter Twenty-seven

After the battle, the war entered a time of suspension. The Army of Northeastern Virginia had failed in its quest for a decisive victory, but the Rebels had similarly failed to seize their advantage. The two armies remained at close but tentative stalemate, thirty miles apart: the Rebels entrenched in Manassas, keeping firm hold on the railroads with cannons fashioned of logs to appear a well-armed multitude, and the well-armed multitude of Federals holding firm in the ring of forts surrounding Washington, having believed the Confederate ruse. The newly recruited Federal troops worshipped the newly appointed and self-consciously dashing Major General George McClellan, because he refused to allow them to engage in battle while still green. This, McClellan decided, had been McDowell's fatal mistake; it would not be his. Besides, neither time nor attack pressed. He had the men for three years and would take as much time as he needed to fashion the necessary army of regulars. In the distant west—hard to believe in Washington that the war extended so far—the two opposing armies eyed the Mississippi and the Cumberland rivers and planned how best to control them. But to everyone, it seemed that both the North and the South had taken a deep breath and never exhaled.

On an afternoon in early September, Stipp ordered Mary to take the day off. *Eat at a restaurant, find a shop and buy yourself something.* Absurd orders for her, but he had grumbled and roared until she stuffed what money she had into her purse and departed. But standing on Pennsylvania Avenue, she didn't know what to do with herself. With the exception of that one night, the whole of August had been spent inside. Now the shock of ordinary life startled her. She had imagined the world had been taken up as she had been, but here were people going off to market or work, posting letters, buying food, and tending children. Theater bills papered a brick tavern wall; a grocer roamed with his cart; cavorting children were cuffed by their mothers; a farmer trundled down the avenue on his way to the market.

*Find a restaurant. Eat something not made of farina or beef. Drink something refreshing.* Stipp's prescription.

He was not a patient teacher.

They had begun her apprenticeship slowly. Each morning, they met for rounds, beginning on the first floor in the ballroom. Her first week was taken up with learning how to wash a wound. Stipp was very specific. She was to remove and discard the old bandage, then dip a sea sponge into a bucket of water and wash away the effluvia, then return the sponge to the bucket. She was then to stuff the wound with lint scraped from old dresses and sheets and sent to them in boxes from across the country. This stuffing kept the wound open. Finally, she was to pour cold water onto the lint, cover the wet dressing with gauze, and then move on to the next patient. She reused the water and the sponge, over and over. She was not to worry about the suppuration. It was part of the healing process; all wounds healed this way. The fever, the chills, the debilitas, everyone suffered from it. Their job was to support the men through the process with good diet and ventilation.

"Like this, or like this?" Mary asked, gently stuffing wounds with fresh lint. She was to feel for the pressure. Too much, and the wound would never heal; too little, and the same outcome would occur.

"Like that. You are too slow."

"I'm being careful. Should we wet the dressings when we remove them?"

"Yes, for comfort. You see that cherry pink color there? The way it seems to bubble? That is granulating tissue. That is a good sign of healing."

After that first week, he let her change dressings on her own, and then they moved on to the fractures. Stipp had put plasters on most of the men, and positioned others in open fracture boxes in which their limbs rested, unconfined. Because of the lack of movement, the men were getting bedsores, which required more dressing changes.

"Should we get the men out of bed?" Mary asked.

"When they can use crutches."

"But we don't have any crutches."

"Make out a requisition."

"We haven't any forms."

"Send the steward for both forms and crutches."

The third week, Mary accompanied him on his medical rounds, which he did separately from the surgical cases. At each bedside she was to observe, examine, question the patient, and then present the symptoms to Stipp.

"This boy can't—"

"Don't be shy now."

"I am never shy. He can't move his bowels."

The boy in question blushed to hear his problem stated so baldly by a female.

"Well, that's a sea change from the rest of the poor fellows in here. Write him up. He must be the only man in the Union army who can't."

"But what should we do?"

"Give him blue mass."

"What is that?"

"Mercury and chalk."

"Will it work?"

"I have no idea. Give it to him and see."

The boy opened his mouth in protest, but they moved on.

"This boy's gums are bleeding. And his bowels. And he bruises. And his knees and elbows ache."

"He's got scurvy. Find him a lime."

"Where do you suggest I do that?"

"At the market." Said with a laugh, for no one had seen a lime in months.

"Aren't you going to help at all?"

"Unless you can grow a lemon tree, there is nothing we can do."

They moved on.

"This one can't breathe."

"Give him whiskey."

"This one can't walk."

"Give him whiskey."

"That one can't stop itching."

"Give him whiskey."

"This one has got diarrhea."

"Haven't they all?"

"We've run out of quinine."

"Give oil of turpentine."

"We've run out of turpentine."

"Then boil some willow bark and put it in whiskey and give it to him."

"We've run out of whiskey."

She was not to think of any of this. *Get out and breathe the air. Get out and see the sky. Leave that surgery textbook here.* She read it obsessively, even though there was no surgery to be done. He had made her hand it over as she left. *Go out and do something pleasant, if there is anything pleasant left to do in the world at all.*

Mary thought, *I should better remember how to do this.* She crossed Pennsylvania Avenue, glanced into restaurants, made a decision.

The waiter slouched unimpressed at her side, surveying her ruined clothes, before clearing his throat. "We do not seat unescorted women."

"But I am here. And hungry. And alone. And I know no one."

The waiter shrugged. "Perhaps in your hotel room, alone?"

"I am a nurse at the Union Hotel in Georgetown. I have eaten there far too many times. Please."

The waiter turned to the owner, who hurried over. "The corner, then," the owner said, and, sniffing, turned away.

"Oysters," Mary said. "And a glass of wine."

It was early for the dinner crowd, early for wine. There were white cloths and tableware and glassware and candles to light when the day darkened. Underfoot, not rotting boards but creamy marble, left over, the waiter said when he brought her wine, from when they had built the Treasury, the embattled, guarded building across the street.

The oysters were slippery, salty. She asked for bread, and he brought five whole slices. And there was butter and jam.

She requested mutton and mashed potatoes and parsnips.

Did she want club sauce or pickles or olives?

Only catsup, please.

Which pastry?

Lemon pie.

Walnuts or almonds?

Both.

Coffee or tea?

Is it real?

The coffee? Of course.

Questions with direct answers, an interrogation unlike the maddening ones in which she engaged with Stipp. There were people for whom this luxury happened every day; at one time, this had happened every day for her. Silverware clinked against china. More patrons arrived while she ate, the door opening and shutting at such frequent intervals that flies flew in and out unimpeded. A fly buzzed at a window's edge. When the door opened again, a breeze fluttered over her face.

The newest restaurant patron stood silhouetted against the door. He held his hat to his chest across a blue expanse of brass button and epaulets. His gaze floated lazily across the room. Mary rose and ran her hands over her dress.

James Blevens. Here.

He spied her and crossed the room, towering over her in a protective half bow. He did not seem to notice her disarray.

They each spoke at the same time.

"Mary Sutter—"

"No one knew where you were, Dr. Blevens, or if you were even alive—"

Into the ensuing cavern of silence, she said, "But you're all right."

He was still hovering over the table in his posture of safeguard. Other diners looked their way and imagined trysts in the shadow of the president's house. The new social order.

"Are you well, Mary?" Blevens asked, and could have sworn she swayed, but he rushed on, stumbling over his words, glad to see her, though his elation was a surprise even to him. He'd been lonely in the city; he'd missed saying good-bye to anyone in the 25th, and the loss of that camaraderie, despite his relief at not being at Fort Albany any longer, had made him eager to see anyone from home, but especially Mary. Their good-bye at the quay had haunted him; a ghost of kindness. Perhaps now he hoped for more. "I've been looking for you. Back at the fort, Christian told me you were in the city. But I've been looking in the hospitals. I should have been looking in restaurants. This is remarkable. I came in, and here you are." He stepped toward her, took her elbow, because while he'd been talking she had gone completely pale.

"You don't know," she said.

"What don't I know?"

"Christian died. On his way home in the train. He was sick. Did you know he was sick?"

James tried to remember when he had last seen Christian; they'd been at the stream, bending to bathe, his strong body stronger yet. He'd been laughing, teasing someone for trying to wash out his socks. *You'll never get them clean; don't even try.* His musculature not in any way diminished like the others', his eyes clear, no hint of the debilitation of the dysenteric plague. A doctor's eye, raking the past for clues. No. Nothing.

"I didn't know," Blevens said. "I am sorry. I didn't know."

They were still standing, their eyes locked. Loneliness yoking them, making them grateful for one another.

"Pneumonia, Mother said."

"I am so sorry."

"Are you finished, Miss, or are you planning on having yet another meal?" The waiter interrupting. His hands were clasped behind his back in a passive gesture that nonetheless seemed aggressive. Hungry patrons shifted at the door; it was now past noon and the rush was on.

Mary pushed a strand of hair from her face. Blevens waited for her acerbic comment on the waiter's bad manners, but it did not come.

Blevens said, "I'm so sorry to have kept you waiting."

Mary looked at him for a moment, confused, and then said, "It is nothing," and sat.

Blevens said to the waiter, "I will order as soon as you do your job and clear away the lady's dishes."

Sullenly, the waiter flung dishes into his elbow and forearm.

"You forgot one," Blevens said, and handed him Mary's wineglass. "Would you like anything else, Mary?"

"More coffee, please."

"Coffee for the lady. And I'll have mutton, with squash and turnips and applesauce. Fruit pudding and raisins. And coffee for me as well. And a pudding for my patient guest, who was kept waiting by me for a very long time. I had rather hoped that someone kind would look after her until I arrived."

The waiter hunched over the dishes and staggered to the kitchen.

"I was never in need of rescue," Mary said. Her voice was desultory, quiet.

"Of course not," Blevens said. He reached across the table and took her hand. "I'm sorry I wasn't with Christian. I was called away."

She searched his face; the memory of disappointment. *Dr. Marsh said he won't see you. No, I can't apprentice you.* "Where were you?"

"The 79th needed a surgeon. I was sent off with them, I didn't get back until after the 25th had left."

"Mutton. Turnips. Applesauce. Fruit pudding. Raisins. Coffee. And one pudding for you, Miss." The waiter set down the plates, frowned, and turned away.

"Christian was well liked." It was important that Mary understood this; important that she understood he would have done anything for Christian. "If I had been there—"

"I tried to see him at the fort."

"Passes are impossible to obtain." He would forgive her, for he could see she hadn't forgiven herself.

"Or when Thomas said he was sick. Thomas came to get me, but I said no. If I'd said yes—the last time I saw Christian was the last time I saw you. At the ferry." She turned her face to the window and wiped tears from her cheek.

Onlookers thought, *It is a difficult romance.*

"I knew he was sick. Thomas told me he was. He came to see me. I should have gone to Christian."

Blevens offered her his handkerchief. He had a hundred questions to ask her, chiefly what she was doing here, but they would have to wait. And he did not want to ask about Thomas. He did not want to cause her further grief. "You couldn't have known. There were a hundred men with fever when I left to go to the battle. How would you have known what to do?"

But he could tell she was not absorbing his stabs at comfort.

They ate in silence, Mary spooning the pudding into her mouth, Blevens sawing away at the boiled mutton, doctoring its toughness with dollops of applesauce.

Mary smoothed her skirts. Blevens and his kindness were good company, a surprise gift she did not want to return. "This is practically the first time I've been out of the Union Hotel since I arrived—"

"The Union? That hellhole? What are you doing there?"

"I am a ma—a nurse. Rather, I am apprenticed to a surgeon."

Blevens leaned forward and took her hand again, this time an unconscious gesture that he would later remember with pleasure. Her hand was calloused and the nails ragged and broken; it felt heavy in his, like responsibility.

Onlookers breathed more deeply. *They will go next door to the hotel and take a room,* they thought. *The war is bringing out the worst in people.* At the door, those waiting for a table had grown surly, but this unruly behavior was not met with as much judgment as Mary and Blevens leaning in toward one another.

Mary did not fight his offer to pay her bill; Blevens left no tip, which the waiter believed confirmed his prior assessment that the two had been undeserving of his regard.

"Can you walk with me?" Blevens asked.

It was only past noon. Time through a different lens. How slowly it was passing today.

F Street was an artery of quietude compared to Pennsylvania Avenue, but it nonetheless pulsed with dust and heat, and as they walked along they hugged closely to the buildings for shade. On a similar day in Albany, they would have strolled along the towpath of the Erie Canal, finding relief from the heat under the trailing willows, but here there was only an occasional overhang to protect them.

At a corner, James looked down the street at a theater where he'd gone the other night to see a musical performance. The novelty of it had delighted him at the time, but the appearance of Mary Sutter had far surpassed it.

"What was it like at Manassas? Will you tell me?" Mary asked.

"I was quite in the rear, well protected."

"But you saw the battle?"

"I was kept well back. I treated the men as they were brought back on stretchers."

This was not completely true, but Blevens did not like to relive the details of that day. Who would have thought that hell would be so *immediate*? High-pitched screams, astonished, brittle gasps.

Mary stopped walking and put her hand to his forearm. "I have assisted in amputations. I have seen men die. I have scrubbed and laundered and witnessed the most vile things. There is no reason to withhold anything from me."

Forgiven his debt. Blevens hadn't realized that he still carried the measure of that obligation with him. After all he had seen, after all the discomfort of the last three months, the debt he owed had burrowed itself into his soul. And no one had asked him for his story, not in the way that Mary was now. He had told parts of it in bars, had even told the clerk at the Surgeon General's office that the failure of the Medical Department was why he was staying, but no one had touched him and said, *Tell me.*

They began to walk.

On that early morning, he told Mary, there was a calm before the artillerymen had even untoggled the prolonges from their guns. The day throbbed with beauty. It was easy to imagine that they were all on a lark. Redolent with fragrance, the summer morning shimmered with that clarity of light peculiar to midsummer, that glassy serenity, when everyone, human and animal alike, lets down his guard and is seduced by tranquillity. He turned his back on the unseemly hubbub of troops invading the countryside and surveyed the unsuspecting hills to the east where, undisturbed, monarch butterflies dipped their noses into lakes of goldenrod, where in a tangle of vines a nest of newly hatched cardinals appealed for breakfast, and toward the sky, where a red-winged blackbird soared above the cattails of a shallow pond. It was possible at that moment to believe that such an idyll was eternal.

With the first crack of artillery, black smoke voided the landscape and wiped the sky of birdsong. James ducked and scrambled toward the back of the line to his assigned aid station, but the stretcher bearers refused to go into the field. Blevens, tortured by the cries of the wounded, seized the portable surgery kit he'd made from the instruments he'd brought from home, commandeered an ambulance, and drove himself into the fray. At the first impassable gully, he abandoned the wagon and slapped the hindquarters of the horse, who galloped headlong out of the maelstrom. Blevens smelled smoke, sweat. Musket balls whizzed past his head. A soldier fell, and then another and another. Why were they standing to fire? Why didn't they lie down and take cover? James fell to the ground and crawled toward them thinking of all he lacked: opiates, scalpel, lint, bandages, adhesive plasters, syringes. Shells exploded and bullets spit, but he heard only his breath issuing in uneven gasps. *Water?* the boys asked, but he lacked even that. There were moments when he was certain he was dreaming.

In the din and racket, James found an oak tree splattered scarlet and rested his head against it. Shattered men carpeted the field beside him, men that James did not think of as soldiers, for they had not yet hardened. They were still, like him, only half a moment past innocence. One soldier was dead, but unmarked. Not a speck of blood, not a perceptible chink in his body anywhere. Perhaps he had died of fright, or of the percussion waves of the artillery invading his body. Time grew elastic. How many wounded per second, per minute, per hour? The lines of battle moved. They ranged forward and backward over the hilly ground obscured by dust and smoke. Every dip, ditch, hillock, boulder, and tree was a surprise. James stumbled over them with the unsteadiness and unwieldiness of a body dizzy with confusion. His tongue swelled from thirst. At one point, he wiped his face and found that he was crying. Riderless horses winged past, only to sink and complain, their haunches or shoulders or legs destroyed.

The head wounds were hopeless, the abdominal wounds impossible. By then, the thirst and humidity, gunsmoke and cannon powder had rendered everyone slightly mad. It seemed to affect even the air. That's what would be said for years afterward. *Conjured our own weather that night. You remember? It was the last beautiful day for a long while. Maybe for the whole war. We turned even the skies, we did.*

"I did what I could, but it was too little," Blevens said. He was trying not to weep. "And then it seemed as if the entire Union army decided in one moment to run. They just changed direction like a flock of birds."

The retreating troops jammed the roads. After a few dusty, confused miles, carried along by the river of men, Blevens reached the town of Centreville, where thousands had hoped to find water, but the town well had run dry. A church was being used as a hospital, and Blevens pushed his way inside. Pews had been pried from the floor and blankets and hay laid down in their place. A hundred wounded men sprawled on the main floor, and another twenty-five lay upstairs in the gallery. Squeezed in among them were perhaps another fifty healthy men taking refuge in the safety of the building. Outside were two hundred more wounded, laid out in four buildings and beneath the trees in a surrounding grove of timber, all of whom needed dressings, whiskey, morphia, lint. Blevens elbowed his way through to where a door torn from its hinges was suspended between two pew ends.

An amputation of a forearm was under way.

Blevens identified himself to the three surgeons working together on the arm, puzzling their way through the operation.

"Have you any supplies?" he asked.

They stared at him.

More troops kept arriving, and one by one, regimental surgeons, attracted by the wounded, pushed into the church, also looking for supplies, but soon cries that the Rebels were coming sent the onlookers spilling back again out of the church and onto the road toward Washington and safety. But without ambulances, it was impossible to carry off the wounded. The surgeons huddled together to consider who should stay, the oily smell of burning kerosene tainting the air. They kicked the ground and calculated the post-victory stance of the Rebel soldier with regard to surgeons. In the end, five surgeons gave themselves up to be captured with the wounded, and the remainder, all volunteers, including James, joined the thousands of men and wagons jolting over the Warrenton Turnpike toward Washington. Dust fogged the air at the passage of wagon, cart, horse, and foot. Had not the rutted road provided direction, James would have been lost. Here and there, overturned wagons blocked the way, and the whole train had to plunge into fields to pass by. The night passed in painful slowness, until at last, footsore, James reached Fairfax, where he lay down without a blanket on the ground under a sky that opened to a downpour.

James was proud of what he held back from Mary. The horses squealing from their shell wounds, soldiers lying on the ground, impaled by fallen tree limbs. How he had vomited twice in the field.

Now he and Mary reached the square where the E Street Infirmary stood in silent, serious judgment. He had brought Mary here without thinking. They had walked ten blocks, past the post office where army wagons by the dozens lined up to procure food from the commissary in its basement, past the reporters hurrying from the *Evening Star*'s offices, past even Mrs. Surratt's Boarding House, where James had stayed one night and found the company treacherous.

Mary surveyed the dark façade of the infirmary. The September sun was no less fierce than June's had been.

"The infirmary wouldn't have me," Mary said.

"The sisters make good nurses."

"None of Miss Dix's charges for you?"

"It is an all-Catholic hospital. I shall be excommunicated from the Presbyterian Church on my return to Albany. I feign religiosity."

A wagon rattled by.

"May I show you something?" James asked.

They entered the building to which the sister had denied Mary access in June. On the first floor, in a closet of a room, was a desk, a stool, a table, and a microscope sitting uncovered on it.

"How?" Mary said.

"It is mine. I had my landlady send it to me from Albany, via Adams Express."

Mary pulled off her bonnet, her ribbons trailing like discarded apron strings.

He touched his hand to the table. "I'm looking at stool samples." He hesitated, but what was embarrassment now? He had seen a man blown to pieces. She had helped to amputate a leg. "I'm trying to solve the problem of dysentery. I've tried everything, but whether I dose the men with Dover's powder or blue mass, nothing seems to work. Rice does, when I can get any."

"Dr. Stipp has tried to purge the men with ipecac. And quinine has worked in a few cases," Mary said.

"Dr. Stipp? William Stipp?"

"Yes. Do you know him?"

"He taught me at Bellevue. I thought he went to Texas after his wife died."

A wife, Mary thought. Texas. How much Stipp hadn't told her. "I know very little of his life."

"I would like to see him."

"He would like that, I think."

Blevens pulled out a slide and made a preparation, after surreptitiously taking a sample from a covered bucket. He adjusted the lens so that it came into focus.

"You are taking the time to teach me something?" A spark of the old Mary.

"It was only the onset of the war that prevented me. I am sorry," he said.

An apology, albeit a late one. She wouldn't call it pride, but instead gratitude, that made her say, "The penitent doctor."

Each held the other's gaze for a moment, and then Mary turned to the lens and tried to make out something in the shadows of the flickering light.

"Look for small, cylinder-like shapes," Blevens said. "Those are rods. And the others, the circular ones, do you see them? Do you see how they propel themselves?"

"I don't see—oh! Yes!" She wasn't conscious of the intensity of her exclamation, but James was. He remembered a cat lying on a table in Dr. Stipp's dining room, the moment when everything had first started to come together for him.

"What are these?" she asked, unable to make out the meaning of a spiral-shaped body floating past.

Mary shifted away from the long neck of the lens to allow him to look. Peering in, James said, "I don't know what is normal and what isn't normal. I've identified albumin—that's a protein, of course. And red and white blood corpuscles. These have to do with the inflammation of the mucosal lining of the bowel, I think. And the rodlike bodies. Spherical elements, all in motion. These are like those described by Billroth, who calls them *Coccobacteria septica*. Once I put a ring of varnish around the cover plate and the movement went on forever."

Outside, the soft murmur of the sisters' patrolling shoes betrayed no hint of the chaos that ruled at the Union Hotel.

"You want something you think you cannot have," Mary said, when the whisper of their footsteps died away. "That's what you once said to me."

Their shoulders were nearly touching. The debt respoken, or at least remembered, perhaps not yet forgiven, as he had hoped. She would punish him for knowing about Thomas. Blevens gazed at Mary, who was regarding him with naked challenge.

When he did not respond, she said, "Silence is not the answer to everything."

"I never said yours was an unworthy cause. Merely that it was what you wanted and that I could not provide it." He meant for both desires.

She studied him then, her gaze as serious as a scholar's, or a minister's, or a physician's. He looked tired, older, as if the battle had removed the last bit of his youth.

"How are you? Some of the men I take care of relive the battle."

She would not tell him about the saw that still sang in her head, the boy clutching his leg, the blood arcing. All she had seen, and yet he had seen more, and worse.

Blevens wasn't sure how he was. But he was glad to see her, felt even as if the world were a better place because she was here, though something about her had changed since he had seen her last. It was not just her alarming thinness, or her faded dress, or the patina of grief. She was more grave, if possible, than before, but also less angry. And her inquiry about his well-being seemed conciliatory, approaching even forgiveness. He supposed it was because she was no longer at the end of her choices; in the face of chaos, she had found a way. He knew how that felt, knew the pleasure of possibility.

He nodded at the microscope and said, "Trying to find an answer helps."

"Answers. Yes."

"I'm sorry I couldn't be there for Christian. And I apologize again for not helping you in Albany."

"We would know less, you and I, if we had stayed."

Forgiveness yet. They lingered over the slide, reluctant to say good-bye, and for a moment Mary thought that she wanted nothing else but to stay here, with James Blevens's arm inches from hers, but finally she gathered her skirts around her and asked him to hail her a hack.

Outside, he took her hand and helped her into the carriage.

"You must come to the Union Hotel," Mary said.

He looked at her inquiringly.

"To see Dr. Stipp."

"Yes," he said. "To see Dr. Stipp."

That evening, Mary said, "Blevens has a microscope. Here."

"Are you certain it was he? The James Blevens I knew?"

"Yes. He said so."

William Stipp set his glasses on his desk and sighed. He had sent Mary Sutter off for a day of rest and diversion and she had ended up in another hospital, peering though a lens with James Blevens, that precocious, bubbling cauldron of questions who had once dumped a cat on his desk. Of course those two would have found one another; they were each other's echoes.

"You say he knows your family?"

"Yes. He knows everyone."

Sadness had been lifted from her; Stipp tried to be glad. He said, "We missed you."

She lingered at the doorjamb for a moment, wanting to tell him more, about how James Blevens had turned her down, about how grateful she was to Stipp for teaching her, even about how much she had seen today, looking through that microscope, but she did not. Something about the wistful look in his eyes stopped her. She wondered if she should ask about his wife, but decided she would not, not today. Grief of that sort should not be roused indiscriminately; discretion was the gift he had given her in her sadness, she would give him the same.

"I'm here now," she said.

Stipp nodded, but was not at all certain that she was. And then she was gone.

# Chapter Twenty-eight

*Fort Marcy*
*25th September, 1861*

*Dear Jenny,*

*I am without words and heartsick. They will not give me leave. You must do all you can to take care of yourself. I blame myself. If I hadn't left Christian, then perhaps he would still be alive—but Amelia wanted Mary. Oh, how I grieve.*

*Amelia will look after you. Do not be afraid, but strong.*

*Did Mary know in July that you were with child? I only ask because she did not mention it, which I find not in keeping with her general good nature.*

*All we do is drill and train, which is necessary since we are not a professional lot, but General McClellan is a fine soldier who is pushing us to be fit for the fight. I hope that very soon the war will be finished. I will come back to you unashamed, proud that I have given what I could, but sore of heart that I am not with you now. I have seen all of Virginia that I care to. We are chopping down every tree in a twenty-mile radius to keep warm at night and to cook our food. The army is a ravenous thing. We may eat up Virginia.*

*I cannot believe that Mary knew and said nothing.*

*Beyond words, I grieve for Christian.*

*Your husband,*
*Thomas Fall*

*11th October, 1861*

*Dear Mary,*

*Your sister's confinement looms; I fear for her as you would fear for her if you were to see her; she grows pale and has the most tremendous headaches. I suspect eclampsia or worse. The baby is large, perhaps too large for her to deliver. I am unequal to the task. Can you come home to help me?*

*I forgive you for not coming home when Christian died. You say you have a hospital full of Christians. Perhaps this is true. But now you must think of your family. I have lost both my son and my husband in the last year; I need you.*

*Thomas writes to tell us that he is at Fort Marcy, near the Arlington Heights. Is that near you? Perhaps you could convince his superior officer of the need to send Thomas home. You could travel together.*

*Amelia*

*21st October, 1861*

*Dear Mary,*

*You must understand how much I love you. There are days when I think of nothing else. Before me, your sister grows ever larger, closer and closer to her time. You know the dangers women like her fall prey to. She is the size of a faerie, a child, a shadow. I am immensely proud of you for finding your own way in the world. I ask only this one thing of you: Please come home, Mary. Please come home and help me.*

*Amelia*

*27th October, 1861*

*Dear Thomas,*

*Please tell me that you were not in the fight at Ball's Bluff. I am in great fear; the papers are so full of rumor that it is difficult to get an accurate account of anything. I worry all the time. The baby grows. I am tired and headachey and no help to Mother at all. She tries to hide her worry, but I know her, and her tricks with other mothers do not work with me. She has written Mary to ask her to come home.*

*Mary did know in July. Perhaps she did not feel right telling you. She did not know you were going to enlist. My heart aches, Thomas. I miss you all the time. Are you pleased with the news of the baby? You didn't say.*

*Your Jenny*

*27th October, 1861*

*Dear Jenny,*

*I am writing to tell you that I was not in the fight at Ball's Bluff. It was a regiment of the state of Massachusetts, and poor fellows. Their bodies are washing down the Potomac and getting stuck against the Long Bridge. We are having a devil of a time fishing them out. We are charged with sitting on the banks and trying to catch them as they flow by, but we cannot grapple them with just rope. The city is gravely depressed, the war at their doorstep, the barbarity of it. But it heartens me, in an odd way. We are all of a mind that we are fighting a fight that must be won. The importance of our quest helps me bear being apart from you.*

*It is growing to be your time. Please do all that Amelia asks of you. Be very brave.*

*Thomas Fall,*

*Your husband*

*2nd November, 1861*

*My dearest Thomas,*

*Have you written? I have not heard from you in over five weeks. Each day, I wait for the mail. Maybe one of your letters has gone astray. If I do not hear from you soon, I will worry. Please write to me. I sent you a letter only a few days ago; I am eager, you see, to hear from you.*

*I am heavy with child. I am glad you cannot see me this way. The baby kicks and turns. I rejoice, for I take this to mean that he is eager and robust. I have decided it is a boy. I try not to be afraid, but I have heard mother and Mary tell such stories. So many things can go wrong. But perhaps Mary will be coming soon. My savior, my sister. Do you mind if I show her our letters? No, perhaps not. How I wish you were able to come home to me.*

*Your most loving wife,*

*Jenny*

# *Chapter Twenty-nine*

The war around Washington, except for Ball's Bluff, had turned quiet after the battle at Bull Run, and had remained so, though in the West battles raged in Missouri, and in the South a Union naval force of seventy-seven ships steaming from Fort Monroe southwards to invade Port Royal, South Carolina, was savaged by a hurricane. But the biggest news came on November first. Abraham Lincoln accepted Winfield Scott's offer to resign, and George McClellan succeeded Scott as commander of Union forces. Congress especially was hopeful that the energetic, optimistic McClellan would seize the opportunity to implement his dashing intelligence toward swift victory. McClellan was already widely beloved; now, with this newest crown of power, he was worshipped. *George McClellan will save us,* the Northern papers said, as Winfield Scott boarded a train for West Point, where he was going to write his memoirs and observe the young general from afar.

Four days after George McClellan replaced Winfield Scott, James Blevens, asleep in his small cell in the center wing of the E Street Infirmary, thought he was dreaming again about Bull Run. The frightful cries, the inability to catch his breath, the crackle of battle were now his nightly portion, and he awoke choking, as he often did, but this November night the curls of smoke did not disappear with consciousness. He sat straight up, confused, and stumbled to the window. In the square outside, the sisters were screaming for help, their shorn, uncovered heads gleaming in the firelight. About a hundred patients—one hundred four, the mother superior would later state—occupied the beds, and nearly forty of them could not walk. It was this fact, which the nun had reported to him the previous evening, that shook Blevens from his stupor. He thrust himself into his shirt and pants, sweat already slathering his skin. He took a swift but longing look at his microscope before leaving it behind to dash into the hallway, where a dense black cloud billowed along the ceiling, its tentacles reaching into the open doors of rooms where the bedridden and convalescent alike were shrieking for help. Through the smoke, he could make out the hunched shapes of the Metropolitan police darting here and there, evacuating the invalids. Blevens dropped to his knees and crawled along the floor, counting doorways carefully, trying to remember which patient was where. He veered into a room. Two of his patients were huddled in bed, coughing. One had a broken leg. The other was a young man who reminded him of Christian. It was the boy's eyes, he thought. He was missing a portion of his left jaw, a section of his bottom and upper lip, and the whole of his left nostril, compliments of his tentmate, whose musket had discharged when he'd been cleaning it. The boy was eighteen and he was named Peter Markeli. Blevens seized a sheet and spread it on the floor. He tore away a strip of sheet and gave it to each of them to hold over their noses. Then he lowered each man onto the sheet and yelled, "I'm going to pull you."

He covered them with their blankets. Through the window, he could see flames shooting through the infirmary roof. The heat made his hands slippery, but he wrapped each sheet end around his wrists and then anchored them in his palms. He dropped to his knees and gasped for air and then plunged forward, dragging the men behind him to the door, through it, down the hallway, toward the front door. It was a mile away. Ten miles. People were yelling. He could hear timbers falling. He stooped to stay below the smoke, but it swirled down as if to ensnare him. The weight of the men wrenched his shoulders, his elbows; his hands burned. He wondered if he would lose his way; he could hardly see. He could hear artillery shells screaming, the horse yelping as it galloped away. He had done nothing at Centreville, nothing at Manassas. Christian had died. Blevens could see the doorway more clearly now, could see the river of smoke spilling out of it. Blue flames rippled along the ceiling. Men were crying. He stumbled toward the door. He was Charon escaping across the river Styx, hauling the damned behind him.

He burst through the doorway, fell to the ground, wheezed. Men rushed forward to carry his patients away in their slings of blanket and sheet.

Blevens put his palms down to push himself up, but fell again to his knees. He held up his hands. Skin was peeling away from his palms and wrists.

A pump wagon appeared. A stream of water shot from a long snake of hose and drops fell around him like bullets. Buckets of water crashed into the inferno. He started up and forward into the square, then collapsed under a single oak tree, while the blaze consumed the night.

No one died. A miracle. Everyone got out. Every single person, bedridden or no. In the early morning chill, the patients were divvied up between the city's hospitals. Some were carried to the City Hall, some to the schoolhouse on Judiciary Square (a hospital for some time past), some to the former quarters of Griffin's Battery, some to the Old Trinity Church on Fifth Street, and many to private residences in the neighborhood.

James demanded to be taken to the Union Hotel.

A week after the fire, Mary gently peeled away the protective cover of his bandages. Blevens's agony had erased between them even the memory of debt; in its place had sprung mutual tenderness. His was the kind of exhausting pain that rendered a man's belief in God pitiable. On a continual dose of whiskey since arriving, he had learned that alcohol was a blunt tool that numbed little but the tongue and brain. Even the slightest graze of wind seared. Only Mary's presence kept him from weeping. After she unwound the last of the gauze, the poultice of slippery elm in simple cerate had to be removed next. As Mary delicately wiped away the waxy substance with a rag, Blevens broke into a cold sweat. Even so, he flexed his fingers to break the beginnings of scars that would seal his fingers together if he did not.

Stipp, watching, leaned over and said, "You'll grasp a scalpel yet."

Next she was to apply a new preparation of the slippery elm, Stipp's contribution to Blevens's well-being, a product of his Texan exile. The

Indians had taught him how to make it, and then how to apply it to skin after sunburn. It was easy enough to get a hold of at the corner apothecary; he had gone there himself to purchase it for his former student. He showed Mary how to mix the gummy secretion of the bark with boiling water and then allow it to cool. Stipp felt some pride that he could come up with a solution to ease James's pain, whom he distracted with medical cases while Mary worked. Stipp had initiated this practice as a diversion from Mary's ministering fingers the morning after the fire, when Blevens, carried in on a litter, had told Stipp that he had directed his bearers to bring him here over anywhere else. Blevens was suffering from exhaustion in addition to his burns, a temporary effect from inhaling the smoke, Stipp thought. More than his exhaustion, though, he seemed to be mourning the loss of his microscope, its beautiful brass incinerated in the flames. Blevens had pleaded with the firemen to please try to find if it had survived, but they delivered a lumpen mass to him instead, which he kept under his bed.

Though Mary had said that he would, Blevens had not come to see either Stipp or Mary in the days after her visit to the E Street Infirmary. Nor had Stipp gone in search of him. They could each plead the tidal wave of sick from the forts. Though McClellan assured the nation that he would soon attack, and that his attack would be *quick, sharp, and decisive,* there had been no more fighting. And though the autumn weather had been mild, the prolonged exposure had flooded the Washington hospitals with sick. The diseases of the damp—rheumatism, pneumonia, diphtheria, paroxysmal fevers—were making their ugly way through the poorly housed troops.

But now, watching Mary lean over his former protégé, Stipp could not help but wonder for whom Blevens had asked to come to the Union Hotel: him or Mary.

Mary took up her cup of salve and was spreading it now on Blevens's hands as Stipp gave quiet instructions: apply it thickly enough so that your fingers do not touch the unprotected burn; rewrap the salved hands with the gauze; give Blevens a pillow to rest his hands on; dose the poor man with another jigger of whiskey.

He was acutely aware of the quiet trust Mary's ministrations engendered in James Blevens, who did not take his eyes from her face; if she was aware of his studied regard, Stipp could not tell. A brief stab of jealousy made him shut his eyes. What an insipid fool he was being. Of course the man was in love with her. Pain was pain, and there was nothing like the agony of a burn, and Mary wielded the magic salve. The young man was a hero, and he might never be able to be a surgeon again, no matter how optimistically he had suggested that he would. Besides, he was drunk most of the time, and in addition he was married, though a marriage of which nothing definitive could be said. Stipp remembered Blevens's youthful adoration of the suffering Sarah. He wondered whether Mary knew of the indiscreet and impulsive marriage. He was given to love, that boy.

As was he. *Don't be an idiot,* he thought. *They are far better matched, if only for their age.*

Stipp inspected Mary's handiwork and nodded. "Well done." Then he forced himself to turn away, toward Peter Markeli, asleep in the next bed, over whom Blevens still kept vigilant though slightly drunken watch.

Because of Blevens's efforts, Peter had not been burned in the fire, though the blow from the musket ball had been devastating enough. Blevens had not been able to close the wound, because not enough skin had remained behind. It was nearly certain that Peter would starve, and soon; while his tongue had survived intact, swallowing proved nearly impossible, and he already looked like a skeleton. He had weakened since coming to them, able to take in only small amounts of liquid, choking and sputtering when he did. Stipp had noticed that Mary had developed a special affinity for Peter. She spent much of her time trying to get him to eat. To illustrate to herself Peter's suffering, Mary had pressed her jaws together but kept her lips open to try to approximate swallowing without a closed mouth. It was a feat that exhausted. At night, Mary prowled the halls and reported that Peter's breathing had seemed to coarsen, even though the restless boy was able by day to walk those same halls in a twisted posture, his body favoring his left side as if forever recoiling, a circus sideshow for the tourists who roamed the hall seeking the thrill they had not been able to obtain at Centreville.

(Privacy, after tenderness, the second casualty of war.)

"He will live just to make you happy, I think," Stipp had said to her one night.

Now Stipp watched as the boy lay back on the bed and obligingly turned his head from side to side as Mary, finished with James, wound a long strip of bandage about his face, his eyes intent, not with fear, but instead with an outright glimmer of trusting adoration.

Blevens, drunk from the whiskey Mary had dosed as anesthetic, blurted, "He looks so much like Christian. Like he's come to life, don't you think?"

Mary's gaze darted to Peter, who met her clear gaze with his own newly feverish one. She gasped, the sharp intake of her broken voice mingling with the sweet smell of the salve.

Stipp, hovering behind, cursed under his breath. Death was a formidable enough foe without making the mistake of figuring love into it.

But wasn't he guilty of the same? *Just to make you happy. You'll wield a scalpel yet.*

Stipp put his hand on Mary's shoulder and said, "Let me do that."

She yielded and fled the room.

Later, when Stipp knocked on her door, he found Mary sitting stiffly upright on her bed, a small fire lit in the fireplace. She was staring straight ahead, at the dark November cold flooding in through the small porthole window. The scene was as unlike Lilianna and the bright golden air of southern Texas as possible.

"His hair is the same—such beautiful dark curls. And the eyelashes. Black curtains. And he trusts me. He believes I will never hurt him."

Stipp's hand felt cold on the doorknob; he had not been invited to cross the threshold. "If I may say, even if you had been with Christian, I doubt very much you could have saved him."

She turned to him, looked him right in the eye. "Will we save Blevens? Will we save Peter?"

*Just to make you happy.*

When he did not answer, she turned away and looked into the fire.

A hand in the air, a turn, and a walk up an arid hill.

Stipp shut the door.

# Chapter Thirty

*12th November, 1861*

*Dear Mary,*

*Are you receiving my letters or are you not answering me? I have heard nothing from you; sometimes I fear you are not even alive. Acknowledge me that at least. I will do what I can with Jenny, but I am uneasy. I see her still as my child, and you as my esteemed friend. It is not fair, I know, but you must come and help me. I know you are grieving Christian, as am I. Let us find solace together.*

*Amelia*

*25th November, 1861*

*Dear Mother,*

*I have received your letters. Please forgive my unforgivable reticence. I plead an excess of work, which is true, but I also have not written because I cannot face coming home. (You know why I cannot; do not make me say it.) And I grieve Christian every day; you cannot imagine how my heart has broken.*

*Please do not be frightened about Jenny. You fear too much your own emotions. Did you not teach me everything about midwifery? By anyone's estimation you are more than capable of bringing Jenny on your own safely to the other side of her confinement. You must trust yourself, though you may believe that it is unfair of me to disregard your distress. But it is not purely self-protection that compels me to encourage you. I have learned that it is possible to endure anything. And I have duty to render here; hundreds of men who need me. In light of such need, I cannot abandon them or Dr. Stipp, who relies on me. (Dr. Stipp is the man who runs the hospital here; he has agreed to apprentice me.)*

Mary lifted her pen from the paper and glanced out the window onto Bridge Street, dark except for a swinging lantern, its owner on subterfuge of his own. How easy it was to justify. Wasn't need the same excuse she had given to Thomas?

*In light of your distress, I beg you to consider my forbearance. I never told Jenny how sad their marriage made me. This at least, must count for something in your estimation. I hate to ask you to be generous to me after all you have taught me, but I entreat you to understand. Jenny has you, which is more than enough; does she also need me? Two midwives in attendance, when men here are dying for lack of food?*

*Please do not think me heartless. Obligation calls me both places, and, trusting you, I choose the greater need. I do not love you or Jenny any less—*

Was that a lie? Did she love Jenny less?

*—but you must understand that either way, I will think poorly of myself, for there is betrayal in both decisions. And perhaps, if I am truthful, I have chosen to protect myself. There, I have said it. Think as ill of me as you like now. But you will do well by Jenny, or else I would come in an instant.*

*Do not worry, Mother, for you know everything there is to know in order to bring your grandchild safely home. I truly believe that my presence would make no difference in the end for Jenny. I ask one last thing: Please keep my distress from Jenny and do not show her this letter. Perhaps it is cowardly of me, but I fear knowledge of my weakness can do her no good.*

*Your loving daughter,*

*Mary*

Mary put down the pen on the little desk she had fashioned from wooden crates. The candle was nearly burned out. There were times at night when despair showed no mercy. Why couldn't she go home and offer her mother this one thing? *I have learned that it is possible to endure anything.* What was she so afraid of? Would it really hurt her to shepherd Thomas's child safely into the world? Or was she, like her mother, too much afraid of her own emotions?

In the womb, she and Jenny had shared everything, their arms and legs entwined in a seeming eternal embrace, a grasp she feared now had spawned more competition than cooperation. But what was fair when selfishness collided with heartbreak? Mary buried her head in her hands. What was required of a sister?

Cold knifed into the window cracks and up through the floorboards as Mary studied the letter she had written, thinking that it was possible that she knew nothing at all of kindness.

She set aside her letter to Amelia, chose a new sheet of paper, and dipped her pen again in the ink.

*Dear Jenny,*

*I am writing to apologize that I am unable to come home for your confinement. The work here is necessary and demanding and there are so few of us to do it. Do not be afraid, my sister, for you know that Mother will protect you and keep you through the storm. Please endure the best you can; it is best not to fret too much, but to accept what labor brings. Let your body do the work, and then you will have Thomas's child, and your happiness will be complete.*

*My love,*

*Mary*

Mary let the ink dry, then folded and stuffed the letters into their separate envelopes, sealing them with wax so that she wouldn't be tempted to read them again in the morning, when a less fraught perspective might change her mind. But her refusal was not abandonment. Her mother was only afraid, out of love. And when Jenny's time came, that same love would render her mother more competent, not less. She was tempted to tear open her mother's letter to tell her that fierceness in a mother was what every laboring daughter needed, when a knock came on the door. It was Monique Philipateaux, carrying a candle, saying that two men had died of their fevers, and would Mary please come, for their roommates were ill as well, and no one knew what to do.

Without a glance at the envelopes, Mary snuffed her candle, threw a shawl over her nightgown, and hurried out the door.

# Chapter Thirty-one

**Register of the Sick and Wounded, Union Hotel Hospital, November 1861**

| Hospital Number | Name | Rank | Regiment or Corps | Co. | Complaint | Date Admitted |
|---|---|---|---|---|---|---|
| *164* | *Mackey Dr* | | *58 New York* | | *Debilitas* | *October 3* |
| *165* | *Reumpf John* | *Prvt* | *75 Pa Vol* | *B* | *Debilitas* | *October 3* |
| *166* | *Schmidt Jacob* | *Prvt* | *75 Pa Vol* | *A* | *Rheumatismus* | *October 3* |
| *167* | *Ecke E* | *Srgt* | *75 Pa Vol* | *G* | *Hernia Ing.* | *October 3* |
| *168* | *Airgood, Wm* | *Prvt* | *54 NYV* | *H* | *Vulnus Punct* | *October 14* |
| *169* | *Beltsford Wm* | *Prvt* | *3 Penn Vol* | *I* | *Toxicum* | *October 14* |
| *170* | *Driscoll Edrd* | *Prvt* | *2 U.S.I.* | *A* | *Rheumatism* | *October 14* |
| *171* | *Sayon Robt G* | *Prvt* | *23 NYV* | *F* | *Diarrhea* | *October 14* |
| *172* | *K Gustavus V* | *Prvt* | *12 NY Bat* | | *Diarrhea* | *October 17* |
| *173* | *Newell Bugler* | | *12 NY Bat* | | *Debilitas* | *October 17* |
| *174* | *Conger Ed* | *Artifcer* | | | *Hemorrhoid* | *October 19* |
| *175* | *Christie Jms* | *Steward* | | | *Debilitas* | *October 19* |
| *176* | *HendersonWm* | *Prvt* | *12 Maine Vol* | | *Icterus* | *October 19* |
| *177* | *Strayline Grg* | *Prvt* | *107 Pa* | | *Varix* | *October 19* |
| *178* | *Harrison Thayer* | | *15th Mass* | | *Vulnus Punct* | *October 25* |
| *179* | *Markeli Peter* | *Prvt* | *75 Pa Vol* | | *Vulnus Punct* | *November 4* |
| *180* | *Blevens James* | | *E Street Inf* | | *Burns* | *November 4* |

"Dear God, Mary, what are you doing up?" Stipp asked.

Mary dropped her pen, smearing the new ledger's pages with ink. The scraping of the pen against the page had been the only sound she had been aware of, though at night the Union Hotel Hospital was a noisy organism. Tamped down, shuttered in by the cold, its occupants groaned and prayed both for daylight and for delivery from the misery of the dying men alongside them, but the collective chorus had disappeared for Mary as she had worked.

She said, "I might ask the same of you."

Stipp dragged toward her from the hallway door and sank down beside her in a chair. A gray army blanket smothered his shoulders. Clouds of vapor escaped from his mouth. He had lain awake in his room for four hours, powerless as life ebbed noisily away from the men in his charge, thinking that he too was closer to dying with every passing minute. He had fled his straw-filled coffin of a bed to discover Mary—young, indefatigable Mary—writing away, scraps of paper and scribbled notes piled around her as she tried to impose some kind of order on the chaos that was the Union Hotel. The manual Stipp had been sent by the Medical Department, *Handbook for the Military Surgeon*, rested at her elbow. Stipp had been looking for the handbook for two days.

"It's past three o'clock," he said.

Mary peered at the tall clock still in its place at the far end of the dining room. It had been too heavy for the owners to cart off when the government had taken over the hotel.

"It's three-thirty."

"Two hours and the day begins all over again. Aren't you tired?" Stipp asked.

"The Medical Department want us to keep track of all our admissions. They want us to backtrack as far as we can remember." Though it was the second week of December, Mary had been recording the names of the soldiers they had admitted in October from the battle near Ball's Bluff, north along the Potomac. It had been another rout—the Union Hotel had been the closest general hospital, and for a period of two weeks they'd received wounded shipped down the C&O Canal on barges and offloaded and carried up the hill on stretchers. Some were from the field hospital at Poolesville, some from a makeshift hospital in a barn on the Maryland side of the river, where several amputations had been performed. The wounded crowded the hotel—it had been a week of no sleep, again. Fresh surgeries, another amputation, this one of an arm. The new dead house Miss Dix had badgered the quartermaster to build them had received the arm like a coffin. Sometime later, a driver came to cart it off, and it lay uncovered in the back of the wagon, and all the people on the streets of Georgetown and Washington shuddered as it had trundled by.

Mary dipped the pen into the last of her ink. A candle burned on the table. The fire had died down about ten, but she was too mindful of the dwindling supply of firewood to light another. "If you're too tired, Dr. Blevens would probably be eager to take your place on morning rounds."

"I'm not tired."

Blevens's hands were much better. The slippery elm seemed to have done the trick. He was leaving within the week to work at the hospital at the Patent Office.

To Stipp, the scratching of the pen sounded like the scrape of knife against bone. Stipp studied the curve of Mary's long neck. He liked to study her when she was absorbed in work, when her thoughts were directed to a task at hand and she had no awareness of anyone around her. He often imagined that when she delivered babies, she exhibited the same quiescent concentration, an aloofness that nevertheless was eminently trustworthy.

"Is Peter any better?" he asked. *How is the boy? The boy is well.*

"He is. He seems to have come around. He drank a cup of water today. And the edges of his wound are not suppurating much."

Stipp nodded. He did not know why he'd asked her; he believed she was far too attached to the boy to judge his medical situation dispassionately. He'd been dropping in on Peter all afternoon and feared that he was worse off than before. He choked too often when he drank; Stipp believed it was affecting the poor boy's lungs. He would not argue with Mary now, though. It was the dead of night and he craved a moment free of pain.

Mary lifted her pen from the page. "I don't know the rank of the men admitted from Ball's Bluff. And if I have to record every person admitted to this hospital into this ledger, we are going to run out of ink."

She read out loud the next page: "Date Returned to Duty, Deserted, Discharged from Service, Sent to General Hospital, On Furlough, Died, Remarks. How are we supposed to know all of this? They don't even know who's in the army when they're in their regiments. Vulnus Puncture. Why don't we just write 'gunshot wound'?" Mary said.

"The Latin makes it less vulgar."

"Or more. Vulnus."

The building cracked in the cold.

"Christmas is coming," Stipp said, endeavoring to keep his voice even.

Mary lifted her hand from the page. The pen hovered in the air, a drop of ink, like blood, forming at its pointed tip.

"You won't persuade me."

"I have seen you reading and rereading your letters. You cannot claim indifference."

"I do not claim anything like it."

"I will write a furlough for you, if Miss Dix won't."

"I have not asked her."

"Shall I ask her for you?"

Mary capped the ink bottle, wiped the nib of her pen, and rose from the table, leaving the ledger's pages open to dry.

"You are very stubborn," Stipp said.

"You make that observation as if you have just realized it." Mary reached for the surgery handbook, but Stipp forestalled her with a hand on top of hers.

"I am almost finished reading it," Mary said.

"Your mother wrote to me. Grief festers, Mary. And you will regret not going for your sister."

"You are not my father."

"No. I am not. But I love you all the same."

Her hair fell like a curtain across her face, and she tugged her curls back into their combs. Stipp loved even the frantic nervousness of these gestures, the way she worked without even knowing what she was doing. "It is just a fact, Mary. And we might as well say these things." He did not say, *Because death hovers in the wings. Stalks the wards. Prowls in the night.*

Her hands stayed as a corona above her head, then she slowly let them fall. She managed to keep the pity from her eyes, but just. "You love me?" She said this slowly, as if he were already dying, or as aged as he felt in the face of such youthful ambition.

The young woman who was so adept at compassion—matter-of-fact and kind without displaying any pity—now looked at him as if she had never learned that to pity a man was to kill him.

He let a lying smile break from his face, withholding all sorrow, though his eyes watered. He was grateful that it was the dead of night, and the creeping dawn ages away. Oh, he felt old for the foolishness of love, for its indiscriminate yet accurate aim.

"You see," he said. "How could I not love you? You are the daughter I wish I had. The one I would be proud of." He said a silent apology to Lilianna, and to Genevieve, his first love. *But darling, life goes on, and this pain is agonizing evidence.*

Would that there were only the scraping of the pen, the illogical, record-keeping rasp, the focus that renewed her, buoyed her up, let her believe that doom was not inevitable. The world was ending, but here was an offer of love.

Irrepressible Mary, speechless. Dr. Stipp vaulted to wisdom. To age. To rank, even. "Don't worry," he said. "It is better, isn't it, than our disliking one another?" Said it with a straight face, as if such lies were believable.

"Of course," Mary said.

Another mercy dispensed, to pretend to believe the second lie. She would feign belief in a third and a fourth, and then another—endless numbers of them—to keep this man from dissolving. She wanted to say, *It is only the war that makes you love me. It is only the night. It is only the chaos. See,* she wanted to say, *the ledger? It is our only hope.*

As if to confirm, Stipp took up the ledger and made careful examination of her entries. The clock tolled the hour. Four o'clock. God, such beastly things were the hours of the night. "I believe your page is dry now." He shut the ledger and handed it to her, as if it were his heart.

They left the room together and separated at the top of the stairs, Mary taking the candle and Stipp feeling his way back to his bed in the dark.

# *Chapter Thirty-two*

The next morning, December the fifteenth, was a day of piercing cold, compounding the general misery within the hospital walls. Mary and Stipp were on morning rounds when they discovered Peter Markeli breathless, perspiring, sitting up in bed, his hands locked around his knees, his sheets and blankets knotted at his ankles, his nightshirt transparent with perspiration. He had torn away his dressing.

"He's been restless all night," Blevens said.

Stipp prescribed 10 grains of turpentine as a diuretic.

"It may force the fluid from his lungs," he whispered to Blevens, in a voice that harbored doubt rather than hope. He told Mary to also rub volatile oil of turpentine over the boy's chest, but the medicine had no effect. All the long day, Peter continued to labor at breathing. From time to time, he grasped at Mary's skirt or sleeve. Late in the afternoon, as the day began its plunge into wintry darkness, he fumbled in his pocket and pulled from his wallet a tintype that he laid on the bed. It was of an older woman, with dark hair neatly tucked beneath a white lace cap, peering from the gray shadows of the portrait.

"Your mother?" Mary asked.

Peter nodded. His mop of curls clung to his forehead. Mary knelt on the bed and helped him to sit forward.

To drown is to brawl with death; Mary's helplessness made her furious. Blevens, his hands nearly healed, but still bandaged, paced. Toward six, Peter's breathing slowed, his chest expanding and contracting in stutters and starts with long, breathless periods in between. Agonal breathing, called that not for the agony of the dying, but for the agony of having to witness it.

The sharp edges of the tintype cut into Peter's palm.

When the tintype clattered to the floor, Mary draped a towel across his ruined face.

Blevens said, "Mary," but she did not answer him; instead, she hurtled through the hotel, looking for Stipp.

In the kitchen, he was hunched over a bowl of cold stew.

"I'll require leave for three weeks," she announced.

The spoon Stipp was ferrying to his mouth paused in midair. He didn't need to ask what had happened.

"You'll come back?" he said.

"I don't even want to go," she said.

Snow began falling in Philadelphia, and by the time Mary had crossed the Hudson on the ferry, Manhattan's ugliness had been shrouded in a cloak of white. Over her dress she wore a shawl and bonnet, and on her feet only thin summer boots. Her winter coat had been left behind in Albany, along with her muff and hat. Along the waterfront, gaslamps glimmered fitfully in the relentless snow. Mary turned in a circle, surveying the slippery cobbles, the shanties and tenements and warehouses butting up against the rows of docks. The ferry conductor had laughed at her when she'd asked if he thought the trains would be running in New York. He had angled a lantern at her, the flickering light betraying a set of wooden teeth. "I don't even know if I'll make it home three blocks, Miss."

The odor of fish clung to the coiled ropes and slippery posts of the wharf. The ferry she had debarked was smacking and banging against the pier. Mary tightened the shawl over her hair and shoulders. She'd sent Amelia a telegram: *I'm coming.* Had she left yesterday, she would have been home by now, tucked into Dove Street, waiting for Thomas and Jenny's baby. She joined the crowd trudging across the open wharves toward the city. Her skirts dragged behind her in the slush of snow and garbage and fish offal. She would find a horsecar heading north, ask directions to the depot. Sleep in the station, if necessary. Her fingers grew brittle with cold.

A woman trudged past, her shoulders hunched against the pelting snow.

"Pardon me. Do you know how to get to the railroad depot?"

The woman swung around. "Which one, Miss? There are six or more. Where are you going?"

"Albany."

"The Hudson River Railroad? Good luck to you. You won't make it tonight."

"Please. I don't know where to go."

Wind howled, tearing at their skirts. The woman shouted, "I think you'd best go to the Chambers Street Station. It's not much really, but 32nd is too far. Go on down West Street here till you get to it," she said, pointing down the dark waterfront.

Mary looked downriver. The storm had not driven the wharf's roustabouts and loiterers inside. Even in the Union Hotel, surrounded by two hundred undressed men, Mary had not felt as vulnerable as she did now.

The woman grabbed Mary by the elbow. "I'll show you. Come on."

The snow was coming on strong now. Traffic thronged the streets. Drivers were shouting and whipping the air above the backs of the horses, loath to inflict pain, but frustrated enough to threaten. In Albany, drivers would have switched to sleighs, but it seemed that no one used a sleigh in the city. Or they had all gotten caught in the storm. The horsecars were packed solid, men hanging out the doors. They were covering blocks now, the wind having abated some.

They came to an intersection where the woman halted and directed a thrust of her chin across the street. "This is Hudson Street. The depot is straight on, a few blocks or so. I can't remember for sure." She staggered away, snow swirling around her as she disappeared into the night. Mary darted across the intersection, zigzagging between horses and carts. The cross streets came at an angle now. Worth, Thomas, Duane. As she stumbled across one street, a huge locomotive loomed out of the storm to her right. A great iron beast, it was inching forward down tracks laid in the middle of the street. Cabbies and wagon drivers panicked and beat the backs of their horses now to get out of the way, while a man on horseback preceding the engine swung a warning lantern, yelling for people to move, goddamn it, or risk dying. A policeman was blowing his whistle in short, shrill blasts. Mary stumbled on, threading through the jumbled traffic, following the path of the train, until the depot reared up, black and comforting. It was little more than a shed, really, meant to turn the trains and send them back north again, though now it was crammed with people who had given up trying to make it to 32nd Street. That morning, Stipp had taken her by the hands, and said, *Take care, now.* It seemed forever ago. Mary gathered herself and shoved through the press of people elbowing and fighting to get to the ticket window, where a harried clerk behind his cage leaned forward to field complaints, his head cocked, his eyes pressed together in a tight squint. The walls reverberated with shouts. Unable to hear what anyone was saying, Mary watched person after person turn disgustedly away from the window.

After about fifteen minutes, she fought to the coveted space in front of the grille.

"Are the trains going?"

"No."

"But I just saw one arriving."

"Have you seen it outside, Miss? It's a blizzard."

"What about tomorrow?"

"Can't say."

"I have to get home."

"Everyone wants to get home. It's Christmas."

"Could you at least sell me a ticket?"

The man pursed his lips and shook his head. "Come back tomorrow at daylight. If there are any trains, I'll start selling tickets then."

Outside, mired carriages and omnibuses had been abandoned in the drifts. The flickering yellow light of gaslamps barely illuminated a string of swinging signs that advertised a row of boarding houses and hotels. Convincing herself that nothing could be worse than the Union Hotel, Mary set out to find shelter.

# Chapter Thirty-three

Amelia let the parlor curtain fall. Last night, at the height of the storm, a telegraph messenger had pounded on the door and presented her with a telegram from Mary. *Home tonight.* Now it was two o'clock in the afternoon the following day, and Mary still had not arrived, though this morning not even the maids had come from their homes in the Sixth Ward, half a mile away.

"Amelia?" Bonnie hovered in the doorway of the parlor, her hand trembling on the jamb, her face a white snowscape of fear.

Amelia leapt for the stairs.

In Jenny's room, the window shades had been drawn against the sharp edges of the December light. Jenny was curled into a ball, the unmistakable pallor of labor stretched across her face, her dress wet through with perspiration.

"Oh, Jenny, you should have called me. How long has it been?" Amelia asked, easing herself onto Jenny's bed, laying her hands on her daughter's belly.

"An hour or so. I don't know for certain."

"The pains are not too bad?" Amelia asked, instantly angry with herself for having fallen prey to the mistake of asking for the answer she wanted. This was why she needed Mary.

Jenny shook her head. "No, not too bad."

Amelia said, "Help me, Bonnie."

Supporting Jenny by the elbows, they helped her to the lying-in room and removed her wet dress and eased her into a dry nightgown. After settling Jenny in, Amelia busied herself around the room, refolding towels, rearranging her basins and instruments, and counting how many babies she had delivered over the twenty-three years of her career. Over three hundred? More, maybe. And so few deaths. She knew everyone said she was the best, a reputation that brought her business, but the judgment was not really anyone's to confer, except perhaps hers. Mary was the best. Mary, who was stuck somewhere between Washington and home on a train, like Christian had been, on his way home to safety, to her arms, which felt as empty now as the mother of a stillborn's. A baby coming and then not coming. But no, she couldn't think that way. Fear bred nothing but more fear. And she needed her wits about her now. What could she control? The atmosphere in the room, the way she moved, spoke, modulated, conveying safety to the laboring mother. She tried to convince herself that the girl in the bed was not her daughter. She began again to recheck her supplies, keeping her back turned, thinking that by touching objects—basin, stethoscope, laudanum vial, scissors—she could shed her skin of motherhood and find the midwife instead.

Jenny's cry, at first soft but then rising, filled the vast spaces of the house on Dove Street.

Amelia shut her eyes. She was not ready yet. Louder and louder Jenny's cry swelled. And then, mercifully, it fell off and became a small gasp that diminished to a whimper while Amelia, her back still turned, wiped tears from her cheeks.

The train rocked as it crept up Eleventh Avenue, past the stockyards and lumberyards and the open-doored abattoirs that lined the river. To keep warm, the livestock bunched together as steam swirled from their nostrils into the brilliant glint of day. The car's coal heater had begun to work and Mary wiped her window to clear the condensation. Every seat was filled, and more people swayed in the aisles.

At dawn, Mary had joined the long line at the ticket window. It seemed hours before a single ticket seller lifted his black curtain and several more before, one by one, the winding line's occupants fell away and it was finally her turn.

"Albany, eh?" It was the same man from the night before. Calmly, he thumbed through a ticket book, working his lips, counting. He consulted a piece of paper with tallies scribbled in columns. Then he said, "It'll be tight," but filled out her destination and the date and handed her the ticket.

"Be at that door at noon," he said, nodding toward the corner of the building. "That should give them enough time to clear the tracks."

But Mary joined the several others who had already planted themselves in line, even though it was only seven. She was not going to risk waiting until noon, was not going to wander outside in search of warm chestnuts for her hands or something to eat, was not going to miss the train and risk another night like last night.

She had tried five hotels before knocking on the door of a sixth, a rooming house, its shabbiness apparent despite the darkness.

"Beds were taken hours ago," the clerk said. He wiped his dripping nose. It was cold inside too, and there was no sign of a stove or fireplace, to say nothing of a handkerchief.

"I'll sit up in the lobby," Mary said.

"Bed count's the bed count. The city commissioners would have my hide if they was to come in here and see I'd let in more folks than we had beds for. And a woman at that." He sniffed and ran his gaze up and down her form.

Mary could feel the pressure rise in her head. She had left Washington on the early train, had eaten only a peppered beef stick in Philadelphia, could no longer feel her feet or ears. She leaned toward the man in his little cubicle of an office and said, "Do you really think that the city commissioners are going to leave their warm homes and come to this boarding house out of all the boarding houses in Manhattan City and fine you for letting me sit up in a chair?"

Confusion raged across the man's angular, ragged features; he was a creature of the night, guarding his squalid hotel with illogic. "Maybe. Besides, we don't rent to a woman alone."

Mary leaned in closer. "I don't know how you think you can stop me."

"I can think of a few ways."

"When I came in just now, there were two policemen on the corner, digging out their wagon. I will go right now to the door and scream that you have harmed me. Is that what you want?"

The man sniffed, but glanced furtively toward the door. "Two dollars," he said.

The posted rate was twenty-five cents. Mary fished fifty cents from her purse and dropped the coins onto the counter. The clerk fingered them as Mary pulled together two chairs and stretched out her legs, her feet firmly encased in her sodden boots, resigned to spending the entire night awake.

Now, on the train, she was ravenous and cold, but she had a seat. And they were finally leaving the city behind, the tenements and ironworks having given way to wilderness and farms. There were a dozen whistle stops between here and Albany. At each, there would be comings and goings, and luggage to load and unload. When she got to Albany, she would have to cross the river. Everything would take time.

The train tracks ran alongside the Hudson, which was three times as wide here at its mouth as it was at Albany, its temperature buffered by the salty tides that thrust themselves twice a day up the river's channel. But when they reached the Catskills, the river would shallow out, and the water would freeze.

As the train pushed northward, the river's current began to slow, but only Mary Sutter perceived it.

"Oh, Jenny, try, honey. Try."

"I can't."

"Yes, you can."

"It hurts. Please. Oh God. It hurts."

"You have to push."

"I feel like I'm tearing open."

"You aren't. Everyone feels that way, but you aren't."

"Mother, if I don't make it name her Elizabeth."

"Don't be silly, darling. You'll name her yourself."

"And if it's a boy, Thomas."

Jenny let out a cry. Amelia had registered every one of them in her gut. Her daughter had been in labor for eight hours. Not long at all, by any standard. But the pain seemed impossible. At least Jenny reported it so. The dreaded back labor. Poor Bonnie, her hands ached from massaging the muscles along Jenny's spinal column in an effort to alleviate the pain. And now Jenny had to push. So soon! Could that possibly be right?

The room, which had seemed so cold before, was now far too warm. Amelia rinsed a cloth and laid it on Jenny's forehead, but Jenny ripped it away. Her moans rose as Amelia entreated her to push and Bonnie to apply more pressure to her back. Forty-five seconds. Jenny began to scream.

Amelia waited until the contraction passed before saying, "Honey, you're not pushing."

"I *am.*"

Amelia assessed her daughter. Pale, tremulous, exhausted; there was something else wrong.

Amelia slathered her right hand with lard and slipped it inside the warmth of Jenny's body. In her agitation, Jenny tried to push her away, like so many women did at the height of their labor, but Bonnie pinned Jenny's wrists and bent down and whispered in her ear. To concentrate, Amelia averted her head, her fingers feeling their way inside for the cervix. Dilated, completely; Amelia was certain of it. Slowly, she turned her wrist, gently running her fingers over the baby's skull, feeling for where ridges met plates, where the V of the baby's occipital bone met the stretched tissue, verifying, relieved that at least the baby was in the proper position. With another twist of her wrist, she attempted to intuit the diameter of the outlet of Jenny's pelvis. Greater than four inches? Less than three? But trying to discern its size was a futile act, even for Amelia, who had coaxed from pelvises narrower than Jenny's babies of enormous size. Amelia withdrew her hand. No matter what the size of Jenny's pelvis, the baby was too big.

Accustomed to panic in others, she hardly knew how to manage it in herself.

She forced herself to take conscious control of her breathing, but she could do nothing about her hands, which were trembling at her sides. The clock was striking nine o'clock. She must have run up and down the stairs twenty times already, flinging open the front door, looking up and down the street, hoping to see her resourceful Mary climbing from a sleigh, valise in hand, bringing her good mind with her. But now it was too late to expect her; no trains ever arrived this late into Albany.

"Bonnie. Come with me."

Outside the shut door, Amelia said, "Listen to me, Bonnie. You must help me. I want you to go to Eagle Street, and find the doctor on call at the hospital. Make certain you ask if he has used forceps, do you understand? Say it. Forceps."

"Forceps."

"And tell him to bring chloroform. And if he won't do it, then you make him tell you who will and where he lives and then you go there and get that doctor. Do you understand?"

Bonnie's eyes grew wide with dread.

"Take my lantern and go as fast as you can. And don't give up until you find someone. I need you to think clearly. Be smart about this. Threaten them, if you have to."

"How do I do that?"

"Tell them it's for Mary Sutter."

Lithe, quick, Bonnie darted off like hope.

On a day in good weather, hurrying, it would take Bonnie ten minutes afoot to get to the hospital. With the snow, half an hour. And then to find and persuade the surgeon? Another fifteen minutes or half hour, when a minute was already passing like an eternity.

"Hurry," Amelia said, but she said it to the air, for Bonnie had already gone.

At the lying-in room door, Amelia hesitated. Her last resort. A doctor and forceps. She did not want to think what the doctor might do to Jenny with those forceps. How many women had bled to death because of doctors' eager machinations? And the dreaded chloroform would ease Jenny's pain, but it would also make her unable to fight.

Either way, Jenny was in trouble.

The injustice might drive her mad, if she let it.

Another cry shattered the air.

Amelia swept in and poured as much laudanum as she dared into Jenny's mouth, though the opiate was a trick, because it didn't really dull the pain so much as make a woman incapable of coping with the contractions. Weakness, to give in, but Jenny's shrieks broke her heart. If Jenny was going to die, then Amelia didn't want her to die in agony. Perspiration cooled from Jenny's body. Amelia washed her down, then covered her up again. She snatched up Jenny's hand when she began to moan, forcing herself to keep her eyes open to witness the battle.

A candle sputtered and then extinguished. Outside, the perennial hush of winter. Inside, Christian's ghost, stalking them.

An hour passed. Two. Amelia bargained down. Jenny might live. She might not. What mattered most was that Jenny knew she wasn't alone.

Mary elbowed her way out of the train car. Ten hours. Ten. The longest a train had ever taken to travel from Manhattan City to Albany. Savagely, she cut through the milling passengers, made numb by the trip and the weather and the cold. At the line of hacks, she cut off negotiations between a man and a cabbie by climbing in and barking, "Dove Street."

The cabbie pretended to be miffed, but he was delighted. The other passenger had been relaying tales of trunks and ladies in need and a wait of perhaps half an hour. "I'll be back," he yelled, as he whipped his sleigh forward.

The river ice had been cleared earlier that day by boys in caps and on skates, pushing shovels along the ferry path so that the sleighs could avoid the ice cutters' holes in the dark. The lantern made a moon of yellow as the sleigh scraped and bumped across the windswept ridges of ice. Albany loomed before her and then they were in the city, flying up State Street, the coal smoke sharp in the frigid air, wood smoke mixing in, the eerie glow of firelight visible through windows. The Gayety Music Hall was just emptying out, and the cabbie resolved to stop there next, for he did not want to go back again across that river. He sped around the bend of Eagle Street. Mary, huddled under the sled robe, marked the outline of the medical school and hospital, glowering against a shroud of black.

At home, no flurry in black dress and white apron emerged to greet her. A single candle burned in a sconce. Melted snow puddled on the floor of the entryway; a pair of galoshes, a man's coat flung across the newel post. A creak, upstairs. And then, muffled shouting.

Mary flew up the stairs. The door to the lying-in room stood open, and at its jamb stood Bonnie, her head turned away from the door, hand to her mouth, an expression of panic distorting her face. The sickly sweet smell of chloroform mingled with the sourness of sweat. On the bed kneeled a man who had planted one knee between Jenny's splayed legs. He was gripping silver handles that disappeared into Jenny.

*Forceps.*

Jenny's mouth was gaping, her eyes staring unseeing at the ceiling. Amelia, her hands clapped to her face, hovered on the far side of the bed, blood splatters staining her white apron. For a moment, Mary could not act. Time, her enemy all day, now betrayed her again by slowing further. A maddening sluggishness seized her. She could not move, could not think fast enough to understand what she was seeing.

*Forceps. A surgeon.*

As if through water, or blood, Amelia slowly shifted her gaze from one daughter to the long-awaited one standing at the door. Apparition of hope, as if to mock.

But then Mary moved. No, not moved: leapt.

She flung aside her shawl and said, "Are the forceps helping? Are you getting anywhere?"

"Damn it, I don't know." Echoes of Dr. Stipp.

"But is the baby coming down?"

The man turned; he was young, as young as Mary, his beard still straggly, sweat streaming down his temples. "Who *are* you?"

"I am Mary Sutter."

His arms, working furiously, now stopped. "You're Mary Sutter?" he said.

"I am."

For a brief moment, he hesitated, then he climbed from the bed for the midwife about whom his mother spoke so highly, and Mary scrambled into his place, blood soaking through her skirt as her knee sank into his place.

"How do I get these things out?"

"If you don't apply continuous traction the baby will slip back," he warned, but nonetheless showed her how to unhinge the forceps, directing her how to angle them as she withdrew them to keep them from crushing the baby's skull, clucking all the while that they were losing all the traction he had just gained.

Accustomed now to chloroformed men, Mary was nonetheless shocked to see Jenny so lifeless, her legs heavy and unmoving on the bed. Naked, exposed, her swollen breasts dwarfed by the tight mound of her gravid belly, she lay as if left for dead on a battlefield. Quickly, Mary felt for the femoral artery and a fluttering but persistent beat reassured her. Then, as Amelia had done hours before, she inserted her hand into Jenny's body, navigating slowly, trying to locate the cervix and the baby's head and the hard ring of the bones of the pelvis in the wreckage of flesh torn by the forceps. Nothing felt normal. She imagined it was what Stipp felt, trying to retrieve a bullet from a ruined thigh.

"It will make no difference what you feel, the baby will have slipped back," the doctor said.

"I could open her pelvis. Unhinge it at the notch," Mary said. "I could, couldn't I?"

The doctor, who until that moment had delivered only ten babies in his one year as a physician, took in the ragged, exhausted woman before him and felt a wave of hope flood through him. "We could."

"Did you bring anything? A scalpel, a knife?" Mary asked.

From his satchel, he pulled a rolled case of flannel and, fumbling, extracted a short knife that Mary seized from him.

"Let me—" the doctor began.

"No," Mary said, because she was already beginning to reconstruct in her mind the colored diagram of a pelvis from *Gray's Anatomy*: the oval sphere of bone, joined at the front at the symphysis by the penetrable cushion of cartilage that formed Jenny's impinged, narrow outlet. It was perhaps an act of faith to trust a diagram, but it was no more an act of faith than Dr. Stipp's trust in her, reading instructions to him in the dining room of a dirty hovel of a hotel, an act that now seemed wildly tame compared to this. How she wished him here, performing the same mercy for her, his fingers flipping through pages, reading her instructions, imbuing her with confidence.

Anchoring her fingers in a V at the bottom of the swell of Jenny's belly, Mary searched for the exact place to insert the knife, feeling for the sponge of cartilage she could see in her mind's eye. Discovering the depression, she touched the knife to Jenny's skin and pushed the sharp tip through. Blood began to stream from the incision. Jenny groaned, rousing from the chloroform, her back arching, but Mary let her hand rise with her, the two now as connected as they had once been in the womb. She kept pushing, until the knife reached the cartilage. The resistance was shocking. She understood now why Dr. Stipp became exhausted and sweaty during amputations. What force it took to dismantle a human being. Then a sudden, satisfactory pop, and the two halves of Jenny's pelvis disengaged. Mary pulled out the knife and screamed at Jenny to push.

The next hour dissolved, melted away by work and fight. While Mary exhorted Jenny to push, slapping and screaming to rouse her, the doctor used suture and needle in between contractions to sew her up. Five stitches, seven? He lost count, but it didn't matter, because he would never be able to cement the bone back together. This young woman might never walk again.

Blood soaked through the sheets, through Mary's dress, through the pillows and comforters, through Amelia's apron.

The baby, a livid shade of blue, finally squeezed from between Jenny's legs.

Immediately, Mary hooked two fingers through the infant's mouth to clear it, then snatched up the baby and turned it onto its belly, balancing it in her palm. A tablespoon of yellowish fluid drained from the baby's mouth. Flipping the child back over, Mary fingered the chin and puckered lips, which were growing cool and ghostly. She held the baby upside down by its feet and slapped its bottom, taking deep enough breaths for the two of them.

She noticed the baby was a girl. Jenny had a daughter.

Mary heard Bonnie crying beside her. Bonnie, the expert in babies who had died, Bonnie, whose former grief now seemed a contagion.

Amelia, broken free of her terror, was tugging gently on the cord. The doctor had stepped back to gather padding and blankets. The placenta slithered out. Amelia snipped the cord and the baby was free. Mary wrapped the baby in a blanket, the baby crying as if she had always known how to cry. Her head was battered, misshapen. But she was alive. A grateful sob broke from someone's mouth; they would never be able to determine whose.

Jenny's legs were trembling: the shock after the trauma. But then the trembling spread from her legs to her torso and to her arms. Spasms shook her whole body. Her face was flushed, but her eyes blank. They rolled back in her head and the convulsions quickened, until every muscle was contorting in disconnected rhythm. Too late to put something in her mouth. Too late to hold her head.

"Shouldn't we bleed her?" Amelia said.

The doctor said, "She's bled enough."

The seizure went on forever. There was nothing to do but wait it out.

When Jenny's body finally came to rest—one, ten minutes later?—Mary touched her fingers to Jenny's wrist.

But the artery no longer pulsed.

# *Chapter Thirty-four*

At the cemetery, a sharp wind howled. The single sleigh and the dray carrying Jenny's coffin had nearly foundered in the drifts at the base of the Menands hill, where it had left behind the icy highway of the Hudson for the ponderous climb up to the Albany Rural Cemetery. Mary had long ago lost feeling in her feet; the heating brick had cooled almost as soon as the sleigh's runners had begun to skim the river ice. Now the horses heaved as they came to rest outside the twin keeping vaults set into the hill, the fog of the animals' exertions rising in the otherwise clear, biting cold. No mourners from the funeral had joined them; Bonnie had refused to leave the baby. In the black branches of a nearby hawthorn bush, a cardinal was flitting from limb to limb, its scarlet beauty against the black-and-white skeleton of winter's sleep seeming somehow merciless, a beauty so stark it seemed to define death.

In the far distance, heavy drifts buried Christian's and Nathaniel's headstones and blocked the paths; Mary and Amelia would not be able to visit them today. Neither would the drifts allow Jenny to be put into the ground beside her brother and father, for not until April or May would the spring thaw render the soil permeable. Four coffin bearers, who had followed their small funeral cortege from the gatehouse, unloaded Jenny's coffin from the dray and struggled through the deep snow toward the vaults. Mary reached for Amelia's hand as they followed behind, wading through the drifts, their black crepe skirts dragging behind, and to Mary's great relief, Amelia took it, the first tenderness she had allowed since Jenny's death. Even just a couple of hours ago in the church, she had stood stiff-spined in the pew to pray, her gaze fixed straight ahead, reluctant, or unwilling, to acknowledge the mutuality of their despair. But as soon as they reached the vault door and had climbed the wedge of snow that blocked more than one entrant at a time, Amelia broke their grasp, which she did not allow to be renewed.

Inside the vault, the bearers had set Jenny's coffin on the floor to light a few candles, which threw ghostly shadows on the series of arches rising in religious splendor from the cobbled and stone floor. Wooden racks filled the room, a hundred caskets were already shelved three deep, with room for hundreds more. The winter's dead. The vault's confines were redolent with mold, but Mary could still smell the black dye in which she had boiled her dress: once to rid it of the bloodstains, a second time to render it this color of night. The double act echoed Jenny's new plight: to be buried once in this chamber, once again in the ground. A twin burial. Icicles hung from ceiling cracks; a cold womb, the company of strangers. As one, the bearers lifted Jenny's coffin from the floor and heaved it into place alongside another, a thud echoing in the chamber as the far end of her coffin hit the stone wall. Amelia began to weep.

Mary swayed in place; she was bludgeoned, exhausted; mere fatigue had passed long ago. Manhattan, the dirge of a train ride, Jenny's death: in between then and now, only two days, but a desert still.

Amelia had barely spoken to Mary since the night Jenny died.

After the doctor had left the house, Mary had whisked the infant from the lying-in room to the parlor, where she frantically tried to comfort the crying child. Because of the blizzard, they could not send for a wet nurse until dawn and the child would not be soothed; she sucked furiously at Mary's finger, only to break off and wail when no milk sprang from it. Even sugar water was not helping; the child refused the rubber nipple. Cold was knifing through the window cracks and floorboards. Only the fire threw light. Upstairs, Bonnie consoled herself by bathing Jenny's body.

Amelia suffered on the divan, watching Mary struggle. She barely recognized her daughter. Severe, dull, angular, her large eyes prominent, her shoulders sharp under her dress, her chin carved to a delicate point. Starvation and work had whittled away the meat of her and left only a skeleton behind. Amelia could barely register the deprivation Mary must have suffered in Washington. The world had changed utterly: Christian gone,

Jenny gone. And now Mary was half her self. She was, if anything, the picture of death.

Futility, to govern one's children. Futility, even, to try to save them. Amelia's hands curled in her lap. An old woman's hands, no longer able to pluck life from death.

Mary was bouncing the crying child in her arms, cradling her to her chest, trying the bottle again and again. The folds of her skirts were still soaked with Jenny's blood.

It was all wrong. Grief curdled, became something else. Amelia marked the change, felt it rise up in her.

"You didn't come home," she said, beginning, yielding. She shouldn't, she thought, but the young are stupid and headstrong, and Mary hadn't listened.

Mary had been waiting, holding back. Centuries had gone by, it had seemed, as the infant had cried. "I tried, I did. I wanted to be here—the train, the snow, you don't know what I did." The caged excuses burst forth; but they did not assuage Mary's own sense of guilt. Stipp had known: *Go home.* She had, but it was too late.

"I wrote to you half a dozen times; I told you I couldn't do this alone. You ignored me. You knew I needed you, that Jenny needed you." The satisfaction of anger, superseding reason, grief. A coup in Amelia's heart, her unshakable generosity of spirit dislodged in a moment by boiling righteousness. Mary had lost a sister, a brother, but it was not the same as losing a child.

"But you are a midwife—"

"I am her mother." *Am. Was.* Amelia shut her eyes. Only one remaining child and a grandchild. But she pressed on, driven by despair. She had foreseen what would happen, had known she would need help. She had even asked for it, had begged Mary for it. Injury of a specific, intimate kind. She would just say it. "If you had come when I asked, Jenny would still be alive."

Mary nearly buckled, would have, but for the baby in her arms. "You blame me?" She had not wanted to hear this aloud, because in restraint there was always the possibility of generosity. She rocked the baby back and forth, as if she were trying to protect her from the story of her own birth. First to the right, then to the left, Mary shifted, light and then shadow falling onto her face.

"You, more than anyone, know how good you are."

They were both standing now, shouting to be heard over the baby, whose cries seemed the repudiation of life itself. Amelia's face eschewed sorrow for fury and indignation. The satisfaction of anger. Later she would regret everything, but latent remorse would not repair the damage. For all the things we say to our children for their own good, very little good ever comes of it.

"Mother, I had to stay in Washington. You would have, too." Justification, a well of it. Her only defense. "You should see the men. I can't describe it. It's as if hell has come to visit."

"You claim need as your excuse? That is all? Nothing of Jenny having Thomas's child? Nothing of the obligations of family? Thomas never loved you, Mary, he loved Jenny. I thought that would have been plain enough even for you to see."

Mary gasped. How much her mother knew.

"What did you say to him, Mary, when he came to see you? Why didn't you tell him about Jenny?"

"It was her news to tell! I didn't know he would reenlist!"

"If you'd just told him—"

"Then what? Then Jenny would still be alive?"

"Yes. If Thomas were here, then you would have come home, and we could have done something for Jenny, we could have saved her."

Was it true? If Thomas had come home, would she have come home too? Would she have fled the misery and work of Washington? She didn't know anymore. But she did know that if she had been home, she would have given Jenny ergot, would have induced labor, would have forced an early birth.

"Why didn't you come home?" Amelia asked.

*Because of the baby she cradled in her arms now.*

None of Mary's experience, expertise, control, and distance were of any help to her now. Neither could she detach herself from this porcelain baby, whose eyes, nose, chin, and mouth resembled not so much Thomas or Jenny as herself, a trick of heritage that verged on the cruel. But the resemblance could have been a trick of her mind. *This is how hearts are broken,* Mary thought. By love and allegiance gone awry.

"Because I want to be a surgeon. I couldn't do it here. Don't you see?" Pale substantiation. Florid truth. Yes, she had loved, envied, but there had been other, valid reasons. "I want to be a surgeon."

"What you want. Nothing should be about what you want. Not when your family is concerned."

"No? Family? Once you didn't come back home when you said you would. Father suffered for years thinking he had abandoned us. But it was you who had left us, you who didn't come back."

The past as predatory ghost; Amelia's worst mistake, come back to haunt her. "Mary, you of all people should know why I couldn't get away. That woman was dying."

"Well, I couldn't get away either," Mary said. "Men are dying; they are boys like Christian." Tears burned. Latent grief newly roused. "I had to choose, Mother, like you had to choose. We are the same."

"We are not the same. It was not you who was dying that morning. Jenny is your sister."

Cold gripped the house, entombing them. The fire flickered, cowering before the elements. Shouting at one another was a divide across which they had never before ventured. Even so, Mary longed for Amelia to scream on. Anger was the salve, the bond, the cement. The only remedy to the unacceptable breach.

How women defeat one another; how need defeats women.

But Amelia did not forgive. Instead, she began to whisper, as if she were speaking to Mary at the age of two, crying in that crib, the house empty.

"You are who you are because of me," Amelia said. "All I wanted was for you to come home. I needed you, Mary. I needed you. And after that day, I never left you alone. That is why you are who you are. That is why you even want to be a surgeon now. That's why you could have saved Jenny."

"You expect too much of me."

"No, I don't. If you are skilled, more is required of you, not less." A compliment, but she said it as a question, as if she were trying to understand her daughter, trying to understand how they had come to this, the two of them at loggerheads. "I trusted you," Amelia said.

Outside, the night crackled. Snow pellets hammered the windows. A gust of wind flew down the chimney and the baby, as if bewitched, finally descended into an exhausted silence.

Bonnie could hear Amelia and Mary shouting downstairs, the baby crying. She had attempted to mop the floor clean, but even when she thought she had washed away all the blood, the water was still stained pink. None of what had happened tonight made sense to her. Her feet were still numb from running through the snow. At the medical school, the night watchman had directed her to the hospital, where she had pleaded with another guard until he sent her to a house a block away. She had pounded on the door until the doctor emerged. The night was dark, the wind blowing, the horses skittish, the doctor swearing as he tried to follow her directions, the gaslamps giving barely enough light to navigate Washington Avenue. "Here!" she had cried at the turn to Dove Street. She had rushed into the house, dragging him behind her, presenting him to Amelia as the ultimate gift, and then—wretchedness. Unimaginable horror.

Now Bonnie lifted each heavy limb tenderly, gently, turning them as the washcloth glided over the skin, the water dripping first down Jenny's arm, then her thighs. There was still her back to do, and then she had to take out the mess of wet sheets and rubber blanket from underneath her and dress her properly and do her hair. Her skin was already beginning to mottle, and her arms and legs had begun to harden. Like Bonnie's baby, just nine months ago.

Could envy kill a person? She had wanted a baby, and now a motherless baby wept downstairs. She had wanted Christian, too, and he had died. What had she done, with all her wanting?

Downstairs, they were still shouting, the baby still crying. And then, abruptly, silence. There was the whisper of Amelia's steps on the stairs, and then Amelia came into the room with the baby in her arms and saw Jenny laid out, exposed, half bathed, the mop and bucket in the corner with the water still pink, and Bonnie, the wet washcloth in her hands.

Bonnie said, "I'm sorry," but Amelia hushed her and gave her the baby and took the washcloth from her.

The infant's eyes were swollen, flowering bruises. Imperfect in life, as her own child had been perfect in death. It was as if time were repeating itself, making up for its mistakes.

The baby was so tired, Bonnie thought. Yes, so tired, as if it had been hard, hard work to be born.

Amelia heard Bonnie cooing, heard the joy in her voice, as she would never again hear Christian or Jenny. It was as if she had forgotten what joy sounded like, so strange was the noise to her ears.

# *Chapter Thirty-five*

At the train depot, Amelia said, "You must find Thomas and tell him."

Mary was taking the 1:15 express to Manhattan. She had stayed in Albany a month, long enough to see the baby thrive, the baby who peered out with serious eyes from the bundled blankets in which she spent her days, toted from place to place by Bonnie, who gave her up only to the wet nurse and then with visible reluctance.

"Thomas will want to know everything," Amelia said.

"Yes."

"You'll tell him what happened." Implying, *your part in it*. Implying that he, too, would blame Mary.

"Yes," Mary said.

"You won't leave anything out," Amelia said from the sleigh as Mary climbed down.

"No. I won't leave anything out."

Amelia nodded a noncommittal acknowledgment, barely perceptible behind her mourning veil. After they had entombed Jenny at the cemetery, Mary had collapsed. Even then, Amelia had maintained her distance; an evening and a morning visit to her bedside to coolly assess her surviving daughter's general health. Exhaustion, the indifferent diagnosis. Mary barely recognized her mother now, so altered was her approach. They were the North and the South; betrayal complete. In her stupor, Mary had dreamed of cardinals and hawthorn bushes. Of Jenny, alone and cold.

The locomotive spit steam. The conductors, who had taken Mary's bag, were blowing their whistles, waving their arms for everyone to hurry on board. Mary raised her hand as if to forestall the train, though the plume of steam from the smokestack was already rising into the brilliant winter day. Amelia could be anyone, could be a stranger, so stiffly she held herself.

"Do you want me to stay, Mother? I'll stay."

"Do as you like."

Indifference, the final, parting wound.

Mary boarded the train, taking a seat on the river side, because she could not trust herself not to press her palm against the window and with her sorrow persuade Amelia that if she could have bent time, she would have, would even have stopped the weather, would have reversed even the direction of the earth's revolutions to have saved Jenny.

As the train surged forward, she forced herself to look across the river to Albany, where the frozen Erie Canal locks hung like guillotines and the Lumber District's white pine towered brown in the anemic snowscape. Coal smoke blackened a thousand chimneys of the glittering Dutch houses squatting in order up the hill. From a distance, Tweddle Hall imposed; a coffin of memory.

To be dismissed by Amelia, no quarter for reconciliation given.

The train was traveling quickly around the bends of the river now, the thicket of bushes between the tracks and the water, skeletons of black against the alabaster snow.

The train sounded an alarm, an exalted, pulsing warning that reminded Mary of Jenny's cries.

# Chapter Thirty-six

"You want a what?"

"A transit pass to Fort Marcy. And some means of conveyance."

"What do you want at Fort Marcy?"

"It doesn't matter. If you can't help me, perhaps I'd better go see the surgeon general." Mary picked up her bag, which felt heavy after the long hours of travel. Manhattan City, Philadelphia, Baltimore, she remembered little of the trip as the trains rocked in interminable, halting passage toward Washington. "Will it take long, do you think? The afternoon, maybe? What time is it?"

Stipp gripped Mary by the shoulders, his hands almost bruising her in his alarm. How diminished she seemed. She had lost more weight in New York. He had expected to have her return fortified, but the sharp jut of her chin had become even more pronounced, her eyes more sunken. "Tell me what happened."

"I separated the symphysis pubis, but it made no difference. A doctor had already ripped her to shreds with forceps. She bled." She stopped then, unable to say that Jenny had died. "I was too late."

He watched her carefully, seeing the uncertainty and doubt. Perhaps it had been unwise to insist that she go. He was still holding her by the shoulders, as if to keep her standing, as if to help her fight remorse. The work of grief.

"And the baby?"

"A girl. She has a wet nurse. She's thriving."

"How is your mother?"

"She blames me."

And then it dawned on Stipp why Mary needed the pass, why she needed to go to Fort Marcy. The post. "You need to tell your brother-in-law."

"Yes."

Mary was exquisite in her suffering, her face wretched with pain. Stipp reached out a hand to touch her cheek. Her skin was luminous even in the failing winter light.

"I'll go with you," Stipp said.

He called Mrs. Philipateaux to take Mary to her room, then he got on his horse and traveled through the evening light to demand two passes to take him and Mary to Fort Marcy in two days' time. On a street corner, a newspaper boy was waving headlines about McDowell's ongoing testimony before the Joint Committee on the Conduct of the War.

The army clerk was recalcitrant, citing the dozen regulations the surgeon was insisting he break. Then he handed over the paperwork and made Stipp sign it himself, absolving himself of any responsibility in the matter at all. What did it matter if the fool of a man wanted to traipse around the countryside and get shot at by Rebels? The roads were a disaster. They would have to go by horseback and bypass all the regular routes. They might even get shot at by the guards on duty at the Chain Bridge, ever ready to defend Washington from the threat of invasion. Yes, the clerk thought, the man could go if he wanted, but he wanted nothing to do with it.

Thomas's boots sank to his ankles as he traversed the open yard between the log and earthen walls of Fort Marcy. The sky was spitting rain and his cheeks were chapped and reddened. Under his coat, he carried his latest ration of bread, stale as a doorstop.

God, how he wanted to go home. He had heard nothing from Jenny, and now he lacked even paper or ink to write and ask whether or not he had become a father. That life had come to this: paper a luxury, though even if he had paper, he no longer had any money to pay for the post. They had not been paid in some time. He regretted everything, but mostly he regretted that moment when he had climbed from the horsecar outside the Department of the Army and gone in and reenlisted. What had he done since? Freeze and starve and learn the true meaning of deprivation. For the Army of the Potomac, entrenched on the shores of the river after which it was named, had not fought since Manassas. George McClellan, the answer to the North's eagerness to bring the war to a conclusion, had instead imposed a long period of preparation, which for Thomas and the troops at Fort Marcy had turned into month after month of boredom.

Up the hill behind him between the rows of tents, a corporal was calling, "Thomas Fall. Thomas Fall. Anyone seen Thomas Fall?" When Thomas hailed him, the corporal said, "I was told to find you. Come on."

The log guardhouse housed a desk and a guard who stepped outside when Thomas came in. Inside, two figures waited in the dim light.

"Thomas."

An upswell of joy fought to the surface, but just as quickly ebbed, though he did not understand at first why. Neither could he say, precisely, what about Mary's appearance frightened him most. In the dim light, he could make out that she was still far too thin, too serious, and that her gaze harbored pity and dread, and something of guilt, but not compassion. No. That was reserved for the man who stood beside her. *Stipp.* That was his name. The doctor at the hotel.

Later, Mary would not recall even saying hello, offering greetings, or inquiring after Thomas's health.

For so many years, she had given people bad news, and now she had an agonizing memory of delivering the truth fast and unvarnished. *The baby is dead*, or *Your wife is dead*. What arrogance she had entertained, that she had believed she knew how to say such things to people. Now, in the bleak cold of the dismal guardhouse, she said, "I've been home, Thomas."

Her voice broke as she measured her next words, telling the story she had gone over a hundred times in her mind, keeping her gaze fixed on Thomas's face.

When she was finished, Thomas sank to his knees. For a long moment, he stayed there as if in prayer, his shoulders hunched forward, his hands obscuring his face, and though his silence cut through the cold air like a scalpel, Mary's feet refused to move. Outside, the fort went about its clatter and nonsense. Through the small window, Mary glimpsed the ruined landscape through which she and Stipp had traveled, the clear-cut forest, the exposed stumps naked in devastation, the ribs and barbs of the newly constructed wooden barricades piercing the cold air, the troughs and trenches that spidered away from the fort, a corduroy road made of logs sinking into the sea of muck.

Thomas's words floated toward her, as if they too were mired in the same muddy sea.

"If you'd have gone home earlier, when Amelia wanted you to, could you have saved her?" he asked.

Jenny's face surged before Mary. If she had left even a week earlier, two, perhaps Thomas would not be asking her this. She would have been there from the start, could say now yes or no, definitively.

"I don't know," she said.

She took a step toward him, but he held up his hands.

She stood in the center of the room as the wind sliced through the chinked logs and rendered the room as cold as the outdoors.

"I'm sorry—"

"Don't," Thomas said, shaking his head. "Don't."

"Bonnie is there. She is good with the baby, Thomas. She is gentle, and generous—"

"I said, don't."

Mary put her hand to the desk to steady herself. "Why didn't you go home, Thomas? You could have seen her, you could have had time with her before—"

"We all want too much, don't we?"

"I beg your pardon?" Mary said, but it was as if Thomas were echoing her nightmares, as if he had read every single thought of hers on the train ride back. She could feel Stipp behind her, straining to protect her from the truth.

"Glory, honor, ambition. What are these worth now?"

"Son," Stipp said, stepping forward, but Thomas heaved himself to his feet and walked past them, out the door into the mud, leaving the savage room open to the cold rain.

---

The towpath of the C&O was infinitely better maintained than the roads at this time of year, which was why Stipp had decided to return to Georgetown along its crowded path, rather than over the potholed turnpike, the way they had come earlier that morning.

Mary was seated on the carriage bench beside him, staring off over the roof of a packet boat into the steep wooded hills rising sharply from either side of the canal. Since leaving Fort Marcy, she had not spoken. From time to time the wagon lurched into a pothole and she was thrown against Stipp, but still she did not speak. He could hardly blame her. The scene at Fort Marcy had been unbearable. Thomas's question had ripped through Stipp's heart. Had he sounded as broken when Genevieve had died?

"Thomas was in shock," he said now. "He'll realize—"

Mary said, "I knew what would happen, I knew it as soon as Jenny said she was with child."

"You can't predict—"

"I should have gone home when Amelia wanted me to." Self-protection was no excuse. *You love too little, you love too much. It was all selfishness. If only, if only.*

Stipp could hardly bear her sorrow. He wanted to take her away, to travel on past Georgetown, across the Aqueduct Bridge, past the entire Confederate army, to the marshes and estuaries of Chesapeake Bay and the sea, where they could wade into the breakers and be taken up by a passing ship. They would travel back to Texas, live with Lilianna. How old would the boy be now? Four? Had it been only a year since he'd seen them? It seemed a lifetime. He thought, *I just won't stop. I'll keep driving and we'll forget the war and all its pain.* They traveled on, passing the slow mule teams hauling packet boats down the canal toward Georgetown and, as they neared the town, row houses and factories and warehouses sprouting from the treed hillside. Mary was remembering another earlier, difficult trip on a towpath in Albany with Thomas, just before he met Jenny and everything changed. She would go back in time, she thought. She would go back and change everything, if she could. Men were shouting as they unloaded and loaded barges at the warehouse doors opening onto the canal, the day crackling with work and the war. Above, on Bridge Street, a horsecar was struggling to turn as a train of army wagons slogged through the mud.

"Mary?" Stipp said.

She turned to look at him, her face masked and unreadable. She bore none of the fierce confidence that had driven her to hunt him down at the Union Hotel eight months ago, none of *I will climb through that window.*

"I'm nothing. I can't help anyone. Why did I think that I could?"

"You're just tired," Stipp said, pulling over to the side of the path to speak to her.

The mule team behind them could not get around them. The driver swore and deckhands jumped off the packet boat to slow it down so that it wouldn't drag the mules with it as it drifted forward. Behind them another packet did the same.

"Back home, afterwards—after Jenny died—my mother and I said things to each other that we've never said before. I said something I wish I'd never said. She'll never forgive me."

"That was only your grief speaking. People say things."

"I betrayed her trust."

"She trusts you."

Mary shook her head. "No. I'm arrogant and clumsy and proud. And I want things I shouldn't want."

Stipp suspected she meant Thomas, at least he hoped that's what she meant, because he needed her to want to be a surgeon. He didn't know how he could live without her. The long month of January had been a dark cave whose only light had been the possibility of Mary's return.

"You'll see. You're just tired," he said, unable to say, *Want me,* but Mary's blank glance confirmed the inadequacy of his reply, and he took up the reins and snapped the horses forward.

When they left the towpath, men were still leaping onto the path from more than a dozen boats, ropes blistering their hands as they dug in to hold back catastrophe.

The hotel had been bedecked with flags and sentinels, its new, official status recently proclaimed by the Surgeon General's office. Outside its doors, a good many of the convalescents were standing about, brightened by even a brief stint in the drizzly February cold. They greeted Stipp and Mary with the restless air of those with untold news.

"They're closing the hospital down."

# *Chapter Thirty-seven*

**Circular Number 18, February the 2nd, 1862**

> By order of the Surgeon General, the general hospital in Georgetown in the former Union Hotel is to be closed the first day of May 1862. The premises are vermin-infested, dilapidated and crumbling, and do not meet our rising standards for military hospitals. The staff is to be divided forthwith among the hospitals at Miss Lydia's Seminary and Georgetown College. Those patients afflicted with small pox and typhoid should be directed to the Insane Asylum for isolation purposes. The building is to be razed.

The army, the circular went on to say, was going to build a new hospital right under the Capitol building on the mall, to be named Armory Square. It would be the pride of the army, the nation. It would transform medical care. It would make people forget that the Union Hotel Hospital had ever existed. There would be regulations. There would be ventilated wards and ward nurses and supervisors. Surgeons would have care over a wing each. The hospital would be advantageously situated near the Long Bridge, eliminating the torturous rides over the city's bad roads to reach the little hotel in Georgetown. Lives would be saved. Order would reign.

Their eyes met. Eight months since they had first met in this room. *A lifetime.* Stipp lit a lantern and the sweet smell of kerosene flooded the room.

"Don't give up hope," Stipp said. "Anything is possible yet." Trying to atone for *You are only tired.* Trying not to panic. He had orders to report to the surgeon general for employment as a regimental surgeon, but Mary was not listed on the government payroll, and so was now unprotected, without a post.

"Perhaps Miss Dix would help you. She has come around, I believe. Or what about Blevens? Surely he would take you. He would be delighted to have you, I'm sure." Tried to say it without the least bit of envy. "Or, I will write you a letter of introduction anywhere—to medical school, perhaps, or Miss Lydia's Seminary Hospital. They treat officers there. It's where Blevens would have gone after the fire if he hadn't come here. You could work there, Mary; it would not be the abyss that it has been here." Trying to keep her from breaking. "Or, perhaps, you could return home."

He would say, *I love you* again, but that was not what she required, no matter how much he required it. If he could retrieve those words, he would, and silence them to the end of time, just to ease her in his presence.

Mary was looking past him. She still wore the funereal hat that she had worn to Fort Marcy, her black cloak wrapped around her.

"People want to believe that we can do anything," Stipp said. "That doctors can erase pain, erase inevitability." *We doctors*, though she wasn't one yet and might never be. "But it isn't true."

Even Lazarus had been resurrected.

"My mother was right. I could have saved Jenny," Mary said. She was speaking now as if Stipp weren't in the room, as if she were negotiating with death itself. She looked up distractedly. The spectral shadows of the kerosene light flared against her skin, illuminating the hollows under her cheekbones.

The dinner bell clanged. All through the hotel, beds scraped, feet thumped to the floor. The future dead, rising to forestall.

She was slipping away, leaving the shores for hell. The lantern flickered: Charon, impatient to be off. A ferry to the other side. Her eyes stared straight ahead, though what was to come was around a bend, uncertain except in certain regret. The safety rope of ambition trailed behind. Slippery; it, too, uncertain. The cruelty of war was such that coincidence, in the past nearly always a pleasant surprise, was turned to sadness: to want to become a surgeon, only to see the chance offered, then ruined before your eyes. To find your brother-in-law, only to have to tell him terrible news.

"Mary," he said. "Why did you want to be a surgeon?" *You won't last.* He did not want the victory; he hadn't even wanted it in the beginning. God's judgment. Or joke.

Mary opened her mouth to speak, but no sound emerged. Had it been conceit to wish to conquer death?

"It doesn't matter what I wanted," she finally said.

The light in the lantern flared and then blew out, as upstairs a door slammed.

Mary rose to take Stipp's hand, a commonplace enough gesture. She ought to touch his face, she ought to reassure him, as he had once reassured her.

At the door, she turned, her hand on the knob.

But before he could say anything, Mary turned and went away into the dark.

# *Chapter Thirty-eight*

To get to Washington, Thomas had understood, you had to follow the C&O towpath southward until Georgetown, but he couldn't just walk down the towpath, because there were patrols on the lookout for invading Confederates and spies. Instead, he had to bushwhack alongside it through the underbrush, which he had started to do in the dark before dawn, after abandoning his post on the great rocks overlooking the Potomac when his fellow guard fell asleep in the deep morning chill. The forest in February in Maryland was a vast, sucking pool of mud, but Thomas slogged ever southward, keeping the canal in view as he fought through the endless frozen thicket rising on the hillsides along the canal. But by noon he was exhausted, his arms and face abraded by the brittle branches, his legs coated with freezing clay. A mile north of Georgetown, a cavalry unit met him just as he left the cover of the forest. They had been on the lookout since dawn, when they'd been alerted to a deserter leaving the Chain Bridge unguarded. They identified Thomas by the look of desolation that they'd noticed in other deserters, the ones truly desperate to get home. They marched him at gunpoint down the path, skirting with difficulty the mule teams towing barges toward the Tidewater locks where the C&O joined the Potomac River, past the Observatory and the Aqueduct Bridge, the farm kids and dogs running alongside, shouting and barking insults. They marched him right into Washington and reached the Central Guardhouse just as the sun grew pale and dropped from the sky. It had been a march of some miles, and Thomas, cold and footsore, sank onto a rectangle of space on the prison floor in the large cell that held the day's accumulation of drunks and pickpockets.

Among the clangs of cell doors shutting and guards shouting, a tuneless whistle drifted over the heads of the milling men.

"Hey. Fall. Hey."

In front of him squatted Jake Miles in a tattered Union shirt, coat, and cap. The war was a war of brothers, acquaintances, enemies. A quick whiff of Jake's breath told Thomas all he needed to know.

*Take care of Christian.* That was the last thing he had said to Jake at the Capitol before he had gone in search of Mary.

Thomas lunged.

He was in such a rage that he did not hear the shouts of his fellow prisoners, the warnings of the guards, did not feel Jake's drunken slaps about his head. Then someone hit him in the back of the head with a rifle butt, and he was dragged off to one of the single cells and thrown onto the floor. He spent the night sleepless and hungry, swatting at mice and roaches. In the morning, he lined up with the rest to be examined by the judge advocate, who listened stone-faced to Thomas's story.

"And where did you think you were you going, Fall?" he asked when Thomas had finished.

"Home, sir."

The judge ordered him returned to his regiment. By two o'clock that afternoon, Thomas was back at Fort Marcy standing on a barrel in the middle of the fort near the bomb-proof for everyone to see. That night, he was allowed to return to his tent, where he collapsed from exhaustion and finally, wretchedly, began to cry.

Grief, the third casualty of war.

The next morning, Stipp stood at the door to Mary's room. Pinned to the pillow was a note.

*Dr. Stipp,*

*The ledgers are in the cabinet in the dining room. Under the pillow is the key to the supply cabinet; keep it from Mr. Mack, he would have it if he could. The nurses all require direction, especially Monique, who charms but is occasionally careless with dressing changes. The stick for unclogging the water closet is in the basement, behind the stairs. Extra bluing for the linens can be had from Jacob Harlow, the egg man; he is cagier than he looks, so bargain hard.*

*Yours,*

*Mary Sutter*

# Chapter Thirty-nine

James Blevens judged Charles Tripler, the medical director of the Army of the Potomac, to be in his mid-fifties. He was a balding, mustachioed man, whose years in the army told of decades in the sun, but he was nonetheless energetic and argumentative. His widely read *Manual of the Medical Officer of the Army of the United States* had been written after his service in both the Seminole Wars and the Mexican War, and he was considered to be the most experienced and knowledgeable practitioner among all the surgeons in the halved army, North or South. Now he was leaning forward in front of the fireplace in his parlor, talking eagerly.

"Egad, man, you want me to choose between microscopes and ambulances? You must be joking. Though that terrible excuse of a surgeon general Finley designed a rattletrap of a beast; did you ever see anyone survive an ambulance ride for the better?"

"Not at Bull Run, no," Blevens answered.

"You were there? Damn it all, I wish I'd have been. I miss war. I'd have court-martialed Finley on the basis of the ambulance fiasco alone. The bastard."

"A microscope is equally, if not more, important than—"

"You cannot be serious. More important than evacuation of the wounded from the field? How are you going to explain that to the mothers whose sons are left behind?"

A glass of whiskey warming in his hand, James Blevens said that of course there would be no way to explain it.

It had been difficult to hunt down the peripatetic Tripler. To be sitting now, finally, in Tripler's well-appointed rooms on New York Avenue in the middle of February was the result of November, Blevens knew, the fire having done the hard work of garnering him an appointment with the revered doctor. His hands had healed well enough, though they were still stiff, and while Tripler was welcoming, the energetic man was swinging his top leg rather agitatedly over the other. Snow was falling all over the city; Blevens had struggled through the drifts from the Patent Office Hospital, where he had gone to work soon after Christmas. He was in charge of the typhoid that was ravaging the troops; so far, nearly a thousand cases had been reported. He suspected that was the disease now sickening Mr. Lincoln's sons, though Dr. Stone, the Lincolns' family physician, had proclaimed their illness to be bilious fever.

"I cannot condone your request for a microscope when I cannot buy a four-wheeled ambulance to save my soul," Tripler said. "Or even get the men to clean out their camps, though making them take quinine in whiskey has certainly made all the difference on fevers. Sick call is nothing now. Did you know the Sanitary Commission is supplying the army with quinine until we can produce enough for everyone?"

"I've observed in the stools of all my patients afflicted with diarrhea some small bacteria, which may be contributing in some way—"

Tripler cut him off. "It is the air that does it. I've moved the men in Arlington off the flats and into the woods, and it has changed everything. The sick do much better in regimental than in general hospitals. The improvement is due to that and the smallpox vaccines. Do you know we've rendered that disease practically null? The ones that have it are the ones who got it before they mustered in. Remarkable, really, it's these small steps, but the volunteer troops don't understand it. But McClellan's getting these boys into shape—he and I, actually. And I suppose the Sanitary Commission. They are a persistent lot. I'm glad for it, really. Ahead of their time; they've been right about hygiene all along. Did you say you were ever in camp?"

"Fort Albany. It was like policing children. Impossible to keep the place clean."

"Precisely my point, eh? Hygiene." Tripler clapped his hands.

"I couldn't agree with you more," James said, recalling the sanitation officer and his long questionnaire. The romantic period: a library, a band, the belief that the problems of the forts could be quickly ameliorated. Futility, but necessary and completely unattainable at the time.

"However, Dr. Tripler, I believe there may be an alternate component to disease, one that cannot be seen with the naked eye, that might be contributing. A microscope would help all of us understand disease in another way; I could establish reports, share information; it is entirely worthwhile, I believe, to establish a place of research now, so that we might come to a common knowledge base that will benefit us all."

"Come now, Dr. Blevens. What you want is impossible. Lincoln has ordered McClellan to move and McClellan is poised." Though he was not. Earlier in the day, McClellan had stormed around this very room, complaining to Tripler about Lincoln's thorough misunderstanding of the intricacies of battle, the still delicate nature of the green Federal troops, the overwhelming numbers of the enemy they were facing.

"What the army needs are ambulances, and ambulances we will have, along with a corps that will be solely responsible and trained for battlefield removal. When the time comes and we face the enemy next, I shall be right at McClellan's side, directing the corps' movements. Did you know that it is the quartermaster who is responsible for ambulances? Not the Medical Department. Upon my word, that's bad planning. To not be under my purview? Can you imagine such a thing? This is why Finley had to go."

Tripler rattled on, complaining of the former surgeon general and the old army regime, how little they understood about modern warfare and the demands of the Medical Department. James nodded along, content for the moment to bide his time. He wanted a microscope. Besides, it was not as if James disagreed with Tripler; everything he was saying was sound and true. But for all Tripler's prescience and efficiency, the importance of research eluded the man.

"Do excuse me, I've been rude running on like this. How are your hands these days?" Tripler asked.

"My hands are fine. I do wish to make the point that I fail to see why ambulances and microscopes must be exclusive. I am asking only for one."

Tripler said, "If only I were able to grant your request. But I've used up a great deal of funds designing a stretcher to be mounted on top of horses. A sort of in-between to go where the wagons cannot. You know, gulleys, deep woods, that sort of thing. It's a bit cumbersome now, but I'll get it right. I'm afraid it takes money to do these things and we barely have any as it is."

Making a great show of not pouring any more whiskey into his glass, Tripler stretched in his chair and yawned. His secretary should have alerted him that Blevens had wanted something besides accolades for pulling patients from that fire.

Reluctantly, James set down his glass.

"Say," Tripler said at the door, nodding at Blevens's hands. "You're ready, I presume, for when the army does move? I could use a good man in the field hospitals. I've established a system of regimental hospitals with good, heated tents, overseen by brigade medical officers with larger hospitals. All this to treat the men quickly and not have to send them to the general hospitals in Washington. I'm shutting down the Union Hotel Hospital; that place is a dump. Hardly up to our new standards. We're modernizing." He clapped Blevens on the back. "Glad you're better. Find your way home in this snow?"

On the stoop outside, James worked a pair of gloves over his still sensitive hands, the palms stiff and shiny. The snow had temporarily conquered the city's perpetual odors. Spring would be coming soon, and with it more changes. He looked down the street, toward the president's house, the outside lit by torches, the snowflakes shimmering in the firelight before melting away. They looked like the small bacteria he had seen gliding across his slides.

James decided to go to the Union Hotel to find Mary, whom he had not seen since she'd left for home so abruptly after Peter's death. When the cab sailed past the president's house, the flags had been dropped to half-mast. Swaths of black crepe now draped the double front doors. A line of mourners was forming.

Willie Lincoln, eleven years old, reportedly very ill, must have died while Blevens had been trying to persuade Tripler of the need for a microscope.

---

In the Mansion, the president was stroking one of Willie's caps, which the boy had flung into the corner of his office only a few weeks before, running in screeching in the midst of a game of tag with Tad. Willie had claimed sanctuary in his father's arms, his thin-walled chest heaving, the ribs like spindled fretwork under Lincoln's fingers.

Early signs of illness? If only he had thought to question.

Willie's cap was so small that it did not even cover Lincoln's palm. Lincoln pulled it to his chest and held it over his heart. Before he gave in completely, he checked to make certain that the door to his office was bolted. It was, but he couldn't remember having done it, couldn't remember even having traversed the long hallway from Willie's room, where he had asked the nurse if she believed in God. Understanding his question, she had instead assured him that God had loved Willie so much He had called for him early.

Lincoln laid his head down on his desk and let the fury break from deep inside his chest, as John Hay stood outside the door, registering each keen in his bones.

Upon imminent threat of removal from his post by an impatient and grieving President Lincoln, McClellan sailed out of Washington at the end of March, following the four hundred dinghies, ships, boats, tubs, steamers, and sailing barques the government had rented to ferry his sixty-five thousand troops to Fort Monroe, situated at the tip of one of the fingerling peninsulas that jutted into Chesapeake Bay. Before Little Mac (as John Hay was now calling the procrastinating general) had sailed away, Lincoln asked him why they should go to the expense of shipping the army a hundred miles away when the army they wanted was still planted somewhere between Richmond and Washington, thirty miles away? McClellan replied that he intended to win victory by taking Richmond from the south in a bloodless war. Grudging that at least McClellan was finally doing something, Lincoln approved the general's odd plan.

# Chapter Forty

*18th May, 1862*
*Near the Chickahominy River*

*Dear James,*

*I've managed to scrounge ink and paper, a small miracle in this mess. The Peninsula is a bog of freezing mud and malaria at the best of times; so many men are sick from measles and mumps that we send them away on hospital ships never to return, to say nothing of the malingerers who study symptoms more than they study war.*

*How are your hands? You are a damned lucky beast that your burns prevented your coming here, though God knows we need you. Thirty contract surgeons from New York and Philadelphia have replaced the hundred regimental doctors who've fallen ill, but I have no faith in these new arrivals. Most haven't seen a scalpel since medical school, if they ever saw one there.*

*The battles are sharp and furious. We march on Richmond, but it is a folly of an advance; the other day we had to detour twenty miles around a river that no one knew was there. When the wounded finally reach me, they have been dragged over mud and through swamps. It is butchery, every bit of it.*

Stipp lifted his pen. He wished he were writing to Mary, if only for solace. God, he was tired. He was so tired. All these men, dying, acres upon acres of them, and there were maybe six, seven surgeons who could do the work. What was he expected to do?

He dipped his pen again into the ink and continued writing.

*Neither are there sufficient numbers of ambulances; your friend Tripler daily complains that the four-wheeled ambulances he so loves have not arrived. We use the bone-jarring two-wheeled ambulances, and the injured are near dead by the time I see them, if they ever get to me, for the roads are a sea of mud. We have great difficulty getting supplies. Scurvy is rampant. We beg for potatoes; they send us cartridges. The hospital tents are circuses of rope and rigging; it takes days to put up just one, and then we must take them down and move again. The trains, when they do come, are nothing but cattle cars; we have no means to fit them up to transport the injured.*

*But this is nothing compared to the injuries I have seen. I seem to be able to save only those who sustain gunshot wounds to their limbs, while the rest die. I attempted to remove a bullet from a liver. Shocking how much blood. We are making it all up as we go. Who has seen such infernal violence before? Napoleon, perhaps. How the men suffer.*

*On a less important note, I am curious to know if you have found Mary. Have you tried searching the hospitals? When you came to see me the night Willie Lincoln died, I was certain that Mary wouldn't stay away long, but now I worry that something has happened. You must reassure me that you have found her and that she is fine. I'd hoped she would return to her mother, but I've no way of knowing if she has.*

*Write me when you have found her.*

*Take care, Blevens. You will find a use yet for those hands.*

*Yours most sincerely,*

*William Stipp*

*When you have found her.* He was giving himself away. On the night of Willie Lincoln's death, when he had told Blevens that Mary had disappeared, he had barely been able to contain himself. He hesitated another moment before scratching out the line entirely, holding the letter up to the air to let the ink blot dry in the spring evening.

Folding the letter into its envelope, Stipp wrote out Blevens's address on Pennsylvania Avenue, both envying and pitying his protégé, who in his handicap wished to be here, but to his great fortune was not. He struggled into his mud-covered boots before embarking on the fool's errand of trying to find a way to post the letter, finally collaring a lieutenant who promised to send it with Tripler's latest complaint to the new surgeon general, William Hammond, about the disaster that was McClellan's campaign.

Two weeks later, Blevens opened the letter in his rooms on Pennsylvania Avenue. They resembled his rooms in the Staats House so closely that some days he awoke and thought he was back in Albany. These he had furnished mostly with tables, across which he had accumulated a dozen specimens of tissue and bone. He was studying maceration technique on bone structure, using a rating system to determine the best method and its effect on ensuing bone quality. So far, a combination of bleach, hydrogen peroxide, hydrochloric acid, boiling water, and soap followed by degreasing proved least injurious to the anatomical integrity of the larger bones, which were the main subject of his inquiry. Thankfully, the cats and dogs of Swampdoodle were forever dying in the alleys, his old mainstay supply; he had discarded the failures into the City Canal so as to not alarm his landlord, whose suspicion had run high when he inspected Blevens's rooms on short notice in early April and discovered his jugs of chemicals. Blevens recalled Stipp, the cat slung across his desk: *Yes, that's it, but for God's sake, don't saw.*

Also on his desk was a list of all the hospitals in the city, from the permanent to the temporary, the Ladies' Seminary to the Insane Asylum. He had searched each one twice, running his eyes over the wards in search of Mary, though he claimed to the nosy hospital matrons to be searching only for tissue samples.

In his reply, Blevens was brief:

*Dear William,*

*I was of little use at the Patent Office. The army has furloughed me for the time, until my hands declare themselves. They remain stiff and clumsy; I content myself with research, but I am ashamed when I hear of the conditions under which you labor. I would be of no use to you; I can barely grip a scalpel.*

*I have not yet found Mary, and I am loath to write her mother, whose fears I do not wish to arouse; Amelia has lost more than all of us in this war. I will, however, if my diligence does not yield results soon, but I cannot think that Mary would go home.*

*I am, ashamedly, your ineffective servant,*

*James Blevens*

# *Chapter Forty-one*

In 1864, George McClellan, in his run as Democratic candidate opposite Abraham Lincoln, would complain that the failure of the Peninsular Campaign was due to many factors out of his control, including Lincoln's great meddling in his plans, his failure to provide crucial reinforcements, the teeming hordes of Confederate troops, the inclement weather, the failure of the navy to properly defend the York River, the idiot mapmakers who mistook a river's location that forced him to march miles out of his way, his recurring bouts of malarial fever due to the criminal lack of quinine, the abysmal roads which were nothing but a morass of mud, the swampy, nearly oceanic terrain, and finally, the wily Robert E. Lee, who decimated the Union troops in the last hopeless battle of Seven Days as they retreated down the Peninsula after the Union's failure to seize Richmond. Nor were the legion of wounded his fault. Charles Tripler had stood at his side at every turn. He could not have helped his inept surgeons or the ambulance corps, even though he and Tripler set up office in a boat on the James River miles away. Worse, Lincoln had denied him troops and even the benefit of the doubt.

McClellan would also conveniently fail to mention the tolerant letters from Lincoln (at which John Hay merely shook his head) as the war on the Peninsula unraveled.

At the end of June, surgeon Jonathan Letterman was sent to Harrison's Landing on the James River to relieve Tripler of his post as medical director.

In the wake of Tripler's departure, Letterman found it impossible to determine the exact number of sick and wounded over the three-month period of battles on the Peninsula, but he guessed the number fell somewhere about eighteen thousand.

# *Chapter Forty-two*

All across Washington in July of 1862, women rose in droves with the dawn, washed away the muggy heat of the night, pinned up their long hair, donned calico and lawn dresses, scrubbed yesterday's dirt and blood from their boots, brewed tea, fried eggs, assembled handkerchiefs, bonnets, coins, hung lavender sachets from their necks, tied aprons around their waists, censored once again the futile urge to weep, and waded into the day to nurse the wounded who poured into the city from the Peninsula.

Churches, offices, homes, and old hospitals flung open their doors. An officer breached the padlocked doors of the shuttered Union Hotel, and Miss Dix appointed a woman named Hannah Ropes there as matron when she couldn't find Mary Sutter. Miss Dix couldn't find her anywhere, even though hospital matrons, in an effort at organization, were keeping lists of nurses in marbled paper notebooks they bought at the corner stationers, inscribing names they would dig out years hence from their trunks in an effort to win the women war pensions. In the notebooks, the matrons' penmanship and spelling would show the toll of haste, the ink splotching as if the pen had been hurriedly set down when its user had been called away to some more urgent task than listing the exhausted, charitable women who tried to help that beastly summer. The barriers had fallen. Miss Dix could no longer dictate who was able to work where, but even she was grateful for the women who arrived at the hospital doors bearing only persistence as their gift. Later in the war, someone in the Surgeon General's office would develop a form to send in each month for listing the contract nurses. But that would be after the summer of 1862, the summer that everyone would remember as the Great Scramble, the summer when it was impossible to keep track of anything.

Not all the eighteen thousand wounded came to Washington. Some had to stay behind, scattered across the Virginia Peninsula in the regimental hospitals that Tripler so loved, others were guarded at Fort Monroe, still held by Federal troops, and a portion were shipped directly from the Peninsula to New York, where, at Bellevue Hospital on the East River, the doctors had just ten minutes' notice that they were about to receive one hundred injured men. In Philadelphia—easier to reach than distant New York—the hospitals overflowed.

But in Washington, the deluge inundated the city.

In a single rented room located in an alley behind Maryland Avenue near the Capitol, Mary Sutter also rose and dressed with the dawn. Her thin-walled room was furnished only with a narrow bed, a small window, a dresser and a chair, an armoire, and a coal stove that coughed soot. The boarding house was not unlike the Union Hotel; perhaps it was its resemblance to her former workplace that had drawn her to the tenement, but she could not say for certain. She would walk from the Capitol past the iron foundry, the gas storage tank, and the many hospitals, her boots negotiating the refuse in the gutters as her hems grew dusty or muddy, depending on the weather.

At her clerk's job in the War Department—won by virtue of her precise handwriting—she copied out circulars and passed them to Secretary Stanton, who never looked up from his desk. In the evenings, she walked more than a mile back through the city along a different route, across the City Canal and diagonally along the mall, toward the great undomed Capitol building under which her boarding house squatted. The absence of the bulk of the Army of the Potomac made the once bustling city seem like the township it had been before the country had gone to war. Fewer trundling caissons, rarely a parade. In the distance, Armory Square Hospital was rising. Already, Mary could see the shells of the pavilions, the outlines where, at President Lincoln's suggestion, gardens would one day be planted between the long buildings.

On Sundays, Mary went to church and sat alone in a pew. Afterwards, she walked for exercise to the Long Bridge to peer across the river at Virginia. At night, she shunned the communal dining room of the boarding house to cook herself a modest dinner on the coal stove. When she dreamed of Jenny, as she often did, it was of them as toddlers, when they still had not grasped their separateness. A few times she dreamed of the time they had been caged together in the crib for the entire day, their weeping mother finally reaching in to console them. Once, she dreamed she had cut Jenny's umbilical cord, the knife clutched in her fetal hand, as, intertwined, the two of them floated inside their mother, Jenny slowly dying.

In the fourth week of July, the perspiring pastor of Mary's church opined from his pulpit that "if one of us is dying, we are all dying. No one is special. No one is set apart. Even if all you can do is pick up a mop."

After the service, Mary sat alone in her room and ate a small meal of bread and salted beef. Five months had passed since she'd last set foot inside a hospital. Through the papered walls of the boarding house, she had heard all the dreadful things of life, though she had tried in coming here to banish them. Sometimes, walking to work, she had nearly leapt into the ambulances carrying the wounded from the hospital ships at the Sixth Street wharves to the hospitals. Instinct was a bastard thing, always insisting.

She changed into one of the dresses she had worn to work at the Union Hotel, crossed the mall, and headed toward the Patent Office, the nearest hospital to where she lived. There, an army of women lifted heads to place pillows, offered brandy punch, wine, whiskey, washed shattered arms, broken legs, gunshot jaws, and worried over abbreviated, festering stumps.

Mary passed them all by, hurried to the alley, filled a bucket, returned to the marble hallways, and began to mop.

In the next few weeks, she scrubbed walls, stripped beds, boiled toweling, discarded dressings, scoured bedpans, hauled water, served meals, and scraped human filth from soiled water closets. A Union Hotel redux. Her shoulders cramped and her feet blistered: a fine punishment. She refused to allow herself to be drawn in, even as her eyes roved over the bandaged legs and arms. Except once, she did kneel down to retie a sling the proper way, positioning the man's elbow lower than his wrist. And another time, she removed a saturated dressing and rebandaged it herself.

But she wasn't a nurse. She did not call herself that. When the surgeons made their morning rounds, neither James Blevens nor William Stipp was ever among them.

"You there, mopping the floors. What is your name?" The matron was not a rude woman, but the arduous days of July, with the hospital overflowing, had taken their toll on her, to say nothing of the humidity and the odors of the men entrusted to her care.

"Mary."

"One of the men told me that you changed his dressing."

"He was mistaken."

"Another said you fixed up a little sling for him."

"He must have been thinking of someone else."

The matron hesitated, then gathered her skirts and headed downstairs, where the surgeon in charge was changing a dressing. Robert Smith was not to be trusted. He drank far too much and eroded the general morale of the hospital.

A few days later, Mary was skirting her mop around the legs of a cot, upon which a boy gripped its spindly sides, his eyes glassy with fever. Earlier that morning, a surgeon had performed a second amputation on the boy's leg to cut away some festering tissue. The boy had survived the surgery, the rigors of the chloroform, the vomiting afterwards, but now his face had gone white.

"I'm thirsty," he said.

"I'll get a nurse."

"Wait." He grabbed her wrist. "Don't leave me."

Mary hesitated, and then set down her mop. She poured him a glass of water from a nearby pitcher and helped him to drink.

He began to talk. "I was at Malvern Hill. That's wet land. Scrubby where it isn't just a swamp. Trees slung low, dragging in the water. Cypress, they said. You see my feet? My one foot, I mean. Nothing but a mess after my boots filled up with water."

The boy's remaining foot was not what concerned Mary. He was restless, fidgety, keyed up.

"You should rest," she said.

"I was up on that hill firing away on the Rebs stuck down there around the bottom of the hill." He edged up onto his elbow, talking fast. "I was hunched up behind a rock, you see, getting off a shot now and then, when a bullet ricocheted off a tree and smashed into my knee. It was like a swarm of hornets took up housekeeping right there in my kneecap. But they couldn't drag me off till night. That was pain, I tell you." His skin was pale and clammy, and little beads of sweat glistened on his forehead. "Down on the flats it was a bog and they dropped me into the mud with all them mosquitoes and the night coming on. Someone stuck a rock under my head so I wouldn't drown. The rain was cold, too, and by the time they hauled me up on that table and the sawbones slapped a cone over my face, I couldn't even talk, couldn't even ask him to try to save my leg. That chloroform smelled sick but I breathed it in. When I came to I was throwing up real bad. They didn't have any bandages so the maggots got in pretty quick, but there's no picking them out. They didn't have any whiskey or tents, so I was outside there maybe, I don't know, ten days or so before they could get me onto one of them ships. And then I thought I was in heaven. They poured kerosene into the maggots. That seared, but at least the maggots were gone."

Mary drew back his sheet. Blood was pooling under his abbreviated, bandaged right leg.

"Will someone call the surgeon?" she cried. There was a rustle in the periphery, skirts swishing, heads raised, but all she could see was the fresh blood, and the boy's mouth, which had fallen open in surprise.

*He is like that boy,* Mary thought. *The boy who watched himself die.* Mary felt with her fingertips for the femoral artery, pressed hard.

"Tell me about your home, tell me where you're from." She wanted to keep him talking, to keep him conscious. The boy needed a looping stitch, needed someone to tie up the artery. Mary pressed harder on the artery, and the flow seemed to slacken.

"Herkimer Falls."

"New York?" Mary asked.

He did not answer.

"Tell me," Mary said.

"Yes, New York."

"Tell me about your mother."

But the boy wasn't talking. He was looking at his leg.

"Your mother?" Mary prodded. "Tell me about her."

Women were hovering, saying something about the surgeon being tied up.

"Then bring me a surgery kit," she said.

"Who will use the kit?" someone asked her.

"I will," Mary snapped.

"My mother didn't want me to enlist." The boy had become confessional. Mary didn't like it, didn't like what it meant.

"I left my mother too," she said.

"You did? You left your mother?"

"Yes."

"Are you sorry for it?" the boy asked.

Mary almost lost focus. *Do you want me to stay, Mother? As you like.*

"The way she looked at me when I was leaving?" the boy said. "Like she'd never forgive me. Now I won't ever get to see her again."

"I need a surgery kit," Mary cried. "Does no one have a surgery kit?"

The women shook their heads. Not one of them possessed such an exotic thing. The boy's eyes were beginning to flutter.

Mary was losing him. She was pressing hard, but the artery was still bleeding. This was why she hadn't wanted to come back. She was easing her agitated sister back down on the bed. Renouncing the hapless doctor and his forceps. Centering the knife just so. Separating the cartilage to save Thomas and Jenny's child. She could almost recall the heft of the scalpel in her hands, the deep pleasure of locating that notch in Jenny's pelvis, the release of the bone at the tip of her fingers. The soaring, triumphant feeling that she had done something miraculous. Laudable. Singular.

The matron rushed up and thrust a kit at Mary.

"Here, press hard," Mary said, and when the matron slipped her fingers next to hers, Mary lifted her hand away, and then tore off the boy's dressing and searched for the failed stitch. She used the long tenaculum to separate the ravaged tissue, found the unraveled stitches, the bleeding artery, inserted the needle, looped the stitch, once, twice, again, and then again, finally formed a knot. She was acting out of memory. She heard someone call her name, but she ignored the call, told the woman to ease the pressure on the artery. Waited, as Stipp had once waited. Waited, until she was certain the suture held.

Reflexively, she put her hand to the boy's wrist. The pulse, though faint, beat.

Mary stared at her hands, at her skirts glistening with the boy's blood, a smell and sight as familiar to her as her lost family.

The matron bent low and said, "Well done. Now, come with me." She wrapped an arm around Mary, steered her away to an office, where she helped her out of her stained dress, and for a moment Mary was almost naked, shivering in the August heat. Then the matron swaddled Mary in a blanket.

"Mary, you said your name was?"

"Yes."

The matron pursed her lips. "You are not by any chance the Mary Sutter who worked at the Union Hotel? Miss Dix told me to look out for a nurse who was interested in being a doctor. That isn't you, is it?"

Identity as a question. Mary wondered if her mother would even know her now.

The matron pressed. "I hear she was quite good. Extraordinary, even. That she had a gift."

"No. She wasn't good at all. She made a lot of mistakes."

"What kind of mistakes?"

"Unforgivable mistakes."

"Mistakes are rarely unforgivable."

"These were." Mary shut her eyes.

"I need you to come back here tomorrow and work," the matron said. "Will you?"

*Come home. I need you.* Mary looked up. If only, if only. Time the terrible trick. Find your way through the black shadow of the past. And if you failed to snatch life from death for Jenny, you must still do it for yourself. You must still try. The impossible dictum. *You will not last.*

The matron pressed again. "You will make more mistakes, my dear. We all will, I'm afraid. But you must help us. Can you help us?"

*Come home. I need you.* There had been a moment when Jenny had bolted upright, as if to stop her, and Amelia had thrown Mary a gasping, despairing glance. But Mary had cut anyway. She remembered trying to stanch the flow of blood, remembered seeing Amelia paralyzed at the bedside, taking in Jenny's last moments.

*Mother,* Jenny had cried.

Perhaps it wasn't her fault that Jenny had died, Mary thought now, but she knew that she would never know, and that not knowing would be her punishment, her own little circle of hell.

She could almost see Albany, could almost imagine Amelia at the door, holding Jenny's baby, could even envision Thomas cradling his infant daughter.

"Will you help us?" the matron asked.

Mary made a noise, not quite yes, but a cri de coeur, soft, like the splash of Charon's oar, or the sound of a train whistle, going home.

# *Chapter Forty-three*

The morning of August 30, 1862, dawned sticky and oppressive in Washington. A gathering storm had stalled in the Virginia hills far to the west and was making the ordinarily pleasant ride in from the Soldiers' Home, where Lincoln and his family had again retreated for the summer, miserable for Hay and Lincoln. All was confusion because the Union general John Pope had been out of communication for days. All summer, the relentless Pope had chased Stonewall Jackson's Confederate troops west from Richmond, but now no one knew exactly where anyone was, even though, Hay told Lincoln now, the telegraph operators on the rail lines near Manassas had been reporting sounds of firing nearby the site of the former battlefield. McClellan was being no help. Ordered by Lincoln to return from the Peninsula, he had reluctantly boarded a steamer a few days ago at Fort Monroe and had sailed up the Potomac, but only as far as Aquia Creek south of Washington, where he was holed up at the naval base sending telegraphs to the War Department every few hours or so asking for updates, and then when updated making excuses as to why he wouldn't send troops to help Pope, asserting that Pope needed to get out of whatever scrape he had gotten into on his own.

"Petulant man," Lincoln said, removing his hat and wiping his forehead of sweat, though it was only six in the morning and the sun had not risen completely above the horizon. "I do believe McClellan wants Pope to fail."

Hay could not understand why Lincoln did not call McClellan to Washington to have him court-martialed.

"I'm beginning to think McClellan might actually be crazy," Lincoln said. "Do you know he had the temerity to recall General Franklin's men after General Halleck thrice ordered them forward to help Pope? And last night, McClellan wanted to blow up the Chain Bridge to keep the Rebels from using it. The man is a coward."

In July, after McClellan had failed so magnificently on the Peninsula, General Henry Halleck had been made commander in chief above him, in an effort to goad the golden boy turned truculent imp into action, but even that had not persuaded McClellan. Coward indeed, or traitor, Hay thought now, but held his tongue. He rode with the president in the mornings not as judge, but as listener. Usually by the time they reached the Mansion the president had talked himself around whatever problem he was mulling.

Now, when they arrived at the Mansion, Lincoln went straight to the War Department, as was his habit, to read the latest dispatches. Edwin Stanton, the new secretary of war and onetime rival of Lincoln's, whom Lincoln had installed back in January to replace the ineffective Simon Cameron, was pacing, his coat jacket slung across his desk.

"I don't know what the hell is going on," he said.

They telegraphed Colonel Herman Haupt for news. Haupt was the superintendent of railroads, stationed most mornings at the central railroad station in Alexandria, where he could direct the military trains full of troops and supplies where they were most needed. Haupt was a reliable source, because he heard everything first, owing to the fact that the telegraph operators were under the guardianship of the railroad.

Haupt replied quickly that the railroad bridge across Bull Run had been burned sometime in the last day. He confirmed that firing had indeed been heard that morning near Centreville and Manassas. At this very moment, he was sending forward five railcars containing a wrecking car, a construction car, two containing fodder for the animals, and another loaded with meat and bread to Fairfax Station. He had also sent forward a telegraph operator with wire and instrument.

"The only man in the army who can write a clear dispatch," Lincoln said when he was finished reading. Satisfied, he left for the Mansion, though throughout the morning Haupt's updates were messaged over to him: *No firing of any importance, bridges are being repaired, provisions sent. It appears that the firing reported before had merely been Pope running Jackson out of the area toward a gap in the mountains, where his army can no longer threaten Washington.*

Lincoln and Hay and Secretary of War Stanton went out to noon dinner. The discussion ranged around McClellan; Stanton wanted the imbecile court-martialed, and thought that Pope deserved commendation for the rout of the Rebel forces. Hay held his tongue yet again. He had learned that Lincoln listened to every suggestion made to him, but judged men on their ability to discern.

After dinner, Hay and Lincoln went to army headquarters to see if they had better information. The War Department was separate from the Department of the Army, and the two were sometimes at war with one another. Each department received different updates; Lincoln had learned to wander between the two. Now it seemed that during dinner, events had changed dramatically. A great battle had begun. Pope had not chased Jackson south; instead, they were facing off on the same battlefield where Irvin McDowell had failed the year before. McClellan was frantically telegraphing from his protected spot on the Potomac, asking what was going on; he could hear the guns from his position on Aquia Creek.

Lincoln and Hay went back to tell the secretary of war. Stanton was agitated, pacing back and forth, flinging open his door to speak to his telegraph operator, then shuttling back again to his desk. Thousands of wounded were being brought off the lines and laid at Fairfax Railroad Station, and there was no one to care for them.

"Letterman is still on the Peninsula, with most of our ambulances, all of our tents, and a good number of our surgeons. My men are posting notices as we speak around town for any able-bodied men willing to work as nurses to report to the Long Bridge for transportation to the front. I sent an order to the guards at the Long Bridge to let volunteers across without a pass."

"Men with no experience? As nurses? At the front? Don't you think they'll be in the way?" Lincoln asked.

"I'm trying to save lives, Mr. Lincoln," Stanton said. "Until Letterman gets here, we are without medical direction. It is essential that someone take charge." He glared at Hay, as if to insinuate that he should have taken charge, because he, Stanton, already had plenty to do.

Walking back toward the Mansion, Lincoln said, "Haupt will have his head."

Hay agreed. "It will just be a bunch of idiots, showing up out of curiosity."

Lincoln regarded his young secretary, whose keen intelligence he cherished. "Keep your ears open. If Haupt wants a meeting with Stanton, I want to be there. I get so little entertainment of late."

"Entertainment? Fireworks, more likely."

"Just what I expect, yes," Lincoln said, as a slow smile worked its way across his face.

Fatigue had hewn Lincoln's craggy face into a visage that appeared a decade older than even the year before. Hay worried about him, but now he marveled again that the president could find the humor in anything, even in the midst of disaster.

Across town at the Patent Office, the evening sun was slanting in through the windows, shining above the ever-darkening cloudbank brewing in the west. Even with the windows flung open, the air in the hospital sweltered. Mary wiped the perspiration from the back of her neck and said, "But I don't understand."

The matron had run up the stairs with a copy of the *Evening Star* and had read Stanton's notice aloud.

"Stanton wants men?" Mary said. "Why men?"

The matron grew alarmed as Mary's eyes flickered; Mary had stolen the paper away and was earnestly reading the notice. It was like holding back the tide with her. She had convinced Mary to help and now she couldn't stop her. Though the young woman said she kept a room somewhere, she stayed overnight many nights of the week, rarely sleeping, instead haunting the long rows of beds, as if she were trying to make up for all those months away.

"You cannot go. It will be dangerous. And besides, try to convince a general that you should be on the field. They will dismiss you as a camp follower." It was worth the shock, the matron thought, because she knew that argument to Mary was a challenge rather than an obstacle, but Mary met her gaze with a familiar steely look. Her resolve had rebuilt itself in a very short time.

"No one would ever think me a prostitute."

The matron nearly gasped. Measure for measure, Mary could certainly hold her own. "Surely, you understand that to go is madness. They will ship the men back here. I will need you here. The men will need you here."

"The last time I waited to do something, my sister died," Mary said. She stuffed a bag with supplies—lint and bandages and a bottle of whiskey—and then a surgery kit that she slipped into her bag too.

"Wait," the matron said, grasping her hand. "Take a candle and matches. It will be dark out there."

"You there! You! You can't go!"

Mary had just been hoisted into a freight car by two men, whose precarious hold on her tightened as the lieutenant screamed at her from the platform.

"Are you mad?" Lieutenant Watson's face was puffy with heat and fury. Around him surged hundreds of inebriated men, who had already imbibed most of the whiskey they had ostensibly brought as medication for the wounded they were intended to nurse. Earlier in the evening, a hard rain had begun to fall, but that had done nothing to deter the hordes now clambering into the freight cars. The lieutenant, in charge of sending cars on to Alexandria from the Long Bridge, had telegraphed Colonel Haupt, questioning the unbelievable order to waive the requirement for a pass. Haupt replied that orders were orders and to send them on, though to make certain that surgeons got on first. But there was no telling who was who, and no surgeon had made himself known to Watson. The rest of the men were not so much nurses as rabble. Watson estimated there must be a thousand men at least demanding to go across, every one of them drunk. Months and months of security abandoned in one night. And now a woman was forcing her way on. He shuddered to think what might happen to her.

He made one last glance up and down the platform as stragglers scrambled into the cars. At his signal, workers methodically moved down the train, slamming the doors shut. Then he dropped his hand, and the engine hauling the rabble spit steam and ash into the rainy night and lurched from the Long Bridge terminal toward Alexandria.

"We are concerned for your safety." Colonel Haupt, a trim, tall man with a full beard, was shouting through a megaphone at the occupants of the cars he had waylaid at the Alexandria station. The volunteer nurses, all men, milled about the platform, stumbling and shouting, utterly drunk. It was ten o'clock at night, and he had so few tracks. He still needed to send troops and ammunition forward, to say nothing of commissary stores and fodder. No doubt these revelers would all skedaddle as soon as they saw what destruction awaited them at the end of the line. It had been stupid of Stanton to authorize a lark for a bunch of curious idiots. And of course, they would have to be transported back, taking up precious space once again. Haupt shook his head. The inefficiency appalled.

"Listen," he shouted again. "You will be in grave danger once you leave this station. We are going to send a train ahead of you with ammunition, and only then will we send you on. An armed regiment will travel atop your cars. Be patient; the delay is for your safety. But do not provoke me. If I see anyone consuming any more alcohol, you will be removed from these premises by armed guard."

Haupt stalked off with his assistant, hoping that his warning would subdue them. In the yard, lanterns were flaring as his men feverishly directed cars onto tracks, hitching them onto engines, the racket and thuds ringing out into the clammy night. The scene would have been beautiful if it hadn't been so panicked, for more than anything Haupt loved a railyard at work. At the beginning of the war, he had left his job building the Hoosac Tunnel in Massachusetts to renew his commission. But now he was remembering why he had left the military. There was nothing so exasperating as a confused chain of command. For days now, he had gotten only a few hours of sleep, and the long night was still before him. He cast his gaze over the riot that was the trainyard, forcing himself to think on what required his attention next.

"When you send that train on," he said to his assistant, "telegraph ahead to McCrickett to arrest them all."

When the train finally jerked to a stop at Fairfax Station, Mary had been standing for thirty-odd miles, clutching her bag to her chest, praying for the ceaseless rocking of the train to end. The men in her car had grown restive; some had been sick. Above the loud hiss of the engine releasing steam, she could hear the railcars' doors being thrown open one after the other, the sound growing louder and louder until finally the doors of her car were unlatched and heaved apart. The car had been stifling, but now, as her companions scrambled out the door and fanned onto the platform waving their flasks and shouting that they had come to nurse, by God, and no one could stop them, a chill flooded the emptied boxcar. Mary peered into a shadowy fog of locomotive steam and mist. Blazing torches illuminated a small station house, around which hundreds of men were milling.

All was chaos. A soldier climbed onto a bench near the station house and fired into the air, then began to shout, trying to be heard in the confusion. In the torchlight, the cold rain made the darting shadows grotesque. Mary hugged her bag to her chest, felt the hard ridges of the wooden case of the surgery kit digging into her ribs. She could hardly make out what was happening; men were lurching and hollering and the soldier was shooting again above their heads and there were no wounded in sight. She dropped from the car to the platform and shuttled along the train, not knowing exactly where she was going, but desperate to leave the drunken crowd behind. Beyond the train, she crept away from the lights of Fairfax Station. A few drunks had spilled onto the rocks and slippery grass surrounding the depot, but no one followed her into the darkness. The night was as inky black as the matron had said it would be. Underfoot, the slippery ground rose and fell away. She could see only a few feet ahead of her. In the distance, a few pinpricks of candlelight glimmered.

"Don't step on me," a voice said, as a hand grabbed her ankle.

The voice was choked, hoarse. She dug in her bag among the whiskey bottle, surgery kit, and dressings for the candle she then lit and thrust high above her head. In every direction, men were sprawled on the ground, packed so tightly together that she would not have been able to have taken another step without stumbling across their arms or legs. Directly beneath her was the soldier who had taken hold of her ankle. His pants had been torn away. A shattered thighbone jutted through the broken skin of each leg. His wounds were raw, mere hours old. Gunpowder blackened his face; tears were tracing gritty rivulets down his temples.

"Are you a ghost?" he rasped.

"No," Mary said.

"You got any water?"

"I have whiskey," she said, and again opened her bag and pulled out the whiskey bottle. With one hand, she pinned the bottle between her knees and uncorked it.

She held the bottle to his lips and he choked the liquor down.

At the train station, soldiers were shoving the men who had come to nurse back onto the trains. A locomotive was being turned and the racket was fantastic. She imagined that it must be what birth was like to infant ears. The great amniotic buffer finally removed.

She turned to the next man, an arm's reach away. He wanted whiskey, too. And the next man after that. The men latched on to her as she bent over them, a sob or a thank-you breaking from their lips. They threw their arms around her neck. Some were sixteen, fourteen. She bent over them and flooded whiskey into their mouths and pried their hands off her wrists and moved on. Someone had lain hay underneath them as a bed, and with every move she worried that she would drop her candle and set them all afire. Amid the general din and the trains screaming and hissing and the mules braying and the men crying out, it was nearly impossible to hear what a single man said to her. She smelled the sour battle scent, the gunpowder and the sweat and the fear. It mingled with the musk of sap and loam and leaves stewing in the rainfall. By habit, she surveyed their wounds, running the candle up and down their bodies, but not even the Union Hotel had prepared her for this. From time to time, her hand settled into a pool of clotted blood or vomit and she would wipe her hands on her skirt and scramble on. There were so many men, and she hadn't even yet gone fifty feet from the station.

In the trees, the birds began to chatter. The night was beginning to fade, but even the morning star, flickering on the gray horizon, seemed to outshine the pale scatter of the miserable dawn. Mary extinguished her candle.

Her whiskey bottle was empty.

She scrambled back to the station, pushing through the unruly crowd. From a small office, a remarkably tidily dressed man emerged, followed by a red-faced colonel who was screaming that no more civilians should be sent, what were they thinking back in Washington? When the two men saw Mary, the colonel abruptly stopped shouting to stare at her. Next to the depot door, chained to the bench, a dozen men were growing miserably sober. The depot clock read four-thirty in the morning.

Mary said, "Do you have any whiskey?"

The men continued to stare.

"Water? What about water? Surely somewhere there is a tank for the trains. We could tap it or fish the water out of it or—"

The two men were staring at her skirts. She looked down. The hem of her dress was sodden with blood to her knees. She leaned over and wrung it out.

"What the hell are you doing here?" the colonel sputtered.

"Just tell me if you have any water."

"There is a well behind the station," the other man said.

A train screamed into the depot. Doors were hurled open. Men surged from the cars and swarmed onto the platform. The colonel roared, "I told those idiots in Washington not to send any more drunks!"

A telegraph operator waded toward them shouting, brandishing a telegram above his head. "We are evacuating Centreville. The Rebels are fast behind our troops. Haupt says they will send no more supplies and we are to send the wounded back to Washington on the trains."

The colonel stalked toward the telegraph operator, shouting, "Let me see that, McCrickett."

Along the railroad line, in the opposite direction from which the trains had been arriving, a long line of ambulances was materializing out of the gray mist, plodding toward the station through the dew and drizzle of the dawn. In between them and the station, a continuous, unbroken multitude of men lay on the rocky ground. She could not see the end of them. She had guessed before that there were perhaps five hundred wounded, but now she saw that there were thousands. The drivers had to stop two, three hundred yards away, for they could get no closer, climb out of their wagon seats, and wrestle their human cargo out of the wagon beds onto the ground. A forest grew on a sloping hill above the station, and Mary could see more men laid under the protective canopy of the maples and oaks.

A phalanx of newly arrived volunteers were brushing past her, bumping her shoulders, stumbling toward the fields. In the door of one of the railcars, though, appeared a young woman, and behind her two more women and two men, who were swiftly unloading boxes onto the platform. Astonished, Mary elbowed through the crowd to reach them.

"What is in those boxes?" Mary asked.

"Socks. Jellies." The young woman reached into the car and pulled down a crate and lifted its lid. Mary gasped. Inside were bottles and bottles of whiskey.

She felt the color drain from her face. She lifted her arm and made a sweeping gesture, which was all she could accomplish by way of explanation. It seemed as if she were mired in seconds and minutes, wading in a slough of impossibility. Behind them, the colonel was standing on a bench, shouting orders for the civilians to line up and be counted into a burial party or as stretcher bearers, for they were going to help load the trains, by God, and they weren't to ride back to Washington until every wounded man was put on a car under pain of shooting.

"May I have two bottles?" Mary asked. She couldn't tell if the woman heard, because there was a great jangle as the locomotive was uncoupled from the train, but then the young woman waved her hand in the air and said, "Yes, yes."

The volunteers were surging into two lines, soldiers jostling them into place. Mary seized the bottles and threaded through the crowd toward the well, where she filled her one empty whiskey bottle after securing the others in her pockets. In the distance, she could see people going from wounded man to wounded man, teamsters and other soldiers and maybe even surgeons. Soon they would all get on the trains. She pushed back through the crowd to where she had left off. A man came up beside her, breathless, an open crate of jelly jars in his arms.

"Miss Barton said to give you these."

"Miss Barton?" she said, turning. The young woman who had given her the whiskey lifted her hand and nodded.

Now Mary was armed. She had jelly and whiskey and water, a bounty, though now she needed to be three, four, a hundred people at once. But thankfully it was only a matter of time until all the wounded were on a train.

She dropped to a boy at her feet. A small branch was embedded in his arm where a bullet had pierced the flesh. She fed him sweet plum preserves with her fingers. His dry tongue lapped at the edges of his mouth.

"You'll be at a hospital soon," she said. "They're beginning to load the trains."

The next man was shivering, his injury not readily apparent until he opened his jacket.

"How is it?" he asked.

Blood blacked his stomach, and the edges of the wound were swollen and beginning to suppurate.

Stifling a gasp, she said, "You'll be on a train soon."

The train, the train. The train was all. The train was hope. They were all going to Washington, where the brand-new Armory Square Hospital was waiting for them. For many months she had seen it rise, the many pavilions, the modern conveniences, the open wards, bed after bed at the ready. She couldn't remember where she had left her bag, with its depleted dressings and lint and the surgery kit, but all that was unnecessary now, for the trains were coming. "Drink this," she said, filling a mouth with whiskey. "They're sending trains." The emptied jam jars became cups for water mixed with whiskey. A swallow, two, three, and then she moved on. Some of the men were barely covered, their shirts and pants torn away by the artillery. She tore strips of clothing and wound them around legs and arms, but the dirty cloth fell apart in her hands. No matter, they were sending trains. She was a purveyor of hope, the assurance of help to come. Mary began to imagine the sound of thousands of railcar doors sliding open at once. The trains are coming. The trains.

From time to time she discovered that she was crying.

Later, the sun emerged from the dark clouds and the ground began to steam. But now the flies began to nestle in the edges of the wounds. She beat them away. Just one of these men needed all of her attention, but there were thousands. A sudden thought came to her that one of them might be Thomas, and she leapt to her feet, off balance, searching for him, but every one of them looked the same: blackened by gunpowder, undernourished, exhausted, torn to shreds, suffering. She wanted to find him and she didn't. She had to put him from her mind. By midafternoon, only a few more trains had rumbled into the station. Men were loaded on and taken away, but it was making no difference, because more wounded were arriving with every moment. From time to time, she ran back to the well to fill her emptied whiskey bottles with water. She worked her way up a steep, rocky incline toward the woods, crawling on her knees, past teamsters searching for lost whips and gravediggers digging shallow troughs. Here, on the hillside, away from the station, it was quieter. She could hear snatches of conversations and individual cries for mercy, which somehow made everything worse.

She was tying a tourniquet of torn cloth around the calf of a soldier when a familiar voice floated above the din.

"It's not bad, you'll do just fine."

She was certain she must be hearing things. Ghosts appearing, because of desire.

"Your tibia, I think. A man can live with just a broken leg."

That voice, with its distinctive, deep growl, the measured words, the innate intelligence. Where was it coming from? She was hearing things. Hearing hope.

She stood and turned in a circle as Dr. Stipp stepped from behind a tree, raised a hand to shield his eyes, and looked her way.

His hair had turned completely gray. Deep furrows creased his sunburned cheeks and forehead. He was gaunt, lean and rawboned, his face a coil of worry and strain, though his eyes were still that fine china blue, but clouded now with fatigue and agitation.

For a full minute, William Stipp could not speak, and then in an instant breached the gap between them, seized her hand, and, ignoring the men who were pulling at her skirts, dragged her past them all and climbed to a rocky outcrop. From this vantage point, Mary could see legions of maimed lying side by side under the trees.

"What are you doing here?" Stipp asked.

Mary fumbled in her pocket to produce Stanton's notice that she had torn from the newspaper, as if that would explain everything, but she was exhausted and her hands shook. Sunlight dappled the ground beneath them. At some point, the sun had emerged from behind the clouds.

Stipp stared at the newspaper cutting and then threw it away. "You shouldn't have come," he said.

"I had to," she said. "I stayed away before."

*Jenny,* Stipp thought. Of course. Mary's skirts and hands were scarlet, her lips chapped, her hair a nest of twigs and locomotive soot. How he had thought of her, all those months on the Peninsula.

"Do you have any morphine? I don't have any morphine," she said.

"There is no morphine. There is nothing. No dressings. No more whiskey. Nothing. We left behind all our medicine wagons on the Peninsula. All we have are the trains."

*The trains. Yes, the trains.*

"I looked for you after you left. Where did you go?" he asked, grasping her by the elbow, but then he let go again and shouted, "God damn it."

Behind them, in the ever-filling valley, another line of ambulances was arriving, while at the station a single locomotive idled, its few cars being loaded by figures moving at the pace of a truculent child. An eternity was passing in the time it was taking to lift a man onto a stretcher and shove him into a boxcar. "God, they're moving so slowly. Don't they know there isn't any time? The Rebels could be upon us at any moment. You'd think they'd have learned. It's the Peninsula all over again." He began to pace back and forth, raking his hands over the dome of his head, which glistened in the suddenly brilliant sunshine. Stipp stopped and shut his eyes for a moment, as if he couldn't stand to see the unraveling scene before him. Then he said, "We don't have a choice. We'll have to transport the ones we can save first. That's what we'll do. Otherwise, we are all doomed. Afterwards, we'll load the rest." He turned toward Mary, relieved he'd found the answer. "I need you to help, Mary. I need you to go down to the depot and sort them."

"Sort them?"

"Organize the wounded into groups."

It took a moment for what Stipp was saying to her to penetrate, and then its meaning entered her like a knife. "You want me to choose?"

"Yes."

"But I cannot choose." She twisted away, stumbling backward on the rocks.

He lunged toward her and grabbed her by the elbow, thrusting her before him to witness the scene from which he had turned away. "Listen to me, Mary. You see all those men? Most of them will die. If not here, then back in Washington. On the Peninsula, no one shot in the belly or chest or head survived, not one, no matter how fast we got to them. Do you understand? We have to save the most men. If we let one on the train who will die anyway, it will doom two."

Mary wrenched free of his grasp. "But what if we treat them here, what if we set up a hospital?"

"There isn't time. I need you to go down to the station and make certain that no one gets on that train who can't be saved."

"But I told them all that they would get on a train. They're waiting. I told them—" But her voice trailed away. Exhaustion was magnifying everything: the wearying hours, the clatter of the trains, the harsh light falling on Stipp's face. "The men are depending on me. I told them everyone would get on a train."

"Now you'll have to tell them something different."

"But I can't decide who will go and who will stay." She was losing her sense of balance; she might topple over the outcrop, tumble down the hill, might prefer that to what Stipp was asking of her. Hovering there, between earth and sky, she thought she heard the distant crackle of gunfire or thunder.

The world declaring the situation dire, as if no one knew.

"Someone has to decide," Stipp said.

"I can't."

"Then go home," Stipp shouted, and turned and walked away.

Mary put her head in her hands. At home, Amelia would be feeding the baby; dinner would be being served on a white tablecloth, upstairs a bed would be waiting, and sheets, and someone to take her bloodied clothes from her, heat her bath water, and gentle her into a clean bed. Perhaps, even, the months of separation might have rendered Amelia grateful to see her again.

*You see, it is a war.* Everything is a war.

"Wait," Mary cried. She hurried after Stipp and seized his arm, and he wheeled on her. He was utterly changed, even from a moment ago. Sweat and blood matted his beard and hair; his eyes were wild and black. That night, so long ago, when he had tried to bar her from the amputation, angry as he had been, he had looked nothing like this.

"You want to be a surgeon? To be a surgeon is to look a man in the eye and tell him the truth. If you can't do that, then get out of here. Go home." He was shouting now, his fury echoing the thunder rising in the distance. Stipp had taken her by the scaffolding of her shoulders as if he no longer trusted her, but now he pulled her into an embrace and whispered, "It is all butchery. Every bit of it. You cannot help them with just whiskey, Mary."

Mary lifted her face to the sun, but it had fled behind the clouds and rain spilled from the sky.

"Choose who you are," he whispered into her ear. "Choose who you'll be."

She cried out then, but softly, and then a look of recognition flared between them, but only for the briefest moment, and then they parted, Stipp along the ridge, assessing, and Mary threading through the men, resisting the urge to stop, to touch, to soothe, to do any of the things she had been doing moments before. But she did not look away, either, for she was already quantifying and tagging the men in her mind, sorting them one from the other, practicing, steeling herself for the work ahead, because she had already chosen who she was a long time ago, the moment she had inserted a knife into Jenny's pelvis.

# *Chapter Forty-four*

James Blevens sat across from John Brinton in the Surgeon General's office at the Riggs Bank Building near the Mansion. Blevens had been called to meet Brinton, who had been appointed to an as yet unnamed post in the office of the Surgeon General. Hammond, the latest man to become surgeon general, was away at the Armory Square Hospital on the mall, meeting victims of the Second Bull Run coming off the trains, trying to get a sense of the numbers and what still needed to be done. Blevens, too, wanted to be there, to see if he could help in some indeterminate way. His hands were still clumsy, though perhaps he could assist, he thought. But for now he was stuck here, trying to understand what this stranger wanted from him. James could hardly keep track of who was in charge anymore. Tripler had been banished; Stanton had made a disastrous plea for the public to become temporary nurses; the new surgeon general was no one anyone knew. The whole business was a great mess.

Brinton, a man of about thirty, leaned across the polished walnut desk and asked, "How are your hands?"

"They're coming along," James said.

Brinton nodded. He understood how self-conscious Blevens was about his predicament: a surgeon who had been kept from going to the Peninsula because he had not been able to adequately control a scalpel. Brinton would not embarrass Blevens further by asking how much progress he had made along that line; it was none of his concern. Indeed, it was to his advantage if Blevens were to remain completely out of field work.

"Hammond has instituted a medical museum."

"A medical museum?"

"A place for research. It is not yet widely known. Joseph Woodward is in charge of the medical portion, I am in charge of the surgical."

Startled, James said, "I think a place of research is essential. So much is known, but hardly anyone has compiled it. I've been looking at specimens, trying to discern cause. Microscopy is helpful, particularly in the stool, but even more so in sputum. The fluids of our bodies harbor more than we think they do. It's entirely possible that contagion is not so much the effect of humors, but of—" James broke off. He was babbling. The months of isolated research had done that to him. "I think a center for research is an excellent idea," he concluded.

"I thought you might think so. In this, I believe we will find some purpose for the carnage, if there can be any. Or at least we can make it so. Not just a silver lining, but silver, or gold itself, in the form of collective knowledge."

"Exactly," Blevens said. "Will you publish the findings?"

"Yes. Something like the *History of the British Medical Services in the Crimea*, but more extensive. A medical history of the war. We'll write up cases. I particularly wish to look at statistics—of disease, efficacious treatment, occurrence, et cetera. So many men are dying of disease. I have particular interest, as do you, in microscopy."

"The *cause* of disease, not just its symptoms." Now Blevens was leaning forward too, his scarred hands on the desk.

"Yes. True causality, discoverable, I think, in the invisible."

Blevens exhaled and sat back and worked his fingers, contemplating the depth and breadth of the proposed work

"But I need help," Brinton said. "At present, what we require are specimens of morbid anatomy, surgical or medical, which can be regarded as valuable; along with the projectiles and foreign bodies that caused the wound. I need someone with an eye and a passion for research who can convince a field surgeon to go to the trouble of retaining examples of tissue and bone. Someone who's been on a battlefield, who would know the pressures. From what I understand, you were at Bull Run."

Blevens nodded.

"We'll need histories, too, summaries to be sent along with the specimens. It will be a lot of extra work for the surgeons. They'll need to be persuaded of the value of it, the need for it. I think you ought to explain that the medical officer who sends in a specimen will have his name attached to the report, credit given. This will provide incentive, I think. I need someone like you, someone who can talk the surgeons into seeing the advantage for them, but also someone who is very adept at acquiring specimens. You understand, this will be the entire army collaborating in research." He studied James, watching for signs of objection, but there were none. "If you are willing, I'll assign you to follow the Army of the Potomac."

"To follow them?" Blevens asked. "But haven't you heard? The army is all here." That morning, a newspaper boy had been hawking the headlines: *"Retreat from Fairfax Is Complete. Lincoln asks McClellan to Head the Defenses of Washington. Rebel Army in Motion."*

"For now, begin with the Armory Square Hospital. See what you can find. Follow cases, explain what we need. And then, if the war goes on—" He stopped speaking and looked down at the massive desk.

*He is ashamed,* Blevens thought. Without the war, there would be no research. Without the war, there would be no opportunity for learning.

They avoided one another's eyes for a moment.

"Someone has to wring the good from all of this," Blevens said.

Brinton brightened. "Yes," he said. "Yes."

Outside, on Pennsylvania Avenue, Blevens passed a line of Pope's defeated soldiers hobbling toward Fort Stevens as citizens scurried to stock their homes in case of siege. How he wished he could tell Mary about the project. On his forays to the various hospitals across the city, he had searched for her, but it was as if she had vanished. From time to time he'd even perused the contract and transient nurse lists pouring into the Surgeon General's office from the hospitals, but that had yielded nothing. Finally, he'd written Amelia, and her reply had hinted of panic and despair. She didn't know where her daughter was, hadn't heard from her since she'd sent her off on the train in February. Wasn't there anything Blevens could do to help? There had been a breach. Jenny had died. Had he heard? Had he seen Mary? The baby was well, though. Thriving. If he found Mary, would he tell her this?

After receiving the letter, James had paid to have his name listed in the City Directory, though he wasn't certain that Mary would seek him out. In his bleakest moments, he worried that Mary had been unable to forgive herself, worried what she might have done, in desperation. If anyone knew how to end her own life, it would be Mary. But he pushed the unholy thought away. He was imagining, out of worry.

He flagged down a hack, climbed in, and headed for the Armory Square Hospital.

# *Chapter Forty-five*

Jake Miles walked the grounds of Armory Square Hospital with a kind of jiggly, excitable gait that betrayed his agitation, shirttails hanging, his suspenders slipping from his shoulders. He'd been appointed guard when no one else knew what to do with him. In the heat of early September it was simply too hot to tolerate the scratchy, shoddy wool of his uniform jacket. Every so often in his assigned circumlocution of the hospital he crammed his hand down the inside of his pants leg to pluck his flask from its harness and knock back a good swallow. During the months of the hospital's construction, when his job had been to prevent the theft of building materials, he'd found shelter in the lee of a pile of scrap wood, but all that had been cleaned up. To sneak a swallow now he had to look around and be quick about it. But in the last few days, the growing heap of limbs outside the surgery window had provided a refuge behind which he could hunker down. He squatted with his back turned, his shoulders hunched, knowing that to passersby on the mall he appeared to be reverently tending the pile, whose presence they greeted first with shock, then revulsion, followed by ashamed glances to verify the savagery.

It was near noon. The sun was white in the Washington sky. Jake could see the doctors through the open window of the surgery doing their depraved work of lopping off arms and legs. Jake had no idea if he was supposed to do something with the pile of limbs rising outside the window or not, but he refused to touch them. The wretched stink nauseated. That was the other reason he required the whiskey.

After tucking his flask away, he rose like a phoenix from behind the pile of limbs and sauntered around the side of the hospital to B Street, where ambulances and carriages bearing visitors had been arriving all morning. Jake idly surveyed the visitors, mostly Washington women swaying up the walk in their wide hoop skirts, but there were others whose object in coming was to search for loved ones. They were just off the train from somewhere distant, their faces a collective mask of grief. As Jake studied them, more as a matter of boredom than anything else, a tall man disengaged himself from a hack and strode up the walkway. There was something in his posture that made Jake feel a sudden longing for Bonnie, though he didn't know why. Something about the way the man walked, or his studied absentmindedness. Jake hid in the corner under the eaves and watched him march past.

Inside the hospital, James Blevens scanned the rows of beds as was his habit, as unconscious to him as his ever-present need to flex his fingers, looking for Mary Sutter. When he saw her, it took a moment to believe it was she. Her dress was torn and bloodstained, her skin tanned and freckled; in her hair were twigs and leaves. Her expression was newly broken. She looked as if she'd been wandering in the woods for days.

She looked up and discovered him. He flexed and unflexed his fingers, wondering what he meant to her.

She came toward him and said, "James."

No one paid them any mind. Outside, limbs were being piled; what was a public embrace?

In the end, every wounded man had made it onto the trains, every one, except those who had died and had been buried in shallow, unmarked trenches. For four full days, Mary had coolly stood at the railcars and made choices, had trod the impossible line. Had tried to reconcile need with mercy. Just before they left on the last train, Stipp had stopped at Mary's car and gazed wordlessly up at her before turning away to prowl the grounds around the station, calling out to the hills to ascertain whether or not anyone else remained before he stepped onto the engineer's car as the train lurched forward, the station burning behind them to keep the Confederates from salvaging anything. Mary hadn't seen Stipp since. She told herself that the men who had died and been buried beside the station in long trenches would have died anyway, comforting herself like she had comforted the mothers of stillborns. As she had comforted Bonnie. As she had been unable to comfort Amelia.

When she was finished telling James the story, he said, "Extraordinary."

"Not so extraordinary. There was another woman there, too. Clara Barton. She brought supplies. Jams and jellies. She was feeding everyone. She was of far more use than I."

"I think it is as Stipp said," James said. He was being careful, for he had never seen Mary so vulnerable. "There wasn't room for everyone."

"But in the end there was."

James waited before he said, "You are not provident, Mary. There was nothing else you could have done."

At some point, they had made it out of the hospital and were standing up against the building, sheltered under the eaves. Observing them from around the corner, Jake Miles suddenly placed the man's long, beak-like face, the sharp gaze, the thin frame. That man was the doctor who'd taken his Bonnie to those Sutters, that woman there who had made a mess of things and cost him his baby and his wife. Tears welled up in his eyes as he remembered how the first night Bonnie had come home, his little boy had clung to his finger while Bonnie had slept, and how Bonnie had waked up and looked at him like that Miss Sutter was looking at that doctor now, as if there were such a thing as hope in the world. For the first time in months, Jake thought of Christian Sutter, how he had poured liquor down his throat, how it had seemed the right thing to do, how he had suffered when he'd gone back to the corner of the train to find Christian as lifeless as the baby Bonnie had carted all the way back to the Sutter house.

James looked up and saw the pale boy peering at them. It took a moment to place him, for he had not thought of him for more than a year. "Jake?"

Jake wiped his tearstained face with the back of his arm and spun away from his perch on a pile of bricks. "Everything is spoiled, you hear me? Everything."

Mary turned and took in the sight of Jake Miles. His face was flushed, his eyes bright and feverish.

"That Christian shoulda never done what he did," Jake shouted.

"But Christian is dead," James said. It seemed brutal to say it in front of Mary, but maybe the boy didn't know. For a moment James considered telling Jake that Jenny had died, too, in order to forever settle in Jake's mind the debt he thought the Sutters owed him, but the boy whirled away around the corner of the building and disappeared.

Mary turned pale and closed her eyes. "He's right. Everything is spoiled."

James wanted to say that everything wasn't spoiled; that one day they would learn something from all of this that would change medicine forever. But for now, he didn't say anything.

For days and days, Mary had been living on courage, but now she could feel it draining away from her. And here was James Blevens, solicitude, like a caress, emanating from his concerned face. "Take me home," she said.

He startled, for he had thought it would have taken days to persuade her to go home.

"To Albany?" he asked.

"No. My rooms."

The tenement in Swampdoodle resembled nothing of Dove Street. James Blevens tapped the driver and said, "This can't be it."

"It is," Mary said, descending nimbly from the carriage, surprising James, because she had rested on his shoulder all the way here in the hack, rousing only to say, turn here, turn there. James paid the driver, jumped from the carriage, and took Mary by the elbow, letting her guide him up to a musty room that might rent on the quay in Albany by the hour. Or something in Five Points. The memory brought him up short. He had not thought of Sarah in months.

*If Amelia could see this*, he thought.

Mary sat on her bed and did not move, and he understood that she would lie down in her dirty clothes and sleep if he did not help her. She did not resist when he undid her buttons, helped her to ease her dress around her shoulders. He had touched women as a physician, and he summoned that detachment now, and the self-control allowed the intimacy. He lifted a blanket from the bed and held it up, and she rose, her back to him, and dropped the dress in a heap to the floor and slid the straps of her camisole and her underwear to the floor also. When she was done removing her undergarments, she sank onto the bed and slid under a sheet and James laid the blanket over her.

He removed his coat and hat and searched under the dresser for her bath basin. In the alley, he pumped brackish water. He ran the wet washcloth over her scratched arms, her smudged face, down the length of her back. He untangled her hair as she slept, painstakingly removing twigs and broken leaves, exercise for his stiff fingers. The window opened to the alley, and the shrieks and bellows of Swampdoodle bounced off the narrow passageway.

It was the sixth of September. Mary had said she'd left on the thirtieth with all those volunteer nurses. Four days out in the field, and then three at the hospital. She might sleep forever, he thought.

And she did sleep through James's coming and going, the clatter of the kettle on the stove and the putting away of the coffee and bread and butter he had purchased for her. The day passed into evening and then into night, and he slept next to the open window in the one chair, his feet stretched before him like a steel gate, guarding Mary from the world.

# *Chapter Forty-six*

That evening, Saturday the sixth of September, Abraham Lincoln climbed toward the roof on the spiral iron stairway he had discovered behind a door in an attic room. Through unfinished walls shrouded with spider webs, he could hear the occasional crash of china drifting up from the East Room. After the week's terrible news, it astounded him that people still attended the regular Saturday night levee, though in the crush the guests' uncertain gaze had followed him more closely than usual on his round of handshaking and salutations. He usually enjoyed these public opinion baths, but tonight he had not wanted to hear the shouted questions, proffered opinions, and clinging entreaties about Lee's whereabouts.

With each ascending stair, Lincoln's heart thundered against his chest wall. He had learned not to panic when his heart betrayed him like this. It calmed usually, over time, though his wife always took fright when he had to pause to catch his breath.

Sometimes he thought his heart might burst, it beat so hard.

Two more steps and he was out the door, taking great, gulping breaths of the muggy stench of Washington. Bent over, his hands to his knees, he willed his racing heart to slow, imagining that if it did not, he might die up here and no one would find him for days. Unlike the divided country, or George McClellan even, his heart began finally to obey, and as a faint northerly breeze began to bestow tepid relief, Lincoln straightened, removed his coat, his tie, and loosened the buttons of his shirt.

No doubt Hay would soon be searching the East Room for him. Or Mary, or Tad, racing between the silk ball gowns and worsted pants legs of the guests to impart him some welcome piece of distraction from the social hoohah.

The problem with being president, Lincoln decided, was that he was rarely ever alone when he needed to be, except in the deep hours of the night, and even then the house echoed with the ghost of Willie. Even up here, he couldn't be certain that he wouldn't once again imagine that Willie was beside him. Lately he had found himself talking to his dead son. The other day, when his pants leg had grazed the arm of a chair, he'd even turned to snatch Willie up in his arms the way he used to.

Before.

Lincoln leaned now against the parapet and gazed westward toward the half-built Washington Monument barely visible against the Arlington Heights, the fort campfires flickering like yellow stars above the moat of the Potomac. Perhaps Mary was right, perhaps the dead did try to communicate from the grave. Her cadre of spiritualists had certainly convinced her, and she derived comfort from their tales, poor woman, though he simply could not tolerate the sitting around of tables and the holding of hands in the dark. What his money sometimes went to. But still, perhaps. Above the clatter of carriage traffic, he strained now to see if he could hear Willie's high prattle, but it was just the lowing of the army cattle grazing on the mall, the raucous banging of a tavern piano from nearby Murder Bay, and the party noises floating up from the East Room.

Ghosts. Or not.

Lincoln peered through the dying evening light at the vulnerable city in his care. Why shouldn't his family share in the general grief? Willie, in Mary's mind, had been more than enough to pay. And if he commanded his grown son Robert to leave Harvard and enter the army, he was certain Mary would imprison the boy in his room to prevent his going. Somewhere out there in the gloaming was a Rebel army intent upon conquering Washington. There had been skirmishes at Fairfax and Falls Church. Closer even than Manassas. For a moment, Lincoln allowed himself to imagine the worst: a surrender, the handing over of the Mansion's keys, the Union irretrievably sundered. It was this that had sent him wheezing up the stairway away from the spying eyes of the nervous party guests.

This, and the need to entertain a single, unadulterated moment of despair: What if he failed?

Almost a year and a half had passed since the war had started. Since this most recent debacle at Bull Run, Lee was marching north, primed either to circle back and attack Washington or to press even farther northward, perhaps even to seize Philadelphia or New York. The maneuver would destroy the country forever, a country built on principle and purpose. It was bruising to think that he might preside over the country's bloody cessation, and then immediately he was conscious of the vanity. The personal vainglory of worrying about how he might be perceived. What history would be written of the destroyed democratic experiment of a young, unsustainable country would be brief in the annals of time, his part a mere whisper. The failure not his alone. But still, what Lee and Jefferson Davis didn't understand was that to destroy a union founded on freedom was to declare all of humanity's endeavors foolhardy.

To fail at this would be to fail at God's work.

Lincoln began to march back and forth along the parapet, the city noises turning hushed and expectant, as if at any moment Lee was going to charge down Pennsylvania Avenue and claim the Mansion for the Confederacy.

Mary's comfort had been that God was taking care of Willie, that it was only their own inability to perceive Willie's attempts to reach them that kept him from them. Some days, Lincoln thought her view insane, and other days felt himself insane for his inability to see God's hand in all of this, and even to believe that God existed.

What would it mean, then, to fail at the work of a being whose existence you doubted?

Lincoln supposed that his failure would mean that he, too, would no longer exist.

He would love to see Willie again.

*Enough.*

He turned violently and toppled against the parapet, catching himself with his free hand, then righting himself, tugging at his clothes, fighting for breath as his heart once again galloped out of control.

If he allowed himself to lose his mind, as he already feared Mary had lost hers, then he would be of no use to anyone.

God's work, then, and whether God existed or not, he would act as if He did, on faith, for he could deduce no other reason in the end for man's existence. He would die one day. Sooner rather than later, a failure or maybe a hero, perhaps a victim of his own quavering heart, perhaps a result of his insistence that men see their hypocrisy for what it was. Something, then, to warrant the last year and a half of misery. Something good to come of all of this, the very least of which, if he were successful, would be an unsundered union.

But it was not just this that drove him. There was a certain decency that had to be imposed. A righting of wrongs. Yes, just as he had shut down the Maryland legislature, so would he shut down slavery.

The language had already come to him. His other idea—forming a colony in Africa or the Indies to which any freed American slave or black man could migrate—had proved unacceptable to the abolitionists who were demanding political equality for the black man. It had not been his intention to liberate, but now? Now it was. The tone of the final document would have to be firm, the intent indisputable. Already he had read one draft to a portion of his cabinet, but now he had decided that nothing less than complete authority would do. After all, this was armed rebellion. Not even the innumerable dead had quelled the Rebels' intransigence. And now they were marching nearby, perhaps even approaching the city's ring of forts. At any moment, Rebel muskets might flash in the night and the last battle might begin, leaving a proclamation he might never get to make unfinished on his desk.

Oh, to fail as grandly as that.

His heart beat more slowly now, though Lincoln could not understand why. A country's imminent failure should rouse even the stars to fainting.

To emancipate. He shut his eyes and lifted his face to the night. To effect such a change. To enact with impunity. He supposed Jefferson Davis and Robert E. Lee wanted the same, believed the insistence that they remain in a union in which they were unhappy an encroachment upon their own personal freedom.

Lincoln simply could not understand a man who could not see his own fallibility. Irony lost in the blind pursuit of cacophonous righteousness. I wish to be free, but *you* may not be free. What he hated most was that they could not see the inherent cruelty in their economy. Their slaves' skin might be black, but it was not as black as the souls who might enslave them.

Contradiction the rule of the land. Right and wrong were as interchangeable these days, it seemed, as the winds, and yet here was one concrete thing he could achieve, would achieve before the end, whenever that came.

What purpose death? What purpose any of it?

Lincoln allowed himself this last moment of melancholy before banishing the remnants of the despair he had indulged, and then he slowly descended through the torrid heat of the attic rooms, entering once again the unnumbered circle of hell reserved for the doggedly hopeful.

On Monday, September the eighth, Lincoln turned to his secretary of war, Edwin Stanton, and said, "Exactly where do you think the Rebels might go after Frederick?"

North of the city, the guns at Fort Stevens were pounding away, practicing in case the Rebels, who had crossed the Potomac at Leesburg, Virginia, on Thursday and were heading north toward Frederick, Maryland, and its stores of Federal ammunition, were to instead turn back to take Washington.

Stanton cleared his throat and tried to compose himself. He was furious. He thought he had sealed McClellan's dismissal, had in fact come today hoping to hear from Lincoln that the indictment he had written with the attorney general had once and for all rid the nation of that timorous little man, but instead the decision that Lincoln had made on September second was holding. George McClellan was again in charge, and in fact had been given leave under General Halleck to do all that was necessary to defend Washington. They were right back where they had been in March, with McClellan all but running the Army of the Potomac—though in the last month he had defied Halleck's orders again and again. In truth, after Pope's abominable performance at Bull Run, it was hard to imagine any Union general less trustworthy than Pope. Next to him, McClellan appeared to be as fearless an invader as Genghis Khan. But McClellan? With Stonewall Jackson and Lee running unfettered through Maryland? Stanton wished the war was still on established Southern ground, not the shifting sands of the state of Maryland, whose legislature Lincoln had recently reduced by half when it was discovered that a good portion of its number were traitorous. Those members were now in prison. If there was one thing Stanton admired about Lincoln, it was his willingness to hatchet any rebellion in the ambivalent state just to the north. These were instincts to trust, but McClellan was nothing but trouble.

"It's difficult to say where they'll go," Stanton said, staunching his wish to rail against McClellan. "If the Rebels do take Frederick, then perhaps they'll head northward. The governor of Pennsylvania has called for militia. They are arming themselves."

Lincoln was pacing. Stanton doubted that the president had slept since the news of the defeat at Bull Run had come through. He'd been a whirlwind of activity, taking charge of the collapsing army, even calling his friend Pope into his office yesterday to have him read directly to him his account of the failure at Bull Run. It had been clear that Pope lacked insight into what had happened. He had blamed everyone but himself. Where, Stanton thought now, was a Union general who did not blame someone other than himself for his own failures?

Lincoln said, "Tell Halleck to have McClellan gather every man, gun, wagon, and mule within his reach and get them back out there."

Lincoln knew the state of the men, knew how exhausted and demoralized they were, because he had visited the hospitals and seen the havoc that had ripped through the troops.

"I've already issued a directive," Stanton said.

"Will McClellan move? It is imperative."

"I believe so." Stanton didn't believe so, but Lincoln was in a mood.

Lincoln exhaled and gazed up distractedly. "Do you know, if we pursue them now, this could be it: we could annihilate the entire Rebel army in the next few days. Surround them, cut them off."

"Or they could take Philadelphia."

For a moment, equal visions of victory and defeat competed, each one as real a possibility as the other.

Stanton heaved himself to his feet. A quagmire, with the best general stuck in a mansion, and the Union's hopes pinned on a man whose record terrified him.

Amelia Sutter laid aside the Albany *Argus* with its news of the Rebel incursion northward and reached for little Elizabeth lying on a blanket at her feet. In the parlor, the evening air still carried the pungent whiff of the last of Albany's summer heat, but Elizabeth didn't seem to notice the noxious smell. Eight months old and thriving, she gurgled and stuffed her little fists into her mouth against the teething pain she didn't seem to mind, either. The darling child was Amelia's only evidence that she had ever had daughters.

*Do as you like.*

And what would she say to Mary now, months later? It was impossible to govern her grief. She'd not had a single letter since Mary had left last February. Now she feared she would never know whether or not Mary was even still alive.

A hundred times over, she'd relived Elizabeth's birth. A choice changed here, a detail there. It was impossible not to despise herself. What mother chastises one twin for the death of another? Insatiable, a mother's need to save her children. Any means possible, including, it would seem, betrayal.

Elizabeth would be dead now, but for Mary.

*Thank you*, is what she would say now. *For trying. For coming back when you didn't want to. And I am sorry your heart was broken.*

"Amelia?" Bonnie was standing at the door with a bottle of milk.

Amelia handed her granddaughter to Bonnie and watched Elizabeth hungrily take the rubber nipple into her mouth.

Bonnie looked up from Elizabeth, as the child, newly dexterous, balanced the bottle in one hand and grasped Bonnie's pinky with her other. "She looks like Mary, doesn't she?" Bonnie asked.

The cry of a thrush escalated in the evening air. Bonnie set the child in Amelia's lap. Amelia supported Elizabeth with her hand to her back as the child fought to sit up, already exhibiting her aunt Mary's predilection for independence.

# *Chapter Forty-seven*

The day after General McClellan left Washington with his exhausted army in search of Robert E. Lee, Lincoln was looking out onto Pennsylvania Avenue from his second-floor office at a young woman poised at the Mansion gate. By the set of her shoulders and the deliberate manner of her posture, she appeared to be on an errand of some importance. He watched as she opened the gate and strode down the slate walkway, her fingers entwined in the trailing ribbons of a bonnet that dangled from her hand.

He turned his attention to the men in the room. John Hay was standing in his usual corner, observing with that perspicacious gaze of his, unnatural in so young a man. Seated in one of the chairs that ringed the president's desk, Secretary Stanton was about to argue that it was clear that what Lee wanted was not New York, but the entire state of Maryland, when the butler interrupted at the door.

"Sir? Do excuse me. There is a young woman who wishes to speak with Mr. Hay. She claims to know him. I informed her that he was in conference, but she refuses to leave until she has an audience."

All three men, including the butler, aimed a mocking expression at John Hay, who had been in and out of love at least a dozen times since arriving in the capital. Now it seemed the women were following him to work, though to hear Hay tell it, he'd had little success in his amorous pursuits and was at pains to find any female company that would oblige him with even the smallest of attentions.

Amused, the president said, "Oh, do bring her in. We'd love to meet the young woman."

Hay began to sputter. This was beyond tolerance. Lincoln was exercising his fondness for diversion at his expense. And in front of Stanton. He could hear Stanton now. *Oh, that Hay is such a dilettante.*

The butler ushered in the young woman Lincoln had observed from his window. Tall, square-jawed, she seemed familiar to Hay, but her tattered appearance silenced both Stanton and Lincoln, ever eager to mock his weakness for the feminine. She was not like Hay's usual women, pampered girls obsessed with the latest fashions in hats and sleeves. Neither would anyone mistake her for any of the more serious daughters of the senators. Hay peered at her: she was not any of the women he'd recently met. The men rose as she looked directly at Hay and said hello.

The president said, "You know this young woman, Mr. Hay?"

Hay took a moment and, finally remembering, said, "Mr. Lincoln, do you recall that I once told you I had met a remarkable young woman on the street?"

"How can I keep track?"

"This one didn't like Miss Dix." Hay turned to Mary and said, "Allow me to introduce you. Miss Mary Sutter, President Lincoln."

The men bowed.

"I've interrupted," Mary said. "I do beg your pardon for not having made an appointment, but I did not know until just this moment that I would need one."

At this pronouncement, Hay smiled. She had become well versed, he saw, in the ways of getting things done in Washington.

Mary said to Hay, "You remembered my name."

"As Mr. Lincoln will attest, I have an affinity for names."

Stanton said under his breath, "Females, especially."

"And this is Mr. Stanton."

Mary said, "I am acquainted with you as well, Mr. Stanton. I was your employee until recently."

Stanton peered at her, finally recognizing her as the young woman who had disappeared a month before, leaving them with extra work.

"Are you nursing under Miss Dix now?" Hay asked.

"Not really, no."

The president and Hay exchanged glances. Just that morning they'd had another letter from Miss Dix, complaining that the surgeons and matrons at the Armory Square Hospital had been hiring nurses themselves and that her authority was being summarily usurped. Something had to be done, or she would not be responsible for the chaos that would ensue.

"I came this morning to ask Mr. Hay for help. I wish to follow the army with supplies. I was at Fairfax. Mr. Hay helped me once before. I was hoping he could help me again."

Stanton, Lincoln, and Hay stood in silence, awed that the young woman before them had braved Fairfax. A regimental surgeon named William Stipp had come to tell them of the abject neglect the wounded had suffered. Ten thousand dead or wounded was the provisional count. But the number was impossible to reconcile, and Lincoln especially had felt helpless. At times, it seemed he could not control anything, least of all the help the wounded needed.

Mary said, "I wish to go today, if possible."

Lincoln thought, *If only once George McClellan had said that to me.*

Stanton sputtered, "But this is ridiculous. Lee could tour Maryland without firing a single shot. It is nonsensical to send a woman chasing after the army when we don't even know where, or if, there will be a battle."

But Lincoln held Mary's gaze as he said, "You understand that you are risking yourself, Miss Sutter. For an uncertain future." His eyes were sharp, quizzical, but alight, too, as if he already knew what she would say.

"None of us knows the future, do we, sir?"

"Write her a pass, Hay," Lincoln said. "And one for the quartermaster for any supplies."

"You can't be serious," Stanton said. "After what just happened at Fairfax?" He rose in a huff and went to the window, his back turned on all of them as Hay bent over the president's desk.

"Thank you, Mr. Lincoln," Mary said.

At the window, watching Hay accompany the young woman down the walkway toward Pennsylvania Avenue, Stanton shook his head. "You have just written that young woman's death warrant."

"I was not the one who sent a thousand drunken men thirty miles on a train, Stanton. Besides, I have more faith in that young woman than I do in most of my generals."

Stanton pursed his lips and said, "She left the War Department in the lurch, you know."

James Blevens cinched the copper banding around the ten kegs of alcohol he had packed into the long wagon bed standing in the lot next to the Surgeon General's office. The stills had been boiling for three days to make enough alcohol to fill them. He had allowed no one to label them, though, for a siphon could easily drain the casks and he feared losing the preservative before he even got to a field hospital. Even the teamster assigned to drive the wagon was eyeing them with sly greed.

James tossed his bag under the wagon seat. On Saturday, he had awakened aching and uncomfortable in the armchair in Mary's room, and had watched Mary sleep for a long while before writing her a note and going to Armory Square to begin the job of persuading surgeons to take histories and to save the amputated limbs. He was met with quizzical exasperation and the forceful suggestion that if he wanted the limbs so badly, he was welcome to go root around in the pile himself and take the limbs back into the wards, where he could try to match them to their previous owners. And he was welcome to take his own damn histories, too, because they were a little busy, goddamn it, and whose shining fucking idea was this, as if they didn't have enough to do, and if he had so much time on his hands, why didn't he pick up a scalpel and give them a hand instead of yammering on and on about specimens and research when men were dying? James managed to catch only one soldier just as he was taken into surgery to ask him some questions, but the surgeons tossed out the leg before James could claim it.

And now, Monday, he was going to follow the army to try to persuade field surgeons of the benefits of research, and he would have to do it under conditions far less favorable than the ones at Armory Square. This morning, Brinton had taken in the reported disinterest of the Armory Square surgeons, sniffed, written out a circular to distribute, and then ordered James to follow the army with barrels of preservative and to make certain he obtained specimens.

James had no time to go back and check on Mary. He had written her a letter and posted it, saying he would be gone for a while, but that he would return as soon as possible and that she was not to disappear again under any circumstances. He had little faith that she would follow his command. It was entirely possible that she would vanish again. She had her own mind, exhibited by her choice of those shabby rooms.

What absolute trust she had placed in him.

The same trust Sarah had once placed in him.

Why he should be thinking of Sarah now was not a mystery to him. He supposed it was seeing Mary asleep. Perhaps it was that in the face of so much death, he wanted to understand his life before it was taken from him. Or perhaps it was that he didn't want to ever lose anyone else again, as he had almost lost Mary, as Mary had lost Jenny.

Everyone was precious now, even the mistaken love of his youth.

# Chapter Forty-eight

It was late afternoon on Sunday, the fourteenth of September, and the sun was angled low over the swell of South Mountain to the west. It had taken Mary and her driver four days to travel the forty miles north from Washington to Frederick, only to get caught now behind the army's long, snaking supply line and its soaring plume of yellow dust as it headed west. All day, Mary and her driver had been trapped behind the procession. The soldiers had marched on ahead, following Robert E. Lee, who had abandoned Frederick two days ago. A corporal had found a copy of Lee's secret orders in a field there, and for once, George McClellan acted. He gave chase, leaving the supply line to follow at its own tortoise pace. Mary estimated that the line was at least ten miles long. Artillery, then food, then hospital supplies at the rear, and behind the ambulances a herd of steer prodded forward by listless soldiers. Food on the hoof, tearing up the macadam, clogging the road.

In the distance, black smoke hovered over the mountain pass. All day, the booms and hiss of cannon and musketry had rolled down the National Road from the northern tip of the Blue Ridge Mountains, but now, late in the afternoon, the pass had grown eerily quiet. The line ground to a halt. The steer headed out into the farmland to graze, but the teamsters sharpened their ears, listening, the silence far less comforting than it would seem.

Mary removed the handkerchief she used as a screen for the dust, welcoming the respite from the jolts and jarring of the last few days. In Washington, the quartermaster sergeant had taken one look at the signature on her letter and had given her trunk after trunk of bleached muslin rolls, papers of pins, scissors, lint, sponges, silk suture, syringes, needles, towels, leg splints, fracture boxes, thermometers, tourniquets, bone saws, forceps, ichthyocolla plaster, and no end of medicines, including a treasure trove of quinine, morphine powder, and chloroform. There were mercury pills, tannic acid, ferric chloride, lead acetate, and numerous flasks of nitrous ether stoppered by lamb's intestine. There was zinc sulfate and spirits of ammonia. Compared to the one bottle of whiskey she had taken with her to Fairfax, she was now the wealthiest woman in the world.

Her driver was a laconic, sober man, unruffled by his assignment to ferry Mary wherever she wished to go. At night he rolled up in a blanket next to the wagon while she slept under it, and in the morning he rose and made her coffee, turning aside when she traipsed into a nearby gully or wood to take care of herself.

James's note was tucked in her pocket. *It is not all spoiled,* he had written. *Have hope.* Her driver hopped down from the seat and sauntered forward to see how long the wait would be. Within minutes, he was back. "Road's blocked. Ambulances are coming, heading toward Frederick."

There were twenty of them—the two-wheeled type—jouncing over the hard road, filled with wounded. The entire army train pulled off the road after it passed.

"Now is our chance," Mary said.

Night fell quickly, evidence of autumn. She and her driver trundled past restless horses and the dark ghosts of covered wagons, lanterns flickering like forgotten summer fireflies, teamsters' snores already sawing into the chilly night. When they reached the end of the supply line, stars emerged to light their way, but darkness closed in as they climbed the wooded slope of South Mountain. When they reached the top, the whole night had passed and dawn was pinking the eastern sky behind them.

The first bodies appeared around a rocky outcrop. They lay sprawled across the road in postures of death next to the detritus of war: broken caissons, splintered wheels, discarded muskets, the carcasses of horses swelling in the morning sun. The driver let out a long, low whistle and stopped the wagon. He hopped down and turned in a circle. "Hello? Does anyone need help? Hello?"

A hollow breeze rustled the leaves.

Mary armed herself with a canteen of whiskey and another of water. Her driver armed himself with a shotgun, and together they trudged from body to body, searching for someone who might still be alive. They counted hundreds of dead, Rebel and Federal alike, hidden behind trees and curled behind boulders.

Even this early in the morning, fatted carrion birds waddled among the dead.

Hello? Hello?

They climbed back into the wagon. At the summit, an inn built of stone housed a doctor presiding over a dozen wounded. He wept when he accepted Mary's supplies of suture, morphia, and dressings.

Mary and her driver crept down the switchback on the westward side through a heavy mist, detouring around more bodies. Ascending wagons carried volunteers from Boonsboro. Mary told them about the doctor at the inn.

About noon, they reached Boonsboro and found the town crowded with the mountain's wounded. Along the main street, Union flags flew from houses and Union soldiers on horseback raced up and down the streets. Confederate troops had passed through the day before; the town's inhabitants had cheered when the Union army arrived.

They pushed southward toward Keedysville and the sound of artillery. Wagons brimming with families and Saratoga trunks flew past them on the road. The sharp whine of occasional artillery fire was whistling ahead. Companies of Union soldiers were lying at rest in the warming afternoon. The air pulsed with excitement. The going was slow now. They were following cavalry regiments, marching soldiers, clattering wagons. The soldiers were cheering and hollering when the shellfire hissed and burst in the distance. There was the sense of energy drawing everyone in. At any point, Mary and her driver could turn around, but they didn't, choosing to head into the vortex. They had come so far. And for Mary, even knowing what was ahead, she set aside fear and apprehension. Or rather, fear and apprehension had become pleasurable, a turn of perception that she did not want to consider, because it was terrible to think that she was attracted to devastation. She didn't quite know what would happen, or what she would do when she arrived. But this time was different. This time she had supplies. And she had already seen the worst, hadn't she?

A marker for Sharpsburg said to turn right, but the wagons went on, following the winding road under sheltering maples and oaks, past well-tended German houses, along a stream burbling over rocks and widening into still, sheltered pools. The road then swung out through fields dotted with harvested grain, the wagons rising and falling with the undulations of the land, green and verdant and formerly wholly peaceful, a place brimming with orchards and prosperity and beauty, but now invaded by an army. They reached a checkpoint beyond which a peach-fuzzed guard would not allow Mary to travel, even with her pass from John Hay.

"But I've brought supplies," she said and ordered her driver to push past, but the guard prevented her and sent a courier to find someone to help him.

A young, hollow-eyed colonel galloped up on a horse.

"Jonathan Letterman, medical director," he said, his eyes devouring Mary's medicine wagon. He had been galloping all over the hills, checking on the regimental surgeons and their preparations, directing them to select barns over houses as hospitals for their better access to hay and water, and for their capacity to house more men at once. Most of the surgeons had no supplies; the ambulances and supply wagons were at least a day away. The Rebels had destroyed a railroad bridge over the Monocacy Creek between Frederick and Baltimore, and all the provisions had had to be removed from the railcars and put onto wagons. He was terrified of the carnage to come. From what he had seen on the Peninsula, even if only in the aftermath, the lack of stores would doom hundreds, if not thousands, to die.

"How did you accomplish this?" Letterman asked, nodding at the wagon.

"I was at Fairfax." Mary handed him her pass and his eyes widened as he read it.

"What did you do there?" he asked, returning her papers.

"I sorted men."

He was about to speak, but stopped as her meaning sank in. After a moment, he said, "And how did you know to do that?"

"I was working with William Stipp."

At the mention of Stipp's name, Letterman drew himself up. Stipp was here with his regiment on the Hagerstown Pike, and though he was loath to let the woman through, she had supplies. There were seventy-five thousand Union men gathered on the hills behind him and uncountable Rebels entrenched under the white spires of Sharpsburg. They might all be wounded or dead tomorrow, every one of them. "All right. I will allow you to enter if you take your supplies directly to Stipp." He nodded to the guard. "Escort her to the Hagerstown Pike and stay there with her until Stipp accepts her."

Upon Mary's arrival, Stipp stood staring, an inscrutable expression on his face.

He said, "Did you bring morphine?

"Yes. Morphine, dressings, whiskey, everything."

# *Chapter Forty-nine*

Thomas Fall was marching toward Sharpsburg with the Sixth Corps along a southerly route, different than the one the main army was taking over the two northernmost gaps of South Mountain. The Sixth Corps was to travel over the most southerly, Crampton's Gap, in order to engage the Confederate general A. P. Hill, who had taken Harper's Ferry to the southwest, on the Potomac River. Now it was Sunday afternoon, the fifteenth of September, and the Sixth Corps were stopped at Burkittsville on the eastern base of South Mountain, pinned down in clover and cornfields, while four Union Parrott guns and two Napoleons answered Confederate guns on the mountain above them.

Thomas was exhausted. Since April, he had marched two hundred miles up and down the swampy, waterlogged Virginia Peninsula, and another thirty into the latest melee at Bull Run, and now, in the last few days, sixty miles double-quick from Washington. He had fought at the Chickahominy, Malvern Hill, the Seven Days, as well as the debacle at Chantilly, where the wounded men drowned in the deluge afterwards. At White Oak Swamp, the muck had sucked at his boots and he had thought he might drown too. In the last months, the imperative to stay alive had obliterated any desire but the most primitive. He had lost whole sections of time. In battle, the upsurge of panic rent his mind in two and he became a shadow, another being who crammed minié balls into his rifled musket and shot into the smoke and confusion and then rose running over corpse and log to fall to the ground before doing it all over again. The bitter tang of gunpowder had stolen taste, smell, happiness from him.

His memories of Jenny had slipped away. She shimmered just out of reach, an indistinct sadness that haunted his days and nights. He wanted to understand how love had wrought disaster, but with each passing day he understood less and less.

He tried to conjure desire, a reason to live, tried to imagine tiny toes, fingers. Jenny's and his, in miniature. He tried to believe that the daughter he had never seen existed at all.

The clover smelled fresh and sweet. After the rain of the last weeks, the ground was wet, but nothing like the mud of the Peninsula. Thomas regretted nearly everything, but one thing he was certain of. He had slayed Mary Sutter with his grief. If he ever saw her again, he would tell her that he knew now that keeping someone alive was more difficult than he had ever imagined.

There was a lull in the artillery barrage, and in its ringing aftermath the order came to rise up from the field and run toward the mountain. Thomas was always stunned when his feet responded, but he flew through the tall grass as the Rebels emerged from behind a stone fence and fired. Still, Thomas and his regiment ran, up the mountainside now, bayonets fixed, hurling themselves at the Rebels, slashing and stabbing until the Rebels turned and ran up the hill. The Federals fired after them, killing them by the dozens, dashing up the mountain, past the abandoned big guns. Thomas hid behind trees and boulders as balls whistled past, until his legs pushed him higher. He had fired perhaps twenty shots. He was aware that around him, in the trees and on the slope, men were falling. But he was not falling. He was pushing ahead, up the mountain. He was a shade, a shadow. He passed wounded Rebels, kicked their muskets from them. He flew over another stone wall. The Rebels were running away, retreating. He fired at their backs. He let out a yell, echoed by men to his left and right. An orange moon rose, highlighting the black branches of trees. An owl hooted. There was no more firing. Thomas could no longer stay awake. He lay down in the underbrush and slept.

In Mary's dream, Jenny was dying again, only this time, Mary withheld the knife. She made no cuts, no intervention. Did not presume to think that she could save her sister. Instead, she pressed herself against the lying-in room's walls, letting the doctor work the forceps in and out, crushing the baby's head between the curved blades in an effort to save Jenny. Her mother was pleading with her to intervene, but she did not trust herself. She was too stymied by the shame of having stayed in Washington until it was too late, too busy condemning herself so that she was unable to act. When the doctor failed, when both the baby and Jenny died, Bonnie cried and her mother waged battle with Mary while the doctor crept out of the house, unaccustomed to the grief of women, though he would have to become so if he ever dared again to dabble in women's lives.

"Mary. Wake up."

"I'm awake," she said, though she wasn't. She was suspended in time, hovering in that space between dream and reality wherein the sleeping mind recasts the past. Not merely dwelling in memory, but changing it utterly, irrevocably.

"Get up, Mary. It's nearly dawn, and it's raining."

Mary's eyes flickered open.

Under a deeply gray sky, William Stipp was standing above her.

"We have to get ready," he said.

The barn Stipp had chosen was located at the far right of McClellan's line, in a swale suffused with cool morning fog. Seven people huddled inside: Mary, her driver, Stipp, and four soldiers assigned to assist him at the makeshift hospital he had crafted amid the hay and cow stalls. In the night, while they had been sleeping, the Union general Joseph Hooker and his division had tramped past them toward a cornfield, where now the stalks were rustling like silk, giving the Union soldiers the misimpression of safety, which allowed them to fling themselves into the corn and disappear by the hundreds, their muskets upright against their chests, a parade of bobbing bayonets glinting above the stalks in the feeble morning sun. For one moment, the scene was beautiful. For one moment, the hills and woods around held their collective breath. For one last, beautiful second, the silvery light on the slender leaves made everyone believe that despite the roar of artillery falling nearby, restraint was still possible.

In that second, the Confederates considered the beauty from their perch on a slight rise on the opposite side of the cornfield and thought of home, where their own fields lay fallow and their children were hungry. They wanted to go home to cradle their starving children and then shoot a hog and scavenge apples and stray oats down by the edge of the river and take the bounty home and feed the family they loved so that their children wouldn't die.

For immortality, they raced into the corn.

By the time that last beautiful second had passed, the field enveloped both armies, the Federals and the Rebels alike, the silky corn thread brushing their weathered cheeks, the light sifting between the stalks, the cool, wet dirt cushioning their bare feet. What boots they had had rotted away on the Peninsula and so it was possible to think that they were at home, barefoot, safe on their own land.

Reveling in the familiar, some of the men forgot what was coming. Or imagined somehow, something different. Some silken reprieve.

But in each row of corn, the enemy appeared as if from nowhere. Face to face, at intimate range, each man was alone with his opponent. Each knelt, fired, charged with his bayonet, stabbed with his knife, and wielded the butt of his musket. Each stepped over and on the fallen, friend or enemy, wounded or dead, groaning or silent, to get to the next man and the next, until few were left alive.

There was nothing beautiful about it.

It took four hours for the men to finish, and when they were done, not a single man who entered the cornfield emerged untouched.

By the thousands, the wounded lay on the ground and thought, *This thirst is not thirst. This pain is not pain. This world is not being rent in two.*

*That howling is only a whisper. That screech is just a murmur. That explosion is nothing but a sigh. That musket fire is but a rustle.*

*I am not here. We are not here. Armies are not here. The country is not depending on this moment.*

*Battles are conversations. An exchange. A dialogue.*

*None of this is true.*

After the cornfield, there were woods and bridges and the holy grail of a sunken road to take. The battle swelled southward along Antietam Creek.

From his vantage point at the Pry farmhouse, George McClellan directed his army, though the rolling hills and his own caution prevented clarity. The attacks had to be scrupulously managed or his army might be depleted and he would have no one and nothing left to command. Across the way, Robert E. Lee, stranded and stationary and blinded by the burning houses of Sharpsburg, regretted invading Maryland, for McClellan's troops were defending this land like his had defended Virginia.

Weariness swept over them both.

Thomas and the Sixth Corps were pouring up the hill from the Boonsboro Road, expecting to be sent immediately into the fray. But George McClellan worried that all his men might die, and he loved them so much that he told the Sixth Corps to take up a position to the extreme right of the line, and to do nothing. Shot and shell burst above their heads. Thomas clung to the earth, the musty smell of bloody dirt invading his lungs.

Then Thomas Fall thought he heard a call to go forward. This is what he heard in the bedlam. Go forward. In all, he took ten steps before a solid shot struck him in his left shin. He cartwheeled in the air and landed on his back. When he came to, the fight was a symphony of smoke that blinked out the sun.

The Confederate general A. P. Hill, having heard the rumble of guns, abandoned Harper's Ferry and double-quicked north in an all-out marathon that endeared him to Lee for the remainder of their lives. Sometime around two, he presented himself to his friend, who flung Hill's men into the maelstrom as if he didn't love them.

Jonathan Letterman was sending an army of stretcher bearers into the woods and fields to search for wounded. The numbers were staggering. Carnage was everywhere. Even he had to turn his head and vomit.

Blood fogged the landscape, obscured the sun, infiltrated even the waters of the creek, which flowed smoky red southward in the direction of Harper's Ferry and the Potomac River. Days later, the citizens of Washington would remark that the Potomac had turned the color of rust, but would not make the connection until news of the enormous numbers of casualties came pouring in.

It was exhaustion that ended things.

The cornfield, rustling so beautifully at dawn, was at evening a sea of stubble and bodies. Down the way, a contested bridge still stood, but the dying festooned its arcing roadbed and graceful footings. In the woods and thickets and sunken road turned bloody lane, so many men had died that the surviving could not count them, though later, when Jonathan Letterman painstakingly pursued the tally, the dead and wounded on this one day would exceed the number accumulated over the three and a half months on the Peninsula.

The cornhusks would not absorb much blood, but Mary laid them on wounds anyway, tossing them aside when the stringy fibers swelled and burst open. Underfoot, the barnyard was a lake of sanguinous mud. The night had seemed to fall very fast. The wounded had started to flood in at midafternoon, and the stores of dressings had been depleted within a half hour. All her supplies, used up already. The fracture boxes, the morphia, the whiskey. She had already torn up her petticoats. It was Fairfax all over again, though this time there were no trains. But it was the noise that bludgeoned. *Sighs and sorrows and heartrending cries resounded through the starless atmosphere.* Dante, Mary thought. But which circle of hell was reserved for the hopelessly useless?

"Mary."

Stipp stood silhouetted in the barn door, a yellow lantern flickering behind him, his amputation saw a black sword at this side. Since morning his face had aged a thousand years. His forearms were scarlet to the elbow and his hands had already swelled from just the few hours of gripping the bone saw. With the back of his arm, he wiped his forehead.

Mary swayed to her feet. They had been up for hours and hours. The dawn was an eon away. She went toward him.

"I need you to do something," he said.

"I can't choose. There isn't enough light, and besides it would be useless. There aren't any trains on which to put the men."

He swallowed hard, resisting the urge to kiss her, to fall again into that well. Instead, he forced himself to look her in the eye. "No. That's not what I mean. You wanted to be a surgeon. Do you still?"

Mary felt her whole body protest, thought suddenly that she was an arrogant, presumptuous person who had chased hope into the Maryland countryside, and would now be punished for every ambitious thought she had ever harbored in her life.

"Yes," she said. "I do."

Stipp led her to his makeshift surgery table. Already, his ankles and feet were swelling in his boots. He remembered this from the Peninsula, knew what pain lay ahead. The hours and hours of amputations. He would have saved Mary the horror, if he could.

He positioned her at the side of a wounded man he had already chloroformed. His left lower leg was lacerated, and the shattered bone exposed. A shame to teach her here, where time was an ever-ticking bomb, but he was not in charge of hell, he was only its perpetual resident.

"Do you remember?" Stipp asked her.

"Yes," she said, though for a moment her mind had gone completely blank. She could not even remember how to cut an umbilical cord.

He made her hold the bone saw and the scalpel to feel their heft. Then he said, "What's first?"

"Set the tourniquet."

"That's right." He helped her to do it, showing her how to tamp the canvas strap with the screws. When it was in place and the skin was beginning to pale, he said, "The skin will be tough. Make as precise a cut as you can."

Instinct, desire, how far these had gotten her, but courage was an entirely other matter. Courage was triumph over desire. When her hand hesitated above the pallid skin, Stipp turned courtly, as if she were already in great pain. "We have only so much time."

She made the cut, tracing a circular line only an inch above the knee, enough to save enough skin to make a flap.

"Deeper," Stipp said.

She complied, slicing through the skin until she reached the striated red of the muscles. Her hands felt awkward, as if they were not hers, or attached to her. The muscles exposed, Stipp showed her how to locate the blood vessels, though when she slipped a perfect loop through each before he could tell her how, he only nodded, as if he understood already that she would know how to do everything.

"I have to dissect the muscles next." Mary was talking to herself now, not to Stipp, remembering, summoning the drawing from *Gray's*, the steps from the surgery manual. The taut ribbon of the quadriceps tendon was pink and stretched over the patella. It snapped back when she cut it, and the suddenness of the movement made her jump.

"That's right," Stipp murmured, and he picked up the thigh so that she could detach the hamstring tendons. Her assistant now, he nonetheless said, "The ligaments will go with the leg. No need to worry about them." Each of them was remembering when the situation had been reversed, when Mary had taught him how to do this, reading instructions to him from the book.

When the bone was revealed, she grasped the handle of the bone saw and Stipp pulled back on the skin and muscle. "Now, take the saw in one hand and anchor the other on the knee. Press down, but when you pull back, pull up, as if you are caressing, and not cutting the bone."

The saw teeth bounced over the shiny, hard surface. The sound of the saw sang in her head. She pushed the memory away.

"You will be able to do this one day without even thinking about it," Stipp said.

But it did not feel that way now. It felt awkward and wrong. After another ineffective swipe, Mary shut her eyes, pushing away the press of time, trying to understand what was needed. Maybe it was something like breech babies, how they required both force and finesse, a two-handed maneuver that felt cumbersome and artificial. You had to hold the baby's torso up in a towel with one hand, and with the other slip a finger into the birth canal, locate the baby's mouth, and draw the chin down to the chest so the neck wouldn't hyperextend and make the presenting diameter too large.

*Force and finesse.*

She slipped into that place deep inside her that was more prayer than thought. Again, she drew the saw over the bone.

"Yes. Exactly. Pressure and not pressure. You feel it. It's a breath." Stipp knew how to talk to her, went on talking in rhythm as she sawed. "Strength, yes. But intention more than force. Yes. That's it. That's right."

And then, suddenly, the bone separated and the weight of the leg fell away.

No baby to manage, Mary was stunned, uncertain what to do next.

Stipp said, "Release the tourniquet."

She unscrewed the tamps, waited for any sign of bleeding from the tied-off arteries, and when they held, Stipp eased behind her and talked her through folding the flap of skin over the cut, securing it in back, lifting the thigh so that she could stitch the skin back together.

When she was done, and the boy had been carried away to recover outside in the damp, Mary looked up. Lanterns blazed on the floor. Her driver and the four assistants were gathered in a half circle a few feet away, watching her. She had no idea how much time Stipp had taken to teach her. She had lost track of time, had lost track even of where she was, the sounds of the war having disappeared as she concentrated, but now the dirty sound of anguish came roaring back. She was afraid that she had wasted hours and hours, that she had been selfish and covetous, knowledge an uncharitable luxury when men had been dying. The driver and the assistants came toward her, and they grasped her by her elbows, murmured words she recognized as admiration. Their faces looked like fathers' faces when she emerged from a birthing room to hand them their infant sons or daughters.

*Imagine that,* she thought she heard one of the assistants say.

"Can you do the surgery without me now?" Stipp asked.

Mary nodded.

"Good," he said, and gave her his set of knives, while he retrieved another from his case. His assistant was setting up another table, quickly fashioning one from the barn stalls. "You'll do only above-the-knee amputations. No others. I'll do everything else. But you'll have enough work as it is. Do it the same each time. You'll get fast, believe me. The assistants will administer the chloroform and manage the induction seizure for you. I want you to think only of doing the surgeries." He had become brusque again, William Stipp at work, but for the first time in a long time, everything seemed right to Mary.

"Your hands will get tired. Don't hunch your shoulders. Take deep breaths." He was going to add, *Don't be afraid,* but stopped himself just in time.

# *Chapter Fifty*

"Not you, too?" The soldier wiped his sweating face with a grimy square of handkerchief and turned to the rest of a small group of soldiers leaning on their shovels beside a half-dug shallow trench. Hundreds of dead, looted of their shoes and other valuables, waited to be buried. Farther down, the work of the early morning appeared indifferent; heads and toes peeked out from the loose dirt shoveled on top.

James had stopped his wagon at the base of a hillock where an embalmer had set up a table outside a tent and was taking payment from families who'd streamed into the area searching out their dead, hoping to find their loved ones before they were buried. Everyone held handkerchiefs to their faces as the stench of death curled like a virulent fog over the once fragrant hills. Nearby, townspeople were fashioning coffins out of a splintered sycamore. A bonfire of horse carcasses rained ash.

"Someone else wants specimens? Who?" James asked.

"What'd he say his name was?" The gravedigger was hoping to keep the conversation going so he didn't have to turn back to his unspeakable task. His clothing reeked of death; he would never get it out. Never.

"A fellow by the name of Brinton," someone offered. "He went yonder," he said, and then watched the inquirer jounce his wagon and its odd cargo over the burned field, winding around bodies still lying in the sun.

James discovered Brinton nearby, at a bridge where the living were dragging the dead from the water onto the stream's shores. But it was not the human dead that interested Brinton. The surgeon was circling a horse that was standing perfectly balanced on two legs. But when James swung down from his wagon seat, he saw that the beast was dead.

"The muscles remain fixed and rigid, you see?" Brinton said, not evincing any surprise at seeing James. He pointed out the stiffening curve of the horse's neck, its open mouth, the remnants of froth bubbling at its lips. "I've seen this same peculiarity in a number of the dead as well. Curious what a violent death can do to the body, don't you think?"

After the teamster jumped ship in Frederick, it had taken James ten days to trundle over the Maryland countryside with his casks of alcohol. Every pothole, rut, rock, gulley, and pebble had registered in his bones, and yet here was Brinton, as fleet as a messenger.

To Blevens's astonished inquiry, Brinton said, "I traveled by horse. Much quicker. And I bought this wagon in Keedysville, though I had to pay a great price for it. But I've done fairly well for myself. I've already managed a few specimens." He showed James the back of the wagon, where burlap bags filled with limbs were pinned with notes. "Don't forget to describe whatever circumstance you can about the death. I'm sending these up to Hagerstown with a teamster today to get them on a train and save them from spoiling in the heat. What are your plans?"

James was furious. Brinton hadn't had to lug kegs of alcohol over mountain passes. "To visit the hospitals. Obtain what I can, as you suggested I do."

"You won't have to visit the hospitals, I don't think. They're behind on the burials."

James paled. "You don't mean for me to hack bodies apart in the field?"

"No. But if something interests you. Not just as a curiosity, of course, but to be of real use. Why not?"

James opened his mouth to speak, but he could not form words. Nor could he tear his gaze from Brinton's tranquil face. Smoke lingered in the crisp fall air, as the detritus of the battle burned in perpetual bonfire.

Brinton lowered his handkerchief. "Dear God, man, what is the difference between this and searching out an arm or a leg in a pile of cut limbs?"

James didn't know, but there was a difference, some sacred distinction that he could not describe. Despite all the specimens he'd collected over the years, he had always been able to separate the person from the object. True, most of what he had purchased was from medical supply houses, and he supposed they had come from cadavers, but they had come already prepared, floating in glass jars or already skeletonized. His scientist mind had been able to distinguish science and the death that had provided it. The specimens he had obtained in Washington had come from surgery, mostly pieces of diseased tissue to examine under the microscope. Now the wind picked up, bringing with it the memory of life before brutality had wiped the beauty from the hills. The land was utterly defaced. He couldn't deface the dead, too.

"I'll visit the hospitals, thank you," James said.

"Think again. The most interesting specimens might be from the ones who died of their wounds. Ask around. Despite the look of things, the burial parties might be far too efficient for our task. See if you can rustle up some information from them. Head injuries, for one. Those all died quickly. Of great interest would be a skull with a fatal projectile in place, for instance. Or a penetration of the vertebrae. Arms and legs will be a dime a dozen soon. We need information on how to treat the ones who die, so that in the future they might not die. Those amputees"—Brinton nodded into the distance—"they'll all live. What's the greater good there?" He tucked his handkerchief in his pocket. "Also, you might want to pick up a shovel for yourself." With that, he strode away and mounted his horse, a sorrel spooked by the lifeless field, and galloped off across the wasteland.

James climbed into his wagon, put his head in his hands, and waited until his nausea passed.

# *Chapter Fifty-one*

The day after the battle, the sight of the crowded yard nearly knocked Mary off her feet. Men lay next to one another without room for anyone to walk in between them. She staggered and caught herself on the doorframe, and a splinter jabbed into her palm, but she did not feel it. Cries for water and for mothers and sweethearts mingled with sobs of pain. It was a great rabble of suffering, and now it was her great rabble.

She covered her mouth with her hand and her eyes traveled over the endless numbers for whom her responsibility was now far greater than it had ever been. She wished William had told her not to be afraid, because she was terrified now.

Only ten amputations since last evening? The end might never come.

She turned in the doorway and tried to catch her breath. What had Lincoln said? *Are you willing to risk yourself?* She did not know he had meant her sanity.

They brought in another soldier and laid him on her table. Mary looked over at Stipp, absorbed in his surgery. He had done all he could for her, had given her exactly what she'd asked for. *What had she done?* She returned to her table just as her assistant put the chloroform cone over the boy's face. They were all in tatters: dirt crusted underneath their fingernails, gunpowder blackening their faces.

There was a crater in the boy's left shin. His eyes were shut tight against the pain, though the chloroform was already beginning to take hold. Mary blinked, once, twice, then put a hand to the boy's wrist and said, "Thomas."

He opened his eyes, fearing death, and instead saw Mary Sutter, aproned and bloodied and staring at him as if he were dead.

After being shot, Thomas had lain in that ditch all night, watching the stars flicker on and off, not knowing if it was the clouds or his dying that obscured them. The pain in his shin had bored like a worm, and then it went completely numb, followed by his hip and his back, and then they all flared up suddenly together and he couldn't move without causing more pain. All night, he'd waited for death, lanterns bobbing in the distance, the drizzle pooling in his ears and eyes. But looking at Mary now, he remembered that he had something to say to her. Something important to say before he died. He racked his brain, searching back through time, back to before the Peninsula, where he had fought at White Oak Swamp and Seven Pines and Yorktown, his feet sinking to his shins in the mud, but before that, to the time when he had last seen her at Fort Marcy. Oh, yes! It was that he was sorry. Sorry that he had once believed her to be perfect. He wanted to say something else, too. He wanted to tell Mary that love was a mystery he had been unable to solve in his life, but he found that he could not speak. He was leaving her, and he could not get the words out. Mary was bending close to him, but her face was blurring and a sweet, thick perfume was falling through the air, filling him with such fatigue. She whispered, and the words were strung out, stretched on a bed of sleep.

"I promise I'll make it right," she said, but he had no idea what needed to be made right. He was falling, but he understood very clearly that Mary had always loved him; had loved him from the moment they had met. Why this had not been apparent to him earlier, he did not know. But now he was falling asleep, falling into an imitation of death, and before he lost his last dizzying hold on time, he thought of Jenny dying and that Mary had been with her, and how comforting it must have been to Jenny that the last vision she had had of the world was her sister, bending over her, trying to save her.

It did not occur to Mary to call for Stipp to take care of Thomas. Instead, she thought of Jenny. A knife goes into a body and something is either repaired or it isn't. Perhaps it really was that simple.

It was strange that redemption, when it finally came, felt like discipline. Mary's movements were certain, her thinking methodical, stemming no longer from fear or love—the same emotion, when love is unrequited—but instead from determination. She was not even bartering with death anymore. She was defying it. At home there was a baby named Elizabeth who was Thomas and Jenny's child and Mary was going to make certain that Thomas lived to know her. She would do this by paying meticulous attention to tying off the arteries, to the precise severing of the tendons, to a vigorous but careful application of pressure to the saw, and finally to the looping of perfect, painstaking stitches. Time, suspended, did not matter. Thomas was Christian and Jenny both, and Amelia too.

When she had tied her final knot and snipped the black catgut, Mary stepped back and saw James Blevens standing not five feet from her, his hat covering his heart. Dust motes were twisting in the sunlight piercing the gaps in the barn walls. Behind her, stretcher bearers were slinging a groaning man onto Stipp's table. Other surgeons, men Blevens did not recognize, swayed at the tables in the late afternoon light. Save the rigors of the patients succumbing to chloroform or an occasional muttered epithet, the barn was a sanctuary of quiet compared to the clamor outside. Mary's eyes were bloodshot, her apron scarlet.

Stipp looked up, saw Blevens, and said, "Holy hell, what are you doing here?"

"Looking at our Mary."

The two men acknowledged one another with a nod—*our Mary*—and then James Blevens said to Mary, "I thought I told you not to disappear."

"I didn't," she said. "I've been with William the whole time."

*William.* James flexed and unflexed his fingers, glanced charily at Stipp, and then let his gaze run again over the broken barn stalls, the heaps of hay, the sawdust scattered on the dirt floor to absorb the blood, and Mary, surgical instruments in hand, a patient at rest on a wooden slab balanced on doubled sawhorses, a pile of legs beside her table. *You will have no lectures, no dissecting lab. What you want is impossible.* But what was impossible was Mary; the last time he had seen her, she'd been safely asleep in her bed.

"Dear God, Mary."

Mary lifted her bloodied hand to her face. Her eyes were hooded with fatigue, and a vague haziness had come over her, as if she were out of focus. He could see the nicks and scars on her knuckles and wrists, the new strength in her forearms. She gazed at him, and when she spoke it seemed to James as if she were speaking through glass, her reply delayed a second or two.

"I'm so glad you're here. Can you help us?" she asked.

Her request was oddly formal, out of keeping with the surroundings, hospitable in this hovel in a way she had not been that first night at Dove Street, when she had desperately wanted him to leave. It was as if she were displaced, out of time, as if everything were reversed. Except that now he was going to disappoint her again. He raised his hands, turning them over to show her his palms with their still-shiny surfaces, capable of holding a washcloth, of separating twigs from strands of hair, but not the delicate work of tying off arteries.

"My hands won't do the work. They may never do the work again."

The same hands that had bathed her. She hadn't asked him about his hands in Washington. She'd been too exhausted to wonder about his health; she, who had slathered his palms with slippery elm, had forgotten, when he had been so kind to her.

"But you're here?" Her assistant was wrapping the leg in cornhusks and making a mess of it.

Blevens nodded at the limbs at her feet. "For another purpose. I've come to take away the legs."

Mary was peering at him as if he were now a subject of study. He could almost picture her refocusing the lens of the microscope, trying to comprehend what she was seeing.

"You've come to take the legs?" she asked.

"Yes, to study them. There is going to be research."

"Research?" But she said it as if he had offered her gold, or an end to the havoc. "You know what to do with them?"

"Yes. Don't you see? Something good has to come out of all of this."

And yet even as she seemed to welcome the notion, she seemed even more distracted. She pointed to the soldier on her table.

It took a moment for Blevens to understand. He took a step closer and said, "What is it?"

"This is Thomas."

Stipp, who had begun his next surgery, listening as he worked, now jerked up his head. "What the hell is the matter with you, Mary? Why didn't you call me?"

"Because I didn't need to."

Stipp and James stared at her and thought, *Sarah, giving the whiskey and opium to her little brother when she had to.* What women were capable of.

"Will you study Thomas's leg?" Mary asked Blevens. "Please. I can't think of it here—" And she nodded at her pile.

James said, "Of course."

The soldier on Stipp's table reared up and Stipp barked for his assistant to give him more chloroform. "James," he said, tossing his instruments to the hay at his feet in order to help hold down the boy, "take her outside. Find her something to eat and then make her sleep." And he watched as James Blevens took Mary's arm and led her away to the barn door, and she disappeared from his sight.

Day after day, night after night, Mary worked beside Stipp, stopping only to rest a few hours before rousing again. She had needed only a few hours of sleep that morning; not even James could persuade her to rest any longer. He arranged for a teamster to take his wagon and specimens, including Thomas's leg, back to Washington, while he stayed to help with the chloroform. They worked for a week; Mary cut off thirty-five legs a day. Exhaustion obliterated sensation. Her back ached. Her knees swelled. She took no notice of the tangle of her hair or the blood on her skirts. By the fifth day, she knew nothing but legs and more legs. In the exhaustion and confusion, she nevertheless checked on Thomas every morning and every night, appraising his sutures, worriedly laying her hand on his forehead, looking for fever. The day after the surgery, he had clung to her and begged for water. She studied him, looking for signs of decline before he fell back to the ground. Day after day, she changed his dressing, tugging on the suture threads to see whether or not they were ready to come out. She had only moments to spare for him. He and his neighbors cared for one another, crawling for better shelter under a sycamore tree behind the barn. They were all sunburned, their faces sunken from thirst and fever.

In the few hours of sleep that Mary stole curled up in the corner of the barn, the dead began to speak to her. They called to her from the fields. *Work faster, work faster! Legs are not enough. There are hands and feet and arms that must be removed. My head, my head, take off my head.* She was more tired than tired, more mad than sane. In her dream, she wandered outside and followed a trail of blood to a stream, where a hundred men lay in the thickets and scrub along the banks. No one had cared for them. Why had no one looked here? Why had no one discovered them? She tore her skirts as she searched among the blackberries and in the elder bushes, flinging unfound soldiers over her shoulder. She must rescue them all. But they were all dead, so she laid them down and descended to the stream bank where the brook flowed red. She wanted only to get clean, to wash the blood from her fingernails. But it was no use, for the water had turned into blood. She sank to the damp earth. On the opposite bank, the dead rose and formed a single file walking up a rise. *Follow us,* the dead said. They were all missing a leg, hundreds of men disappearing into the woods. She wanted to follow them, but something kept her back.

"Mary."

She was logy with sleep, unable to find a way to leave the nightmare behind.

"Wake up, Mary."

Stipp handed his instruments over to his relief, and drunkenly took Mary by the elbow as James Blevens watched from the head of a surgery table, where he was administering chloroform. The two stumbled outside to dip their hands into the horse trough. Then they sank under a poplar tree. The Medical Department was lumbering to life; Jonathan Letterman's organization, formulated on the Peninsula, coming to fruition. He had formed wagon trains of ambulances and one was assembling on the road. In and among the wounded, fifty men were calling to one another, making decisions about who to send and who to leave behind. Mary watched them perform and envied their camaraderie. At Fairfax, she had been alone.

She said to Stipp, "They will make mistakes."

"Yes," he said.

Mules pawed and brayed in a pen nearby. Steam rose from the laundry cauldrons; a crone from a nearby farm was bent over her task. From somewhere nearby came the smell of a hog roasting. For half an hour, Mary and Stipp stared at the milling crowd with their backs pressed into the corrugated bark of the tree, its little barbs and rivulets reminding them that to be alive was to know pain. Unconsciously, they clenched and unclenched their fists, working the strain out of their burning finger joints.

"Are you hungry?" Stipp asked.

"Yes," Mary said.

Still, they did not move. Mary had an idea that she was thirsty, too, but to rise and obtain something to drink seemed an enormous task. The act of locating a cup, impossible. Finding a pump or a well, unmanageable. As if her own legs had been amputated.

"I don't know if I can do this anymore," Mary said.

That Stipp knew she meant the work, they both understood. This is the way of love and catastrophe. Everything is evident.

"You can," he said.

Mary turned to him and touched his face, as he had once touched hers, a long time ago. She traced the coarse outline of his beard, ending at his lips, which opened under her fingertips, as if to joy.

He helped her to her feet. It was difficult going. He led her by the hand to the well, from which he drew a bucket of water. He gave her some to drink and then carried a bucket to a scrub of bushes that lent privacy. Stipp guarded at a discreet distance, looking away from her. On the Peninsula, there had been other women to watch: camp followers, laundresses, the coarse and the pretty, whose relative rarity among the masculine had heightened their femininity. The light over the fields was taking on the golden edge of evening. When Mary finished washing her hands and face and had poured the scarlet water onto the ground, she walked toward him, her hands scrubbed clean, her dress weighty with her futile attempts to clean it.

Far past the years of the war, when even specific memories of which battles Stipp had worked in had faded and all the faces of the wounded had coalesced into one, he would remember this moment, and the way the sun set behind Mary as she came toward him.

# Chapter Fifty-two

Five days after the battle of Antietam, Abraham Lincoln read the perfected draft of the Emancipation Proclamation to his cabinet, who, after arguing for four hours, heartily endorsed it.

On November 5, Lincoln gave orders to General Halleck to fire George McClellan, who would not follow the retreating Lee into Virginia despite direct orders.

McClellan replied that he would step down immediately, then wrote to his wife and said, "They have made a great mistake! Alas for my poor country!"

# *Chapter Fifty-three*

On a day in early October, James Blevens was preparing to leave Sharpsburg. He said to Mary, "May I kiss you good-bye?"

They were standing not far from the barn, which they were evacuating for a hospital down the road that the Medical Department was fashioning out of Sibley tents. It was for the injured who could not tolerate the trip over the mountains to the hospitals of Frederick. Thomas was among them; Mary and James had doted on him, but now James was leaving.

"Must you go? What if Thomas falls ill?"

Two weeks had passed since the battle, and the men were suddenly hemorrhaging or sinking into fever. Soldiers whose flesh wounds had at first appeared to be healing would begin to complain of burning, and their wounds, previously thought inconsequential after being thoroughly probed by the hand of a surgeon, would, for mysterious reasons, suddenly begin to suppurate and require amputation. Or a primary amputation would require a second operation to ligate arteries that gushed when traction was applied to the sutures. Erysipelas—reddened tissue that then turned black and ulcerated—spread among the men, and they were languishing, falling ill with pneumonia, developing fevers. James was taking skin samples back to Washington. He promised to write if he learned anything that might help. But the mystery was driving Mary mad. She had wanted to be a surgeon, had become one, but now, after the surgeries were successful, men were dying anyway.

"Always Thomas," James said, worried for her. She was at risk, and the condition of her heart mattered more to him than almost anything else in the world.

"He is my sister's husband."

"He is your sister's widower."

Mary looked away, not wanting to think about that. She had been unable to save her sister, but she had saved her sister's husband, for whom she now felt an overwhelming panic. Thomas's demeanor worried her. He followed her every movement as if she had hung the moon, but something was not quite right. Day by day, she kept close watch on him, changing his dressing herself, but he displayed more vulnerability than strength. He was not the Thomas she remembered, but then she wasn't even certain she was remembering him correctly. What did she know of him, really, except that he had lost his parents, loved her sister, and foolishly reenlisted when he could have gone home?

Once, when the whiskey she had given him had not yet dulled his deep pain, he said through his teeth, "You would not have tolerated domesticity."

Mary let her hands fall into her lap. She was seated on the edge of his cot. "But you loved her, didn't you?"

His gaze did not stray from her face. "Yes," he said. "Yes."

And she had gone on with her dressing change, the intimate ministrations that proffered no difficulty for her with other men, making her move more deliberately and carefully than with anyone else. He was her twin sister's husband.

Now Mary said to James, "You want to kiss me?" She was bone-tired, stripped bare. She thought it was possible that she might kiss every man at Sharpsburg. What was life for when death was so greedy and spiteful? She remembered James's hands gently washing her back and arms, his burned fingers in her hair, the generous restraint, when she might have turned to him, if he had asked.

He touched her face. "I will never have the chance again."

"Are you going to disappear into Washington forever?"

"No. I'm going to try to find my wife to tell her that I want her to come to Washington to live with me."

Mary fell silent. She thought then that she knew nothing of men, would never know anything of them. Dead wives, hidden wives. All she knew of men was what their damaged muscles and bones revealed: that they would sacrifice their fragile skeletons to violence, but would keep their feelings about women secret forever.

James went on, as if at confession. After the carnage, real love had suddenly seemed to be not so much likeness of mind as responsibility met, and a promise, however foolishly entered, kept. "It was a marriage from when I was very young. I don't even know her very well. But she was a lot like you. Very brave."

"Will she come?"

"I don't know. I'm not even certain of where she is or what she is doing."

"Then why kiss me?"

"To apologize for what might have been."

It came back to her now, that faraway beginning in his surgery, when she had begged him to teach her things she hadn't yet understood, things that she now understood too well: the human body's complexities, resiliencies, secrets, and hidden places. Its vulnerability. She had even seen the tight pack of organs, the bowels, the liver, the stomach, and even once a heart, nestled deep inside a destroyed chest. She did not need James's microscope anymore to understand that life existed or did not exist based, at least in part, on the goodwill of man. Really, in the end, everything had turned out to be as simple as that.

She took James's face in her hands and drew him to her and kissed his cheek.

"Has the war given you what you wanted, James? Have you learned enough?" Her taunt, from their first dinner together. But now she was rueful, weary. "How little the two of us understood, sparring over death."

Of what would transpire, whether James would ever see his wife again, the further seductive barbarity of his research, the exhaustion of an inveterate desire fulfilled, James and Mary knew nothing that morning, standing opposite while the country was still at war. But Mary and James were not at war.

"Good-bye," James said.

Mary raised her hand and then stood watching on the road until he disappeared around a bend on the road to Keedysville.

# *Chapter Fifty-four*

In November, the cold weather hit Sharpsburg like a sledgehammer. The tent hospital, full to the brim with convalescents, burned everything it could find: frozen cow pies, bad coal, wilted swamp grass. The hospital was dubbed Smoketown for the way the smoke caught in the fir tree canopy of the grove where the tents had been pitched for extra shelter from the elements. Mary begged for more blankets from the quartermaster and tucked them around the shivering men, kept the stoves going with the help of stewards and soldiers whose convalescence allowed them to get up and about, but the nights were mostly freezing affairs to be endured. Mary slept in a coat and gloves and two pairs of socks. She would have slept in her boots if she could. Mary and the nurses—mostly women from Sharpsburg whom she had trained—kept the tents ventilated during the day to keep out the bad air, but the men kept falling ill nonetheless.

One day in mid-November, she and Stipp stood over Thomas, who had developed a fever. Mary surrendered for a moment, stopping her whirl of activity, her curls frizzing around her face. Stipp believed that in the last weeks she had regained some of her health, though perhaps it was only his pride speaking. Mary had laid poultices of willowbark to draw out the inflammation, and made Thomas drink willowbark tea around the clock. Her entire tent of charges grew sick of it, but they were also faring better than some of the other tents, where men were developing gangrene. James Blevens had written that the disease was traveling from patient to patient in the hospitals in Frederick, infecting their wounds. Most of the men were dying.

Stipp said, "You're going to take him home, aren't you?"

They were outside the tent now, having slipped away to the field beyond to talk, as they usually did, the nurses and other doctors given to gossip about the surgeon and his woman protégée. *It just isn't right.* This was the women speaking out of jealousy, for they had seen the devotion in Stipp's eye and envied her the love. They also said, *He is so old.* But he looked old only to the villagers, who would themselves age a decade when the winter and disease worked its pitiless scythe on their patients. Stipp was not yet fifty, but he had seen as much as God. This much Mary knew.

"I have to. If I don't take him home, Amelia will never forgive me." Mary had written Amelia to tell her where she was and that she was with Thomas.

"It is a fool's errand, Mary. Impossible. How will you get him there? The gap is snowed in."

"I'll take him north to Hagerstown and take a train from there." From there to Philadelphia, through New York, on to Albany. Sometimes it was hard to believe that Albany still existed. Or anywhere else, for that matter. There were only these tents, these men, this life. The world was a cluster of Sibley tents, campfires, duty. She had grown to love the scent of the pine needles crunching underfoot, even the smell of the boric acid they had begun to scald the incisions with, and always, the ever-present woodsmoke hovering in the trees.

"You love him. You're going to marry him, aren't you?" Every day, Stipp awoke, unable to believe his luck. Here was Mary, swathed in blankets and hat, trudging beside him, their breath frosting in the morning air, discussing incisions and pneumonia, the conversation ranging between the fitting of wooden legs and the treatment for wasting, and all the time he was afraid that one day she would exhaust his knowledge and be done with him. He had seen Thomas grow more dependent on her day after day, though the affection he could not say was unequal to any of the others'. They all loved her. Gentleness combined with competence seduced beyond measure. Now he said it again: "You'll take him home and marry him." And knew himself to be a fool as soon as he uttered the words.

Not wanting cruelty, he evoked it with his own fear. The world over, the besotted write their own demise, unable to escape love.

Mary lifted her head, the pale sunlight circling her like a crown. Underneath, the hay was stubble, sharp and broken.

"I'm not yours," Mary said. The words were out before she had even practiced them in her mind, but they were the right words, the ones she intended to say.

"I didn't mean to be so hard on you. Back at Fairfax—you didn't need to see any of those things. I should have helped you."

The two of them were linked by that experience, would be for all of time. Moments of those days had crystallized and fixed in her mind. *Choose who you are*, he had said.

"That is not why I'm going."

"You're leaving me."

"He'll die if he stays. Don't you see?"

She put her hand to Stipp's face, and that simple action nearly undid him. He had brought this on himself. How he had thought of her all his lonely months on the Peninsula, the bitterness and horror, the counting of the dead upon the fields, measuring one man's vitality against another's. And now she was doing the same. Measuring Thomas's need against his.

He could not hear Antietam Creek bubbling in the distance (though Mary could; she had stood on a wooded shore near water before, contemplating love), could not even hear the clatter of the hospital tents, the nickering of the horses in the corral, or even his own breathing. Men were dying and autumn leaves were falling, and the northern world was turning away from the sun.

"Are you certain, Mary Sutter? Because my heart will break if you leave me again."

"But I have already broken my mother's heart," Mary said, and then, in the measure of a breath, rested her hand on his shoulder, kissed his cheek, and turned.

At the train station in Hagerstown, Stipp gazed at Thomas, who was watching them intently from the train car in which they had secured him, his crutches tucked beside him. Stipp said, "Are you coming back?"

Mary shook her head. "I don't know."

"You're leaving me."

"Just for now."

"For your own good, don't come back, Mary. Stay at home."

As the train pulled away, Stipp raised his hand to shield his eyes from the sun, and conjured a view of a funeral cortege leaving an East River dock, a lithe Mexican girl climbing to an adobe hut, a young woman going to her bed in the dark.

As the platform grew smaller, Mary raised her hand to shield her tears from Thomas, and conjured a view of a curly-headed brother slumped in a train, an exhausted sister dying in her bed, a man handing her a ledger, as if it were his heart.

The train's cars rocked Mary as the Hudson River, steely gray in the late November afternoon, formed tiny ice crystals that would slowly transform the river to glass. On the seat next to Mary, Thomas dozed, his fever ebbing for now, his stump wound dry and cool. Inside the railcar, the lamps were lit, but the setting sun had brightened to such a blaze that the candles flickering in the lamps seemed only a mirage. At Sharpsburg, the light had failed in just this way, slipping from the autumn sky behind the low hills, the last rays illuminating the rows of tents earlier and earlier each day, the slanted roofs shining like pearls.

At the train station in Albany, she hired a carriage to carry Thomas to the ferry and across the river and all the way home. It was night now and State Street exploded with light and civilization.

Thomas said, "My baby girl won't know me."

"No," Mary said, "but she'll love you."

Amelia emerged from the parlor, and put her hand to her mouth. From behind her, Bonnie appeared with the baby, who looked so much like Mary, it was as if Elizabeth were Mary's lost child.

"Is that my daughter?" Thomas asked.

Shyly, Bonnie stepped forward, reluctant, heartbroken. She could see the end of all her happiness. But the baby would not leave her. She clung to her, her head tucked into her neck. Mary watched how Bonnie turned

Elizabeth and made her feel safe as she took Thomas's hand, supporting his crutch so that he could grasp a tendril of his daughter's blond hair to see how much of Jenny still lived.

Mary shed her coat, but hung it over her arm, as if she were staying only for a moment, as if at any second she might be asked to leave. But Amelia came across the floor and took it from her and hung it over the newel post.

"You came home to me," she said.

"Yes," Mary said.

In their embrace, mother and daughter could feel all the members of their family gone now but for Elizabeth; they sank into one another, linked with regret and grace, as are all the reconciled.

# *Epilogue*

The late afternoon of September 25, 1867, brought a sudden rain, and with it, darkness. The lamplighter on Bleecker Street was already making his rounds, the end of his long pole flickering in the unnatural twilight, the heavy odor of gas skulking behind him through the mist.

A figure hurried past the man and his ladder, pushing his eyeglasses back in place as he hunched against the rain that cut through the cold afternoon; he should have hired a hack, he thought, or at least brought an umbrella, but he had needed the time. After five years, he still needed the twenty blocks between his home and his destination to compose himself. The going was harder for him now. He had a limp, the war having stolen quickness from him. From time to time, he consulted a letter, tucking the onionskin pages back into his coat pocket to keep them from the rain. At Thompson Street he turned north, and after several blocks reached a brownstone where the neighborhood became Washington Square.

Bolted to the side of the house an oval plaque announced, *Doctor M. Sutter, Physician and Surgeon.*

And there she was—tall, imperious, reigning from the top of the brownstone's steps, still as plain as he remembered, though her hair, beginning to turn when they had first met, was now flagrantly, gloriously silver, piled on her head in the same negligent mess as before, but a crown nonetheless. A sign of the stress of the war, though she was as unaware of her looks now as then. Anyone seeing her on the street would have guessed her age at far past twenty-seven, shamefully unaware of her service and its toll.

Her hand skimmed the wet iron railing. His, too.

They reached one another halfway up the steps.

Five years was an eon in which to have unlearned the other's habits, cues, distinctions, but Mary Sutter took William Stipp's hand in hers and said, "So you needed more time and got caught in the rain?"

And William Stipp said, "Impatiently waiting on the stairs?"

Both carried, despite their martial postures, an aura of sorrow, though the ghosts of smiles flickered across their faces. They would have recognized one another from a mere turn of the head observed from hundreds of yards away on a moonless night in January. Why had he not flown through the streets, hired the fleetest cab? Of what had he been afraid? *I am a foolish, stupid creature,* he thought. The world was relentlessly spinning, and he had wasted half an hour getting soaked in the rain.

The vestibule echoed; his coat dripped upon the pattern of black and white tiles. Mary took the wet garment from him and laid it upon the bench. In the foyer, stairs climbed heavenward.

Outside, the clouds suddenly parted, pouring sunlight into the high-ceilinged parlor, highlighting the coves and plaster cornices as if the universe itself were proud of Mary's accomplishments. William Stipp turned in a circle, taking in the gleaming instruments, the two exam beds, the shelves of books, their covers lettered in gold leaf. A black doctor's satchel waited on a shelf by the doors. In the corner, an oak desk with a capped inkwell, a box of paper, a newly changed blotter, and envelopes on parade. He pictured Mary writing the letter he carried in his pocket now: "I live in New York. Please come." She had written, he was here, and now there was all this evidence of a life built without him.

"Dear God, Mary, you did it. On your own."

"There's more."

She led him deep into the house, to a kitchen. A woman was kneading dough on a floured board. Through twinned windows, a sheltered garden glistened with raindrops. By the fire, a young girl about six years old left a book behind on an armchair. Exact replication had been avoided, but in the eyes, in the steep angle of the cheekbone, the resemblance was unmistakable.

He started, but Mary put her hand to his forearm. "Elizabeth is my niece, Jenny and Thomas's daughter. And I would like to introduce my mother, Amelia Sutter."

Amelia Sutter betrayed her intelligence with a piercing gaze and deep smile. "So you are Dr. Stipp. I believe I owe you my gratitude for sending my daughter home."

"I could never make your daughter do a thing she didn't want to do."

"Nor I."

He wondered how the woman felt upon meeting him; she was nearer his age than Mary was, but her smile reflected nothing but recognition. Kindred spirits who loved a remarkable young woman.

"I believe you know my son-in-law, Thomas Fall?" she continued. "He's out, but he'll return soon. He is eager to see you."

Stipp gripped the back of a nearby chair. So. Now he knew. "Is he well?" (Defaulting to the old mantra: *How is the boy? The boy is well.*)

"His stump bothers him some, but he is able to get along, thanks to Mary. After Thomas healed, we all came down with her to Manhattan City so she could attend Elizabeth Blackwell's School of Medicine. She was their first graduate."

Stipp forced a murmur of acknowledgment for the proud mother. So *that* was why his letters had never found Mary. How many times had he written Albany? Ten? And all his letters returned.

Mary picked up a tray arrayed with a tea service of cobalt blue china, smiling at his distress, misinterpreting it as surprise. "I had to talk myself into the luxury. I got used to the deprivation, and then when it was no longer there—?" She shrugged. "In some ways I liked the struggle better, I think. It clarified what was important."

The dining room walls were bare, and a set of dark furniture intensified the impression of incompleteness, as if the room were waiting for someone to finish it. Stipp sank into the captain's chair at the head of the table, and Mary sat next to him, near enough to touch. They concentrated on stirring and sugaring, rituals to distract them from the past, but which instead reminded them both of cold mornings around a cookfire, getting ready to make the rounds of the hospital tents, grateful for just a cup of hot water to warm them. Oh, if they had only known then what they knew even now, only five years later—infection not understood in the way it should have been. Even a year or two, and Lister's findings would have changed everything. If they had just washed their hands between patients, then all those deaths could have been prevented. James Blevens and his microscope, given more time, perhaps he would have rescued everyone. But Mary was mixing up her grief. So many things to grieve. Jenny, Christian, and Mr. Lincoln, who had asked her how much of herself she had wanted to risk.

"You disappeared, Mary," Stipp said, his gaze steady, his blue eyes reflecting the sharp blue of the china.

"But I'm here now."

The war had etched even more seams into Stipp's face, though some of them had been in place even in 1862. They grew deeper now, and he said, "So you married Thomas? I wish you had told me before I came today; I would have been prepared."

Once again, Mary settled her hand on his arm. Ever the midwife, easing hope into being. Other days at this hour, her foyer reverberated with the cries of her patients. She was shocked that no one had tried the bell; but today was Sunday and the house was still. The servants too were off. A planned isolation, though not too isolated. She could hear her mother and Elizabeth in the kitchen, could almost feel their worry; before Thomas had gone out he said, *The man has waited a long time.*

"William, Thomas is not my husband. He loved Jenny, as much as a man can love anyone, I think. He mourns her still, as do I."

Stipp glanced away from Mary and then back again. He did not want to overstep, but he had waited an eon, believing one thing, only to discover another. "But you did love him?"

Unconsciously, Mary unpinned and repinned her hair in that gesture of agitation so familiar to Stipp, recalling the night at the Union Hotel when he had proclaimed his love for her. (A different dining room now but with no less urgent a circumstance; lives were still at stake.)

"He was the first man who believed in me," Mary said. "How could I not love him?"

"And yet you are not married now?

"It was not that kind of love."

Stipp was staring at her, she him, though neither of them moved toward the other. Their own violence, born of years of restraint.

(Once, Stipp had said to Mary, *I don't need you*. And she had said, *Don't be a fool.*)

"As soon as the train pulled out of Hagerstown I knew," Mary said. "I wrote you at Antietam, but you'd disappeared. The army didn't know where you'd gone; their records are a mess. And then the other day I was looking for a patient's address in the City Directory, and there you were." Mary had had to read the line twice: *William Stipp, Surgeon.* Had put her hand to her heart.

Mary had turned as still now as if she were sitting for a portrait. How that silhouette had haunted Stipp: the ramrod-straight back, the wide shoulders, no picture of feminine beauty, but irresistible all the same. He had fled Sharpsburg, unable to stay where she was not, and disappeared into the maw of the war: Gettysburg, the Wilderness, and the tedious siege of Petersburg, where Grant's final assault ended the war. He could hardly believe it when the surrender came. Four years of his life, mired in death. He would not have wanted Mary to have experienced any of that, but the interminable years had seared into his bones his own phantom pain of amputation. His body remembered her, and he had to fight now not to take her into his arms.

"Every day," he said, "I've thought of you."

And then it was all before them, all the heavy sadness of their goodbye, when it had seemed that their lives would be broken forever. You would think that sorrow would dissipate, and it does for most, but when you spend years missing someone, it becomes an ever-flowing spring. After the war, Stipp had gone to Europe to try to erase the memories. In the echoing tomb of the Louvre, he had seen the *Mona Lisa*. Both misery and amusement had emanated from that face; Mary's smile now was like the portrait's, hiding an emotion no one could discern, not even him. He had once read an essay by a man named Walter Pater, who claimed the woman in the painting had been dead many times and had learned the secrets of the grave.

Less than a year ago, he had returned to Manhattan City. Many of his patients were from the South, relatives of Rebel soldiers whose lives he had saved. *This Federal doctor fixed me, what a wizard. And he has this nurse named Mary. They saved my life.* Each time some new patient recounted this tale of recommendation, he would be newly reminded of Mary. He'd say, "Oh, Miss Sutter went on with her own life. No, I don't know where she is. You know how it goes." There had been talk of a reunion of the Army of the Potomac, and he'd already imagined strolling past the nurses' pavilions, scanning smiling, proud faces, hoping to find Mary in search of him. Once, he thought he had seen her on the streets, but it was only a woman with the same sturdy shape, the same imperious posture, the same cautious air.

Until, yesterday, a letter.

William Stipp put his hand to Mary's cheek. War had nearly driven him insane; loving Mary had been his only refuge.

"You need me," Mary whispered.

But Stipp knew Mary's declaration was as much a confession as it was a statement. She could as easily have said, *I need you.*

Mary smoothed the collar of Stipp's shirt. He lifted her hand in his and slowly raised it to his lips.